Colin Wilson is one of the most prolific, versatile and popular writers at work today. He was born in Leicester in 1931, and left school at sixteen. After he had spent years working in a wool warehouse, a laboratory, a plastics factory and a coffee bar, his first book *The Outsider* was published in 1956. It received outstanding critical acclaim and was an immediate bestseller.

Since then he has written many books on philosophy, the occult, crime and sexual deviance, plus a host of successful novels which have won him an international reputation. His work has been translated into Spanish, French, Swedish, Dutch, Japanese, German, Italian, Portuguese, Danish, Norwegian, Finnish and Hebrew.

By the same author

COLIN WILSON

Ritual in the Dark

GraftonBooks

A Division of HarperCollins*Publishers*

GraftonBooks
A Division of HarperCollins*Publishers*
77–85 Fulham Palace Road,
Hammersmith, London W6 8JB

Published by Grafton Books 1991

Previously published by Panther Books 1976

First published in Great Britain by
Victor Gollancz Ltd 1960

Copyright © Colin Wilson 1960

ISBN 0-586-04391-8

Printed and bound in Great Britain by
Collins, Glasgow

Set in Times

For Bill Hopkins

I should like to acknowledge the help of the following: Richard Buckle, for refreshing my memory on details of his Diaghilev exhibition and suggesting many improvements in Chapter One; Bill Hopkins, Stuart Holroyd, Laura del Rivo and John Braine for detailed criticism of the book; Dr Francis Camps for advice on matters of forensic medicine; John Melling and Joy Wilson for preparing the manuscript for press; Philip Stephens for advice on legal matters and police procedure; Pat Pitman, for reading the manuscript for mistakes, and for some stimulating (if unlikely) theories about the identity of Jack the Ripper; finally, Victor Gollancz for constant sympathy and help, and for his many suggestions for improvement.

Part One

Chapter One

He came out of the Underground at Hyde Park Corner with his head lowered, ignoring the people who pressed around him and leaving it to them to steer out of his way. He disliked the crowds. They affronted him. If he allowed himself to notice them, he found himself thinking: Too many people in this bloody city; we need a massacre to thin their numbers. When he caught himself thinking this, he felt sick. He had no desire to kill anyone, but the hatred of the crowd was uncontrollable. For the same reason, he avoided looking at the advertisements that line the escalators of London tubes; too many dislikes were triggered off by the most casual glimpse. The half-clothed forms that advertised women's corsets and stockings brought a burning sensation to his throat, an instantaneous shock, like throwing a match against a petrol-soaked rag.

A thin brown drizzle fell steadily; the passing traffic sprayed muddy water. He buttoned the raincoat and turned up its collar, then opened the woman's umbrella he carried suspended by its loop from his wrist. The crowd thinned as he crossed Grosvenor Crescent; he walked more slowly, enjoying the noise of the rain on the umbrella.

Outside the gilded wrought-iron gates he stopped and fumbled for his money. The doorway of the house was hidden by a striped tent surmounted by a Russian onion dome; on either side of this stood statues of two enormous Negroes, leaning on the marble archway that formed the entrance to the tent. He lowered the umbrella, shaking it

9

to dislodge the raindrops. Behind the Negroes, the walls of the house looked black and desolate.

The entrance hall smelt of damp clothes. A queue of half a dozen people was waiting at the boxoffice. The inside walls of the tent were covered with red and gold striped paper.

There was some delay at the box office. A middle-aged man was protesting with a foreign voice:

Nevertheless, I am a student at the London School of Economics. It is merely that I have forgotten my card. I have a British Museum Reading Room card if that is any good . . .

Sorme produced a book from the side pocket of his jacket, and began to read. The queue moved forward again.

He became aware that the man in front of him was looking down at his book, trying to read its title from the page heading. He looked up, and met a pair of narrow, brown eyes, that turned away immediately with embarrassment. In that moment, he had registered a thin, long-jawed face that in some way struck him as oddly familiar. It was ugly, in a pleasant way, covered with small indentations that could have been pock-marks. A moment later, the man bought his ticket, and Sorme had a chance to observe him more fully. The examination brought no recognition. He was taller than Sorme, although Sorme was slightly over six feet tall. His dark grey suit was well cut. The thin face had high cheekbones, and eyes that slanted. It was so familiar that Sorme stared a moment too long, and suddenly found himself looking into the slanting brown eyes again. They smiled at him briefly as the man turned away, and Sorme was suddenly certain that he had never him before. The ticket-seller was asking: Student?

Yes.

One and sixpence please. Catalogue?

The stairway that led out of the tent curved round the canvas walls, and exposed the rusty scaffolding that supported it. He walked quickly, disliking the unpleasant memories aroused by the scaffolding. The stairs led to a doorway that had been constructed from a first-floor window, and formed the entrance to the exhibition. The first room immediately dissipated the mood of dislike. It had been designed to look like a Paris street, with iron railings, and a view of the Seine between the houses. Under the leaves of an overhanging tree, a huge poster displayed the words: THEATRE DES CHAMPS ELYSEES. BALLETS RUSSES. The enormous drawing of Nijinsky as the Spectre of the Rose was signed by Cocteau.

The place was warm; there was no one else in the room, and he lost the feeling of tension that the rain and the crowds had induced. There was a sound of music coming from a loudspeaker in another room. He slipped the book back into the jacket pocket, plunged his hands deep into his raincoat pockets, and gave himself up completely to the sense of nostalgia evoked by the room. He stood there for a few moments unmoving, until he heard footsteps and voices on the stairway, then walked quickly past the poster of Pavlova that faced Nijinsky, and mounted the narrow wooden stair to the second floor.

The music was louder there. He recognized the final dance from *The Firebird*, the soft, drawn-out horn call. It sent a warm shock of pleasure through the muscles of his back and shoulders, and stirred the surface of his scalp. People were already mounting the stairs behind him. He hurried on into the well-lit room. There was only one other person in it: the man who had stood in front of him in the queue. The voices and footsteps that came from the stairway drove him forward into the next room. A violent hatred arose in him of the talking people who talked away emotions into words. A drawling, cultured voice was saying:

. . . and we nearly got a snap of him. He was there on the beach, just changing into a pair of bathing trunks. Lettie grabbed her camera, but she wasn't quick enough . . . he got them on. Should have been worth something – a shot of Picasso in the raw . . .

The music had stopped. The voice faltered, embarrassed at the silence. Abruptly the music began again, a violent, discordant clamour that exploded in the small room and drowned all other sounds. He recognized Prokoviev's *Scythian Suite*, and smiled. The din was shaking the glass case in the middle of the room; it isolated him as effectively as silence. He examined with satisfaction a design by Benois.

The rooms were not crowded. He worked through them slowly, returning to the first room when the people behind him – an army officer with two girls – caught up with him.

An hour later, the loudspeakers were relaying *The Three-cornered Hat*, and he was again on the first floor, in the portrait gallery. The heat was making him sleepy. There was a curious scent hanging in the air which he half-suspected of possessing an anaesthetic quality. As he paused in front of a portrait of Stravinsky, he noticed the bust. It stood on a cube of marble, directly below an oil painting of a ballerina in a white dress. The inscription underneath said: *Nijinsky, by Una Troubridge*. He had remembered then of whom the stranger reminded him. It was Nijinsky.

Somewhere, a long time before, he had seen a photograph that caught the same expression, and the thin, faun-like face had impressed itself on his mind. As he stared at it now, the resemblance was no longer so obvious. Automatically he looked around to see if the man was anywhere near. He was not. Idly, he wondered whether he might be any relation of Nijinsky, his son perhaps. He could remember no son; only a daughter. Anyway, the bust was not really like him. It was not really like Nijinsky either; it had been idealized.

The man was in the Chirico room at the top of the stairs; he stood, leaning on an umbrella, examining one of the designs. Sorme crossed the room and stood close to him, where he could watch his face out of the corner of his eye. The resemblance was certainly there; it had not been imagination. By turning his head a little more, as if examining the design to his left, he could examine the face in profile.

Without looking at him, the stranger said abruptly:

He should have done more ballet designs.

For a moment, Sorme supposed he was addressing somebody on his left-hand side, then realized, equally quickly, that they were alone in the room. The man had not turned his face from the design he was examining. Sorme said: I beg your pardon?

Chirico. He never did anything better than these designs for *Le Bal*. Don't you agree?

I don't know, Sorme said, I don't know his work.

The stranger looked at him and smiled, and Sorme realized that he must have been watching him in the glass covering the design ever since he came in. He began to feel slightly irritated and embarrassed. Something in the man's voice told him instantly he was a homosexual. It was a cool, slightly drawling voice.

You know, the man said, I could have sworn I knew you when you came in. Do I?

I don't think so.

The eyes rested on him detachedly; he had the air of a Regency buck studying a horse. Sorme thought: Damn, he thinks I'm queer too.

I thought you knew me, the man said, you looked at me as if you knew me.

His voice was suddenly apologetic. Sorme's irritation disappeared. He cleared his throat, lowering his eyes.

As a matter of fact, I *did* think I recognized you. But I don't think that's possible.

Perhaps. My name is Austin Nunne. I was quite sure I knew you.

Austin Nunne . . .? Did you write a book on ballet?

Yes. And a slim volume on Nijinsky.

Sorme was excited and pleased, as the memory returned: the photograph of Nijinsky.

Of course I remember you. I've read them both. So that's why I thought I knew you!

You surprise me. It's a very bad photograph of me on the dust jacket.

No, I haven't seen that. But the photograph of the Nijinsky bust. Wasn't that in your book?

The Una Troubridge? Oh no. Karsavina found this one in a junk-shop in St Martin's Lane. I didn't even know it existed. But I think I know what you mean. The photo of Nijinsky in *L'Après-midi*. The head and shoulders?

Sorme suddenly felt irritated and depressed. He felt that his enthusiasm had placed him in the position of an admirer, a 'fan'. Nunne suddenly turned away, saying in a bored voice:

Anyway, they're neither of them very typical of Nijinsky. To tell the truth, I used that *L'Après-midi* photo because friends said it looked like me.

Sorme looked at his watch, saying: Well, I hope you didn't mind my asking?

Not at all. Are you in a hurry to go? Have you been all round?

No. But I've been here for an hour and a half. I don't feel as if I could take any more.

You're undoubtedly right. It's my fourth time around. I saw it when it opened in Edinburgh.

Sorme said embarrassedly: I must go.

Look here, why don't you come and have a drink? It's about opening time.

Sorme hesitated, and at the same time felt angry with himself for hesitating. He was interested by the feelings of attraction and repulsion that Nunne aroused in him. He had no particular dislike of homosexuals, but was aware that the consequences of being picked up by one could be difficult. He said uncertainly:

I don't know any pubs near here.

I do. Lots. Come and have a quick one. I always like meeting people who are interested in ballet. How are you travelling? Tube?

Yes.

That settles it. They're beastly at this hour. You'd much better hang around for a while.

Sorme followed him down the stairs. Nunne said over his shoulder:

You haven't told me your name.

Gerard Sorme.

Sorme? That's an odd name. What is it, French?

I don't know. My family come from Yorkshire. My father thinks it's a Yorkshire version of Soames.

They were passing through the portrait gallery. Sorme asked him:

Do you notice that odd scent?

Yes. Do you know what it is?

No.

It's called 'Mitsouko'. It was Diaghilev's favourite scent. Oriental. You'll smell it much stronger in here.

They were passing through a room lit by blue bulbs,

that had been designed to look like a haunted theatre. There the scent was overpowering. It seemed to emanate from old ballet costumes that hung in the blue air, surrounded by backstage scenery. The scent followed them down a short corridor, through a room hung with caricatures, and out on to a wide staircase that had been decorated with a tableau representing the legend of the Sleeping Beauty. The music met them loudly as they came down the staircase. Nunne walked jauntily, swinging his umbrella. He had the graceful walk of a dancer. There was a faint touch of the theatrical in his manner as he descended the staircase. He asked Sorme:

What made you read my books? Are you interested in ballet?

I used to be once. Not now.

Where do you study?

What makes you think I'm a student?

You've got a student's ticket sticking out of your top pocket. Anyway, you look like one.

They were outside again, standing near the immense Negro statues, and the drizzle fell steadily.

I'm not a student, Sorme said, but for some reason everyone supposes I am. I suppose it's the scruffy appearance.

He was wondering how he could indicate to Nunne, as quickly and as tactfully as possible, that he was not homosexual. He started to raise the umbrella, but Nunne stopped him:

Don't bother. That's my car over there. Let's run for it.

It was a long, red sports model with a canvas hood. Nunne yanked open the unlocked door and Sorme slid past the steering wheel, into the passenger seat. The car made a neat half-turn and glided forward towards Wellington Place. Nunne grumbled:

16

I suppose there'll be a bloody traffic jam all the way from here to Piccadilly Circus.

Sorme stared at the moving windscreen wipers, and at the red light of the traffic-signal that burst in red drops over the unwiped area of the windscreen.

Nunne began to sing softly to himself:

Cats on the rooftops, cats on the tiles . . .

The car turned into Dover Street. Nunne said softly: It's our lucky day. Come on, move out, old son.

A car in front of them was pulling out from the pavement; Nunne slid neatly into the empty space and braked abruptly. He said:

Three cheers. We've arrived. Open your door.

Sorme stepped out on to the pavement, and immediately raised the umbrella. Nunne slammed the door shut. He said, chuckling:

For God's sake put that thing down. The local coppers will think you're soliciting.

Soliciting?

They'll think you're trying to advertise your sex to the local queers.

I'm not queer, Sorme said bluntly. He lowered the umbrella. Nunne said, laughing: Don't be silly. I wasn't serious. I didn't suppose you were.

They crossed the road, avoiding a taxi. They turned again into Piccadilly. Nunne steered him towards a lighted doorway:

Here we are. After you.

The air was pleasantly warm. Sorme was helped out of the raincoat by a man in a red uniform, who handed the coat and umbrella to the cloakroom attendant. The man nodded at Nunne as if he knew him well:

Evenin', sir.

Evening, George.

There were only two other men in the bar. Nunne indicated a corner seat for Sorme; it was deep and comfortable.

What are you having?

Beer?

They don't have draught. You can have a lager.

That's fine, Sorme said uncomfortably. He was trying to remember how much money he had on him, and how long it had to last. He crossed his knees, and felt the trousers damp. He stared down at the frayed turn-ups, and at the leather strips sewn on to the cuffs of his jacket. The poverty of his appearance did not embarrass him, but he had never entirely lost a sense of its disadvantage. He thought: I wonder if they'd let me into this place on my own? and decided it was unlikely.

Nunne set the glass of lager in front of him. He seated himself opposite Sorme in a rush-backed lounge chair, and poured the entire contents of a bottle of ginger ale into a large whisky. He took a big gulp of it, then set it down, sighing:

Ah, it'll be the death o' me yit, jist like me poor feyther. Cigarette, Gerard?

No thanks, I don't smoke.

You don't mind me calling you Gerard?

Of course not.

Good. And I'm Austin.

Sorme tasted the beer. It was ice-cold.

Tell me, Gerard. If you're not a student, what do you do?

Nothing much. I'm writing a book.

But how do you live? Journalism?

No, I've had a very small private income since I was twenty-one . . .

Which was . . .?

18

Five years ago. I just about scrape along. So I'm really one of the idle rich. Except that I'm not rich.

Are you idle?

Pretty idle.

Like me, then. I thought I recognized a fellow spirit as soon as I saw you. What were you reading, by the way?

Sorme pulled the dog-eared paperback out of his pocket. He said laughing:

Sex for beginners. By Frank Harris.

My Life and Loves. I never read Harris, is it good?

It's quite astonishing.

How? In what way?

I never cease to gasp with amazement at the way he leaps in and out of bed. I wonder whether such men really exist.

Why not?

I mean with such a promiscuous appetite. It astounds me. You remember that Nijinsky slept with his wife for several nights before he made love to her? That's natural. That's the way it should be.

You're interested in Nijinsky?

Yes.

Why? You never saw him dance.

Sorme stared into his glass, trying to find the words that expressed it precisely. It was impossible; he didn't know Nunne well enough. He said:

It's difficult to explain . . .

Wait. Let's get some more drinks first.

Not for me. I can't drink any more beer.

Have a scotch, then.

All right, but let me . . .

No, no, no. You sit still.

He signalled to the waiter, calling: Two large scotches and two dries.

Go on, Gerard. About Nijinsky.

Sorme asked, laughing:

Why are you so anxious to make me talk? What do I know that might interest you?

A great many things, I should imagine. I already know some interesting things about you.

Such as?

That you're twenty-six, have a small independent income, and don't like work. That is interesting in itself. Too much leisure demoralizes most people. You can see it in their faces. You, on the other hand, have an interesting face. It is not a self-indulgent face. Immediately, I wonder: What does he do with his leisure? You haven't enough money to waste it flying aeroplanes, or gadding off to other countries, as I do. What *do* you do with your leisure?

Sorme said: Nothing much. I try to do nothing.

The waiter set the drinks down on the table. Nunne dropped a pound note on the tray.

Prosit, Nunne said, raising the glass.

Cheers, Sorme said.

The waiter handed Nunne his change and Nunne dropped a coin on to his tray. Sorme drank a large mouthful of the scotch. Tears came to his eyes. He took out his handkerchief and blew his nose vigorously, then, noticing the colour of the handkerchief, pushed it hastily back into his pocket. Nunne looked up from the book on the table, and tossed it over to Sorme.

I can't imagine that sort of thing appealing to you.

Sorme shrugged, and emptied the bottle of ginger ale into the scotch. It was a considerable improvement.

I read a lot.

Nunne smiled at the evasion. He sipped his drink thoughtfully, staring past Sorme's head. He asked slowly:

What is this book you're writing about?

I'll give you one guess, Sorme said.

Nijinsky?

Right.

Really? Does it cover any of the same ground as my book?

Not really. This is a novel.

He drank down half of the scotch and dry ginger, and realized that he was feeling relaxed and contented. Now he was no longer worried about the nature of Nunne's interest in him, he was beginning to like Nunne.

Tell me about your novel, Nunne said.

I can't do that. It's not really about Nijinsky. It's about Nijinsky's state of mind.

What do you know about that?

He believed in himself. Most people don't.

Half a dozen more people had come into the bar, businessmen. A young man with a young woman in furs.

Sorme felt the talk rising in him, checked only by a desire not to bore Nunne. He leaned forward, saying:

When I think about Nijinsky, then I look at these people, I feel a sort of incredulousness. You know he says in the *Diary*, Life is difficult because no one knows the importance of it. I picture him walking round the streets at night like a high pressure boiler, almost bursting . . .

He stopped; Nunne's face was perfectly attentive, listening with a gravity that was flattering to him.

You see, I see it this way. Supposing that at the end of your life you had a vision of everything – everything in the universe, all at once. A sort of vision of God. It would justify everything. If you could have a vision like that it would make the world different. You'd live like a fiend, like a possessed man. Because you'd know it meant something, that it wasn't meaningless. Look. None of these people live a whole life. They only live a few odd days at a time. It's like never eating a full meal, but getting an occasional mouthful every few hours. Or like not hearing a symphony in one sitting, but hearing two or

21

three notes at a time, spread over several months. That's how they live. Well, some people don't live like that.

Nunne interrupted smoothly: How are you so sure Nijinsky didn't?

No, he didn't, Sorme said.

Nunne offered him the open cigarette case; Sorme shook his head saying: Thanks, I don't. Nunne lit a cigarette, looking at him over the lighter. He breathed out a mouthful of smoke, saying contentedly:

You really are a very odd person, Gerard.

Sorme finished the whisky, staring hard at Nunne. He signalled again to the waiter, and waved a hand at the two glasses. He said deliberately:

It's not oddness. I am convinced that life can be lived at twenty times its present intensity . . . somehow. I spend all my life looking for the way to it. I envy madmen. But somehow I never get closer to it myself. But I cling to symbols. Nijinsky is one of my symbols.

The waiter set down two more large whiskies. Sorme said:

I'll get these.

No. No. Please.

As the waiter went away, Sorme asked: Why should you pay for my drinks?

Because my father's disgustingly rich.

Oh.

You look shocked!

No. Tell me, what do you do with your time?

Ah, there you touch a delicate subject. I have developed fifty different ways of wasting it. I write books – not very good ones. I attend all the concerts and operas and ballets. I fly to Vienna and Milan and Berlin for concerts. If I was just a little more worthless I'd drink two bottles of pernod a day and kill myself in a year. As it is, I fly a plane and like fast cars.

Sorme said, disingenuously: You're not married, of course?

No, I never met anyone I wanted to settle down with. For some reason, I prefer bitches. I don't suppose you understand that?

No, I don't really. I hate bitches – of any sex.

You obviously lack a masochistic leaning.

I hate pain of any sort – to myself or anyone else.

Ah, you talk like a moralist, Gerard. One shouldn't be a moralist.

You don't understand. It's not a matter of morality. It's what I said before – you have to work on the assumption that there could be a vision of the total meaning of life. And if that's possible, everyone ought to live as if that was the aim.

Ah, you *are* a moralist, Gerard. You ought to meet my aunt. You'd like her.

Why?

She's a moralist too. She disapproves of me. Jehovah's Witness. Believes the Last Judgment'll happen any day now. That's what you want, isn't it? People believing in the Last Judgment.

You're damn right. It's just what I want.

Shall I tell you what I want?

What?

Something to eat. Shall we go and have a meal?

Where?

Anywhere. Leoni's or Victor's or somewhere.

I have to go.

Oh no. It's not the money that worries you, is it? I've got lots on me. Look.

Nunne produced his wallet and waved it vaguely under Sorme's nose. Sorme caught a glimpse of a wad of notes. He realized that Nunne was becoming drunk: he also

23

suspected that he was behaving as if he were more drunk than he actually was.

No, really. I'd rather not.

But you must. I don't want you to go yet. You don't want to go yet, do you?

No, but . . .

Well, we can't drink any more on empty stomachs. I'm getting disgustingly drunk already. Had no lunch. So we'd better go and eat. C'mon, boy.

As the uniformed man helped Sorme into his raincoat, Nunne said:

Let me into a secret, Gerard. Why on earth do you carry a woman's umbrella?

Sorme took the umbrella from the man, and handed him a shilling.

It's not mine. It's my landlady's daughter's. She insisted on lending it to me when I came out today.

They came out into the rain again. Sorme felt fortified against it and happy. It was the first time for several years that he had been drunk, and the sensation delighted him. Nunne grasped his elbow and squeezed it, asking:

Has this girl got a thing about you?

I suspect so. At least, her mother does. And she suspects me of taking base advantage of it – or of being about to. She gave me notice last week.

Really? What do you intend to do?

Nunne backed the car slightly, then pulled out expertly.

I'm moving to another place tomorrow morning.

Whereabouts?

Kentish Town. I'm living in Colindale at the moment.

My God, that's up Bedford way, isn't it?

Not quite that far. It's near the newspaper library, which is rather useful. But the new place'll be more convenient for the British Museum.

And is the daughter moving with you too?

No fear. She's a sweet girl, but I don't want to go to bed with her.

How virtuous of you. Get out of the way, you stupid bastard.

This was addressed to a taxi-driver who was turning his taxi in the middle of Brewer Street. Nunne honked his horn twice. It had a braying, brassy tone. As the taxi came past them, the driver shouted:

Tike yer bloody time, can't yer?

Swine, Nunne said serenely. If we lived in the Middle Ages I'd have him hanged, drawn and quartered for that.

The car shot forward, narrowly missing a pedestrian who came out from between two parked cars.

Fool! Nunne screamed.

You should drive a juggernaut chariot. It'd be more in your style.

Nunne said indignantly: All drivers should be more dangerous. That would reduce the number of careless pedestrians. Eventually, there'd only be careful ones left.

What about when you're a pedestrian?

I'd carry a gun. All pedestrians should carry tommy guns to shoot at dangerous drivers. That'd make London *far* more interesting.

The car cruised down Dean Street. Nunne said:

Not a single bloody parking place in Soho . . . Ah! We are in luck tonight.

An Anglia pulled out of a row of parked cars. Nunne slid past the empty space and backed into it. He turned the engine off.

You're so good-tempered, Gerard. You obviously don't hate people as much as I do.

Sorme said, smiling:

You obviously don't know me as well as I do.

* * *

25

Nunne commanded good service. The manager came to their table and made a polite speech about being delighted to see him. Their waiter was obsequious; he exuded a desire to please.

You seem well known here.

Sorme was not interested; he said it only to make conversation.

I've changed my restaurant a dozen times in two years. I haven't been here for over a fortnight, so they probably assumed they wouldn't ever see me again.

Why do you change?

Nunne masticated and swallowed slowly the last mouthful of smoked salmon. He said, sighing:

Sheer pettiness, Gerard. I get offended about little things. I know damn' well I'm being silly, but I get offended all the same.

Sorme regarded him with mistrust, mixed with a certain disappointment, feeling as if Nunne had confessed to a tendency to shoot at old ladies with a revolver. Nunne seemed not to notice. When the waiter filled his glass, he drained the Chianti without lowering it.

Nunne had ordered roast duck, cooked with paprika and cheese. When it arrived he stopped talking and gave full attention to the food, speaking only to reply to acquaintances who came past the table. When this happened Sorme did not look up; he was aware of being regarded with curiosity. He could almost feel the conjectures being made, and he ate quickly and mechanically to conceal the irritation.

He had difficulty in dissuading Nunne from ordering a second bottle of wine. His motives were purely selfish; he knew that if he drank another half bottle, he would be sick before the end of the evening.

The rain had stopped when they left. Sorme walked contentedly beside Nunne, now feeling happier in the anonymity of the Soho crowd. His feelings about Nunne were mixed. He calculated that the meal he had just eaten was the most expensive he had eaten in his life. The sight of the six pound notes Nunne had dropped on to the waiter's plate had shocked him; it represented a week's food and rent. The most he had ever paid for a meal had been ten shillings. He felt a certain gratitude for Nunne's generosity, now that he had ceased to suspect his motives. But a faint dislike rose in him periodically. There was something distinctly repellent about Nunne. It had to do with the combination of coarseness and femininity in him. The brown hair was long and silky, almost beautiful, a woman's hair. The teeth were irregular and yellowish; two at the front were pointed, canine. When he looked closely at the face, no scars were visible; it was hard to determine what produced the pock-marked effect. When he had asked Nunne, as they drank coffee and vodka, Nunne had said briefly: Car accident, and drawn his finger along a faint, hardly perceptible line that ran across the left cheek, parallel with the jaw.

What would you like to do now, Gerard?

Do you think I might buy *you* a drink now?

I see no reason why not, dear boy. Let's go into the *French*, shall we, that is, if we can sit down.

The pub was crowded. Nunne was immediately hailed by a short, leathery-faced drunk.

Carl Castering, Nunne said. This is Gerard Sorme.

The man seized Sorme's hand, and looked into his face with the liquid eyes of a drunk.

You're very good-looking, Gerard. Don't you think he looks like Rimbaud, Austin? Don't you, though?

Sorme allowed his hand to be caressed between two damp palms, then withdrew it. He asked Nunne:

What will you drink?

Straight scotch for me.

27

Sorme asked the drunk: will you have a drink?

The leathery face turned to him coquettishly.

Why, that's awfully sweet of you. Yes, I will. Scotch and water.

Sorme finally attracted the barmaid's attention. He passed two whiskies back to Nunne and his friend. They stood, wedged together in the crush, holding their glasses tightly.

Nunne said: Carl is one of the best photographers in London, Gerard.

Castering leered at Sorme, then suddenly regarded him seriously:

I would like you to sit for me, Gerard. Would you do that?

Only if I'm present, Nunne said lightly.

Why? Don't you trust me with him?

I was joking, Nunne said.

He said to Sorme: Drink up and let's find somewhere less crowded.

Sorme obediently threw back the whisky. It no longer made his eyes water.

Outside, Sorme asked him: Is he a friend of yours – Carl?

Swine, Nunne said shortly. Masochist. But a damn good photographer.

They walked slowly along Old Compton Street, keeping close to avoid being separated by the crowd. Outside the Cinerama theatre Nunne was saluted by the uniformed man who controlled the queue.

You seem to know everyone.

He worked as a chucker-out at a place I knew once.

They stopped to look at the coloured pictures, displayed behind glass, that showed scenes from the film. Sorme, glancing up at Nunne, suddenly caught a look of

revulsion and absorption. Nunne was staring at a photograph of a switchback car swooping over a hump. A
pretty, plump girl stared at the camera, holding her dress
over her knees, but the sides of the dress, caught by the
wind, revealed the tops of her stockings and suspenders.
Nunne turned away abruptly, saying:

Let's go, Gerard.

Sorme said, laughing: I didn't think you liked women.

Nunne said: What do you mean?

Nothing; you were staring at that girl as if she fascinated
you. The look passed over Nunne's face again, then
disappeared. He said, smiling:

She does. Come on.

They walked back to the car.

Where now, Gerard?

Sorme said, dubiously: I'd like a little quiet.

So would I. What about my flat?

Where is it?

Near Portland Street station.

I'd rather stick to somewhere closer to my way home. I
ought to think of getting back.

Where do you live?

Hendon. Until tomorrow.

Of course. All right, we'll head that way. I know rather
a good little pub in Hampstead we might go to. Quiet.

Hampstead? Is that on the way?

Certainly. We can cut over to the Hendon Way.
Straight route.

They moved slowly along Old Compton Street. Nunne
blew the horn; it emitted a gentle, warning note. Nunne
said, grinning: Excellent invention this. I can adjust the
tone and volume of the horn. Loud and blatant for the
open road; gentle and, as it were, coaxing for London
crowds. Come on, shift, you stupid bastards, or I'll turn
the cow-catcher on. This is the only part of London that

reminds me of Hamburg's Reeperbahn. Do you know Hamburg, Gerard?

Sorme said abstractedly: No. He had been staring at his watch for half a minute without registering the time. It was ten past nine.

As they passed Chalk Farm station, Nunne said suddenly:

I know. Let's go to my aunt's place. She'll give us a drink.

Who's your aunt?

You'd like her. Her name's Gertrude, and she's not really my aunt, but she's terribly sweet. She lives all on her own in a house in the Vale of Health, and never sees anyone. She likes me to drop in. Unless she's holding a meeting.

What kind of a meeting?

Jehovah's Witness. It's her only vice. But she's really rather sweet.

Sorme said with dismay: You're not serious, are you?

Why not?

About her being a Jehovah's Witness?

Oh yes, quite serious about that.

But – I mean – they're quite up the wall, aren't they?

Couldn't say, dear boy. I don't know a thing about them. She's never tried to convert me. Anyway, we don't have to stay if you can't bear her. But she'll give us a drink, anyway.

Sorme relaxed into the seat. He had a feeling that he would not get home early after all, and he was too drunk to care deeply. The prospect of changing his lodgings, which had worried him for a week past, now seemed unimportant. He closed his eyes and tried to calculate how much he had drunk. The car braked suddenly, throwing him forward.

Nunne said: Sorry, old boy. I get used to driving my

other car, and it brakes gentler than this. Smashed it up last week.

The road was completely deserted. On one side of it the Heath rose steeply; Sorme stepped out and slammed the door. The cool air wakened him; the car-heater had come close to sending him to sleep. Nunne was groping in the leather pocket behind the door; an electric torch clicked in his hand. Sorme followed him through the gateway, into complete blackness. About fifty yards away a light was burning in a doorway, trees shed rain from their leaves as the wind rocked them; Sorme turned his face up to catch the wet drops. He said dreamily:

Does your aunt enjoy living in the middle of nowhere?

She hates it, actually. She's always threatening to move nearer town, but the Heath's so lovely in the summer.

The light that burned in the porch was a square lantern, with a pointed electric bulb inside it. Nunne rang the doorbell. A moment later, a light appeared behind the glass panes that covered the upper half of the door. A woman's voice called: Who is it?

Austin.

Austin!

The door was opened by a small, slim woman.

This is Gerard Sormes, Gertrude. Gerard's a writer.

Do come in. I was just thinking about going to bed.

Don't worry. We shan't stay all night.

I didn't mean that. Stay as long as you like.

She led them into a long, comfortably furnished sitting-room.

Are you hungry? Have you had supper?

Yes, thanks. An hour ago.

Would you like a drink?

Rather!

You know where it is. Help yourself. I'm having some cocoa.

31

She switched on the electric fire, and went out. Nunne opened the sideboard, and took out a bottle of whisky. Sorme glimpsed an array of bottles in the cupboard; he asked:

Does your aunt entertain a lot?

Not much. She mixes with two lots. A sort of Hampstead literary crowd – most awful lot of goddam squares you ever saw – and her soul-savers. They're about as bad. She takes care never to invite them here on the same evenings.

Why?

When her soul-savers come, she hangs up a banner: Beware the Demon Drink – over the booze cupboard. When the literary crowd descends, she has to hire a navvy to cart them home in a wheelbarrow.

The woman came in again, carrying a cup on a tray. She asked:

How is your mother, Austin?

In excellent condition, thanks. She's coming to London next week.

Will she be staying with you?

She'll be at my place. I shan't be there, though. Going to join some friends at St Moritz.

She sat down opposite them. There was something about her that Sorme found very attractive. He would have guessed her age to be about forty. In some way, she managed to give the impression of being well-dressed without seeming to care about her appearance. The tweed skirt was well-cut, but it had started to come unzipped at the waist. The mouth and chin were firm, slightly schoolmistressy. But there was something curiously anonymous about her: she was the kind of person he would not have noticed if she had sat opposite him on the tube.

I didn't catch your name.

Sorme. Gerard Sorme.

Nunne said: I thought it was Sormes.

No.

What do you write, Mr Sorme?

Sorme said embarrassedly: Austin shouldn't have introduced me as a writer. I've only ever published a few poems in magazines.

Are you a Catholic?

He said with surprise: No, why?

I wondered . . .

Nunne said: He's an atheistic freethinker, with inclinations to Catholicism. Aren't you, Gerard?

Austin, behave yourself!

She smiled at Sorme, as if excluding Nunne from the conversation.

You're not a freethinker, are you?

No . . . I don't suppose so.

What are you then? Nunne asked.

Gertrude said reproachfully: Austin, do behave yourself. Have you been drinking?

Certainly not. Not much anyway. Another, Gerard?

Sorme said hastily: No thanks. I haven't finished this.

Nunne had given him a tumbler half full of neat whisky, and he was wondering whether he could find some opportunity to pour it back into the bottle.

I really don't think you ought to, Austin. It can't be good for your tummy.

Nunne stood up, a little unsteadily:

No doubt you're right, Gertrude. 'Scuse me, dears.

He went out of the room. Sorme watched her eyes following him.

He really is rather drunk, isn't he? she asked him.

I dare say he is. I am, a bit.

You don't look it. Are you used to drink?

No.

I didn't think so. Have you known Austin long?

For some reason, a sense of shame made him reluctant to tell her. He said:

Not very long.

You mustn't let him lead you into bad habits!

I don't expect so.

What religion *were* you brought up in?

I don't know. C of E, I suppose. But I never had to go to church or Sunday school. I hated both.

And have you any religious beliefs?

The bare minimum.

And what are they?

Sorme heard Nunne's footsteps outside the door. He said smiling:

I'll tell you some other time.

Nunne came in again. He said cheerfully:

I thought Friday was your meeting night?

It is. It's over now.

Oh. And how's old Brother Horrible?

Who on earth are you talking about?

Fatty. Tartuffe with the butcher's complexion. What's his name?

Really, Austin! You get worse. What have you got against Brother Robbins?

Nunne sat beside Sorme again, having refilled his glass. He said, winking:

He's after you, Gertrude.

Nonsense!

I saw it in his eyes. He's thinking what a nice match you'd make. Nice cuddly little wifey.

Sorme noticed with surprise that she had coloured. He stood up, saying: Excuse me.

It's upstairs, Nunne said, second on the left.

The hall and stairs were carpeted with blue pile that made his footsteps noiseless. There were two prints of paintings by Munch on the stairs. In the warmth and haze

34

of the alcohol, it seemed one of the most charming houses he had been in.

He switched on a light, and found himself in a small bedroom, containing a single bed. There was a large framed photograph of a blonde girl on the dressing-table. He peered at it with interest, then kissed his lips at it. He backed out of the door and went into the bathroom. A lineful of damp clothes hung across it; he had to duck under them to reach the lavatory. He murmured softly: I should seduce her and come and live here. Perfect conditions for working.

He washed his hands at the basin, humming quietly.

When he turned away, he walked immediately into a wet towel. He wiped his face on his hand, and reached up to touch a blue nylon waist slip. Water dripped down his sleeve. He swore under his breath, smiling.

When he came into the sitting-room again, Nunne said: I think we'd better go, Gerard. Gertrude wants to go to bed.

Of course.

Are you going to finish your whisky?

I don't think I will. I've had rather a lot.

I didn't think you were. So I've finished it for you.

She said, laughing: You really are disgraceful, Austin. I don't know how you manage to drive that car. *Do* be careful.

Tush! Did you ever know me to have an accident?

It's a miracle ! she said.

Nunne heaved himself to his feet. He seized her and planted a kiss on her forehead. Sorme regarded her, smiling. He would have liked to do the same. Nunne said:

Goodnight, dear aunt. Lock the doors now. Make sure old Brother Barrel-belly's not under the bed.

She turned to Sorme:

You will come again, won't you? You can find your way here.

I'm not so sure that I can, he said, smiling.

I'll give you the address.

She tore a sheet of headed notepaper from a pad in the bureau and scribbled on it. He slipped it into his back pocket.

Goodbye. *Do* make Austin drive carefully.

Sorme shook her hand; her grip was as firm as a man's.

She called from the front doorstep:

Keep to the right of the drive. There's a pool of water there.

Nunne's torch wavered erratically over the ground. Sorme kept close to him to avoid stumbling. As they emerged into the street, Nunne said:

She likes you, dear boy. I got a little lecture on corrupting you. I think she wants you for her Bible class.

Not for her literary evenings?

Oh, perhaps. I don't know. I should think from her questions . . .

His voice trailed off. He opened the car door, and collapsed into the driving seat.

Ouf! That's better . . . Well, where now? It's only ten past ten. We've still time for another drink. Or you could come back to my place and have a couple.

No! Really, it's quite impossible. I must get back. *Any* other night but this.

Ah yes. You've got to move in the morning. How will you do it?

Take a taxi.

Would you like me to pop over and help you?

No, no. Don't bother.

Nunne lit a cigarette, and tossed the match out of the window. His headlights suddenly lit up the road. The car surged forward jerkily, then stalled. He said:

Sod it. Left the bloody hand-brake on.

Sorme said: Look, drop me on the Edgware Road, and I'll get a bus home. Or better still, drop me off at Hampstead underground.

No, no. I'll take you home. You're not letting Gertrude's comments on my driving worry you, are you?

No . . .

Good. I'm a perfectly safe driver, even when I can't see for scotch.

What about your other car . . . ?

Oh, that wasn't my fault . . . Somebody built a wall in the middle of the road.

Didn't they nab you for drunken driving?

Fortunately I wasn't drunk. That was the trouble. Morning after. I felt like hell.

Nunne's driving seemed neither better nor worse for the drink. He turned off the engine and allowed the car to freewheel down the hill to Golders Green, singing mournfully:

Cats on the rooftops, cats on the tiles . . .

Sorme said: Was your aunt ever married?

She's not my aunt.

Was she ever married?

No. Gertrude is a most mysterious case. No one knows all the facts. She had a *father*.

A what?

A father. You know some people have got a mother who won't let them off the dog lead? Well, she had a father.

Why should that stop her from marrying?

How should I know, dear boy? Use your imagination. If it's as lurid as mine, you can think up all sorts of reasons.

Sorme suppressed the comments that rose to his lips.

Nunne was not the person to make them to. Nunne startled him suddenly by saying:

Anyway, I doubt whether she'd be any good in bed.

Sorme glanced at him. The cigarette was hanging loosely from the side of his mouth. He said:

No, I dare say you're right.

It began to rain again. He sat there listening to the steady click of the windscreen wipers, then said suddenly:

By the way, who's that delicious blonde girl in the photograph?

Which photograph?

I walked into a bedroom while I was looking for the lavatory. The first on the right. There was a photo of a lovely little blonde on the table.

Oh, that'd be Caroline. Her niece. I haven't met her. Why?

All delicious little blondes interest me.

You are a cow, aren't you? Always on the lookout for sex.

Sorme laughed. They were passing Hendon aerodrome. To change the subject, he said:

By the way, did you say you fly a plane?

Yes. Got one down at a place near Leatherhead. You must come over for a weekend. I'll take you for a trip.

Your own?

My father's actually. He never uses it.

Turn left here, please. It's by that next lamp-post.

The car stopped with a jerk; this time Sorme had braced himself for it. He said:

Well, I owe you quite a lot for this evening.

No you don't. I owe you a lot. I'd have been bored stiff on my own. Have you got any booze in your room?

I'm afraid not. At least, only some beer.

Excellent. Let's drink that. Or are you too tired?

Not at all, Sorme said. Come on up.

As they opened the front gate, Sorme said quietly:

Don't make a noise until we get into my room.

Are they asleep already?

No, probably watching the TV.

They tiptoed up the stairs, Nunne walking in front. A door below opened; a woman's voice called:

Is that you, Mr Sorme?

Yes.

Oh.

The door closed again.

Sorme switched on the light and closed the door.

You don't know how lucky you are to have no landlady. I detest landladies.

He lit the gas fire and turned it on full. The room was small and had too much furniture in it. Two cheap suitcases, bound with string, stood near the door. The table was completely occupied by the remains of a meal and an empty drawer. A large cardboard soap-carton, half full of books, stood in the washbasin in the corner. Sorme took off his overcoat and hung it in the wardrobe. Nunne was seated on the bed; he lit a cigarette:

I had an awfully nice landlady in Hamburg.

Sorme took the empty drawer and fitted it back into its place in the sideboard.

I've had too many landladies. I've had so many that now even pleasant landladies make my flesh crawl. That's the main advantage of this new place – the landlady doesn't live on the premises. Even the decentest landladies end by persecuting me.

Don't be neurotic, Gerard.

You'd be neurotic if you'd had as many as I have. Stupid, petty-minded old cats who leave little notes in your room. They don't like visitors after ten o'clock. They don't like you to have women in your room. You never know when some triviality's going to upset them and make them give you notice. If I were a dictator I'd open concentration camps for landladies. Mean, trivial, materialistic old sods. They poison our civilization.

He moved the carton of books on to the floor, and let the hot tap run, then washed two glasses, and dried them with the hand towel.

Poor Gerard. You ought to find yourself a flat.

Sorme took a quart bottle of ale from the bottom of the wardrobe, and poured into the two glasses. He handed one to Nunne, saying: Cheers.

Nunne took a sip, and set it down on the table. He said:

I'm sorry I'm going away just as we're getting acquainted.

Sorme sat in a wooden chair near the fire; he said sententiously: There'll be plenty of time.

Without a doubt. Give me your new address, will you? and I'll give you mine.

They exchanged address books; both wrote silently for a moment. The warmth made Sorme's stockinged feet steam. He suppressed a yawn. Nunne moved to the end of the bed, where he could see the fire, and stretched out his hands towards it.

Gerard. What you were saying earlier. About looking for some other way to live . . .

Yes?

You ought to see a friend of mine. Father Carruthers, at a hotel in Rosebery Avenue.

That must be where Brother Maunsell lives: there are quite a number of priests there. Do you know him?

No, I don't recall him.

You're not a Catholic, are you?

No. My mother is. Carruthers is her friend, really, but I'm sure you'd like him.

Sorme sipped his beer slowly. He had no real desire to drink it; it tasted bitter and wholly disagreeable to him.

What do you think this Father Carruthers could do?

I don't know. I like him. He's awfully clever. He knows a lot about psychology – he was a friend of Adler.

That sounds dangerous.

Why?

I can't imagine the Church approving. Does he talk about neurosis instead of sin?

Yes. Well no, not exactly. You'd have to go and see him. He's written a book on Chehov.

Sorme shifted his chair further back; the fire was too hot. He said, for the sake of saying something:

I probably will.

Nunne tilted the beer glass and emptied it. Sorme pushed the quart bottle over to him. Nunne allowed the beer to slop into the glass; the froth immediately brimmed over and ran on to the tablecloth. He leaned forward and sucked up a mouthful of the froth, until it ceased to overflow. He looked up at Sorme suddenly over the brim of the glass, saying, with a casualness behind which Sorme could sense the control:

You seem to have an awful down on queers, Gerard.

Sorme said, shrugging:

No. On the contrary, I always get on very well with them.

But you don't like them?

It's not that I don't like them. I disapprove of the queer mentality.

What on earth is the queer mentality?

I shouldn't say.

Do say. Don't mind me. I wouldn't take it personally, I assure you.

All right. Most queers I've known have been too personal. With them, everything is personal. It all depends on people. I can't imagine a homosexual visionary, or a homosexual Newton or Beethoven. They seem to lack intellectual passion – the capacity to become fanatically obsessed by purely intellectual issues. They're like women-everything has to be in terms of people and emotions.

You *do* talk nonsense, dear boy. How do you know Newton and Beethoven weren't homosexual? Neither of them got married. What about Schubert, Michelangelo?

Sorme said, laughing:

OK. I'm sorry I spoke.

No, but answer me! I'd like to hear your views.

No. I'm too tired. When you go tonight, I've got to finish packing. I'll have to be up early tomorrow to start moving.

Nunne looked at him; his eyes were serious, almost pained. Abruptly, he shook his head, and drank the rest of his beer. He stood up, saying:

All right, I'll leave you.

Sorme immediately felt guilty:

You don't have to go yet. It's hardly eleven. You could stay for another hour.

No, I'd better go. Why are you smiling?

You're like a jack-in-the-box, Sorme said. Why don't you sit still for a while?

This was not the real reason Sorme was smiling. He had thought: He has taken it personally. Everything is personal for them. But he was glad Nunne was leaving.

Bye-bye, Gerard.

Where will you go?

Nunne shrugged:

Home, perhaps. Or a club I know in Paddington. Bye-bye.

Goodbye, Austin. Thanks for the evening.

Don't come down, Nunne said.

He went out quickly, closing the door behind him. Sorme stood there, until he heard the front door slam. His landlady immediately called: Who's there? He said angrily to the door: Oh, drop dead! The car door slammed. He looked out of the window, in time to see the rear light disappearing into the darkness.

He emptied the rest of his beer into the sink, and washed the two glasses, then systematically washed the rest of the crockery on the table. When he had told Nunne he wanted to finish packing he had been sincere; but now he felt sleepy and drunk. The room was hot and stuffy. He turned the gas fire off and opened a window. Before undressing, he swallowed three dyspepsia tablets with a glass of milk. The sheets felt pleasantly cool. He yawned in the dark, and stretched in the bed, experiencing intense sensual satisfaction from the contact of the sheets. He thought of Nunne flying to Switzerland, and felt a faint envy, which he immediately suppressed. Sleep came quickly and easily.

Chapter Two

He liked the new room. When the boxes had been unpacked, and the radio and record player were arranged on the chest of drawers, it seemed smaller than he had anticipated. A fire escape ran past the window, which looked out on a piece of waste ground and on a church. He had also the use of a small kitchen that was probably a converted lumber-room. It was reached by a narrow flight of stairs opposite his door: he was to share this with a Frenchman who lived in the next room.

The move exhausted him. He had awakened without a hangover, but feeling tired and dry-mouthed. When he had finished arranging the room, he felt the sweat running down his sides and along his thighs. He set a kettle to boil on the gas ring; he could hear the thump of his heart, and the roar of the traffic in the Kentish Town Road. The bed stood under the open window; the breeze cooled him. He fell into a doze, and was awakened suddenly by the whistle on the kettle.

He made tea in a two-pint thermos flask, and poured it out through a strainer. He put a record on the gramophone, then sat down at the table, staring at the glowing nipples of the gas fire, sipping the tea. Someone tapped on the door; he called: Come in.

The man who opened the door said: I hear we are to be neighbours and share the kitchen.

Come in, Sorme said. Would you like a cup of tea?

Thank you, I would.

The French accent was not strong, but quite perceptible. Sorme stood up, holding out his hand.

My name's Gerard Sorme.

Edmond Callet. How do you do?

Do you mind sterilized milk in your tea?

Not at all.

He took the whisky-cap off the sterilized milk bottle that he had brought from Colindale; the milk was three days old. He turned down the volume of the gramophone. The Frenchman asked: What is it? Prokoviev?

Yes, the Fifth Symphony. Do you like music?

Very much. I used to play the oboe in the orchestra in my home town. Lille.

But you're not a professional musician?

Oh no. I'm an engineer.

When he smiled, he showed a mouthful of regular, white teeth. He had a handsome face, with a square, powerful jaw. Sorme found himself liking him instantly. Callet sat opposite him, in the armchair.

I hear you're a writer?

Yes. Who told you that?

Carlotte. The girl who cleans up. We have some strange tenants in this house. You have the worst one above you.

The worst? Why?

He's mad. And he plays gramophone records all night.

Christ! Does he thump around, though?

No, I don't think so. He plays records. You won't see him during the day. He sleeps.

That's all right. I sometimes work most of the night too. Do you object to the noise of a typewriter?

No. I use one myself. The only person who might complain is the girl in the room underneath.

I see. And who else qualifies as 'strange'?

The Frenchman made a puzzled grimace. Sorme explained:

You said there were several strange tenants?

Ah, yes. Well the old man above you is the worst.

There are two homosexuals who live on the ground floor. They won't bother you. They sometimes quarrel all night. They are all right except when they are drunk. Then they get noisy.

Doesn't the landlady object?

No. She doesn't live here. The German girl is supposed to keep an eye on the place. Carlotte. She lives in the basement.

The record came to an end. Sorme turned the player off. Immediately, they heard the sound of someone knocking on the door of the next room. The Frenchman opened the door, saying: Hello?

Phone for Monsieur Callet, a girl's voice said.

I'll probably see you later. Thanks for the tea.

You're welcome, Sorme said.

He poured himself a second cup of tea, and switched on the record player again. The heat was making him drowsy. To wake himself up, he began to rearrange his books in the bookcase behind the door. He flattened the three cardboard cartons that the books had been packed in, and heaved them on top of the wardrobe. They met some obstruction and slid down again. He climbed on to a chair, and looked on the wardrobe. There was a pile of books there, pushed to the back against the wall. There were four tattered copies of P.G. Wodehouse, and three volumes in the *Notable British Trials Series*. One of these had a label inside: Erith Public Libraries. The date stamped inside seemed to be several years earlier.

He lifted them down, blowing the dust off them, then sat down at the table to examine them. A quarter of an hour later he was still reading the first volume he had opened, *The Trial of Burke and Hare*. It made him feel slightly sick.

Someone knocked on the door. He called: Hello.

The Frenchman looked round the door.

Hello. Lotte asked me to give you a message. Someone phoned for you this morning.

Oh? Did he leave a message?

Yes. She didn't get his name, but he left a telephone number. Here it is.

Sorme took the torn envelope flap. He said:

Thanks. I'll ring him now. Where's the phone?

Unfortunately, he left a message asking you to ring him before three. He said he was leaving London at three.

Sorme looked at his watch. It said half past four.

Oh . . . thanks anyway.

The Frenchman asked conversationally: What are you reading?

Oh, a book on murders.

Did you read about that murder last night?

No.

In Whitechapel. Another girl found beaten to death. It was in the midday paper. Do you want to see it?

Sorme said, chuckling: Don't bother. I intend to eat a meal today. This stuff makes me feel sick.

When the door closed again he tossed *The Trial of Burke and Hare* on to the bed, and opened one of the Wodehouse volumes.

In the night, he woke up and remembered Nunne's aunt. Until then he had completely forgotten about her. He reached for his trousers, and felt in the dark for the back pocket. The sheet of notepaper was still there. He struck a match, and read: Gertrude Quincey, The Laurels, Vale of Health, followed by her phone number. He propped it on the chair beside the bed to remind him to phone her in the morning, and lay down again, in the night that now smelt of burnt sulphur, and thought about her. Her figure was slim and attractive; there was something demure about her manner that he found exciting. She was probably fifteen years his senior; perhaps less; perhaps only ten. He speculated idly on the advantages of persuading her to become his mistress, even of marrying her. It would be pleasant to be looked after. But in ten years' time, in fifteen? There was also this business of her being a Jehovah's Witness. Somehow, that did not fit in. He thought of Jehovah's Witnesses as rather slovenly-dressed working-class women.

It would be interesting to find out how serious she was about the Bible classes. Or if her convictions made chastity obligatory.

He knew, with sudden certainty, that there could never be any question of wanting to marry her. It would be a sell-out. There was an intuition of certainty in him that told him that a sell-out for security could never be necessary. He thought instead of making love to her. The idea carried him into sleep.

The following evening he tried phoning her; there was no reply. He depressed the receiver-rest and rang Austin's number; a girl on the switchboard told him that Mr Nunne had gone away for a few days. He returned to his room, feeling curiously disappointed.

Half an hour later he was reading when he heard footsteps ascending the stairs to the old man's room. Someone knocked on the door. A girl's voice called: Mr Hamilton! There was no reply. The footsteps came down the stairs again. Someone rapped on his door. He called: Come in.

The girl who stood in the doorway said:

I'm sorry to disturb you . . .

He said: You're Carlotte?

Yes. There is a policeman at the front door . . .

To see me?

O no! He says someone has thrown a bottle into the

street. I think it must be Mr Hamilton. But he won't answer the door. What shall I do?

What makes you think it's him?

It must be. Monsieur Callet is out. Who else could it be?

What do you want me to do?

Could you – go up by the fire escape? He may answer you.

Where's the policeman?

Downstairs.

He climbed out of the window on to the fire escape. A shaft of light came from the open door above.

In the room, the old man squatted on the floor, his back to the door, naked. The choir sang:

> *Stella matutina*
> *Salus infirmorum*
> *Refugium peccatorum . . .*

He stood there, uncertain, wondering whether to return quietly to his own room. When the record stopped, he coughed and knocked on the door. He expected the old man to turn, or start guiltily. Nothing happened. The old man took off the record and selected another from the pile in front of him. Sorme said:

Excuse me . . .

The old man said over his shoulder:

Come in. Don't stand there.

Sorme advanced into the room.

I'm sorry to trouble you, but there's a policeman down below enquiring about a bottle that somebody threw into the street.

As he spoke, he saw the window was open: it overlooked the street.

The old man said: You are German, are you not?

49

No, English. So would you mind . . .?

Yes, all right, all right. Do you like the Roman litany?

He felt irritated and helpless. The old man had a bottle between his knees, with a glass inverted over the neck. The gramophone was a big wooden box; the circle of green baize was loose on the turntable; the wires ran across the room to a radio on the bookshelf. He felt chilled in the draught that blew across the room, and noticed with surprise that the old man was sweating.

I only came to tell you that the policeman seems pretty annoyed. Throwing bottles out of windows causes a lot of trouble . . .

Tell me, my young friend, do you believe in mortification of the flesh?

He felt suddenly violently angry, and would have enjoyed snatching up the gramophone and smashing it on the perspiring bald head. It was a feeling that he was somehow the victim of a drunk old man. He crossed the room to the door and tried it; it had been locked and the key removed.

The old man said thickly: Sit down and have a drink. What part of Germany do you come from?

Sorme turned round, and was suddenly shocked and repelled by the blotchy nakedness; a tainted spittle of disgust rose in his throat. The old man poured gin into the tumbler, and then inverted the glass over the neck of the bottle again. He shook the bottle so that the glass clinked, and smiled:

You can't get out that way.

He flung out his right arm, pointing; Sorme followed the direction of his finger to a wall cupboard. The door stood open.

Do you know what this is, my young friend, my little German friend?

No.

'S a map, isn't it? A map. But do you know what it is?

There was a map pinned to the inside of the door; it seemed to be drawn in ink.

Of course you don' know. An' I'm not goin' a tell you . . . It's my secret . . .

He crossed the room quickly and went out of the fire door again. The old man called: Hi, wait a minute! Sorme went down the fire escape and climbed back into his own room.

Well? the girl said.

It's no good; he's drunk. You'll have to tell the policeman it won't happen again. He's too drunk to listen.

She turned and left the room without speaking. He closed the window and knelt by the gas fire, warming his hands. From somewhere downstairs he could hear a deep male voice speaking. The gramophone above was playing again. He was puzzled by the violence of the killing instinct that the old man had aroused in him. Even now, it would have given him pleasure to stand in the doorway and empty a revolver into the repulsive nakedness. The strength of his own hatred surprised him.

His hands were grimy, from touching the rail of the fire escape. He washed them in the kitchen, gradually relaxing as he leaned over the sink, his hands in the warm water. When he came down again the girl was waiting in his room. She stared back from the bookcase as he came in:

Oh – I'm sorry. I hope you don't mind me coming in . . .

Not at all. What happened?

He says he will have to report it. That's all.

Will you have a glass of wine?

She looked as if about to refuse. He took the bottle out of the cupboard, saying: I'm having one.

Please. Just a little, then.

It was the bottle he had opened the day before and was

still nearly full. He poured wine into a tumbler and handed it to her.

Sit down.

Thank you.

She sat in the armchair by the fire. She had a strong, pointed face, with high cheekbones. Her mouth was full, but strong, not sensual. If she had been slimmer she might have been almost beautiful. Her English was perfect.

What do you think we ought to do about him?

He said: I'm all for killing him. He disgusts me.

What did he say?

Nothing intelligible. He was pretty drunk. He was sitting on the floor in the nude.

Nude. You mean naked?

That's it.

He pulled a hard chair up opposite her and sat down.

I don't understand him. It is strange that he has not killed himself. He drinks all the time.

Who is he? Do you know?

He was an engineer. His wife died. I think he has money. Sometimes he talks in Hyde Park about religion.

What about religion?

I don't know. Some Russian sect who believe in dancing round a bonfire. And he talks a lot when he's drunk. About murder.

Murder?

Yes. He pretends he has a great secret . . . about – what do you call him – Jacques L'Eventreur?

Jacques . . . Jack the Disemboweller? Oh, you mean Jack the Ripper?

What does he say about him?

I don't know. He talks a lot when he is drunk.

Why does Mrs Miller tolerate him? Why doesn't she throw him out?

Why should she? She doesn't have to live in the same

house with him. He pays three pounds a week for that room. No one else would pay so much.

He finished his wine, and poured some more. She had not touched hers yet. She said: He frightens me. Once he stole a pair of my shoes . . . There was a ring at the front doorbell. She jumped up immediately:

I have to go. That is for me.

Did you get them back?

Oh, yes. I found them in his cupboard. Goodbye. Thank you for the wine.

Not at all. Come up some evening when you don't have to go out.

He sat, staring into the gas fire, then leaned over and picked up her untouched wine. It tasted warm. He said aloud: I must get a woman. I'm getting sex-starved. He thought of the women who stood outside the Camden tube, their eyes following the men who walked past; then realized immediately that he had no desire for a prostitute. It would have destroyed his appetite, like a meal in a Rowton House. He finished the wine, and sat down at the typewriter.

That night, the vastation happened again. He woke up feeling hot and slightly drunk. He was still fully clothed, lying on the bed. Opposite his eyes, the radio droned softly; he had fallen asleep listening to a late night chamber concert. The room was in darkness, except for the light from the wavelength panel, and the red glow of the neon lights from the cinema over the way. His mind formed the question as he stared across the room: What am I doing here? It seemed arbitrary; he might have been anywhere or anything. A sense of alien-ness oppressed him, and he tried to focus his attention on it to discover its precise nature. Immediately, an orgasm of fear twisted his heart, and drained the strength out of his will. It was an awareness that his own existence was not capable of detaching itself from existence to question it. Existence faced him like a blank wall. There was an instinctive desire to penetrate the wall, to assert his reality beyond it, and a terror that came with the recognition that he was trapped in existence; that no detachment from it was possible. The terror was like losing an arm: too violent to hurt.

He came back to his own existence, lying on the bed, with a jerk of relief. He swung himself off the bed, and crossed the room to switch off the radio, thinking: Absurd or not, I choose to be here.

Back in bed again, he tried to recreate the fear, and the perception that caused it, and failed. It had drained him, like sexual fulfilment, and his mind formed words instead of sensations. The only thing he could recall was the sense of alien-ness, a feeling: I do not belong here. He wondered vaguely, losing the struggle to keep awake, whether the insight was not some kind of guardian, a benevolence whose aspect was othingness.

He woke up again in the night, and felt curiously disgusted with his body, as if it were already dead flesh. Suddenly, he realized what it was that disgusted him; it was the idea of his own non-existence.

He woke up with an immediate sense that something was happening. He looked at his watch; it was half past ten. Someone was banging on the door of the old man's room. The voice of the German girl called:

Open the door, please. Someone wants to speak to you.

The old man's voice shouted something. It sounded muffled. The knocking was repeated. The old man called again; this time his voice sounded clearer:

Who is it?

A male voice said: Police officers. Would you mind opening your door?

Sorme sat up in bed, thinking immediately of the bottle. There was a noise from overhead, a movement of bare feet on the floor. Then something heavy moved, an article of furniture. The male voice called again.

Would you let us in, please?

There was no reply, only another dragging sound across the floor. The knocks on the door became heavy and peremptory. Suddenly, the old man's voice, shrill and breathless, shouted:

What do you want?

The German girl said soothingly:

They only want to ask a few questions.

What about?

The policeman said: Open the door, and we can talk.

The old man's voice was harsh, hardly recognizable; he shouted:

I know you. I know your tricks.

There was a note of hysteria in it. The policemen were now conferring with the girl in low voices. In the room above, the bare feet padded across the floor. Something clanged as it fell. The policeman shouted: If you don't let us in, I'm afraid we shall have to force the door.

Sorme swung himself out of bed and pulled his trousers on. He looked around for his slippers, and then remembered he had left them in the kitchen. His door opened suddenly, and the German girl looked in. He was still on the floor, looking under his bed. Her voice said:

There's no one here. You can come in.

He straightened up as a man came into the room. The girl whispered: O, I'm sorry. I thought you were out.

He felt embarrassed, his hair tangled, still wearing the pyjama jacket. He asked:

What it is?

55

Sshhh! We don't want him to hear. This gentleman is a policeman. He wants to get on to the fire escape. Do you mind if he comes through your room?

No. Of course not.

The plain-clothed policeman said gruffly: Thank you, sir.

Sorme heaved up the lower window frame. It went up with a shriek of unoiled pulleys. The girl grimaced. The policeman had picked up a sheet of newspaper from the table, saying quietly: Do you mind, sir? He laid it on the bed, and stepped on it to climb out of the window. He was a short man, with a pointed, bird-like face. He stood there for a moment, staring up at the room above, then went quietly up the fire escape. Sorme lowered the window six inches to lessen the draught. He asked the girl: What's it all about?

She shrugged: He must be mad. They only want to ask him a few questions.

About throwing that bottle?

Oh no. Not that.

What has the old boy done?

She said mysteriously: It is about a murder. They think he might know something.

They heard a sudden blow on the door above as someone tried to force it. The old man's voice screamed:

You're not coming in!

The girl ran to the window and looked out. The policeman called:

Tell Bert to come and help, would you? I'm afraid we'll have to break the door. Sorme hurried to the door, but before he reached it the other policeman ran into the room, wrenched up the window, and clambered out. The girl said:

What does he think he's doing, the fool? No one wants to hurt him.

She flung herself on the bed again and craned out through the window. The door above gave way with a crash. The old man's voice shouted despairingly:

Don't come near me.

The girl turned round and stared at him. There was a sudden shriek of pain that made them both tense. Sorme said: My God, what's he done? Perhaps I'd better go and help.

As soon as he climbed out of the window, he saw the black smoke that poured through the doorway. He took the stairs three at a time. Flames and smoke made it impossible to see into the room. One of the policemen was shouting: Open the window! The flames abated for a moment, and he could see that the fire seemed to be immediately inside the door. He recoiled against the rail of the fire escape, then threw himself forward into the room. Smoke filled it like a dense brown fog. The old man was writhing on the floor. He seemed to be on fire. Both policemen were trying to smother the flames with blankets. Sorme wrenched open the window on the far side of the room, and breathed gratefully the clean air. When he turned back into the room, he was able to see that the fire was coming from a paraffin tin that lay on its side near the stove, still gushing oil. He took a running kick at it and sent it through the door and into the yard. The old man rolled under his feet, still screaming, and made him fall on to the bed. He regained his balance, and heaved the mattress off the bed and into the middle of the flames. Immediately, the area of flame was reduced to a few square feet, lapping around the edge of the mattress. One of the policemen called hoarsely: Good man! They stopped using the blankets as beaters, and threw them into the flames. Sorme opened the wardrobe, and threw all the clothes he could find. His eyes and throat were smarting from the fumes. He began to stamp on the flames that still burned, cannoning into the policeman as he staggered drunkenly, coughing in the smoke. On the floor, the old man was silent.

The draught through the room was clearing the smoke. Sorme left the policemen to stamp out the flames, and started to tear away the trunk and armchair that had been pushed against the door. He turned the key in the lock, and pulled it open. In his eagerness to breathe clean air, he almost fell down the stairs.

He resisted the impulse to close the door behind him and cut himself off from the smoke and stink of paraffin. He sat on the top stair, his back against the banisters, breathing deeply. After a few minutes the smarting died out of his eyes. He felt begrimed from head to foot with smoke. When he had ceased to feel that he was suffocating, he went back into the room again. Both policemen were standing outside, on the fire escape, panting. The fire was out. The old man was lying, perfectly still, in the middle of the floor. Sorme turned and went downstairs again. Three people were inside, looking out of the window. He turned away with disgust, and went up to the kitchen. There, he turned the tap on full, and held his head underneath it. He pulled off the pyjama jacket and rubbed his body with a wet sponge, which soothed his hot flesh with a luxurious coolness. His body ached and throbbed as if he had been beaten. He soaped the sponge and his face and chest, and then, lowering his trousers, the lower half of his body. When he had dried himself he felt better. His hair, which he had allowed the water to soak, dripped on his shoulders and down his neck. He rubbed it vigorously with the towel, then combed it. He went downstairs again, carrying the pyjama jacket.

His door was now closed. In the room, both the policemen were sitting without their coats and jackets. The old man lay on the bed, moaning gently. The two men looked at him and smiled when he came in. One commented:

Blimey, I thought we'd had it that time, didn't you, Jack?

The one called Jack glanced at the bed, saying:

Stupid old bastard. What's he have to do that for?

The other one looked at Sorme; he said:

Thanks for the help.

Not at all. Are you arresting him?

No. We just wanted to ask him a few questions.

Their faces and hands were grimy; both were still sweating. Sorme asked: Can I offer you a drink?

I'll say you can! the policeman called Jack said.

What of? the other asked.

Wine or beer?

Beer for me.

And me.

He opened a quart of light ale, and poured into two glasses and a china mug. He drank his own down in one long draught. He pushed the bottle towards them, saying:

Help yourselves.

Thanks. We will.

Where's Carlotte – the German girl?

Phoning the ambulance.

The girl came back into the room as he spoke.

They will be here soon. How is he?

The man called Jack shrugged:

Can't tell at his age. He's not badly burned, but there's the shock . . .

The old man was lying on the bed, his eyes open, breathing heavily. He began to groan. Sorme said:

I'll go and dress, if you don't mind.

He took a pair of neatly folded trousers from the drawer, and a shirt and tie. Both policemen refilled their glasses, emptying the bottle; they ignored the old man.

The girl came out of the room after him. She said:

You can wait in my room if you like. The ambulance should be here soon.

He was about to refuse, then changed his mind:

Thank you. Where is it?

I'll show you.

She went down the stairs ahead of him. He asked her:

What do you make of it all? What's it all about?

I don't know, I know no more than you.

For some reason, he had expected a dismal room, but her living-room was large and comfortably furnished. The floor was carpeted. She switched on a tall reading lamp that stood by the settee; it diffused a pink, warm light. An electric fire, set in the wall, was burning. Left alone, he dressed and combed his hair, then looked through the volumes on the bookshelf; they were mostly in German. He noted that her bed in the corner of the room was a wide divan, thinking automatically: Big enough for two; then thought: No, never wise to have a mistress in the house; she can watch you too closely. Nevertheless, he looked with interest through the photographs on the sideboard, and noted no young men among them. There were two family groups, and a picture of the girl, looking about ten years younger, with her arm round the waist of a fair-haired girl; they were both dressed in Bavarian costume.

The door behind him opened. He had expected the girl, but it was the policeman called Jack who came in.

Ah. Would you mind if I asked you a couple of questions?

Of course. What about?

Would you mind just sitting down?

He produced a notebook and a ballpoint pen; Sorme sat on the settee.

Now, let's see. You've only been here since Saturday, so I don't expect you know much about the old boy?

Nothing at all, I'm afraid.

But you went up to his room last night?

Only for a few moments.

I see. You didn't get any idea of any papers he kept in there, did you? Something he might want to burn?

I'm afraid not, I wasn't in there for more than a minute and a half.

The man said, sighing:

I . . . see. Ah well. Would you mind describing what happened last night?

Sorme gave an account of his interview with the old man, repeating, as well as he could remember, everything that was said. The policeman interrupted him only once, to ask:

Did you get a chance to look at this map?

None at all. I just walked past him.

It was behind the cupboard door?

Yes.

A street map?

As well as I could judge, yes.

Would you recognize a map of Whitechapel if you saw it?

I don't know. I might. I suppose it *could* have been Whitechapel. I suppose Carlotte told you about this cranky idea about Jack the Ripper he has?

The man said gloomily: Yes.

He closed the notebook, and returned it to his pocket. He said: Well, I suppose that's all.

Sorme said: Is it a secret, or can you tell me what it's all about?

Just a routine check-up over the Whitechapel murders. Somebody reported him as a suspicious character. We've got to check.

What are these Whitechapel murders?

Don't you read the papers?

Not unless I have to. And I don't often have to!

The policeman lit a cigarette, and stood up, looking for an ash-tray. He said: You're a lucky man. Have a look in today's papers. You'll find all about it.

How were they committed? What weapon, I mean?

Several. Hammer, scissors, a knife.

And how many have there been so far?

Four.

Sorme said: But what makes you suppose they were all committed by the same person? If the weapons were different, surely . . .

The policeman interrupted him, smiling:

Look here, it's no good asking me. Have a look at your paper. I'm not in charge of the case. I'm just doing a routine check.

Who is in charge?

Inspector Macmurdo, Scotland Yard.

A doorbell rang suddenly in the flat. The man said:

Ah, that'll be the ambulance.

He went to the door; before he could reach it, they heard the sound of footsteps running down the stairs. He opened the door and stood there, listening. Sorme said:

You know, it's very odd . . .

What?

Well, the way he went on today. He seemed to think you wanted to arrest him.

Very odd. I'd like to know why.

I think he's a little insane.

I'd better be going. Thanks for the help . . . and the beer.

Not at all.

He found the morning paper on the kitchen table. The headline on the inside page read: Biggest Manhunt Ever. He took it into the living-room, and sat in the armchair to read it. The front page carried the picture of a plump, thick-lipped girl. The text read:

'The hunt for London's maniac killer continues. Yesterday, every available police officer was diverted on to the biggest Metropolitan manhunt yet for the murderer who has now struck four times in eleven months. Late on Saturday night, Detective-Inspector Macmurdo, in charge of the case, told reporters that the police now have reason to believe that the killer of Gretchen Widman, the forty-five-year-old ex-model found stabbed to death on Saturday morning, was also the man who claimed the lives of Martha Turner (January 6th), Juanita Miller (April 3rd), and Catherine Eddowes (August 17th).

'Martha Turner was killed by a hammer-blow in George Street, Spitalfields. Juanita Miller was stabbed with a pair of scissors. Catherine Eddowes, like Gretchen Widman, was stabbed with a knife.

'The police are now almost certain they are hunting a maniac sadist, with a recurring urge to kill. Since Saturday morning, police have been conducting door-to-door enquiries throughout Whitechapel.

'Stallholders in Petticoat Lane Market were questioned about a man who carries a razor-blade and slashes female underwear that is hung up for sale.

'Yesterday afternoon the telephone room at the Yard received over two hundred calls from people who thought that they might have information about the killer.

'Late last night, Detective Inspector Macmurdo said:

'"There has been no further development. The police are still hoping to make an early arrest."'

The girl came in as he finished reading. She said:

Your room's empty now.

He stood up, saying: Oh, thank you.

Would you like a cup of tea?

Thank you very much. Yes.

She called from the kitchen:

The policemen told me you did very well.

He said, laughing: It's not often I get so much excitement before lunch.

He stood in the doorway, watching her as she spooned tea into the pot, then lifted the simmering kettle. He said: Don't you warm the teapot?

Never! I am sure it makes no difference. My English friends say it does, but I can detect no difference.

Maybe, he said noncommittally.

She shot him a sudden friendly smile.

All right. Next time I make tea for you, I warm the pot.

He said seriously: Do you think there's any chance of the old boy coming back?

I hope not, she said emphatically.

Have you read this morning's paper yet?

Not yet.

It says the police had two hundred calls yesterday about this Whitechapel murderer. It looks as if one of them was about the old boy.

She handed him tea in a delicate china cup. Sorme said: Thanks . . . Of course, it's impossible that he *could* have had anything to do with the murders, isn't it?

I think so.

They went back into the living-room; she sat on the settee.

I suppose he has an alibi, anyway – playing records all night.

He sugared his tea and stirred it, saying musingly:

Still, he could wangle that all right. All he'd need would be an automatic record-changer and a pile of long-players. That'd make a good detective story, don't you think? A man who always keeps his neighbours awake to give himself an alibi. Then one night he leaves a pile of long-players on, sneaks down the fire escape and commits a murder, and sneaks back two hours later. Perfect!

You should suggest that to the police.

He said: I would if I thought there was any danger of that old bastard coming back here. Frame him. Declare I saw him creeping up the fire escape in sneakers, with a bloodstained hatchet in one hand! That'd fix him.

She said with unexpected compassion: Poor old man. He should have a family to take care of him.

Irritated by her implied reproach of his callousness, he said cheerfully:

I dare say he has. I expect they're in hiding to try and avoid him. Come to think of it, I bet that's who denounced him.

You shouldn't be so unkind about him.

He hasn't kept you awake all night with his bloody records!

He sipped his tea. It was very bad tea; it was weak, and had not been left to stand long enough. He added more milk to cool it, and drank it in gulps. She said: More?

No thanks. I'd better go. By the way, have you looked in his room?

No, why?

I wonder if it's badly burned?

Why? Do you want to move in there?

It might be an idea, he said. In case the next tenant turns somersaults all night. Or trains a dancing horse.

Chapter Three

The voice at the other end of the line said:

Newsdesk.

Is Mr Payne there, please?

Speaking.

Hello, Bill. This is Gerard.

Hello, old boy! How's it go?

Listen, Bill. Something rather odd's just happened in this place I'm living in. The police have just tried to arrest an old man as a suspect for the Whitechapel murders.

Has any other newspaper got on to it yet?

Not as far as I know.

What happened?

He barricaded his door and set fire to the room.

Christ! What happened then?

They broke the door down. He's in hospital now suffering from burns.

Hold on . . . All right, give me the address. It's Colindale, isn't it?

No. I've moved to Kentish Town.

Good. That's fine. Do you think you could get down here?

To the office?

Yes. No. To Joe's in Carmelite Street. You remember that café we went to with Gret?

OK. I'll get there right away. See you in half an hour.

Wait. Hold on. Give me the address, and we'll send a man there right away.

All right, but would you do me a favour? Don't mention my name. The landlady might resent it. Get your man to say he found out from the police, or one of the neighbours tipped your office. OK?

OK. Give me the address.

He walked back quickly, his hands deep in his raincoat pockets. The November sky looked cold and marble-grey.

He leaned the bicycle against the window of the café in Carmelite Street, and locked the back wheel. The road was being repaired, and the noise of the pneumatic drill filled the air with vibrations that drowned the noise of machines from the printing works opposite. The café was beginning to fill with the lunch-hour crowd. There was no sign of Payne in either of the two rooms. He took off his raincoat, and placed it on an empty corner table to reserve it, then went to the counter to order. When he came back to the table a man was sitting there. Sorme said without enthusiasm: Hello, Bobby. The man said:

I'm well, Gerard. How're you? Ah hope ye don't mind if I sit down?

The watery eyes regarded him with anxiety. He said:

No. I'm waiting for Bill Payne.

That's all right. Ah'll go when he comes. Well, you're looking well, m'boy.

Sorme looked across at the tired, unshaven face, and repented his brusqueness. The Scotsman looked as if he hadn't eaten or slept for several days. He said:

Can I offer you a cup of tea?

No thank ye, Gerard. Ah've just had one. But Ah'll tell ye what you could do. Ah'm expirin' for want of a smoke, and Ah've only a threepenny piece to ma name. Could ye lend me a couple of bob – or a shillin'd do.

Sorme said embarrassedly: I dunno. I suppose so.

He pulled out the wallet, and, removing a folded ten-shilling note, handed it to Robert Drummond.

If you can change that, you can have two bob.

Thanks, man. Ye're savin' ma life.

Sorme looked at his watch; it was half past twelve. Drummond came back, and dropped four florins in front of him. He held out the open packet of Woodbines. Sorme shook his head.

Thanks, I don't.

Ye're lucky.

Sorme noticed the trembling of the hand that lit the cigarette.

The Scotsman sat down, and sighed a cloud of smoke. He detached a shred of tobacco from his lower lip; his eyes closed:

Aahh! My first today.

His eyes opened, and looked directly at Sorme for the first time.

Well, lad, what've ye been doin' since I saw ye last?

Nothing much. Tell me, Bobby, do you know anythlng about these Whitechapel murders?

Only what ah've read in the papers. Why, do you?

No. Until yesterday. I'd never even heard of them. I never read the papers.

Drummond said: Did I ever tell ye about the murder I got involved in in Glasgow?

No.

Well. Ah wasn't exac'ly involved. But the girl livin' in the room next to me got strangled one night. And the funny thing was, I haird her cry out. And I just lay there and did nothing.

Why?

Why? It's hard to say.

He stared, brooding, over his second cigarette. The woman called: One liver and chips. Sorme collected it from the counter and paid. When he sat down, the Scotsman said slowly:

Yes, I can tell ye why. Have ye ever wanted something badly – wanted it a lot more than it's worth?

Occasionally, Sorme said. He shook tomato ketchup on to the plate.

She was a shapely girl, y'understand, not pretty. An' she didn't have regular men friends, as far as I could make out, but she wasn't a hardened virgin either. Men sometimes stayed overnight – not always the same man, y'see? And it was a temptation – to knock on her door one night on some excuse and say: How about it, ma dear? An' I don't think she'd have refused – I don't think so.

Sorme asked, through a mouthful of liver: Why didn't you?

He shrugged, stubbing out the cigarette:

I can't say. Ah was younger then . . . shy.

He looked at Sorme and smiled suddenly. It was a curiously candid smile.

But on the night it happened, I haird her cry out, and thought she was having a nightmare. I thought: Why not now? an' got half way to the door. Then I started to sweat and shake. I'd thought about it so long, I wasn't prepared to get it so suddenly. So I lay in bed, feelin' ma heart thumpin' and tryin' to work up the courage. Then I haird someone movin' about, and thought: She can't sleep . . . But I didn't go. And the next day, they found her strangled.

Did they ever catch him?

Yes. They caught him. He was a soldier. He'd killed her for the three pounds she had in her handbag.

Sorme said: Ugh, what a swine. Poor girl.

Here's Bill, the Scotsman said.

Sorme turned around as Payne came into the room. He waved to him. Drummond stood up, saying:

I'll leave you.

Sorme said: If you don't stop chain-smoking, you'll need another packet in half an hour.

Ye're right, Gerard. Thanks for the loan.

The hand, unwashed, covered with light ginger hairs, pressed Sorme's forearm. Payne called from the counter:

Tea for both of you?

Not for me. – Ah'm just goin'. G'bye, m'dear.

Goodbye, Sorme said.

Payne brought the two teas over. He said:

What did he want?

Nothing. Just to talk.

Talk? Didn't he put the bite on you?

Only for two bob.

I knew it. He usually tries to tap me when he sees me. That's how I knew he'd bitten you already.

You look ill, Sorme said.

Payne's face was bloodless. It was a thin face, with a clean-cut profile and cleft chin. When he was tired, his skin took on the greenish tint of the albumen of a boiled duck egg.

I am. I'm half dead with sleepiness. I've done two shifts running. The other man's away with 'flu.

Did you send a reporter?

Yes, he's on his way there now. I told him the story came from the police. Tell me what happened.

Sorme repeated the story, beginning with the bottle-throwing incident. Payne drank his tea slowly, and listened without interrupting. He asked:

Do you know which hospital they took him to?

No idea.

Never mind. We can soon check on that. It sounds interesting. You say he was trying to destroy something – papers? That sounds as if the police might have a line on him. But I doubt whether he's the man they want.

Why?

70

He was a small man, you say. The pathologist's report says that the girl was stabbed by a tall man. They can tell from the angle of the wound.

I never read the papers. Tell me all you know about this case.

Nobody knows much. Only what the headlines say.

Yes, but I haven't even read the headlines. I'd never heard of this murder case until the other day.

You ought to read the papers, you know, Gerard. No writer can afford not to.

I suppose so, Sorme said dubiously. He finished his tea and stared ruminatively at the caked sugar in the bottom. He said:

Tell me about these murders.

Haven't you read anything at all?

Only about this girl on Friday. Where was she killed?

Somewhere in Whitechapel. I wasn't on the newsdesk Friday night.

He was looking past Sorme's head towards the door. He waved suddenly, calling: Martin.

He told Sorme: Here's the man who can tell you. He was on one of the murders.

The tall, raincoated man waved from the counter. Payne moved across to the inner chair to make room for him as he crossed the room. He said:

You know Martin Mason, don't you, Gerard?

I didn't, Sorme said. How d'you do?

The man had a thin, beaky face, with bird-like eyes. The shoulders were narrow and stooped. He nodded briefly at Sorme, carefully placing his hat under the chair.

Martin, Gerard wants to know about these murders. Give him the gen.

Doesn't he read the papers?

No, Sorme said patiently, not unless I can't help it.

Nonconformist, eh? Mason said. He had a smooth,

71

nasal voice, with no tone variation; the kind of voice that seems perfectly adapted for sneering.

Sorme smiled to disguise his distaste; he said:

I heard you were on one of these murders?

I was, Mason said, stirring his tea. What do you want to know about it?

Which one?

The third – Catherine Eddowes.

I thought it was the second, Payne said.

No. That was the Spanish dancer, Juanita Miller. Jimmy and Sam covered that. Superb woman.

What about the other case? Sorme said. Did you see her?

Yes, but only later, in the morgue. And she was all covered up. She wasn't much to look at. Little, middle-aged woman.

Sorme asked: Was it a sex crime?

They can't tell.

Why not?

She was a prostitute.

What about the other women?

Same, Mason said. He smiled, like a conjurer bringing off a trick. Sorme found his dislike concentrating on the blotchy, beak-like nose.

The Spanish girl wasn't, Payne objected.

She wasn't much better, Mason said, glaring. She slept with so many men they couldn't even check up.

Tell me, Sorme said. Is it quite definite that they were all committed by the same man?

Not certain, Mason said. Juanita Miller and Catherine Eddowes were both knifed. But it wasn't the same knife. The knife was found by the body in both cases. In one case a Boy Scout's bowie-knife, in the other a little kitchen affair. But the really surprising feature is that the murderer must have got blood on him, yet he probably returned through London in the early hours of the morning.

Not so difficult, Payne said. London is fairly deserted then.

Sorme said: There could be three explanations of that. He might have been a local man, and not had far to go. He might have had a car. Or he might have carried a coat over his arm which he dropped while he killed the girl, and put it on afterwards to conceal the blood.

Oh, there are more explanations than that, Mason said. We published a letter from someone who thought he might have escaped through the sewers.

Impossible, Payne said.

I think so too, Mason said. But until they catch him, no one can know definitely, can they?

His eyes rested meditatively on Sorme. He asked abruptly, as if trying to take Sorme by surprise:

Why do you want to know?

Sorme glanced at Payne. Payne said:

It's all right. He works for us.

It's like that, is it? Mason said.

Not exactly. It's just that . . . well, I've been drawn within their orbit, as it were.

He turned to Mason to explain:

The police tried to question an old man about the murders in the place where I live, and he barricaded himself in his room and set it on fire.

Have they any idea why?

No. I think he's a little cracked.

Or he might not be . . . Mason said.

Oh, I think so.

You could be right. But I'll tell you one thing. The police must have a pretty good reason for announcing that they think the four murders were committed by the same man. It's just not good policy. It centres the public

73

interest on the idea of the Killer at Large, and then people start writing letters to *The Times* and asking questions in Parliament about the efficiency of the police. They must have some reason for risking it.

What's your theory? Payne asked.

That they have a good idea who the man is. And they want him to feel that the net is closing. To scare him into giving himself away.

Perhaps, Payne said.

Can you think of any other reason?

Payne said, shaking his head:

If they had an idea of who he was, they'd close the net quietly. They'd watch him and wait for him to try it again. Sexual killers always try it again.

Sorme said: This girl – the one you saw.

The middle-aged woman, you mean? Catherine Eddowes?

Yes. How was she killed?

I've told you. Knifed.

But how? Cut-throat, or stabbed in the heart, or what?

They counted nearly sixty wounds.

Mason smiled. He obviously took pleasure in Sorme's shocked expression.

He must be a maniac! What about the other murders?

Mason drew deeply on his cigarette, smiling.

Less spectacular.

They need to be, Sorme said.

Mason turned to Payne:

Have you heard these rumours about Janet and Ken?

Which one? I heard about his wife screaming at Janet over the phone.

Sorme stood up.

I think I'll go, Bill. You two want to talk shop.

OK, Gerard. I've got to get back in a minute anyway. We'll probably be sending you a cheque soon.

That'd be useful, Sorme said. He shook hands with Mason. See you soon.

Bye-bye, Gerard.

He stopped at the counter to pay for the meal. Outside, the noise of the pneumatic drill was deafening. He unlocked the bicycle, and wheeled it on the pavement to Fleet Street. He stood there, hesitating whether to go towards the Aldwych or Blackfriars. Finally, remembering that his landlady might be in the house, he decided against returning to his room, and went towards Farringdon Street. His stomach felt watery and rebellious. It was the talk of murder. It had settled on his senses like a film of soot from a smoking lamp, coating them with a greyness of depression. He noticed also that he cycled with less confidence. The depression brought a sense of his body's betrayal. He stared up Ludgate Hill at St Paul's, thinking: London in November has no daylight. Only dusk. And London in July has too much daylight. Unreal, or too real.

The newsvendor's placard read: SEARCH FOR MANIAC KILLER. He turned towards Rosebery Avenue. Why should I care? Poor sod probably a paranoiac. Bored and confused. Kills as a protest. Stop the world. I wanna get off.

The grey front of the Rosebery Avenue hostel had a pumice stone quality that chilled the skin, like water. He rang the bell; behind him, the bicycle suddenly fell on to the pavement, the rear wheel spinning. He was leaning it against the wall again when the door was opened. He said:

Hi, Robin! How are you?

Gerard! Good heavens, what are you doing here?

The thin, damp hands clasped his. Robin Maunsell pulled him gently over the threshold.

75

I was just passing, Sorme said. Is it a bad time to call?

No, of course not. Do come in. Have you had lunch?

Yes, thanks.

How lovely to see you.

He peered into Sorme's face, smiling. Sorme withdrew his hand, feeling the pleasure that he had experienced tensing and congealing. Maunsell threw open a glass-panelled door, and led the way into the room, the cassock round his feet making the gentle, swishing noise of a gown.

You'll have a cup of tea, won't you?

Thanks. Yes, I'd love one.

Light the fire while I go and see about it.

Sorme groped in his pocket for matches; finding none, he wandered automatically towards the bookcase and scanned the titles. All were volumes of theology by writers he had never heard of. The windows of the room were of frosted glass, and overlooked the street. Vague silhouettes of people rippled past.

Haven't you lit the fire?

Sorry, I've no matches.

Oh, silly!

Maunsell produced matches from the pocket of his habit; kneeling, he lit the gas fire.

Let me take your overcoat. Do sit down. How are you? And how's your disgraceful sex life?

Sorme said, grinning:

You take a brotherly interest in my sins.

Of course; I wouldn't like to see you damned. But I dare say you'd like to be damned, wouldn't you?

I am, Sorme said. We all are.

Oh, I hope not.

He sat in the armchair with prim suddenness, clasping his hands in his lap. Sorme said:

I think you commit my sins vicariously, Robin.

Oh dear no. I'd really absolutely *loathe* to live your sort of life, really! But do tell me. How's – er . . . thingermer-jig – the one you were going to bed with the last time I saw you?

Sorme stared at the fire; he said solemnly:

Dead. She died of tetanus on top of St Vitus's dance.

Really? I'm sorry . . . Oh, but you're joking! Aren't you? No, be serious. If you don't want to tell me about your love life, let's talk of something else.

I came to talk of something else, as a matter of fact. Tell me about Father Carruthers.

Why? Where have you heard of him?

A friend told me about him. Chap called Austin Nunne. Do you know him?

No. There's a Mrs Nunne who comes here. Perhaps he's some relation?

Her son. Austin suggested I should talk to Father Carruthers. What do you think?

What about?

I'd just like to meet him, that's all. He sounds interesting.

He is. Terribly clever. He's written several books. He's written a life of Chehov, and a book on Dante. He's writing a book on Marcel at the moment.

Could I meet him, do you think?

Well, yes, it shouldn't be difficult to arrange. But listen, will you promise me something? Well, never mind . . . I'll go and see about that tea.

Sorme stopped himself from crossing to the bookshelf, knowing there was nothing to read. He was beginning to regret coming. He had forgotten how irritating Robin Maunsell could be. The idea of speaking to Father Carruthers had also lost its attraction, for some reason. He yawned.

77

The door opened, and a young priest looked in. He said:

Ah, excuse me. You are waiting for someone?

He spoke with a foreign accent that Sorme did not recognize.

I wanted to see Father Carruthers, Sorme said.

I think he is asleep. I will go and see.

Sorme started to say: Don't bother . . . but the door closed again. A moment later, someone kicked the door. Sorme opened it for Maunsell, who carried a loaded tray.

Good boy. It's lovely to see you again, Gerard. But you've got a terrible pallor. Have you been overworking?

Can you imagine *me* working?

Oh yes. You're not the ornamental type at all. You ought to work. Why don't you take a job?

Why should I?

You wouldn't get so bored. And you *do* get bored, don't you?

Yes, I get bored.

Then you should take a job.

Maunsell poured milk into the cups from the china jug, and sugared them.

Why should I take a job? All right, I get bored. What does that prove? That I don't know what to do with my time. And what do you suggest? Waste it by working. It's not logical. By the way, before I forget . . . someone popped his head round the door and asked me who I wanted to see. And I said Father Carruthers, and he went off to see. Priest with a foreign accent, very young.

Ah, Father Rakosi. He's a Hungarian refugee. You *are* silly.

Anyway, he said Father Carruthers would be asleep.

I expect he will be. He doesn't often get up, you know. He suffers from some obscure stomach complaint. But you ought not to have let Father Rakosi go off to see.

Why?

Well, *I* was going to see.

Oh, sorry. He'd gone before I could stop him. Would you pass the sugar, please?

Someone tapped on the door. The Hungarian priest came in again. He looked surprised to see Maunsell.

Excuse me . . . I thought you were waiting to see Father Carruthers?

I'm sorry . . . Sorme began.

Maunsell said: Is he awake?

Yes. He says he can see people for the next hour.

You'd better go up, Gerard. We can have a talk afterwards.

The priest smiled, nodded at them, and went out. Sorme called: Thank you.

You are silly, Gerard. Why didn't you wait for me?

Sorry. I didn't realize he'd arrange it so quickly.

Oh, never mind. You'd better go up now.

I can drink my tea here, can't I?

No, you hadn't better. Take it up with you. Come on. I'll show you the way.

Sorme followed him up the thickly carpeted stairs. On the first landing, a blue plaster madonna stood in a niche, her hands raised in blessing. Maunsell knocked gently on the door at the end of the corridor. He pushed it open and allowed Sorme to pass in.

This is Gerard Sorme, father. He's a friend of Mrs Nunne.

The priest was sitting up in bed, surrounded by white pillows. He wore a nightgown of some coarse blue material. Maunsell closed the door, and left them alone together.

Not Mrs Nunne, Sorme said. Her son.

Ah, Austin. I haven't seen him for a long time. How is he? Do sit down.

His face struck Sorme as one of the ugliest he had ever seen; without actually being deformed, it was crudely and gratuitously ugly, with the strong lines of a gargoyle. The jaw was too big; it would have had the effect of overbalancing the face if it had not been for the forehead, which also jutted, and had a sharp, vertical crease down the middle, as if someone had hit him with a crowbar. The large nose was slightly flattened; the mouth was wide, and spread across the face like a fissure. The eyes were small, almost colourless. If a lamp had been suspended overhead, they would have disappeared completely in the shadow of his brows. Sorme tried hard to remember where he had seen the face before, or where he had seen one like it. Then he remembered: the bust of Charley Peace in the Chamber of Horrors at Madame Tussaud's. The thought made him smile. The priest smiled back friendlily. He seated himself in the armchair near the fire, saying:

Austin's fine, father. He suggested that I should come and see you.

What did you say your name was?

Sorme, father, Gerard Sorme.

Sorme? Sorme . . . I know the name. It's a rare name, isn't it?

I've never met anyone else with it, outside my family . . .

The priest held up his hand to silence him. The furrow in the brow might have been an incision. For a few seconds, he frowned, concentrating.

Ah, I remember! Father Grey of Campion House. Did you ever know him, by any chance?

Sorme felt unaccountably guilty; he said:

Yes, I did. He instructed me once.

Good! the priest said. He was smiling happily again. I

don't often forget a name. Yes . . . Father Grey talked to me about you once. Why did you give up instruction?

I . . . I . . . I didn't get on with Father Grey to begin with.

Why not?

He seemed to want to convince me that Catholics were decent blokes after all. You know the sort of thing? Beef-eating, beer-drinking RAF padre style. And he had no time for mysticism. He spent three instruction periods convincing me that St Peter was really the first Pope. I got fed-up.

The priest said sympathetically:

I understand. Father Grey isn't everyone's idea of a Catholic . . . which is no doubt just as well.

Sorme grinned, waiting. The pale, blue-grey eyes contemplated him steadily. The priest said, smiling:

Well, you keep coming back, don't you? Why?

Sorme frowned, shrugging. It was difficult to find an answer. The soft voice pressed him:

Do you think you'll become a Catholic one of these days?

I may, I suppose.

But do you expect to?

No, not really, father. I don't mean it's impossible . . .

Quite. But have you no idea what you're looking for?

No, father, not really.

None at all?

Well, I suppose I have some idea. . .

Can you tell me?

Well . . . I suppose I hope to find somebody I can talk to.

What about?

I shan't know until I find somebody I can talk to.

He felt the answer was silly, and was irritated with himself. The priest's eyes rested on him calmly, as if completing an examination whose last stages consisted

81

simply in looking at Sorme. He felt a desire to get up and go away. The priest asked suddenly:

Do you know Austin well?

Not well. I met him for the first time on Friday. I haven't seen him since.

How did you meet him?

In the Diaghilev exhibition. I talked to him.

You spoke first?

No, he did. We talked about Nijinsky. Then we went off and had a meal together.

And then what?

Then I went home. And he went home. Why are you asking me this, father?

Only curiosity.

Irritation rose in him, looking at the undisturbed face; it was an odd sense of shame about the incident, considered in retrospect, that frayed his nerves. He said bluntly:

Are you wondering whether anything else happened between us? Because I'd rather you asked me frankly.

The priest shrugged slightly.

Did anything else happen?

No.

It doesn't interest me particularly, you understand. What you tell me is completely your own affair. I have no wish to force your confidence. But, as you can guess, I know Austin very well indeed.

Sorme caught up the unspoken meaning instantly.

Quite. Which is why I'd prefer you to ask me anything you want to know quite frankly. I don't know Austin at all well. We just ate a meal together and talked. But I don't share his . . . tastes. Any of them.

The priest inclined his head.

I like your frankness. Then tell me: When Austin spoke

to you and you went off together, did you have any idea of his . . . sexual peculiarities?

I guessed he was homosexual. That worried me a little. But I didn't feel he was just picking me up.

Did he tell you later that he was homosexual?

No.

I see. And did he speak of anything else?

Sorme stared hard at him, failing to understand.

Anything else? What else?

I see. I was simply curious.

Sorme could see that the priest wanted to drop the subject, but his curiosity was touched.

Do you mean he has *other* sexual peculiarities?

That is not for me to say, is it?

Sorme stared hard at him for a moment, then said:

I see.

The priest smiled immediately.

Please don't think I'm snubbing you. But as you probably know, Austin came to me a year ago with certain problems of his own. Now he sends you along, and, naturally, I wonder whether yours are of the same nature. But I cannot talk about Austin's problems. He can do that himself if he wants to. Presumably you're here to talk about yourself, not about Austin?

Sorme said embarrassedly:

I dunno that I've got anything that could be called a problem, father.

Well, no. That is not necessary, I agree. What kind of work do you do?

I write.

For a living?

No. I've got a small allowance. Just enough to live on.

You're very lucky! What do you write?

A novel, at present . . .

Do you take any interest in politics, at all?

83

He said with surprise:

None whatever.

Do you ever go to church?

I often go into churches – preferably when there's nobody else there.

Do you have any friends to discuss your ideas with?

Not really . . .

The priest smiled at him; the deep eyes were transformed when he was amused. Their good humour made Sorme feel completely at ease. He said:

You're rather a difficult case, aren't you?

Why, father?

You do nothing at all. Except write. That leaves an immense amount of time and opportunity for introspection. Then you go to see a priest in the same way that a man who never takes any exercise goes to see a doctor. Have you ever thought of seeing a psychologist?

The tone of banter made the words seem casual, but Sorme sensed their seriousness. He said:

Why should I? I'm not suffering from any illness. Besides, I suspect all psychologists of being fools and quacks. I don't think there's anything wrong with me. Nothing that's not wrong with all the human race, anyway.

Then why do you want to speak to a priest?

Sorme contemplated the grotesque, gnome's face, and groped for an answer. He said finally:

Not because I think I'm ill, anyway.

The priest laughed:

All right, we'll accept that. So you're not ill. But you feel you are frustrated, somehow. Is that it?

Yes. But not personally or sexually.

A sense of misunderstanding and failure to contact irritated Sorme. It was the assumption underlying their conversation that disturbed him: the assumption that there was something wrong with him.

When you say sexually, you mean physically?

Yes, I suppose so.

I see . . .

The priest nodded, staring at his interlaced hands.

Well, well. I can see why Father Grey was so puzzled by you. It's difficult to learn anything from you.

I'm sorry, father . . .

Let me try another question. What would you say is the centre of your interest in life? What do you really want?

The feeling of lack of contact became stronger; he had absolutely no inclination to try to express himself to the priest. While he was aware of the pale eyes watching him, he felt rebellious and annoyed. He made an effort to forget the priest and the vacuum that seemed to exist between them, to concentrate only on the ideas to be expressed. He stared into the fire, saying slowly:

I'd say all my life centres around an idea. An idea of a vision. I don't mean . . . the kind of vision the saints saw. Not that kind. Another sort.

Can you explain yourself more clearly?

I . . . I can give you an example of what I mean. Sometimes I wake up in the night with a sort of foreboding. Then I feel arbitrary. I feel somehow absurd. I feel, Who am I? And What am I doing here? I feel we take life too much for granted. We take our own existences for granted But perhaps it's *not* natural to exist. It happened the other night. You realize how much you normally take for granted, and feel a sudden terror in case you've no right to take anything for granted. Do you know what I mean, father?

He looked at Carruthers, and was immediately aware of having captured his attention. He began to feel better. The priest said:

I understand. Go on.

That's one aspect of it. Then there's another, that I think is completely different. A couple of months ago I picked up a girl in a café. I know her slightly – she studies at the Slade School. I went back and slept with her, and everything was fine. But the second night I slept with her, something odd happened. Quite suddenly, I didn't want her. I don't know quite why. I just lay there at the side of her, and felt a complete lack of desire to make love to her.

The priest said amiably:

That must have been embarrassing.

Yes. But that's the odd thing. I lay there feeling embarrassed, and wishing I could understand what was the matter. I felt ashamed and irritable. It wasn't that I didn't want the girl. It was some other feeling conflicting with it. So I lay there, trying to discover what the other emotion was. And suddenly I felt a tremendous excitement. It was so strong that I felt I'd never want to sleep again. It didn't correspond to anything in particular. It made me think about mathematics. I thought: I am lying here in the middle of London, with a population of three million people asleep around me, and a past that extends back to the time when the Romans built the city on a fever swamp . . . I can't explain what I felt. It was a sense of *participation* in everything. I wanted to live a million times more than anybody has ever lived. Do you know what I mean, father?

I think so.

It was an excitement, you see. I was suddenly aware of how many people and places there are outside myself.

But you just mentioned mathematics. Why mathematics?

Well . . . because I thought about mathematics. At least, I didn't *begin* thinking about mathematics. I was feeling irritated with the girl, and the idea that she wanted me to make love to her. Then I thought about something I'd read that day in a book on witchcraft. About a woman named Isobel Gowdie, who claimed she had sexual intercourse with demons while her husband was asleep beside her . . .

What made you think of that?

This girl I was sleeping with. She's a completely spoilt, neurotic girl, a nymphomaniac. I suddenly felt sick of her lukewarm little titivations, her everlasting sexual itch. She had sex for the same reason that she chain-smoked. Boredom. Then I remembered Isobel Gowdie. At least sex *meant* something to her. She wanted to be possessed by the devil. She was probably bored stiff on a Scottish farm in the middle of nowhere. So she invented demons and devils.

There was a light tap on the door. Sorme started violently. A woman wearing an apron came in.

Mr Bryce and Mr Jennings have arrived, father.

What, already? All right, ask them to wait just a moment, would you, please?

As she went out, Sorme stood up.

I'd better go, father.

Sit down again for a moment. They're early. They can wait. What you've been saying interests me very much. Have you ever spoken to anyone else about these things?

No, father.

I'd like you to come back and talk to me again. I'm not asking you because I think you need to talk to me – although perhaps you do. But what you say has a great deal of interest to me. Have you read my book on St John of the Cross?

No, father.

It's over there, I think. Bottom shelf. Take it away with you, and look through it, if it doesn't bore you too much.

87

The chapter on the vision of God should interest you particularly. These experiences you speak of. . . I'm inclined to think that they're the root of all visionary insights.

Sorme opened the glass doors of the bookcase, and found the slim, black-bound volume. The desire to get away had risen in him again, but this time it was for a different reason. He was suspicious of the relief he was beginning to feel in talking to the priest.

Can you come back tomorrow?

I think so, father.

Good. I'll expect you. Give Austin my regards if you see him.

He's in Switzerland at the moment.

He took the priest's outstretched hand, and was surprised at its warmth. The flesh looked desiccated and cold.

Tell Mrs Doughty to send the two men up, please.

Certainly. Goodbye, father.

Goodbye.

Outside the door he stood still for a few moments, frowning towards the plaster image of the Virgin at the end of the badly-lit corridor. Then he recollected the copy of the book he still held, and slipped it absent-mindedly into his pocket. He walked slowly towards the stairhead, his footsteps muffled by the carpet. The housekeeper startled him by appearing suddenly from a doorway on his right. She asked curtly:

Is he ready now?

Yes. He says will you send them up.

He went quickly down the stairs. The street door stood open. He went out, groping for his bicycle clips. Behind him someone called: Hey, Gerard!

Hello, Robin! Sorry. I'd forgotten you.

You don't have to rush off, do you?

I have to go in a few minutes, he said untruthfully.

Well, come on in for a moment.

He followed Maunsell back into the reception-room. The fire was still burning. Maunsell closed the door by nudging it with his backside, asking:

Well, how did you get on with him?

Oh, fairly well.

Did you tell him about your disgraceful sex life?

A little. He talked about St John of the Cross. Then someone interrupted us.

He must have talked about St John of the Cross for a bloody long time! You've been gone half an hour.

I'm not keeping anything from you, really.

Aren't you? Really? All right, I'll believe you.

Tell me, Robin. You say you don't know Austin Nunne at all?

Not much. I've seen him a couple of times.

Oh. You don't know anything about him?

No. Not much anyway.

Do you know if he's queer?

Yes . . . I think so. Why? Don't you know?

Yes. I think he is. I just wondered . . .

Wait. I *do* know something. You mustn't tell anyone, though.

No, of course not.

I gather he's a bit of a sadist.

How did you gather that?

I overheard something Father Carruthers said to Dr Stein one day after Mrs Nunne had left.

What did he say – can you remember?

No. It was just an impression I got. I may be wrong. But for heaven's sake keep it to yourself. If anyone ever accused me of telling you, I'd deny it.

Of course. I won't tell anyone. Who's this Dr Stein?

Oh, a friend of Father Carruthers. They used to be at theological school together. Stein's a psychiatrist. Why?

Nothing. I'm just very curious about Austin, and about anyone who's interested in him.

I see. You're not falling in love with him, are you?

For Christ's sake! Are you serious?

Well, I don't know. I'd say there's a definite touch of homosexuality in you. It'll burst out one day. Probably surprise you.

You really are a fool!

You see. I bet I'm right.

Garn!

Maunsell said, chuckling:

You see . . . I bet I'm right.

I've got to go.

You *are* a cow. When are you coming again?

Tomorrow probably. Father Carruthers asked me to look in again.

I say! He's taking you under his wing!

Maybe.

Well, come in early and see me first. Will you?

All right. I may not come at all. I'll phone first.

Good. I always answer the phone.

Sorme stood with his hand on the doorknob; he asked:

Can't you remember exactly what it was that Father Carruthers said to this man Stein?

Maunsell looked alarmed:

No! For heaven's sake! Don't mention it to *anyone*. I may be wrong. He might easily have been talking about someone else.

Sorme realized that Maunsell regretted telling him; he said casually:

Don't worry. I'm not really interested. See you tomorrow.

All right. Come early.

Maunsell let him out of the door, saying: Bye-bye, my dear. Sorme lifted his foot on to the crossbar of the bicycle to clip his trousers. He felt suddenly exhausted and discouraged.

Chapter Four

As he wheeled the bicycle into the yard it began to rain. He covered it over with the tarpaulin. The light in the basement flat was on; as he turned away to leave the yard the curtain stirred and the girl looked out. He grinned and nodded, and her face disappeared abruptly. As he was about to insert his key in the front door, it opened. He said:

Thanks, Carlotte.

I'm glad you came. I'm going out. There's a message for you.

Really?

Someone rang you from Switzerland. He's going to ring back this evening.

Switzerland!

He rang just after you left. He'll ring back about seven.

Thanks very much. Has everything quietened down now?

Yes. Only we've had two reporters here.

Reporters, eh? What did they want?

Oh, details about the fire. Mrs Miller talked to them. I think she likes the idea of getting into the papers.

Mmmm. That's interesting. Did she tell them about me?

I don't think so. Why?

I was hoping to get the George Medal.

He saw, from her blank expression, that she didn't understand. He felt too tired to explain. As he advanced to the foot of the stairs, he asked:

Where's Mrs Miller now?

Back in her own house. Why?

Nothing. I'm just delighted.

This time she laughed. He noted the bouncing of her breasts as she passed underneath him, and was disturbed by it. He thought: Why do I always want a woman most when I'm nervously exhausted? His legs ached as he mounted the stairs. In his room, he lit the gas, set the kettle on it, and sank into the armchair, yawning. His thoughts revolved round the German girl. The idea of making her his mistress was more appealing than it had been earlier. He put this down to his tiredness thinking: the body's exhaustion inflames the imagination.

The kettle began to steam. He reached out to the thermos on the table and found it half full of cold tea. He was too lazy to go to the lavatory to empty it. He shook it up, then poured the tea down the sink, turning on both taps to wash away the leaves.

What the hell could Austin be phoning me for? Where did he get the number? Soon find out. He looked at his watch: it was ten past five. Two hours. I must eat. Hungry. But after tea and a rest. The steam rose from the flask as he poured water into it. Like Vaslav. I am god. Wonder if he is a sadist? They need to beat somebody. Must ask him.

The hot tea and the heat of the gas fire were too much for him. He retreated to the bed. As he drank he began to feel sleepy and thought irritatedly: Why should I feel sleepy? I didn't get up till eleven. Nervous shock, perhaps. He resisted the impulse to lie down and close his eyes, and felt immediately overwhelmed by the desire to sleep. He stood up, and looked vaguely around the room for something to do. There was a case on top of the wardrobe, still not unpacked; he opened it on the bed, and began sorting out ties and handkerchiefs. In the bottom of the case he found the three Van Gogh prints, slightly corrugated with damp, that had been pinned on the walls of his old room. He selected the space over the mantelpiece for the *Field of Green Corn. The Starry Night* he placed at the head of the bed, where he could see it every time he faced the wall in bed. He pinned the *Cornfield with Crows* in the centre of the opposite wall near the door. He stood opposite the *Field of Green Corn* for a long time, trying to recapture a mood, without success. He concentrated, staring at it:

To renew the fiery joy and burst the stony roof . . .
For everything that lives is holy, life delights in life.

And Nunne. And the old man. And a sadistic killer of four women. My body is not ill – it is my soul that is ill. Contempt. What else is there to feel? Not my body, but my soul. Poor Vaslav. He died.

The sleepiness came back and he restrained it. Dirt. Fatigue. This room. Not anonymous, my room, a prison. The wind blew a gust of rain against the windows. But it is my consciousness. Sick and exhausted, I choose it. I choose it. It is mine. Violence. That's it. I contain violence. I don't want to be soothed. The violence is in the muscles, in the throat. When it explodes, I become myself. Everything that lives is holy.

He noticed the fading warmth on his shins. The flames of the gas fire were low. He groped in his trouser pockets for a shilling. In the back pocket he found a folded slip of paper; written across it in a neat feminine hand: Gertrude Quincey; phone any day after five. He searched the pockets of his jacket without finding a coin. Pulling on his raincoat, he went downstairs. On his way back into the house again, five minutes later, he stopped by the hall telephone and smoothed out the paper on the coin-box. Her voice answered almost immediately. He pressed Button A, saying:

Hello. This is Gerard Sorme speaking.

Gerard who? Oh, Austin's friend! Hello! How are you?

I'm fine. I thought I'd like to take you up on that offer to come over some time when you're not busy.

Yes, please do. Would you like to come to tea?

Well . . . perhaps. Are you going to be home this evening?

There was a perceptible hesitation. Finally she said:

Yes . . . What time?

He wondered why she sounded so dubious, and felt chilled:

I don't mind. Make it some other time if this evening's not convenient. Would you prefer to make it next week?

He had decided abruptly that if she put him off he would not contact her again. But her voice answered quickly:

No, do come this evening. I was simply wondering whether anyone else is likely to come. But I don't think so. Come round at about seven, if you like.

Thank you. I can't make it at seven. Austin's ringing me.

I thought he was abroad?

He is. He's ringing me from Switzerland.

Really! Well, come afterwards then. I'll expect you.

She hung up while he was still thanking her. Again he had difficulty in suppressing the irritation. He went upstairs swearing under his breath. All people are swine. In his room, he put two shillings in the gas, and relit it. He poured more tea from the flask, and tasted it. It was too strong. He put on the record of Prokoviev's Fifth Symphony and lay on the bed. Before the first side was half played, he had fallen asleep.

He woke up suddenly in the dark, and peered at his watch. The luminous hands seemed to be indicating eight o'clock. He fumbled to the light switch. It was precisely eight o'clock. The room was hot. He slipped his feet into slippers and hurried downstairs. There was no one about. He went down to the basement flat and knocked. When no one replied, he opened the door a fraction; the room was in darkness. He swore obscenely under his breath. As he started back up the stairs, the phone started to ring. He snatched it before it had time to ring a second time. The woman's voice said:

Is Mr Sorme there, please?

Speaking.

Oh! This is Gertrude Quincey. Are you coming over?

Yes. I'm awfully sorry, but I fell asleep. I think Austin must have rung and got no reply. No one seems to be in.

Oh dear . . .

Don't worry. I'll start out immediately. See you in half an hour.

Good. I'd put some food out for you . . .

Thanks awfully. See you soon.

He hung up, and glared at his watch. His hair felt tousled and his eyes were still myopic with sleep. Almost immediately the phone began to ring again. A woman's voice said:

Is Mr Sorme there?

Speaking.

Would you hold on a moment? I have a personal call from Switzerland for you.

Thanks.

Nunne's voice sounded surprisingly clear and close.

Hello, Gerard!

Hello, Austin.

Hope I haven't kept you waiting? I've been trying to get through for the past bloody hour.

No. I've only just woken up.

Good. How are you, dear boy?

96

I'm OK. What's the idea of spending a fortune on long-distance calls?

Well . . . It's not really important. I want you to do me a favour.

Certainly. What have you done – forgotten your tooth brush?

Nothing as bad as that! Can you hear me clearly?

Yes, very clearly.

Good. You sound rather far off. Now listen, Gerard. I'm thinking of returning to England . . .

Good.

But I'd like you to do something for me first. Would you go along to my flat, and ask the porter if anyone has been enquiring for me while I've been away?

Yes. Is that all?

That's all. Just ask him if anyone has been enquiring, and who.

All right. What then?

If no one has been there, would you telegraph me here? Simply put: No one. If anyone *has* been enquiring, put: Please ring, and I'll ring you tomorrow. Is that OK?

All right. You want to get details of anyone who's enquired about you?

Yes.

Who are you trying to avoid?

Yes, I *am* trying to avoid someone. A rather unpleasant man. Can you do that?

All right.

You've got the address of the flat?

Yes. When will you ring back?

The same time tomorrow night – *if* anyone has enquired. Get full details, won't you? You might also ask the girl on the switchboard. Do you mind?

No, not at all.

Good. You'll go along there, won't you? Don't just phone.

No, I'll go along.

Good. Let's just recap. Go to my flat, ask the porter if anyone has been asking about me. Also ask the switchboard girl. If . . .

If no one, telegraph you: No one. If anyone, get details, and telegraph you: Please ring. OK? Better give me your address.

Oh yes, of course. It's Pension Vevey, St Moritz. And I'm staying here under the name of Austin. Mr B. J. Austin.

Blimey! You are mysterious!

Not really. But don't give my address to anyone else, will you?

Good lord, no! Who should I give it to?

Good man . . .

The pips sounded. Nunne said:

Bye-bye, Gerard. You got that address, didn't you? Pension Vevey. V-E-V-E-Y. All right?

All right. Goodbye, Austin.

The rain had stopped, but the road was still wet and treacherous. He disliked riding on wet roads; the mudguards were inadequate, and the rain wet the bottoms of his trouser legs. He bent low over the handle-bars, and went into bottom gear to get up Haverstock Hill. Hills exhausted him; he usually wasted more energy swearing than pressing the pedals. A car came past, spraying him with muddy water; he stared after it with irritation and envy.

A clock struck the half hour as he turned out of Well Walk into the East Heath Road. He dismounted and walked up the hill.

He rang the doorbell, then leaned against the wall,

perspiring and breathless. A light appeared on the other side of the glass panel. She stood there, smiling at him, looking cool and attractive.

Hello. Come in. You made it quickly.

I'm awfully sorry I'm late . . .

Don't bother. Luckily, it was a cold supper. Yes, hang your coat up there.

She was wearing a black-and-green dress of some shiny material, that left most of her arms bare. She had the figure of a slim teenage girl. He looked at her with admiration as she preceded him into the kitchen.

I hope you don't mind eating in the kitchen? It's easier.

Of course not.

You haven't eaten?

No. I fell asleep at about six. Austin rang me immediately after you'd rung.

Really? What did he want?

Oh . . . it seems rather odd. He wants me to find out if there are any messages waiting at his flat for him.

Strange. I wonder why he couldn't have rung them directly?

Sorme dried his hands on a small tea-towel then sat down at the table. She asked:

Soup?

Please.

As she stood over the stove, her back towards him, he could examine her figure at leisure. Her hips lacked roundness; they were almost a boy's hips; but the slimness of her waist appealed to him. He was trying to imagine how she would look undressed, when she turned round. He looked away hastily. She placed the bowl of soup on the cork mat, leaning across him to do so. If he had leaned forward slightly, he could have kissed her upper arm. The smell of her body was clean, but unperfumed. He asked her:

Do you live here completely alone?

Yes.

No one at all?

She said, smiling:

I'm very seldom alone. There's nearly always someone here. Members of the group usually come three or four evenings a week. Then I have a niece who stays frequently . . .

The Jehovah's Witnesses?

Yes. Then I have many friends in Hampstead.

He took a mouthful of the soup, and realized how hungry he was. A sensual gratitude rose from his stomach, and made him smile at her. She sat opposite him, and took a partly-sewn tweed skirt from a white paper carrier which carried the inscription: Harrods. She took out a needle that had been pushed into the edge of the fabric, and began to sew carefully. He asked casually: What are you making?

A skirt.

Do you always do your own dressmaking?

Usually.

He finished the soup and pushed the plate away.

That was excellent.

Good.

She stood up silently and opened the refrigerator; it was taller than she was.

You're not a vegetarian, are you?

He said enthusiastically: Positively not! The plate contained a leg of chicken and three slices of ham.

Help yourself to salad.

Thanks.

Would you like a glass of beer?

I'd love some!

He ate hungrily and drank half a pint of brown ale. It gave him pleasure to see her sitting opposite him, her head bent over the sewing. He helped himself to more salad, selecting with care the leaves of chicory and fragments of green paprika. He asked her suddenly:

Were you never married?

He knew the answer already, but wanted to see her reaction to the topic. It surprised him. She looked at him with obviously suppressed irritation, and answered:

No.

I hope you don't mind my asking?

Not at all.

Her voice still had a sharp edge to it. He went on eating, and poured a second glass of beer, wondering why the question had annoyed her. He said carefully:

You make me feel that I shouldn't have brought it up.

She went on sewing. He began to think she intended to ignore him, as a measure of her disapproval. Then she began to speak, still looking down at the sewing, her voice level and precise:

It doesn't annoy me to be asked. What annoys me is the assumption that usually underlies the question. Male bachelors are quite ordinary and acceptable, but unmarried women are called 'spinsters' and regarded as somehow incomplete. It's all this nonsense of Byron about love being a man's pastime, but a woman's whole life . . .

Normally, her sentiments would have struck him as dubious. But the meal had left him feeling good-humoured and in her debt. He said hastily:

I agree completely. It's utter nonsense. Of course women have every right to be as independent as men . . .

She interrupted:

I didn't say that. I don't believe most women *are* as naturally independent as men. But I have my own work to do, and marriage would . . . distract me.

And what *is* your work?

She smiled at him suddenly, and the school mistressy

101

expression was replaced by a charm that made her appear younger.

Are you really curious?

Very curious, he said seriously.

She went on sewing.

I used to think about being a . . . a woman with something to say.

A writer?

Yes. Not necessarily, though. When I was a girl I had a book of lives of the female saints – St Catherine of Siena and St Teresa of Avila and the rest.

You wanted to be a saint?

I don't know. I was too young then to know what being a saint meant.

Do you know now?

A little better, I think. I've been reading Simone Weil. She was a saint. I could never be like Simone Weil.

Why?

Because . . . oh, because I'm not clever enough and not strong enough and not . . . oh, I don't know . . .

And yet you don't want to marry and have a family?

Perhaps I might – if I met the man I wanted to settle down with.

She looked up and noticed his smile. She said:

I know what you're thinking. Another woman who needs the right man. I've met so many of them. Waiting for Mr Right.

He said:

But in your case, it's not merely that. You'd like to do something worthwhile with your life?

She said, with a touch of tiredness in her voice:

I don't believe marriage should be a dead end for women, anyway. Most of them behave as if it was a sort of last judgement . . .

And what do you think?

Oh, I . . . I think . . . It sounds pompous, but I think that all human beings ought to try to make the world a little better to live in, as well as living their own little lives.

And do you think that being a Witness helps?

I think so. I don't think of myself as a Witness. I think of myself as a Christian. And the Witnesses are the only group among Christians who are trying hard to oppose the way things are going.

He opened a second bottle of beer, and poured it into the tumbler.

And which way *are* things going?

Oh . . . people are becoming more mean-spirited, more petty-minded.

Don't you think they've always been that way?

He was plying her with questions because he could see she enjoyed talking, and because he liked listening to her voice and watching her averted face. He was thinking that it would be pleasant to kiss her.

In a way, yes. But in the Middle Ages men and women devoted their lives to other people without making a fuss about it – monastic orders and Christian laymen. They did it naturally, out of love of God and their fellow human beings, and no one thought it odd, or accused them of being do-gooders. And it seems that nowadays – well, it's everyone for himself . . .

And how do you hope to alter that? By converting people?

She looked up and smiled; the tiredness was there underneath it.

I don't know. Sometimes I have friends in the Witnesses over for supper, and I think they . . . they seem to be rather naïve, in spite of their seriousness. And sometimes I talk to these people who call themselves intellectuals, and they seem futile, in spite of their cleverness.

Sorme said, smiling:

I'm afraid you have the makings of a first-class heretic.

She said softly:

Perhaps I have.

Silence fell between them; he watched her hands as they held the fabric, and observed that it was easy to sit with her, unspeaking, feeling under no obligation to speak. He wondered how far the beer was responsible for making him feel so relaxed.

She said suddenly:

Did you know that Austin went into a monastery?

No. When?

Not long ago. Hardly a year. But he came out. It wasn't what he was looking for . . .

Were you glad or sorry?

Glad, of course. It was a Catholic monastery. But he still hasn't found what he's looking for.

No?

He pushed his plate further away, and leaned back in the chair. She said softly:

Poor Austin.

There could be no mistaking the affection in her voice. He said curiously:

You're fond of Austin?

Of course! I watched him grow up. I was nine when he was born. I used to take him out. He was a very strange child.

How?

Sometimes he seemed quite angelic. He was a very good-tempered little boy altogether. But at other times he behaved as if he had an evil spirit. He'd get moods when he had to break things, or hurt something.

Her eyes were looking beyond him; he could see she enjoyed talking of Austin. Suddenly they came back to him. She had noticed that he was no longer eating.

104

Would you like coffee?

No, thanks.

Tea?

No, nothing, thanks.

Let's go into the other room then. There's some brandy if you like.

Ah!

She insisted on his going first into the sitting-room. He said: Thank you for a really delicious meal.

Not at all. It was only scraps. Will you have a little brandy?

If you're having some too . . .

Perhaps I will.

He sank into the armchair, sighing with satisfaction. When she handed him the brandy glass, he said happily:

Thank you. You're an angel!

He felt immediately that it was a mistake, then felt surprised to notice that she was slightly flushed. He was charmed; it made her look like a schoolgirl. He turned the stem of the glass in his fingers, saying:

It's big enough to drink a pint of beer from!

It's supposed to be!

Is it?

Haven't you ever drunk from a brandy glass before?

Never. I had a nautical grandfather who used to let me sip his brandy. But he drank it from a two-pint mug, with hot water and lemon . . .

She laughed at him: it was the first time he had heard her laugh. She held her glass up towards him:

You're supposed to hold it like this – to warm the brandy with your hands. That is, if it's good brandy, which this isn't.

Tastes all right to me!

Yes, but it isn't. A good brandy tastes far more gentle and smooth . . .

He said, laughing:

I'm afraid you have the making of an epicure!

Immediately she became serious. She said quietly:

No.

He waited for her to go on; then, when he saw she had finished, said, with raised eyebrows:

No?

No. I don't think I care for good living . . . I once lived in a women's hostel in the East End for a fortnight. It didn't make me long to be home. Except for the dirt. But dirt is bad anywhere . . .

What on earth were you doing in a women's hostel?

Helping.

Ah, I see.

She rearranged the needlework on her knee, and began to sew. He sipped the brandy, watching her with admiration. The glow of the electric fire was red on her stockings, and was reflected from the shiny material of her dress. Her serenity and gentleness filled him with a desire to touch her. An instinct in him warned him that she feared intimacy. He watched her sewing, and speculated about her past. Austin's father-theory sounded plausible. Certainly there was something. He began to wonder how he could lead her to speak of it. Her sudden coolness when he spoke of marriage made him cautious. He said finally:

Tell me about Austin.

What do you want to know about him?

What's this about a monastery?

I don't know. You should ask him.

Where was the place?

In Alsace – on the Rhine, I believe. Austin won't ever speak about it. Not to me, at least.

And you've no idea what happened?

Very little. Austin's mother is a Catholic, and there was

a time when she wanted Austin to be a priest. Nothing came of it. Austin's father wanted him to go into business, but he didn't show any inclination for that either. He simply started to drink heavily. Finally, he got into rather a lot of trouble, and his father decided to send him out to Brazil. Luckily, his mother decided to interfere with that scheme. She persuaded his father that he needed to see a psychiatrist. Which he did. He thought it was all non-sense, but he could see it would be better than Brazil. He even managed to persuade the psychiatrist to tell his father that he wasn't suited for business!

Sorme said: Poor Austin! It sounds as if they just wouldn't let him alone.

Quite! It was a pity, really, that he was the only one.

What happened then?

Then . . . then he started to take an interest in ballet, and said he wanted to write a book. So they made him an allowance, and simply left him to his own devices – which was what they should have done in the first place. And, as you probably know, he *has* written three very good books, and begun to make quite a name for himself as a journalist.

What about this monastery affair, though? When did that happen?

Quite recently. He went off to Germany to live three years ago. He stayed there for over a year, and we didn't hear much from him. Then one day, he simply wrote to say he was in a monastery in Alsace, and hoped to become a monk. His mother was delighted, of course. She was quite sure that he wouldn't remain in the monastery after he'd become a priest. But nothing came of it. He spent about a month there – as a paying guest. Then he came back to England. Since then he's been writing a novel – or so he tells me. Probably you know more about that than I do?

No. He didn't mention it to me. But then, I haven't known him long. Have *you* always been very close to him?

She said quietly: He's always come to me when he's been unhappy or dissatisfied.

He looked at her, and felt again the beginnings of desire for the slim body. He said:

I wonder why?

Why?

Why he always came to you?

We were always fond of one another. He always trusted me. I think I was the most tolerant nursemaid he ever had!

Observing the softness of her expression as she spoke of Austin, Sorme wondered if she could be in love with him. Then, as she folded the skirt and slipped it back into its paper carrier, he decided it was impossible. Her attitude was far more that of a girl who worships a younger brother. He asked her curiously:

Were you an only child?

The change of subject seemed to startle her. She looked at him blankly for a moment, then said quickly:

Yes.

She stood up, and folded the top of the carrier bag. Again, he became aware that speaking of herself embarrassed her. She said:

Excuse me. I have to make a phone call before I forget.

I'll go upstairs, if you don't mind.

In the bathroom, he could hear the murmur of her voice as she telephoned. The room was agreeably warm; he felt drowsy and well-fed. He found the warm water, and the orange scent of the soap, so agreeable that he removed his shirt and washed his neck and face. He wiped the steam off the mirror, and regarded his pink face with approval. There was a two-day growth of beard on his chin, but his complexion was fair and it was hardly noticeable. He wiped away the soap from behind his ears, and made a face at himself in the mirror. Below, the doorbell rang. He went closer to the door and listened, but could hear nothing. She must have opened the door without replacing the phone, for the sound of her voice continued. As he came out of the bathroom, the phone pinged as she replaced it on its rest. She was in the kitchen as he came down the stairs; he asked her:

Has someone arrived?

My niece.

The girl was kneeling in front of the fire when he came into the room, warming her hands. He said:

How do you do?

She glanced up at him, then stood up, smiling.

Hello!

It was the girl whose photograph he had seen in the bedroom. The short blonde hair looked as if it had been recently cut and waved. When she smiled, he noticed that the two front teeth were irregular, one slightly overlapped the other. He guessed her to be about sixteen. She said:

I'm Caroline. Who are you?

Gerard Sorme.

Are you one of Aunt's Jehovah's Witnesses?

No.

I didn't think you were. You don't look like one!

Her smile left him in no doubt that she intended it as a compliment.

No? What do I look like?

I don't know. She considered him with her head slightly on one side, then giggled. It betrayed her age, and contrasted with the controlled, sophisticated drawl with which she spoke. He was slightly repelled by her air of sophistication.

Miss Quincey came in.

Oh, you've introduced yourselves? Would you like a drink, Caroline?

Yes, please. Can I have a glass of sherry?

I didn't mean *that* kind of a drink, Miss Quincey said. Your mother told me not to let you touch alcohol.

But I'm frozen, Caroline said plaintively. Feel.

She laid the back of her hand against Miss Quincey's face.

All right. But don't have a lot. I'm making some tea. She asked Sorme: Would you like some tea?

Please!

Don't let Caroline drink too much sherry!

She went out of the room again. Caroline said: I'll be hiccupping on the carpet when you come back!

Sorme looked at her with warming interest. Miss Quincey's appeal to him introduced a flavour of intimacy. It placed him in the position of her guardian. He watched her moving bottles in the cupboard. She asked:

Are you drinking?

I was, he said. Brandy.

Have a refill!

He saw that Miss Quincey's glass was still untouched. He said: I don't think Gertrude intends to drink this. Perhaps I'd better.

I dare say you had, she said. She sat on the settee, and crossed her knees. She had shapely legs. She was wearing a simple black dress with elbow-length sleeves.

Well, tell me what you do, then! I can't guess.

I write . . .

Do you! A writer. Lovely! I've always wanted to know a writer.

Really? Surely I'm not the first?

Almost. Daddy used to be friends with a novelist called Dennis Scott years ago. I fell for him good and hard! He was terribly good looking . . .

He said, smiling:

I see. And did anything come of it?

Come of it? Lord, no! I was only about ten.

Sorme said teasingly: You must have been delicious!

She said: Oh yes! in a slightly American manner. It was a return to her drawl, which had begun to disappear.

And how old are you now?

Seventeen. I'll be eighteen in three months. What do you write?

Tell me what you do first.

I act. That is, I'm learning to act. At Lamda.

Where?

Lamda. The rival of Rada. London Academy of Music and Dramatic Art. It's in Kensington.

I see!

He was suddenly able to place her. Her combination of naïveté and sophistication had puzzled him, like her complete lack of shyness. He realized that probably in two years' time she would speak with a drawl all the time, and call everybody darling; in the meantime, her manner was a hybrid of schoolgirl and theatre. She said:

I suppose you live in Hampstead?

No. I don't, as a matter of fact.

Oh. I thought you were one of Aunt's arty friends.

No. I'm a friend of Austin's.

Austin! I've never met him. I've always wanted to. Is he charming?

He wouldn't interest you, Sorme said, smiling.

No, why? Unexpectedly, she seemed to understand: Oh, I see. He's like that, is he?

You shouldn't know anything about it!

No? Why not? We've got two in our clsss. They go around with their arms round one another.

That must be annoying for everyone.

It *is*. There's one girl who's got a terrible crush on one

111

of them – the one called Ernest. She's really got it bad. I think queers are rather attractive – in a repulsive kind of way. Don't you?

He said, smiling: I wouldn't know. My tastes don't lie that way.

She said: Good! He wondered whether it meant what it seemed to mean. He was trying to determine whether the warmth of her smile was intended for him particularly, or whether it was part of a general manner she had picked up at the drama school. She leaned back on the settee, and stared up at the ceiling. He looked hopefully at her knees, but the dress had not travelled far as she stretched. She said:

Tell me what you write.

Not now, he said. Some other time.

She looked at him sideways.

When?

He felt a shock of pleasure that was controlled and softened by the effect of the brandy. Before he could reply, Miss Quincey came back in. She glanced disapprovingly at Caroline's position, which the girl seemed to feel without catching the glance: she sat up and began to rearrange the cushions. Miss Quincey said:

I didn't expect you until late, dear.

I know. I meant to come from the theatre, but they called the rehearsal off. I'm darned glad too. I'm really exhausted. We've had such a day! Am I interrupting any profound discussion?

No, dear, Miss Quincey said comfortably. She was pouring tea.

Gerard . . .

The use of his name surprised him. She was holding out a teacup.

Oh, thank you . . .

What have you been talking about? Caroline asked. Her voice was drawling again.

Mainly about Austin, Sorme said.

Oh!

Caroline, Miss Quincey said. The girl took the cup.

Are you hungry?

I am a bit. I haven't had anything since lunch time.

No tea?

Couldn't be bothered. I was learning my part.

Oh dear. You really ought to. I'll get you something in a moment.

Don't bother. I'll find myself a sandwich.

Sorme asked her: What part are you playing? He was not interested, but Miss Quincey's food-talk was beginning to irritate him. Caroline said vaguely:

I forget her name. She's the wife of a poet . . . We're doing a play about the French poet Rimbaud. I'm the wife of his best friend.

Verlaine?

That's right. I have to recite a poem in French. I hope my accent's all right. It begins . . .

Drink your tea, dear, Miss Quincey said.

All right, the girl said meekly. She sipped her tea.

Miss Quincey sat down. She asked:

What on earth did I do with my brandy?

Oh . . . I drank it. I'm sorry. I didn't think you wanted it.

That's all right. I didn't really. I just didn't want to waste it . . .

She had contrived to make him feel guilty, and given him an odd sense of kinship with Caroline. The girl looked at him over the top of her cup; her eyes looked bright. He stopped himself from answering her look. She set her teacup down, and stretched like a cat, her breasts curving. There was a faint noise of something giving way. She said with annoyance:

Damn. My bra's bust!

Caroline! Miss Quincey said.

The girl ignored her; she raised her elbow and felt down the back of her neck.

That's twice today, she said. Have you got a needle, Aunt?

Miss Quincey got up silently, and crossed to the sideboard. Sorme was aware of her irritation and disapproval. Caroline seemed oblivious of it. He said, smiling:

I hope it didn't happen under embarrassing circumstances?

He felt Miss Quincey's eyes on him. Caroline said:

No. Luckily I was on my own. But I know one poor girl who lost her pants in rehearsal . . .

She began to giggle breathlessly. Miss Quincey returned with a needle and a reel of white cotton. Caroline took it without looking at her. She said:

It was so funny . . . She had the kind that stay up with a button . . .

Caroline! Miss Quincey said.

And the button bust . . . She nearly broke her neck with a pair of nylon briefs round her ankles . . .

Really, Caroline!

But it was *funny*, the girl said defensively. She looked so silly trying to get offstage without falling over . . .

Sorme felt a desire to irritate Miss Quincey further. He asked:

What would you have done if it had been you?

Miss Quincey sat down again, as if the conversation had become too risqué for her to take any further responsibility. Caroline said:

I'd have stepped out of them and gone on with the rehearsal.

Oh, really, dear! Miss Quincey looked flushed.

But it *happens*, Caroline said. What's wrong with being frank about it?

Miss Quincey said, with surprising mildness:

It's not a nice subject, dear.

Nice, Caroline said scornfully: You are silly, Aunt!

Sorme looked apprehensively at Miss Quincey, but she sipped her tea quietly, almost abstractedly. The girl stood up.

I'll go and get this sewn. Then I'll cut myself a sandwich, if I may.

I'll do it, dear.

No, don't bother.

She went out of the room, taking her teacup with her. She turned and flashed Sorme a quick smile at the door. When the door had closed, Miss Quincey stared into space, a faintly perturbed expression on her face. She said finally:

I do worry about her.

Why?

She continued to stare, without replying. She said suddenly:

Oh well, I dare say it doesn't matter . . . She'll get married . . .

Of course, Sorme said.

She looked at him.

It's different for you. You're a man. Besides, you're older than she is.

What do you mean?

She began to sew again, not replying. He watched her curiously, wondering what her feelings were. He could think of nothing to say that would open the subject. He asked finally:

Don't you approve of the drama school?

It isn't that . . .

He waited, staring into the fire. She was looking at him, but he kept his eyes on the red bars. She said:

I try not to force my beliefs on other people, you see. I don't force them on Austin or Caroline, or on you, do I?

No.

But . . . Well, I'm supposed to, really. It's a part of our belief that everyone should have a chance to . . .

He waited for her to say 'repent', but she went on:

. . . hear about our message.

Sorme said:

Perhaps you don't believe in it to that extent?

Oh yes, I believe, she said; her voice was as unmoved as if she was admitting to the possession of a front-door key. People have different ways of behaving about their beliefs. I don't mind speaking to strangers about it, because they are under no obligation to listen. But if I forced it on those nearest to me, I'd feel guilty. Do . . . you understand me?

Quite. Perfectly.

All the same, when I see Caroline living as if nothing mattered but getting on the stage, I feel worried.

He said: Ask her to come to one of your Bible classes . . .

The suggestion was not made seriously; he had no interest in talking about Caroline. She said immediately:

Oh no. I don't think she'd be in the least interested. I know she wouldn't. No . . . I'm afraid she'd need to be approached by someone nearer her own age.

Preferably someone she'd get on with, Sorme said, remembering the pale-faced, dowdy girls he had seen singing hymns at the Speakers' Corner on a Sunday afternoon. He looked round to meet her eyes, and was embarrassed to find them regarding him with troubled seriousness. She said:

You might be able to do it.

Me? But I'm not a Jehovah's Witness, after all.

You could attend one or two of our meetings.

Of course. But that doesn't guarantee that I'd finish up with your beliefs, does it?

That doesn't matter. You're a fundamentally serious person. That's the important thing . . .

I'm glad you think so.

But it *is* the important thing, isn't it?

Possibly, he said carefully. But there's an immense difference between my outlook and yours, for all that.

Is it so great?

He said:

I act on the assumption that the world is meaningless, that life is meaningless.

Meaningless? She looked almost scared.

Quite.

But how . . . how can it be meaningless? Surely you don't believe that? No one could believe it.

Why not?

Life wouldn't be worth living . . .

Not at all. It is pleasant to live. That's quite a different thing from believing life has a meaning.

She was regarding him with a doubtful, penetrating look, as if suspecting him of making fun of her, and being prepared to laugh when he acknowledged it. He smiled at her. She said suddenly:

But what do you write about if you think life has no meaning?

Ah! That's a good question. I'll tell you. I want to write a book about all the different ways people impose a meaning on their lives. It's to be called The Methods and Techniques of Self-deception. It will deal with every possible way that people hide themselves from the meaninglessness of life. I shall start with a chapter on businessmen and politicians called The Efficient Man. Then there'll be a chapter on the artists and writers and theatre people called The Aesthetic Man. Then a chapter on revolutionaries and men motivated by envy and discontentment. And, finally, several chapters on all types of religious self-deception . . .

Her face had begun to clear as he spoke. She was smiling as she interrupted him:

But that's a wonderful idea! I agree completely with you. A book like that would make our work much easier. After all, it's really a religious conception, isn't it? People won't think about the really important things . . .

I shall write a chapter on the Jehovah's Witnesses too. I intend to be impartial.

But you know nothing about us.

I do. A little. You base everything on the Bible, don't you? That's a good starting-point.

She said excitedly:

But you say life is meaningless. The Bible contains the meaning of life. How can you condemn us without knowing the Bible?

He said patiently:

You don't understand. That isn't my point. My point is that our experience is *bitty*. We live more or less in the present. If we were honest, we'd acknowledge that life is a series of moments tied together by our need to keep alive, to defeat boredom. Our experience is all in bits. But the Surbiton businessman sticks it together by believing that the purpose of life is to get him a bigger car. The politician sticks it together by identifying his purpose with that of his party. The religious man sticks it together by accepting the guidance of his church or his Bible. They're all different kinds of glue, but they all have the same purpose . . . to impose a pattern, a meaning. But it's all falsifying. If we were honest, we'd accept that life is meaningless.

She asked practically: And what good would that do?

It might make us less lazy and complacent. It might make us turn our lives into a search for a meaning.

But you just said it was meaningless?

Anything is meaningless until you've discovered its meaning.

That's quite a different thing! That's quite different from saying it has *no* meaning. But supposing there had been a few men who *had* seen the meaning? Men who had a vision sent from God . . .?

What good would that do me? Why should I take anybody else's word for it? I'd want to see the meaning myself.

He was so intent on her face that he started when the door behind him opened. Caroline said:

Do you mind if I bring my sandwiches in here? I won't make any crumbs.

Miss Quincey said: Yes, dear. Do. Her voice was level, and betrayed no annoyance or surprise. Sorme felt baffled by her placidness. Caroline said: Thanks. She came into the room, carrying a tray. Miss Quincey shot a quick smile at Sorme that was almost coquettish. She said:

Anyway, it's most brave of you to try to take all the responsibility on yourself. I hope you achieve what you want.

Sorme glanced at Caroline, feeling embarrassed. She asked: What's brave of him?

He said: Oh nothing . . .

He remembered then that he had still not promised to attend one of the meetings, or to 'speak to' Caroline; he felt suddenly pleased with himself.

Caroline said: Gerard looks terribly serious!

Sorme grinned at her:

I've been talking about all the people I'll have shot when I'm dictator.

So long as I'm not on the list . . .

He looked at her, and started to say: Shooting's the last thing I'd want to do with you, then checked himself. She was looking through the *Radio Times*, chewing the sandwich. She said suddenly:

Ooh, can we have the radio on, aunt? There's a recording of Dylan Thomas reading his own poetry at ten-fifteen.

Sorme looked at his watch; it was ten minutes past. He said:

Maybe I ought to go anyway. You go to bed early, don't you?

You don't have to go, Miss Quincey said. I don't always go to bed at ten o'clock! The other night was an exception.

Caroline asked: Don't you like Dylan Thomas, Gerard?

I've never read him, Sorme said. He stood up. I think I'd better be off anyway.

He would have welcomed spending another hour with either of them alone, but to have them both together was frustrating. He sensed obscurely that he was making headway with Miss Quincey; and that she wanted him to stay.

You're not going early because of me, I hope? Caroline said.

Not at all. You wouldn't drive anyone away, I assure you.

Thanks!

I've got a book that might interest you, Miss Quincey said. I think you ought to read it.

Who's it by?

Well, our books are always issued anonymously, but I do happen to know who wrote this one. It's by Brother Macardle of Manchester. I've met him. He's a brilliant man – a biochemist.

She was searching through the bookcase as she spoke. She said:

I . . . can't see it. It must be upstairs. I won't be a moment.

Sorme followed her out of the room, and took his raincoat from the hat stand. He went back into the sitting-room to put it on. Caroline looked at him, chewing. She said:

I'm sorry you've got to go.

Maybe we can meet again?

I'd love to. I'd like you to tell me about your book.

He belted the raincoat.

When are you free?

Almost any evening – and just occasionally in the afternoon. He was being deliberately casual, yet listening hard for the sound of Miss Quincey on the stairs, afraid she might come back too soon. He asked:

Are you free tomorrow evening?

I . . . think so. If I'm not, where can I contact you?

He gave her his phone number, and she wrote it in a notebook which she took from her handbag. He asked:

Where shall I see you?

Where do you live?

Camden Town.

Miss Quincey's step sounded on the stairs. She said quickly: Six o'clock at Leicester Square Underground?

That's fine.

She was returning the notebook to her handbag as Miss Quincey came into the room. He felt absurdly tense and embarrassed. Caroline, looking completely unhurried, bit into the sandwich. Miss Quincey held out a green-bound book to him.

Have you got a copy of the Bible?

Er . . . yes, of course.

It's not of course. Most people haven't.

121

No?

No. I soon found that out when I did some door-to-door work with Brother Robbins. We visited thirty houses in one road in Putney, and only two had a Bible.

He slipped the book into the inside pocket of his raincoat. It was not large.

You'll find it marked in many places. It's one of the best books we've ever published, I think. It gives you everything we believe in a nutshell. If you intend to write about us, you ought to base it on that. But you'll need a Bible to refer to as well.

Thanks . . . Er . . . when shall I see you again?

In front of Caroline, he felt his phrasing was preposterously ill-chosen.

You ought to read that first. No, I don't really mean that. You're very welcome whether you've read it or not. Come any time. Not over the weekend though.

Later this week?

Yes . . . Not Wednesday or Friday, though, unless you want to attend a meeting. And Thursday I've got some people coming. You could come tomorrow if you wanted to.

Not tomorrow. I think I'm doing something.

Then it will have to be next Monday at the earliest. Will that be all right?

Yes, that's fine . . .

He turned at the door. Caroline was still eating.

Goodbye.

Bye-bye, Gerard.

He deliberately refrained from calling her 'Caroline', feeling a constraint in Miss Quincey's presence.

At the front door he said:

Look here, I feel rather guilty about this . . .

About what?

About coming here and eating your food. I don't want you to feel that . . . well, you know . . .

Oh nonsense. I know you don't. There's always food here whenever you want to come in. Don't feel guilty.

He said: Perhaps I might take you out for a meal one evening?

She smiled, shrugging, then suddenly met his eyes, and seemed to colour slightly. She said briskly:

Well, we can talk about that.

He took her hand.

Goodnight.

Goodnight, Gerard.

To his surprise she took his hand in both hers, and squeezed it. He turned away quickly, and hurried down the drive. She called:

Can you see all right?

Yes, thank you.

The dark closed around him as the door clicked to.

Chapter Five

She yielded immediately, and with no sign of surprise. When he tried to press her backwards on to the settee, she pushed him away gently, saying: Not here. Someone might come. He asked: Where then? She smiled, and nodded towards the bedroom. Before she was through the door, she had begun to pull her dress over her head. He slammed the door and locked it. He said happily:

My god, sweet, you've got a superb body.

Someone hit the door behind him, banging it hard. He was surprised; there had been no one in that room a moment before. She looked alarmed, and reached for her slip, which she had thrown on to the bed. The knock came again. He said:

Never mind that. Let's hurry before . . .

The knocking became more insistent, and he became aware of the voice shouting: Telephone for you. The dream dissolved; he sat up dizzily in bed, and looked at his watch. He shouted:

OK. Thanks very much.

Carlotte's steps retreated down the stairs. He pulled on his dressing-gown, thrusting his feet into slippers. The dream became an unreality, and was forgotten before he had had time to dwell on it.

The front door stood wide open; he closed it before picking up the phone. The operator's voice asked: Mr Sorme?

Speaking.

A personal call for you from Switzerland.

He said: Blimey, again?

Beg your pardon?

Nothing. Put it through, please.

Gerard? Is that you?

Yes.

Have you been yet?

He let the annoyance sound in his voice:

No. I've only just got out of bed!

Oh I'm terribly sorry! Did I wake you?

Yes. But never mind. Was that all you rang me for?

Normally he would have apologized for the inconvenience he had accidentally caused, but sleepiness made him irritable. Nunne's voice said:

No. Can you hear me well?

Yes, perfectly.

Gerard. . . I want you to do me rather a favour. Would you?

Yes. What is it?

I'd like you to go to my room, and collect something for me, and take it back to your own room. Would you?

All right. But will the porter let me in?

Yes. But it's not my usual room . . . It's not my flat I'm talking about. I want you to go to another address. Have you got a pencil?

He groped in the pocket of the dressing-gown, and found the cheap ball-pen he usually kept there. His address book was not with it, but there was a chocolate wrapper, which he tore open.

All right. I've got a pencil. Go ahead.

The address is twenty-three Canning Place. That's Kensington, off Palace Gate. Have you got that?

Yes. Twenty-three. What do you want me to do?

There's a man called Vannet in charge of the house. He's a friend of mine. Ask for him, and he'll let you into my room.

Will he?

125

Yes. I'm going to phone him now.

All right. What then?

When you get into my room, you'll see some clothes in a corner near the fireplace. I want you to pack them in a bag, and bring them away with you. But don't let Gerald Vannet see you, will you? Make sure he isn't in the room. And whatever you do, don't tell him why you're going there. I'll tell him you want to collect an address I've left behind. All right?

Yes. But why all the secrecy?

I'll explain to you later. But keep the clothes in your room, and don't tell anyone, will you?

All right. Anything else?

Yes. There may be some books lying around the room. Take them and put them back on the bookshelf, will you? And make sure Vannet isn't hanging around to watch you. Sit down and make yourself comfortable, as if you intend to stay half the day. Would you do that?

All right.

And take a taxi. I'll give you the money when I see you. Or, better still, ring Silver Cabs, and quote the number of my account. It's seven two three. Ask for Jakey.

That doesn't matter. I'll cycle.

No, don't do that. Ring for a taxi. I wouldn't be happy otherwise. Will you do that?

All right.

Listen, Gerard. I'm sorry to be such a nuisance. But there's no one else I'd trust. Don't forget. *Please* don't mention it to anyone – especially Vannet. Will you?

No. All right. And you still want me to send you that telegram?

Yes, please. If you would.

When shall I see you?

Probably tomorrow. I'm not sure. But probably.

126

OK, Austin. Look forward to seeing you . . .

Carlotte passed him on the stairs. She said your friend must be very rich, to telephone from Switzerland.

I'm afraid he is. Eccentric, too.

In his own room, he lit the gas fire and put the kettle on to boil. He climbed back into the still-warm bed, and listened to the hiss of gas, the water simmering. He closed his eyes, and thought of Austin. Very rich. More money than sense. Looks as if he might be a damned nuisance. I wonder why all the secrecy? Can't tell. Queers get odd ideas. Maybe he has to keep it a secret that he's queer? Not likely. Most of them advertise it. Trusts me? Why? Perhaps because I know no one else in his circle.

His thoughts flowed into a dream. Austin was lying behind a barrier of stones on top of a mountain; he was pointing towards a house in the valley, and saying, 'Don't show yourself. He has sharp eyes. Lie flat.' They were in Switzerland. Behind them, on a small plateau, stood Austin's aeroplane; it looked like the Spitfire that had stood by the gate of the RAF camp where he had been stationed for his National Service.

He woke up and saw that the kettle was boiling. He made himself tea and got back into bed to drink it, still wearing the dressing-gown. He reached out for the nearest book in the bookcase. It was *The Trial of George Chapman*. He sipped the tea, looking with morbid interest at the face of the sadistic poisoner, the powerful jaw and deep-set eyes. The face looked scarred.

He asked the cabman: You're Jakey?

Yes, sir. But you're not Mr Nunne, though!

No. I'm not. Mr Nunne phoned me from Switzerland an hour ago and asked me to do some errands for him. Do you know his address?

127

Yes, sir, but I'm not sure it's all right me takin' you when you're not Mr Nunne. It's his account, you see . . .

Yes, but he's in Switzerland. He's only just phoned me. He gave me his account number.

Yes, but I don't know that, do I?

Sorme said irritably: He told me to ask for you because you wouldn't make difficulties!

The man said gloomily: All right, jump in. I'll risk it.

Sorme got into the cab swearing under his breath. It annoyed and affronted him to be regarded with suspicion. As the taxi moved off, he began to feel better. It had been a long time since he had travelled by taxi. It gave him a sensation of carelessness and relaxation. He placed his feet on the leather bag he had brought to pack Austin's clothes in, and stared with pleasure at the traffic. He remembered Caroline, and again felt contented and pleased with himself. It was not a frequent sensation; a degree of self-criticism and analysis that accompanied everything he thought made it rare. His thoughts tended to be logical and verbal, like telepathic communication or writing; intuition played only a small part in his mental processes. When tired, he hated this tendency to carry on mental conversations with himself, but was unable to stop it. Now he thought happily: I have tried to avoid complications. But they come all the same. I have tried to simplify my life, to concentrate on the only thing that's important. And the simplicity destroys my ability to concentrate. And now things are happening that should make things worse, and instead I feel certain and confident again.

He felt a sense of disappointment when the taxi drew up opposite Great Portland Street Station. The driver asked:

Is that the lot?

No. I've got two more errands to do. Would you wait?

The man said resignedly: Right y'are, guv.

A man in a red uniform came to meet him as soon as he came out of the revolving door into the hallway.

Can I help you, sir?

Sorme said: Good morning. Mr Nunne asked me to call and find out if there are any messages for him.

The man's manner became perceptibly more respectful.

Hold on a moment, sir. I'll ask the telephone girl. I won't keep you a moment, sir.

Thanks.

He turned as he was hurrying away, to say:

Would you like to take a seat, sir?

Thank you.

They were deep, comfortable armchairs, as in a hotel lounge. In the bowl of the potted palm that stood beside the chair there were several cigarette butts. The lift descended as he sat there. He watched with curiosity the white-moustached old man and the young girl in furs who stepped out of it. Both had the air of unconscious grace and poise that comes from never having to think about money. There was no envy in his contemplation of them: only an almost proprietary kind of affection. He felt that no real barrier existed between themselves and him; on the contrary, he had a strange sense of advantage over them. The girl took the old man's arm and squeezed it. He thought: She is either his mistress or his daughter. Or granddaughter. He looked at them friendlily as they went out of the revolving door, then transferred his attention to the reflection of himself in the mirror opposite. He was mildly surprised that he felt no envy for Nunne and his way of life. He examined the awareness, and realized that it was based on a sense of belief in himself and of confidence in his own powers that was always latent in him, yet which only rarely became conscious. He smiled to himself, and said softly, Delusions of grandeur and distinct paranoiac traits; the patient Sorme should be kept under observation . . .

The man came back. He said:

I've got a few phone messages, sir. People who want him to ring them back.

Thanks. Nothing else? No one has been here enquiring about him?

Enquiring? No, sir. Why, sir, is he expecting someone?

I think so. It doesn't matter. Can I have the phone messages? He's phoning me from Switzerland this evening.

Certainly, sir. The girl's copying them out now. She won't be a moment.

Thanks.

He crossed to the mirror and looked at himself closely. The leather bands around the cuffs of his jackets showed below the sleeves of the overcoat. The grey whipcord trousers looked baggy; one of the turn-ups was hanging down. He thought: I must buy more trousers and get my hair cut. I look a wreck.

In the taxi he glanced at the two sheets of paper headed 'Phone Message'. The messages were written neatly with a ballpoint pen; they were dated from the previous Friday. 'Will you ring Mr Beaumont before ten this evening?' 'Major Dennis will not be able to join Mr Nunne for dinner on Wednesday.' He looked through the rest, then folded the papers and put them in his wallet. They told him nothing more of Nunne. Nunne was becoming increasingly the centre of his curiosity.

The sight of the Post Office at Notting Hill Gate reminded him of the telegram; he tapped on the glass, and asked the driver to stop at the next Post Office. He had forgotten what Nunne had asked him to say in the telegram; after consideration, he worded it simply: No enquiries, and signed it: Gerard.

The driver asked: What number, sir?

Is this Canning Place?

Yes.

Would you mind driving to the end of the street and waiting for me there? I shall be about ten minutes.

The end? Right.

He noted the surprise in the driver's voice, and was about to explain; then he felt irritated with his own embarrassment, reflecting that it was none of the man's business anyway. He stepped out of the cab, saying:

I shall want to return to Camden Town afterwards.

Afraid I'll have to keep the clock tickin', sir.

Right you are.

Number twenty-three was half way down the street. It was a tall, Victorian house with steps leading up to the front door. When he pressed the bell labelled 'Vannet', a voice spoke from a circle of wire gauze above the bell-pushes:

Hello. Who is it?

He addressed the wire gauze:

My name is Sorme. Austin Nunne asked me to call.

Oh yes.

The door clicked open. The voice said:

It's the second door on your right.

He went into the badly-lit hallway, closing the door behind him. The door was inscribed: Gerald Vannet, in white plastic letters. When he knocked, the voice called: Come in.

The man was levering himself out of an easy chair as he came into the room. He was six inches shorter than Sorme. He wore a loose green tee-shirt with a silk muffler underneath it. The flannel trousers had a knife-edge crease.

Well, I'm delighted to meet you! You're Mr Sorme.

131

Austin rang up about an hour ago. Won't you have a drink?

His voice was a neighing drawl, on an almost soprano note.

Sorme said uncertainly: That's very kind of you . . . He was thinking of the taxi.

You're not in a hurry, are you? Austin said you might want to spend an hour or two here. You haven't got a taxi waiting, or anything?

Sorme's immediate inclination was to admit that he had, until he recollected Nunne's insistence on secrecy. He said quickly:

No. I'm not in a hurry.

Lovely. *Do* sit down. I'm afraid the room's in a bit of a mess. I've not been up long. We had a party last night. What will you drink? Whisky, or gin and martini? I'm afraid I've nothing else except a little wine.

Gin and martini then, please.

Sweet or dry?

The room was stuffily warm, with two electric fires burning. It was a large and very comfortable bed-sitter. The carpeting was a plain fawn colour, and looked as if it had only just been hoovered. Nothing in the room suggested a party, or the untidiness associated with late rising. Sorme took his gin and Italian, and sat on the bed. Vannet stretched himself out on a piece of furniture that combined armchair and divan, with curves moulded to his body. He smiled at Sorme over the top of his glass, and then drank as though toasting some secret that they shared. He said:

I may say, it isn't like Austin to send his . . . friends along to see me. You are a fairly *new* friend, aren't you?

Fairly, Sorme said.

Vannet grinned, and took another sip of whisky, managing to imply that his tact would forbid further questioning. He said blandly:

I manage to meet all Austin's friends sooner or later. Where'd you meet him – the Balalaika?

No. What is it?

Ah! I can see you haven't known him for long! You'll see the Balalaika soon, no doubt.

What is it?

Oh, it's a . . . well, a sort of a . . . It's a club.

He simpered over his glass.

I see, Sorme said. I shall look forward to going there.

You ought to go tomorrow. Wednesday's drag night. World-famous female impersonators! Oh, my dear!

He said this with a nasal Cockney accent, fluttering his hand stiffly from the wrist.

I'll ask Austin – if he's back, Sorme said.

Are you expecting him?

I'm not sure.

A pair of china blue eyes regarded him penetratingly for a moment, then dropped coyly. Vannet said:

Well, *if* you want to see it, and Austin's not back, *I* could probably get you in . . .

That's kind of you! But I can see it some other time.

That's what you think! You don't think they do it every week, do you? They have to *arrange* it. Then they pass the word around quietly. So the police don't get wind of it. They don't intend to be *raided*, don't you see, dear? Don't mind me calling you dear. It doesn't mean anything . . . But if you'd like to see it, I'd be delighted . . .

Sorme grunted, and nodded noncommittally. Vannet stared wistfully into his glass, and asked:

Is Austin in Switzerland alone?

As far as I know. Why?

Oh, I'm not prying. But he had his eye on a rather nice little dish at the Balalaika on Friday.

Friday, Sorme said.

Yes . . . why? It was Friday, wasn't it? Yes, I remember.

I was with him on Friday evening, Sorme explained. But he left me before midnight.

Oh, this was well after midnight. He was looking far gone. . . . Cigarette?

No, thanks. Tell me, do you own all this house?

Yes, why? You looking for a room?

Again, the look was suggestive and coy. Sorme finished the martini.

No. I've only just moved into a room. Camden Town. But it seems a most impressive place. With all the gadgets.

Thank you. You touch me on my weak spot. This place is my pride. I own two more – in Highgate and Islington – but my heart belongs to twenty-three Canning Place. Another drink?

No, thanks. I ought to get a move on.

An instinct told him that a second drink would mean at least another hour of conversation.

No. Perhaps you're right. It wouldn't improve your studies.

A buzzer sounded suddenly in the room, making Sorme jump. Vannet picked up a small microphone that stood by the chair, and flicked a switch. He said tartly:

Bugger off. I've got a visitor.

He smiled at Sorme, and pressed the switch again. A complaining voice said:

I don't want to get you out of bed. I want Frankie.

He's not here. He went hours ago.

When? the voice demanded through the microphone.

When? Don't ask me. I'm not his bloody mother. Hours ago. Do you want to come in for a drink?

No, thank you! Not after that! He's got to meet this producer chap at one. You've no idea . . .?

Yes, I have. Try flat seven – Dilly's.

134

Oh, you awkward bastard. Why didn't you say so?

Vannet put the microphone down. He said:

Useful little things, these. They save my poor old feet. Not to mention the tenant on the top floor. Where were we?

You were saying something about my studies. I didn't quite follow you.

Oh yes. Austin said to leave you down there so you could study, or something.

I shan't be there long. I only want to look something up.

Oh. Pity. I was hoping you'd be here for lunch.

No. I must get back, I'm afraid.

He stood up to emphasize his intention of leaving. Vannet heaved himself regretfully off the curved armchair. He said:

Oh well, if you have to go.

Sorme was afraid he had offended him, but the intimacy of Vannet's smile as he opened the door reassured him:

I'll hope to see you again. And if you do want a room . . .

He led the way across the hall, and opened the front door. Sorme asked:

What about Austin's flat?

That's in the basement, Vannet said. Sorme caught a glint of amusement in his eyes, and guessed that Vannet had been curious as to whether he had been here before. He followed him out into the street and through the gate in the area railings. A glance at the end of the street showed him the taxi still waiting there.

It's quite self-contained, Vannet said. You can't get into it from the house.

I see.

Vannet opened the front door. Immediately, a smell of

some perfume met them; Sorme recognized it; it was the perfume of the Diaghilev exhibition, Mitsouko.

After you. The door is to your left.

The room was in complete darkness. He groped for the switch. A soft pink light came on, showing a room that was similar to Vannet's bed-sitter. The air smelt of strong tobacco. Sorme looked into its corners, but saw no clothes. He set the leather grip down on the table.

This is it, Vannet said. There's another room through there. I'll leave you now. Make sure you slam the door as you go out. Enjoy yourself.

Thank you.

Vannet held out his hand. He said softly, almost pleadingly:

And if you'd like another drink, or a bite to eat, come into my place when you leave.

Thanks, Sorme said uncomfortably. But I don't think I'll accept this time. Perhaps another day . . .

Bye-bye . . . I don't even know your Christian name.

Gerard.

It's like mine – Gerald! Ah, well. Bye-bye, Gerard.

Goodbye. Thanks for the drink.

Come again!

The front door closed noisily. Sorme crossed the room immediately and opened the other door. The smell of Mitsouko was suddenly stronger. He switched on a light. Four wall-lights came on, filling the room with a blue glow.

It was smaller than the other room. The walls were almost completely hidden by velvet curtains that stretched from floor to ceiling. The hangings were black; they contrasted with the carpet and divan, which were wine-red. He said aloud: Christ! Shades of Edgar Poe! He suddenly felt grateful to Vannet for leaving him alone; it relieved him of any necessity to comment on the room.

He sat on the divan-bed, and stared around. The room repelled and attracted him. He looked up at the ceiling, which had been painted night-blue. He stood up to stare more closely at the pictures that were spaced along the walls between the hangings. Two were Gauguins; they looked like originals or skilful copies. On either side of these were spaced four obscene drawings, signed and titled in a Chinese or Japanese script; these seemed to have been sketched with a fine brush dipped in Indian ink. One showed a naked giant of a man, with a proportionately large member, landing from a raft on a beach; across the beach hordes of laughing women rush to meet him. Its companion-picture showed the same man leaving the island, shrunken and withered, while the women tear their hair and wail. The other two drawings showed the same giant performing feats of strength: in one case, shattering a copper vessel with the immense member; in the other, holding off hordes of armed bandits by using it as a club. He observed that all four drawings bore in the bottom left-hand corner the minute letters: OG.

He slid aside the plain-glass doors of the bookcase. The bottom shelf was devoted to an edition of the Marquis de Sade. He took down a volume of *Les 120 Journées de Sodome*, and observed that the title page bore no publisher's imprint. The other shelves contained volumes in French and German, uniformly bound in blue leather with silver lettering, and copies of limited editions of Petronius, Apuleius and Sappho, all lavishly illustrated. Finally, the top shelf contained several works on medicine and psychology, with volumes of Bloch, Stekel, Krafft-Ebing and Hirschfeld. The French and German volumes seemed to be mostly of nineteenth-century romantic writers. He opened the volume of Lautréamont, and found it thick with dust. Some of its pages were uncut.

He returned to the other room and investigated its

doors. One was a clothes cupboard; the other led to a large kitchen in which everything seemed new, although when he looked more closely he realized from the undisturbed dust that no one had used it for a long time. Beyond the kitchen was a bathroom, in which the smell of Mitsouko was overpowering; it came from the bath, where the fragments of a large bottle were scattered. He pulled out the plug and turned on the tap; after a few moments, the water flowed hot, and clouds of scented steam rose around him. From the size of the fragments, he judged that the bottle must have held at least half a pint.

From somewhere above his head, he heard the sound of a telephone ringing. It reminded him of the reason he was in Nunne's flat. He turned off the tap and returned to the bedroom.

At first sight, he could see no sign of the clothes Nunne had mentioned. Then he tried looking behind the hangings, and found them immediately. They were lying beside the fireplace, which had been sealed up with black-painted hardboard. At the top of the heap lay a pair of women's stockings. It seemed to be a complete women's outfit. He was surprised; he had expected that the clothes would be Nunne's own.

He opened the leather grip, and tried to push them inside in a bundle. They were too bulky; he had to fold them, and place them in one by one. There was a black raincoat with a torn lining, and a shabby navy blue skirt. The stockings were of good quality nylon, but the rest of the underclothes were evidently not new. Finally, there was a pair of black suède shoes, one of the high heels was broken off and missing. He packed these on top, and closed the grip.

The thought of the waiting taxi worried him; he had no desire to leave the flat immediately. Finally, he went out and dismissed it, telling the man that he was being delayed. He felt guilty as he watched it drive away, but the guilt gave way to a sense of relief and relaxation as he closed the front door behind him. Excitement produced a watery sensation in the bowels.

In the sitting-room he switched on the electric fire, and knelt, warming himself at it for a moment. Then he crossed to the sideboard and opened the cupboard. It contained an array of liqueur bottles, mostly full or half full. With a sense of having the whole day to spare, he took them out one by one and sniffed them. Some he knew; most of them he had never heard of, or only seen on the shelves behind bars. He found a shelf of glasses in the other cupboard, and proceeded to line up a dozen along the sideboard, and pour a drop of liqueur into each. He pulled up a chair to the sideboard, and tasted each glass in turn: the Calvados, Chartreuse, Benedictine, anisette, maraschine, allasch. In some cases the taste was so agreeable that he poured more into the glass. After ten minutes he realized that he was becoming slightly drunk. There were still bottles untasted. He decided to leave them until later. The room was becoming warm; he removed his coat and flung it over an armchair. He said aloud: You lucky bastard, Austin. He returned to the other room, and was glad of its relative coolness.

When he pulled at the curtains, he realized that they moved on rollers; if necessary, they could be drawn to cover the walls of the room completely. He drew them back until they were all bunched in corners of the room. It made little difference to the appearance of the walls. They were painted black. A door in the corner was also painted black. The space where the window had been was boarded over like the fireplace; from the other side of the room, it looked like a continuation of the wall.

The wall at the far end of the room, which had been

completely covered by curtains, had two paintings hung on it. One showed a man in evening dress walking along a busy street; he was leading a pig by a length of blue ribbon; in the middle of his forehead was an enormous eye. The other showed a man in shirtsleeves, lying on his back under an apple tree in moonlight. The fruit and leaves of the tree were painted in deep greens and reds and blues; they possessed a misty and lyrical quality that contrasted with the completely yellow figure under the tree. The titles of both pictures were painted at the bottom of the canvases; *Les Amours Jaunes*, and, *Self-portrait by Moonlight*. Both were signed: Glasp, and dated 1948.

The other door led into a small closet, whose back wall was lined with bookshelves. He switched on the light to look through them, and found them disappointing. There were many standard works of English literature, and some volumes which he guessed to be Nunne's college text books. There were several children's books; when he idly took down *The Bumper Book for Boys* he found a signature: Austin Nunne 1935, inside the cover. An abridged edition of Frazer's *Golden Bough* seemed to have been given as a school prize in 1940; it had evidently been thoroughly read; the text was covered with pencil-marks. It fell open at an early page as he leafed through it. He turned to the light to read a quotation marked in red ink:

'The notion of a man-god, or of a human being endowed with divine or supernatural powers, belongs essentially to that early period of religious history in which gods and men are still viewed as beings of much the same order, and before they are divided by the impassable gulf which, to later thought, opens out between them.'

He carried the book into the bedroom, and sat on the divan to read it. A curious sense of Nunne's presence was beginning to grow in him. Once he looked up startled, expecting to see Nunne standing in the doorway, looking at him. He said aloud: I am yesterday, today and tomorrow, and I have the power to be born a second time. The sound of his voice released his tension, but left a sense of disquiet that puzzled him. He felt as if something unpleasant was about to happen, a sensation like the end of a nightmare. Then he noticed the grip, standing beside the fireplace. The disquiet was connected with the women's clothes he had packed. As he tried to analyse it, he remembered that Nunne had asked him to return any open books that might be lying around to their shelves. He could not recollect having seen any. For some reason this worried him. He went into the other room and looked around, finding none. In the bedroom he pulled aside all the curtains, and peered between the divan and the wall. Finally, he raised the edge of the divan cover and looked in the three-inch space between its bottom and the floor. A book lay open, face downwards on the carpet. Its title was: *Criminology, Its Background and Techniques*. He turned it over, and found himself looking at a photograph of a woman with her throat cut. The caption under the picture read: Note defensive wounds on hands. He dropped the book on the bed, feeling sick, and went out to the kitchen.

There, the daylight made him feel better. He ran the tap, and stared at the water that ran in a smooth stream. It soothed him. The room he had left seemed in some way unclean; he felt no desire to go into it again. It was the first time he had seen a photograph of a violent death; it seemed to taint the air he breathed with tangible disgust. He felt almost as though he had discovered a mutilated body in Nunne's cupboard.

He told himself that the disgust was stupid, that he had no right to be shocked by physical violence. After a while

141

he returned to the bedroom, and made himself take up the book again. This time the photograph made less impact on him. He sat on the bed with a sense of bravado, and looked through the book. It seemed to be a well-documented textbook for the use of the American police. A whole chapter dealt with stolen cars, with photographs of the marks made by tyres on mud; another dealt with fingerprints and footprints. It was the final chapters of the book which examined causes of death and identification of the dead, that contained most of the photographs of violence. He found himself turning the pages with a tension that was like being prepared for a physical blow. He made himself read the captions before he looked at the photographs: when he had finished looking through these, he returned the book to the top shelf, among the volumes on forensic medicine. Still standing on the divan, leaning against the wall for balance, he opened some of these, and glanced into them. The photographs had ceased to shock him; he felt only a heaviness of continual disgust in his stomach. When he lowered his eyes to the shelf underneath, containing Mallarmé, Nerval, de L'Isle-Adam, Schopenhauer, he experienced a sense of unreality. It seemed to him that these men had known nothing of the reality of death when they wrote, that somehow the photographs made nonsense of the obsession with sin in de Sade and Baudelaire.

As he stood there, his feelings seemed to black out, like a sudden breakdown in a film; for a moment, he was overpowered by a sense of his own absurdity. It was the vastation that had come to him on the previous Sunday in the night. It was as if he was watching something over which he had no control, and that terrified him. He sat down on the divan. The feeling began to disappear. He tried to capture it, feeling strongly that he must outface it and examine it. It disappeared completely.

He became aware of the coldness of the room. He sat there, scowling into space, trying to analyse the fear. It was difficult, but he was certain it had to do with his own identity. He thought about the words that had come into his mind as he had stood there. Absurd. Arbitrary. He said aloud: It is because I might be anyone or anything. Or not exist at all. But if I didn't exist . . . I. Exist. They mean the same thing.

He began to walk up and down the room, thinking in words, as if talking. It was elusive. I. My own. The legitimate me recognizes nothing as its own. All is alien. Even existence. I must disown existence too. If I exist, I am trapped.

A new idea came to him. Limitedness. I don't want limits. It is limits that are alien to me. The universe, space, time, being. Nothing must be limited. I am god. I am yesterday and today. I am the god Tem, maker of heaven, creator of things which are. If I am not, life is meaningless.

He took down a volume on forensic medicine, and stared at a photograph of a man who had been killed in a railway accident. It failed to revive the vastation. The death in the book no longer represented reality. Like Baudelaire and de Sade, it was still two moves away from reality.

After washing and drying the liqueur glasses, he walked to Kensington High Street and caught the tube. He was glad of the lunch-hour crowds. Silence and the sense of uncertainty had left him tired.

The Scotswoman opened the door; when she saw him, her face tightened. He said quickly:

The father *is* expecting me.

He was. It's time for his rest now.

He was irritated by her manner, but repressed the resentment, saying politely:

I'm sorry. I'll come back again another day.

She hesitated, then stood back and opened the door:

Come on inside, an' I'll see how he feels.

He said quietly: Thank you. He kept his voice lowered in case Maunsell was downstairs; he had no particular wish to see him at the moment. The woman went upstairs without bothering to show him into the waiting-room. He was glad she didn't waste words. When he approached the glass-panelled door, he heard a murmur of voices from outside. He stood in the dark hallway, leaning against the banister. The woman appeared on the stairs, beckoning him up.

He can't spare more'n a few moments. He should be asleep. He's been at it all day.

I won't keep him long, Sorme promised.

As soon as he encountered the faint disinfectant smell in the corridor, he was reminded of his talk on the previous day; a feeling of anticipation came over him as he reached the door. It disappeared immediately when he saw the priest, the curiously ugly face above the pyjama jacket; instead, he experienced the same slight disappointment he had felt on first meeting him.

Father Carruthers was sitting in the armchair by the fire. A plaid rug and an eiderdown were wrapped around the lower half of his body.

Come and sit down. How are you?

Sorme laid the raincoat on the bed, and sat in the other armchair.

I'm fine, father. I'm expecting Austin back today or tomorrow.

Good. You've heard from him?

He's phoned me twice since yesterday.

The priest grunted, and regarded him steadily. Sorme realized what he was thinking. He said:

They weren't just social calls. He seems to have something on his mind. Has he always been inclined to get excited over nothing, father?

In what way?

Well . . . being strange and secretive. Acting like a conspirator. I'm a little worried . . .

I've never known it. In what way is he strange?

Sorme told the story of the phone calls, and ended by describing the flat.

While he talked he was aware of having the priest's complete attention.

The priest asked finally:

I would like to know your exact reason for speaking to me of all this.

The question embarrassed Sorme. He considered his answer carefully. He said slowly:

Austin fascinates me. And I don't fully know why he fascinates me. And . . . well, I like him. Do you see?

He said this almost defiantly, because he could think of no other way of expressing it. The priest smiled, and the ugliness dissolved in the benevolence that flickered at Sorme.

I understand.

Besides . . . that flat of his . . . it made me feel I know him a lot better. And that I want to know him a lot better.

The priest closed his eyes. He talked with his face turned towards the fire, as if talking to himself.

What you tell me of this flat is new to me. And to some extent it is a surprise to me. But, after all, there is perhaps no reason to be surprised. It probably explains why Austin stopped coming here. Romanticism is a dubious refuge, but it is not a dangerous one. And no one remains in it for a long time.

145

Sorme interrupted: You think he'll come to the Catholic Church eventually?

I think that it is not impossible.

Sorme considered this, staring into the fire. The eyes in the white, invalid's face remained closed. He said:

Romanticism . . . I see your point. That accounts for de L'Isle-Adam and Huysmans and the rest. But what about the crime photographs? And de Sade.

You have answered yourself. De Sade – another romantic. Sadistic pictures . . .

I don't know that they were sadistic. They were just revolting.

For the sadist, the revolting causes pleasure.

Is Austin a sadist, father?

He asked the question quickly, and without thinking. Almost immediately he wondered if he had gone too far. The priest's eyes opened and regarded him; the voice said calmly:

Shall we say . . . he has tendencies . . .

Sorme said bluntly:

Look here, father. If you think I'm talking out of turn, tell me so flatly. I don't want to pry.

The priest said, smiling:

Yesterday, I hardly knew you. Today, you know a great deal more about Austin, and I know you a little better. I think we can speak frankly.

Sorme felt relieved; the removal of the ambiguity made him more relaxed. He smiled broadly:

Thank you, father. That's kind of you. You see, I *do* feel a sort of tentative responsibility for Austin. I felt rather touched when he said I was the only person he could trust.

Quite.

But I don't understand at all. Those women's clothes, for instance . . .

Where are they now?

Sorme said with sudden alarm:

I left them downstairs in the hallway.

That doesn't matter. They'll be quite safe.

Sorme scowled at the palms of his hands. He said hesitantly: Father, I'm going to tell you what I've got on my mind, and if you think it's tosh, just tell me so.

I will.

Well, look here, it's like this . . . Yesterday morning, two policemen tried to interview an old man in the house where I live . . . about the East End murders. Now I'm sure they had no special reason – no real suspicions of him. He was just an odd sort of crank, and perhaps he's been in some sort of trouble with them before for a sexual offence, and he's probably one of dozens they'd interview. Now Austin's asked me to get some women's clothes out of his flat. Supposing he's expecting the police to want to interview him about the murders? Supposing he's known to them as a man with sadistic tendencies? Does that make sense?

The priest said:

You don't seriously think that Austin might be involved in these murders?

Good lord, no! Of course not. But the police wouldn't leave any stone unturned, would they? And the clothes belong to a woman. What do you think?

It is possible . . . it is possible. But that would not explain Austin's secrecy.

Why not? It might. Anyway, perhaps he is in some sort of trouble. After all, a man with perversions can land in trouble pretty easily. Perhaps it isn't the police he's worried about. It could be that someone's blackmailing him . . .

He stopped, with a sense that such speculation was

futile. The priest's eyes flicked up to his face and were lowered again.

You may be right, but the best way to find out is to wait until Austin comes back, and ask him. It is not at all improbable that the police might question him in connection with the Whitechapel murders – *if* he is known to them as a sexual invert. In cases of sadistic murder they spread their net very wide. They have to, since there is no other way.

How do you mean, father?

In the average murder, someone has a motive, and it is simply a matter of finding it. In a sexual crime – unless the criminal is caught in the act – the police have nothing to go on. I was in Düsseldorf at the time of the Kürten murders. The number of suspects the police interviewed over three years ran into hundreds of thousands. So it is not at all impossible that Austin may be one of those questioned.

Sorme said, smiling:

Or me . . . or anybody else?

Quite.

Sorme stood up. He said:

Look, father, I'm not going to keep you any longer. I know you're supposed to be resting. Thanks for listening to me. I had to talk to somebody about it or bust.

You were right to come to me. But some time you must come here to talk about yourself.

Thank you, father.

One more thing. I have a friend – a German doctor – who is working with Scotland Yard. When you have talked to Austin – if you think he needs help – get him to contact me. Dr Stein might be able to save some trouble.

Thanks, father. I'll do that.

He picked up his coat, and opened the door. As he did so, he remembered a question he had forgotten to ask:

By the way, father, do you know a painter named Glasp?

Yes.

Austin has some paintings by him on his walls. How old is he?

I . . . I'm not sure. About twenty-six or so.

Twenty-six? He must be very talented. Two of the paintings are dated nineteen forty-eight. That means he'd be about seventeen when he did them.

He is very talented – or he was. He is also very poor, and he's been in a mental home twice. Perhaps Austin will introduce you to him.

Do you know where he lives, by any chance?

I'm afraid not. I haven't seen him for some years. Father Rakosi may have his address. Austin is sure to.

He's a Catholic?

Yes.

The door opened as he stood with his hand on the knob. It was the Scotswoman.

Time for your rest, father.

Sorme said:

I'll come again soon, if I may, father. Goodbye.

Goodbye.

In the hall, he encountered the Hungarian priest. He said:

Pardon me, Father Carruthers said you might know the address of a painter called Glasp.

Yes. Do you want it?

If it's no trouble, please.

Wait just a moment. I can get it for you.

He went into a room next to the waiting-room; a moment later, he reappeared with a notebook:

It is number twelve Durward Street.

Sorme wrote it down in his own address book. He asked:

Where is it?

East one, Whitechapel.

Do you know his Christian name?

The priest looked surprised:

You do not know him?

No. I've seen some of his paintings. I thought I might go and see him some time.

I see. You will not find him sociable. His name is Oliver. He is not easy to talk to.

Sorme slipped his address book into his pocket.

Thank you, father. Maybe I'll write him a letter. Good afternoon.

Outside, he looked around automatically for his bicycle, until he remembered he had travelled by Underground. He walked towards Chancery Lane station, swinging the leather grip. Glasp's Christian name had confirmed his suspicion that the obscene drawings had been sketched by him: they were initialled O.G. But this in itself meant nothing. It was only another fragment of the jigsaw puzzle that fitted around Nunne.

He had thought so much about Nunne that Nunne's reality was becoming shadowy. He thought: I am negative. That's the trouble. I am negative, and I am interested in Nunne because he is positive. I am like a stagnant pond. And Nunne is a stone that has disturbed the scum.

He walked towards Kingsway, and the mood of gloom and self-irritation deepened. He was aware that, to some extent, this was because he had not eaten since breakfast. The faint intoxication induced by the liqueurs was beginning to wear off too.

In the Underground he came close to falling asleep. He wiped the tears out of his eyes with his handkerchief, and immediately yawned again.

Tired. That's the trouble. I'll eat and sleep when I . . . oh, damnation.

He remembered Caroline, and that he was due to meet

her in two hours. The thought depressed him. He considered phoning her and telling her that he couldn't make it, but the idea troubled him even more than the thought of being at Leicester Square by six o'clock. Finally, he left the train at Camden Town, and went to a ready-made tailors to buy trousers.

Before he had been with her for a quarter of an hour he realized he liked her, that he was going to enjoy the evening. There was no kind of constraint between them. He observed that this was because she took him for granted, as if it was the tenth time he had taken her out and not the first. She treated him casually, like an intimate of long standing. It was something he had noticed also in Austin's manner.

The restaurant was in a basement in the King's Road: it was entered through a coffee bar. Half a dozen voices called her name as soon as they came in, and a bearded youth, wearing a duffle-coat, flung his arms around her and kissed her, crying:

Alloa, me luv, it's grand ter see yer!

She introduced him to Sorme, saying: This is Frank. He's playing Verlaine in the play we're doing.

The young man had a plump, immature face; his beard was scanty and silky. Sorme found it hard to imagine anyone less like Verlaine. The youth said:

Howdy, pardner? Ah hope you ain't a fightin' man, 'cause ah ain't brought ma six shooters. Coffee for both of you?

We're having a meal downstairs, Caroline said. We may see you afterwards.

Come to the party. It's on the bomb site opposite the art school. Bring a bottle of wine.

We might do that, she said. They pushed their way through the crowd of youths and girls who lined the

151

counter and the high stools along the walls. Sorme heard someone say:

There's Miss Beddable for Nineteen Fifty-eight.

The downstairs was divided into two halves by a lattice screen, and lit by table lamps made from Chianti bottles. When an olive-skinned waiter hurried towards them, he expected him to address Caroline by her Christian name. But he only said:

Table for two, sir?

The menu cards were enormous, almost as large as a sheet of newspaper.

Some of this stuff's rather expensive.

Don't worry. I robbed my money box this morning.

She surveyed the menu, and asked finally:

Do you like escargots?

He admitted that he had never tried them.

Let's both have some. Do you like garlic?

Love it.

Good. Shall we be pigs and have a dozen each?

When the snails arrived, she instructed him in the use of the small tongs, and insisted that he drink the melted butter from the shell, after the soft, black body had been extracted and eaten. They had another gin and lime, followed by a bottle of hock. He began to feel relaxed and slightly irresponsible. He admitted to her:

I wasn't looking forward to this evening at all.

No. Why not?

I was a little nervous that we wouldn't get along. Do you know something? I haven't taken a girl out for the past five years.

Good Heavens! What did you do? Take a monastic vow?

No. Just stayed in my room, mostly. Or in the British Museum Reading Room.

But why? You're not shy . . .

152

No. I was looking for something . . . if you see what I mean.

She asked, smiling: For what?

The roast chicken arrived, and gave him time to consider his answer. He said finally:

The same thing Rimbaud was looking for. A vision.

She said immediately: I've been trying to read a book about him, but it's full of French quotations. He wanted to derange his senses or something, didn't he?

Yes.

Did you try that?

No. I tried some disciplines. But nothing happened.

And what do you intend to try now?

Funnily enough, I'm closer to it now than ever before. Do you know what a catalyst is?

No.

It's a thing that causes a chemical reaction without getting altered itself. You make sulphuric acid gas by heating oxygen and sulphur dioxide. But you have to heat them over platinized asbestos. Otherwise nothing happens. But the platinized asbestos doesn't change. Well, Austin has been like platinized asbestos for me. I had a lot of elements inside me that didn't mix. I had a lot of knowledge that didn't mean anything to me. Since I met him last Friday, I've started feeling alive for the first time in years.

She asked, pouting:

Don't I come in anywhere?

Of course you do. If it hadn't been for Austin, I wouldn't have met you, would I?

How *did* you meet Austin?

He told her while he ate. He was still telling her after the meal, when they went upstairs for coffee. Half way up the stairs, she stopped and turned her head towards him, whispering:

153

You know, I'm a little tipsy.

She swayed backwards slightly, and he put both hands around her waist to steady her. She gripped them in hers for a moment and pulled them tight, then released them. He was feeling too well-fed and somnolent to be excited by the gesture, but it increased the sense of comfort and certainty he felt with her. As they drank coffee, she asked suddenly:

Do you think Gertrude's attractive?

He stared hard at his cup, and said critically:

Yes . . . she's attractive.

But not your type? she prompted him.

No . . . It's not that. It's the simplicity of the way she sees things. She puzzles me.

Puzzles you? Why on earth should she puzzle you?

She's either brilliantly dishonest or so primitively simple-minded that I can't even conceive of it. Mind, I can understand people being simple Bible Christians, and thinking the Bible's the beginning and end of everything. But she doesn't strike me as having that type of mind. You'd think she'd read Virginia Woolf, and patronize the local young writers.

She does!

Yes . . . I suppose she does. Do you know anything about her life before she came to live in Hampstead?

No. Mummy's never talked about her. But she did drop something once when I wasn't supposed to be listening. There *was* a man once.

And what happened?

I don't know, really. Why are you so interested? Have you got designs on her?

You brought the subject up!

I expect I did. Anyway, I think she's got designs on you.

On my salvation, you mean.

Well . . . She's rather lonely up there. That's why I go up to stay some nights. I think she'd like it if you went up there more often.

Hasn't she any other close friends?

No. She used to see rather a lot of a painter once. But that stopped . . .

You mean she had an affair?

Oh no. He was half her age. A man named Glasp.

Oliver Glasp?

Yes, why?

I've heard of him. A friend of Austin's, I think.

Yes. I think Austin took him there for the first time.

Why did he stop going there? Do you know?

Yes. He had some kind of a breakdown and went into a mental home. She never talked about it much, but I think they quarrelled as well.

They had both finished their coffee. He asked her:

Shall we go?

She slipped down off the stool, and picked up her gloves. He asked:

Where would you like to go now? Back into Soho for a drink?

I don't mind. Where would you?

Let's walk anyway. I've had too much to eat.

The night was cold and windless; there were no stars.
She asked:

Would you like to visit a couple of girl friends of mine? They live on a boat on Chelsea Reach.

How do we get there?

It's a ten-minute walk.

Shall we buy some wine to take?

That's a good idea. I don't suppose they'll have anything to drink. They're both actresses, but they're out of work at the moment.

They bought a bottle of hock at a wine shop, and

walked on past the town hall. A hundred yards further on they could see the glow of a bonfire.

That'd be the party Frankie mentioned. We don't want to go, do we?

I don't.

The fire had been built on a piece of waste ground that was divided from the road by a low wall. The land itself was about ten feet below street level; it was reached through an entrance in the side street. The site was crowded with students, most of them holding bottles or glasses. A crowd of them were dragging a tree trunk across the fire. It was too big to lie flat; it formed a kind of bridge across the centre of the fire, supported at its far end by branches.

Let's go down for just a moment, Gerard?

Sorme trailed reluctantly behind her as she walked to the side street. There the ground sloped naturally on to the site.

He asked with misgiving:

Do you know many of them?

A few. But we don't want to get involved. Let's just have a warm and then go.

Somewhere, a portable radio was playing dance music, but no one was attempting to dance. In the shadows, towards the wall, couples were stretched out on the grass. Most of the crowd stood around the fire in a wide circle. It was too hot to stand close. In the blaze, Sorme could distinguish an old sofa and the remains of a door. As they stood there, someone leapt over the tree trunk where it lay across the centre of the fire, and landed clumsily on the far side, sending up a shower of red sparks. A few students began to cheer spasmodically. The youth turned round and leapt back the other way, flinging his arms in the air and shrieking as he jumped. Sorme said, disgustedly: Bloody fool.

That's Ivor Fenner. I used to go out with him.

Sorme repressed an irritated comment and turned away, shrugging. She took his arm, saying:

Let's go.

As they came back on to street level, he said gloomily:

It all makes me feel as if I'm fifty. I detest students.

They're all right.

Individually, perhaps. En masse, they're loathsome.

Before they had walked more than fifty yards they heard a distant clang of bells. The fire engine passed them and pulled up opposite the bomb site. Caroline said:

They're going to put it out. Let's watch.

When they reached the site the waste ground was already empty of students; they clustered around the walls, looking at the fire. Sorme and Caroline stood at the end of the wall, and watched the long, white jet of water that hissed across the grass and curved on to the fire. Immediately, clouds of steam rose, and the flames disappeared. The water hit the end of the tree trunk, and set it jerking across the grass. A groan went up from the students. Someone shouted:

Rotten spoil-sports!

The fire was out. It had taken less than three minutes.

As they walked away, Sorme found himself feeling ashamed of the irritation he had felt earlier; it was not that he sympathized with the students, but that he revolted automatically at the idea of the authority that could put an end to the party. She looked at his face as they passed under a streetlamp, and asked:

What are you annoyed about, Gerard?

He laughed, becoming aware suddenly that he had been scowling:

I'm not annoyed. I suppose I'm never satisfied.

How do you mean?

I disliked those students because they seemed a sloppy

and undisciplined mob of adolescents. That makes me an authoritarian. But I detest the authorities when they stand about in uniforms and give orders. So I dare say I'm an anarchist. An authoritarian anarchist!

They had turned into Cheyne Walk. The breeze that came from the river was cold. She turned up her collar, and pressed her head against his arm. They crossed to the wall that overlooked the river, and stopped to stare at the water. The lights from the Albert Bridge wavered up from the ink-coloured dark. He became aware that she was looking up at him. He bent to kiss the cold lips, and felt the tip of her nose icy against his face.

She said:

I don't care what you are.

There's no reason why you should. You don't have to live with me like I do.

She said stubbornly:

I wouldn't care if I *had* to live with you.

He kissed her again and wondered, as he did so, how many times before she had been kissed in the dark, and by how many men. He stopped himself before his speculation went further, but was not soon enough to stop a feeling of resentment towards her.

They crossed the bridge that led out to a landing-stage. From this, a narrow gangway of planks ran out along the side of the moored houseboats. He said:

I'd better go first. It's as black as your hat. Which boat is it?

The third along.

What do we do if they're not in?

We could wait for them. Or go home.

As he came level with the third boat, he observed that there were no lights on.

It looks as though they're out. What now?

Let's go on board. The door might be open.

He clambered over the side of the boat, and helped her over. She asked:

Have you got any matches?

He found a match, and lit it. She pulled at a door, which opened.

Thank heavens! We can get in, anyway.

He followed her curiously. An electric light came on, revealing a small kitchen, with two Calor-gas cylinders standing beside a gas stove. She called:

Anyone home? Yoohoo! Barbara! Madeleine!

He noticed a corkscrew hanging on a hook on the wall.

We can have some wine, anyway.

He tore off the lead foil, and opened the bottle. There were no glasses, but he found two china cups on a shelf. Caroline said:

Come on in here.

It was a small bed-sitting room, containing only a wide single bed and an armchair. It was barely six feet square.

This is Barbara's room. Madeleine's is next door, but that's smaller still.

Where do they eat?

In the kitchen.

And where do they receive visitors?

There's another room through there, but they're painting it at the moment.

He handed a cup half filled with wine. She asked:

What shall we drink to? Shall we drink to us?

To us.

He met her eyes as he lowered the cup; she turned her face up to be kissed. He could taste the wine on her lips. They still held the cups. She said:

I wonder what Aunt Gertrude'd say if she could see us now?

I dread to think.

He flung his coat over the armchair, and sat on the bed.

159

Do you think Barbara would mind if I sit on her bed?

Of course not. Move over.

What about my shoes?

Take them off.

He unlaced them and slipped them off, then moved over to the wall. She immediately lay down beside him and closed her eyes.

Don't you want your wine?

In a moment.

He bent over her, and allowed his lips to move over the soft and still cold skin of her face. She said softly:

That's nice.

Her fingertips touched around the back of his neck; her tongue darted between his lips. He straightened up, breathing deeply.

We ought to stop, you know.

Had we?

Yes. Before it's impossible!

She opened her eyes and smiled at him:

I wouldn't mind you being my lover.

That's a highly immoral proposal!

It isn't. You'd be the first.

It's still immoral! Anyway, you're too young to have a lover.

That's silly. Of course I'm not. Anyway, I nearly had one a year ago.

What happened?

He asked me to go to Brighton for a weekend with him. And I said yes.

And did you?

No. I got a sore throat the day before and had to stay in bed.

He said, with mock severity:

That's a fine way to go on! I'm deeply shocked.

She levered herself into a sitting position, and reached out for her cup.

You're not really. Are you?

He asked curiously:

Was it that pimply moron who was leaping over the bonfire?

Ivor! Good lord, no! I wouldn't go to bed with him! No, this was an actor. He was thirty-five, and he'd been divorced twice. And for about three weeks I'd thought I'd go crazy about him. I thought I'd never be able to live without him.

But nothing happened?

No. We quarrelled after that weekend. Then he had to leave. His company went to Liverpool. So that was that.

He drank the rest of his wine, and began to laugh. She asked:

What is it?

Nothing. Just the contrast between you and your aunt.

She said emphatically:

God forbid I should ever be like her!

You won't be!

She put the cup down, and dropped her head on to the pillow: her lips pouted to be kissed. He said:

No. It's not good sense. I get blood pressure and an urge to undress you.

You can't. Not here. Barbara might come.

Let's lock the door?

You can't. It won't lock.

How do you know?

Barbara told me. When she has her boy friend here, they have to wedge the door with the armchair.

Won't she object if she comes in and finds us on her bed?

No! She's a sport. Anyway, we can hear her coming over the side. Then you can get into that chair and look respectable.

He kissed her again, and made no effort to repress the

161

excitement that began to rise. She thrust out her lower lip as she kissed, so that he could taste the moistness and smoothness of its inside. After a few minutes he raised his face from her, and sat up. She asked:

What is it?

It's no good. I'll explode if we keep it up. Are you sure she's likely to be back soon?

I don't know. I don't know when she'll be back.

He started to put his shoes on.

Let's go now. We'll leave her the wine as a present.

Where do you want to go to?

Anywhere. Back to Soho. We can have a drink. It's only ten o'clock.

She stood up in her stockinged feet, and put her arms round his neck. He had to bend his shoulders to shorten himself by fifteen inches in order to reach her face. There was impatience now as he kissed her. He had accepted that nothing could come of it at the moment; further contact with her demanded that he put constraint on his impulses. She seemed to sense this, she broke away gently, saying:

All right. Let's go.

After he had left her at Tottenham Court Roat station he felt relaxed and satisfied. He stared out of the window of the bus as it passed Goodge Street, and allowed his mind to dwell on the memory of her acquiescence. It was not that he suspected he might be falling in love with her; there seemed no likelihood of that. It was simply that he was charmed by her. She was too naïve, her mental processes were all too obvious for him to take her seriously. There was no element of mystery or intoxication, neither had there been any sort of a struggle. Without preliminaries, she had allowed him to see that he excited her, that she would be willing to allow herself to become infatuated with him if he had no objection. He had no objection; the idea of becoming her lover was pleasant. It was as simple as a commercial transaction.

He yawned, and wiped the moisture out of his eyes with a handkerchief. The girl in front of him stood up and transferred a small white pekinese from her lap to the floor. She was pretty and smartly dressed. He glanced at her and looked away, pleased by the indifference he felt. It struck him that he was hardly ever free of desire; at any hour of the day or night, the thought of a woman could disturb him and arouse the dissatisfaction of lust without an object. It was a luxury not to care.

It was a return of the sensation he had felt that morning, watching the girl get out of the lift: a sense of ease and power, a complete lack of envy. He could think of Nunne with complete detachment; not because he felt that Nunne's advantages were accidental or temporal; on the contrary, it seemed there was something in Nunne that made money and luxury inevitable. But, in itself, this was nothing to envy. In his mind, Nunne stood for physical existence, a direct sense of physical life. His natural background would be the spotless deck of a yacht in the Mediterranean, the whiteness of sunlight on snow near Trondheim; the rocks sticking out of a salmon fishing river in Galway. Sorme responded to these thoughts as he responded to Caroline; but underneath them, something oppressed him. There was a futility inherent in physical life that frightened him.

He had begun to feel the cold as he got off the bus at Prince of Wales Road. He shivered, tensing the muscles of his shoulders, and walked quickly across the road. The relaxation had disappeared, and he had begun to feel a sense of anticipation he could not account for. It began to take definite shape when he turned out of the Kentish

Town Road, and noticed the Jaguar parked outside the house.

He looked on the hall table for letters or phone messages. A torn envelope read: Mr Sorme: Mr Nunne rang. It was signed: C.

He saw the slit of light under his door before he opened it. The room was clouded with cigarette smoke. He said:

Hello, Austin. How long have you been here?

Chapter Six

Nunne said: I was just about to push off. I began to think you might be out all night. How are you?

Fine. Have you eaten?

Hours ago. I've been drinking too. Have some brandy.

He indicated the flask on the table. He was sitting in the armchair, his feet on the seat of a wooden chair on the other side of the rug. The gas fire was burning, turned low. Sorme sat in the opposite armchair, and poured a little brandy into a glass. He said:

It's good to see you. What time did you get in?

Five o'clock. I tried phoning you right away, but you'd left.

In the four days since he had last seen him, Sorme had forgotten many things about Nunne. He had forgotten that the drawling, cultured voice grated on his nerves, and that something about the pock-marked face repelled him. The Nunne who sat opposite him had very little in common with the person he had been thinking about on the bus. He said:

I've been out with Caroline Denbigh – Gertrude's niece.

Who? Oh, Gertrude. Caroline! I don't think I've seen her since she was a little kid. But she's only thirteen or so, isn't she?

No. Seventeen.

Oh. Has she fallen for the Sorme approach?

I wouldn't know.

Nunne said, sighing:

I expect she has – like all of us. Will you take her to bed?

Sorme looked at him closely; his face was serene, faintly ironical.

That depends . . . I may.

The irony became unmistakable.

And would you enjoy it?

Sorme said: You've got a good point there. Perhaps not. Oh, I'd get some sort of a kick out of it . . . but what it might lead to . . . I don't know that I'm ready to buy the consequences.

Nunne poured more brandy into the tumbler.

Well, never mind Caroline. You got the clothes, I see.

Yes. Did you look for them?

I did. Many thanks indeed. Did you have any difficulty getting them?

None. I met Vannet. He tried to persuade me to stay to lunch. I didn't.

He would. That man has the curiosity of Pandora.

Then I spent an hour in your flat. Oh, and – I tried some of your liqueurs.

Good. I should have told you to help yourself.

I also looked through your books. I spent a fascinating couple of hours there.

Nunne hunched his shoulders, tensing his arms, then stretched them and yawned.

I'm really very grateful to you, Gerard.

He sagged in the chair suddenly, as if he had been coshed from behind; his eyes continued to stare at Sorme levelly, speculatively. He said:

I suppose you're rather curious about all the mystery?

Sorme shrugged.

Not particularly.

He had a strange sensation, as if he and Nunne were both caught in some slowing-down of time, as if they could sit and stare at one another for hours, days, with no sense of urgency. It was not entirely the drink. Nunne said quietly:

You're a very generous person, Gerard.

Not at all.

Do you mean to say that you're not curious about my flat? And about the phone calls?

Sorme thought for a moment. He said:

No. I don't say that. I'm curious to know *you* better.

Nunne smiled at him. It made him aware that Nunne was tired and depressed; there was exhaustion behind the eyes; they refused to participate in the smile.

Why are you curious about me?

Sorme took another sip of the brandy. He said carefully:

I . . . I like being alive. It sounds obvious, but it's true. I never stop wondering why I'm alive and worrying in case it's all a mistake . . . but for what it is, I love it. But the trouble is, I get tired. I think about it too much. And sometimes, if I'm lucky, some things give me back a sense of being glad I'm alive. A Mozart symphony, a hot frankfurter sausage in a cob, the smell of acetone. They revive my curiosity about living. They give me a new grip on being alive. Or sometimes a book does it. Almost never a person. I sometimes think people are the most uninteresting things in the whole universe. They only reflect the defeat I always carry around with me. Well . . . you're one of the few people I've ever met who arouses all the interest in me. I sense a lot of things about you that worry me a little – the crank, the fanatic, the pervert.

He noticed the slight start of surprise at his use of 'pervert', but it didn't worry him. He was certain of what he meant. But Nunne's exhaustion worried him; he was aware of it all the time. While he had been speaking,

Nunne had uncapped the bottle, and carefully divided the remaining brandy between their two glasses. His eyes were dull as he pushed the glass towards Sorme. He said:

You called me a fanatic and a pervert . . . Do you know exactly the nature of my perversion?

Sorme's heart began to beat fast; he stared steadily at Nunne, hoping to conceal it. He felt his cheeks and neck growing warm.

No. But I can guess.

You don't have to guess. I'll tell you. I'm a sadist.

Sorme's heart was thumping so hard that he was afraid it was showing through his pullover. Controlling his voice, he said:

In what way?

Nunne emptied his glass, and stared at him.

You know what a sadist is?

Yes.

Nunne smiled.

I wonder if you do? What do you think it is?

Someone . . . who enjoys pain.

He knew his voice would shake if he tried a longer sentence. His ears were on fire.

Yes, Gerard . . . that is what a sadist is. But that's nothing. That's only the dictionary definition. It doesn't take account of a lot of things. Like the tension before, and the fear afterwards.

Sorme made no effort to control the excitement that almost suffocated him. He relaxed in the chair, and tried to imagine that Nunne's voice was a gramophone record. The voice said:

The fear never stops. You feel like a carpet when a lighted coal's fallen on it – just a hole where the heart should be, with burn round the edges. Sex is supposed to be a normal desire of the body. But what about when it's an accumulation of tensions you can't define? While you feel it, you can't define it. And when it's over, you feel empty, and still you can't define it.

Sorme began to feel better. He said:

Excuse my ignorance . . . but what's to stop you satisfying your needs? There must be people who . . . well, do it professionally.

You don't understand, Gerard. There are, that's true. But . . . I can't explain. You see, if you feel sexual desire you can be pretty sure you'll find a woman who wants to take what you have to give. But the whole point of sadism . . . is that it wants to take what someone doesn't want to give. If they want to give it, it's not the same.

But I *do* understand, Sorme contradicted him. I feel the same frequently. Nothing shatters me more than a woman who wants to be made love to. Even if I'd been sex-starved for six months, I'd be nauseated if I got into the same bed as a nymphomaniac. And if I'd spent six months trying to seduce a girl, and thirty seconds before I was ready to take her she suddenly moaned: Take me, for God's sake, I'd lose my desire immediately. I'd be incapable of making love to her. Isn't that the same kind of thing?

Not quite. You merely want a completely passive partner. There are probably millions of girls who want to be completely passive.

Sorme said, grinning:

I wish I could find them.

He thought, as he said it, of Miss Quincey and Caroline, and felt a pang of pleasure at the memory of his evening.

Nunne did not smile. He said patiently:

Nevertheless, they exist.

Sorme interrupted him:

Look here, Austin, aren't you making too much of this? Anybody can learn to live with his . . . needs . . .

169

well, without tormenting himself. I've known homosexuals who made a tragedy out of it and spent all their time talking about persecution and frustration. And I've known homosexuals who make a perfectly good job of it, and quite enjoy being queer. Isn't it the same for you? Isn't it just a matter of taking your peculiarities for granted?

That is not the question. The question is to make society take them for granted.

Nunne reached for the brandy bottle, then saw it was empty. His hand dropped, as if exhausted. He said, with apparent irrelevance:

Have you ever read de Sade, Gerard?

No. Only some expurgated bits, anyway.

De Sade was right about the sadist. The true sadist could only find full self-expression as an oriental despot. You see? There's no give and take. Just take.

Pretty bad for the character, I should think.

Ah yes. One would have to be quite callous about it . . .

And you're not?

Not normally.

Sorme said, smiling:

Then use the frustration to create. That's the classical remedy.

Nunne straightened up in the chair, saying abruptly:

Look, let's go and find some more drink.

Do you really want more?

Nunne said in a flat voice:

I shan't sleep tonight unless I'm drunk. And I want to talk to you.

All right. Where do you want to go?

We could go to my flat . . . or to a club I know.

Sorme shrugged, standing up. He no longer felt sleepy.

All right. Whichever you prefer.

Nunne's hand rested on his shoulder as they crossed to the door. He said:

You put up with me very well, Gerard.

Not at all.

The wind was cool around his face in the open-topped Jaguar. The streets were quiet; in the whole length of Albany Street they saw no one. Sorme looked at Nunne's profile as he drove, and tried to connect it with the idea of cruelty. It was difficult. In the light of streetlamps, he appeared tired and pale, not particularly sensual.

They encountered no one in the hallway of the block of flats; the room labelled 'Porter' was empty. Sorme looked across at the chair where he had sat earlier in the day; it was difficult to realize that it had been less than fifteen hours ago. Days seemed to have elapsed since he had watched the white-moustached old man and the girl in furs step out of the lift.

Tired, Gerard?

He realized that he had yawned.

No. Not at all.

The lift stopped at the third floor. The white, marble-like stone of the floor and walls gave the corridor the appearance of a hospital. Nunne led the way, fumbling with a bunch of keys. He stopped opposite a dark, panelled door, and inserted the key. Sorme found himself thinking that he preferred the basement flat in Canning Place; the atmosphere was less chilly.

After you, Gerard.

Daylight lamps came on, illuminating a large, comfortably furnished room that dispelled the feeling of doom. It was furnished completely with a contrast of light wood and a sky blue. The carpet and ceiling were of the same shade of blue; two of the walls were pale amber; the other two were covered with bookshelves of the same colour. The furniture was mostly of blue leather. Above the fireplace, the wall was covered with an immense reproduction of Michelangelo's *God Creating Adam*. Sorme said:

My god, what a superb place! You *are* lucky.

It doesn't belong to me. It belongs to my mother. But she never uses it. Do sit down.

Nunne crossed immediately to the liquor cabinet, and pulled it open. He said:

What will you have? The same again? Or some wine?

While he spoke, he poured more brandy into a glass, and took a large gulp. Sorme said:

I'd prefer wine, if you've got it.

He was looking in the bookcase near the door. It seemed to contain nothing but volumes on philosophy. There was an edition of Schlegel in ten volumes, and volumes of Kant, Fichte and Schelling in German. The shelf above these contained a row of bound volumes labelled uniformly: *Crelle*. He took down the first volume; it seemed to be a work on mathematics. Nunne came from the kitchen, carrying a tall bottle of Rhine wine.

Afraid this isn't cold. The fridge is off.

Are all these books yours?

Yes. Left me by an uncle. Fascinating things.

He handed Sorme a large wine glass filled with the straw-coloured wine. He placed the bottle on a table beside the settee, saying:

Help yourself.

He poured more brandy into his own glass, and collapsed into an armchair. He looked like a sawdust-filled doll, inert.

Sit down, Gerard. I'll show you round my books next time you come.

Sorme sat on the settee and sipped the wine. To avoid the necessity of starting a conversation, he took another drink from the glass. Nunne said:

172

Gerard. If I went off to South America or somewhere, would you come with me?

Sorme looked at him; he said cautiously:

Are you serious?

Very. I'd like to go to another country – somewhere I could start again.

Why?

Because . . . I get tired.

You shouldn't rush around so much. Why don't you try renting a room in the East End – Whitechapel, say – and not telling anybody where you are?

Something in Nunne's smile produced a tension in him. Nunne said:

Whitechapel?

Oh. Perhaps not. I'd forgotten these murders.

Nunne stared at him for a space of thirty seconds, as if trying to remind him of some question. He said finally:

Quite.

Sorme began to wonder how much more brandy Nunne could drink and still remain articulate. So far, Nunne showed no sign of becoming drunk, but his movements and speech were growing heavier, duller, as if an immense weariness was overpowering him. Sorme himself felt only slightly drunk. He had no desire to drink the wine in his glass; it tasted like lemon juice and water to his palate. Nunne said:

I want to get right away. Away from cities. I get sick . . .

Sorme said nothing. He could think of nothing that would not be cancelled out and invalidated by the facts. He thought: It's his problem.

Tell me, Gerard, have you ever felt really unintended? As if you can't choose any course of action because you're no more than flotsam?

Yes. Never for very long, though.

I do, Nunne said, as if he hadn't heard. You know, when I was at Oxford I used to know a chap called Nigel Barker. Terrific bloke. Most talented man I ever knew. Splendid cricketer, classical scholar, mathematician. Best all-round sportsman in Balliol, but not one of these brainless sportsmen. Got some prize or other for Greek verse. I'd have sworn he'd have a charmed life – really cut out to do something big. Well, he went and broke his silly neck falling off a horse. Didn't kill him, but he's half paralysed. Funny. Makes you feel everything's all wrong somehow.

Sorme said:

You know your trouble, Austin. You've got an over-developed sense of your own worthlessness.

Nunne halted the brandy glass before he drank, and stared at Sorme over the top of it, with surprise.

You've got something there. Sense of my own worth-lessness. That's it. You know, we had a chaplain at Balliol who used to give me talks about that . . . About how the men who don't serve God never get on in the world.

He emptied the glass, and seemed to lose himself in speculation. He said finally:

You're right about the worthlessness. I was always a worthless bastard if ever there was one. Neurotic little bugger all the way through my childhood, in trouble all through my teens. Always smashing up the car or driving it through somebody's back garden. You'd think if there was any justice in the world I'd break my stupid neck, wouldn't you? Not somebody like Nigel.

Sorme found Nunne's self-accusations embarrassing. He was in no position to contradict them. He said uncertainly:

You're creative, anyway. You write books.

Books, Nunne said sneeringly. By any standard of good writing my books are worthless, and I know it. So do you.

What if they were? I'm not saying they were – but what would it matter even if they were? You're still free. You can write books that aren't worthless.

Could I?

Why not? A lot of writers have started from a sense of worthlessness . . . Baudelaire, Dostoevsky. . .

Nunne said softly:

Baudelaire. Everything in the world exudes crime . . .

When Sorme stared at him, puzzled, he said abruptly:

Don't mind me. I'm just a little drunk and tired.

His eyes, resting on Sorme, confirmed what he said; they looked blank and lifeless. He seemed to make an effort of will, and something like amusement came into them.

But you're OK, aren't you, Gerard? You're balanced and sane and level-headed?

Sorme suspected that Nunne had some secret joke. He said cautiously:

No, I'm not balanced. I'm just stagnant.

Oh, come! Let's not have any of that!

Sorme said, grinning

Stagnant, sullen and sex-starved.

Well, you shouldn't be sex-starved, anyway. I'm sure Caroline would oblige. Or that beefy girl who let me in.

Sorme smiled at the tartness in his voice.

No doubt. But I probably wouldn't enjoy it. You know, we had a phrase for it in the RAF. We called it 'having your oats'. That really catches its meaning – the straightforward physical act – having a nibble, a screw, dipping your wick. But that's not sex. Sex is the opposite of all that. It's the opposite of this feeling of being worthless, unintended. It's an overwhelming sense of power and security. It's the complete disappearance of the feeling of being mediocre. It's a strange conviction that nothing matters, that everything's good.

175

Nunne said with interest:

Does it really mean all that to you?

Sometimes.

Then you're lucky.

Maybe. Maybe I'm not particularly lucky. Everybody's lucky, if only they knew it.

Even sadists and hopeless neurotics?

Everybody. You know, you say you often feel worthless. So do I, sometimes. But, fundamentally, I know I'm not. When I was a kid, my parents used to say I was born lucky. And the funny thing was, I always felt lucky, fundamentally . . .

Then you *were* lucky, Gerard. I wasn't. I had a loathsome childhood. My father bullied me, and my mother sat on me like a hen hatching eggs. She practically suffocated me. My main feelings in my childhood were shame and furtiveness. *That's* what my childhood was like. What do you say to that?

I understand it. I used to feel the same pretty often. Anybody does when they're children. Unless you spend most of your time day-dreaming. It's just the feeling of total lack of purpose in a child. You don't start to possess your own soul till you become an adolescent. And that sense of purpose, being your own master, is the greatest thing that can happen to you.

Nunne said:

Provided you're not up to your neck in a treacly mess of emotions.

Throw them off. Strangle them. I did. Anyway, you get moments of insight into yourself that make up for everything.

You do, perhaps.

Yes, I do. You know the Egyptians all believed they were descended from the gods? That's the feeling. For the Egyptians, man was a sort of god, a god in exile. For the Christian Church, he was an immortal soul, poised between heaven and hell. Today he's just a member of society with a duty to everybody else. It's the steady devaluation of human beings. But that's our job, Austin, yours and mine. We're the writers and poets. We can fight the inflation. Our job is to increase the dignity of human beings, try to push it back towards the Egyptian estimate.

He began to feel excited and happy as he talked, and grateful to Nunne for releasing this sense of certainty. Nunne was listening with an expression of interest, but there was no response in his face. Looking at him, Sorme remembered his image, being burnt out inside, like a hole in a carpet. That was it. Something had short-circuited Nunne inside. His capacity to respond had been burnt out by guilt and fatigue. Nothing Sorme could say would strike any response; there was nothing to respond. Sorme stopped and stared at him, feeling the futility of saying more. He said finally:

You know, Austin, I wish you could tell me what's worrying you so much.

Why, nothing. Nothing you don't know about.

I don't understand. What's the use of being conscience-stricken? If you've done something bad, why waste time regretting it? If you can't stand by your action, then forget it. Dismiss it. Start again.

Nunne sat up in the chair. Sorme was aware of the effort it cost him. He smiled tiredly at Sorme.

Listen, Gerard, let's forget it, eh? I can't explain to you. I will one day. Don't get the idea it's a mystery. It's not. But let's not talk about it.

Sorme said:

Austin, I'm going to leave you. You look dog-tired.

I am. I shall take a strong sleeping-draught. Do you mind very much if I don't drive you home?

177

Of course not.

I'll send you in a taxi . . .

No!

Yes. I really insist.

Don't be a fool. I'd enjoy walking.

When he came back from the lavatory a few minutes later, Nunne was returning the phone to its rest. He said: The taxi will be here in a few minutes. It's on my account, so don't pay.

He yawned, then stretched, and looked at himself in the mirror, saying:

Hair of a woman and teeth of a lion. One of the beasts in Revelation. Why was I born so ugly?

Sorme sat down and picked up the wine glass.

You really are an idiot, Austin.

Nunne reached out, and touched Sorme's hair briefly. He said:

Dear Gerard.

He picked up the phone again and listened for a moment. He said:

Hello, is that the night porter? Mr Gregory? Ah, this is Mr Nunne speaking. Do you think you could put my car away for me? It's outside now. No, I'm sending a friend down with the key in a few minutes. Thank you. Goodnight.

Sorme said:

By the way, Austin, can you tell me anything about this chap Oliver Glasp?

Nunne lit a cigarette.

What do you want to know?

Well, who is he? He seems very talented.

Do you know his work?

Only the paintings in your flat.

You might like him. Except that he's quite the most quarrelsome person in London. He has no skin.

178

Has he . . . any peculiarities?

He's not queer, if that's what you mean. I never enquired into his sex life. He's been in mental homes – tends to fly into sudden rages and throw things. He also has some obsession about pain. It's his favourite word – at least, it was when I knew him. We quarrelled – I couldn't stand his touchiness. At the time, he was trying to be an ascetic – sleeping on the bare wires of his bed and all that . . .

The phone rang. Nunne said:

That will be your taxi.

Back in his own room, he collected the brandy flask and the glasses, and took them upstairs. The kitchen smelt pleasantly of fruit; a bowl of apples stood on the table.

He felt physically tired, and yet curiousiy excited. Talking to Nunne had given him an intuition of change. He thought, with sudden complete certainty: I have wasted five years. Stuck in rooms. The world was alive. I have done nothing.

Poor Austin. Sadistic and listless, sensual, caring only about people and places. I am freer than he is; yet for five years I have behaved like a prisoner. Why?

He opened the kitchen window and leaned out. The night air smelt fresh. He felt buoyed up by an intuition of kindness and gratitude. It came again: the sense of life, of London's three millions, of smells in attics and markets.

As he stood there he heard a door close. He turned around and listened; it had been the Frenchman's room. Probably Callet would come up to the kitchen. The idea of conversation gave him no pleasure. He went quietly down the stairs, and back into his own room.

Instead of switching on the light, he crossed the room and opened the window, then climbed out on to the fire escape. He sat there, staring into the darkness, faintly lit by lamps and the neon sign of the cinema. A light came on above him; it was in the kitchen. Looking up, he could see Callet's shadow move across the glass. He congratulated himself on his foresight. But the light disturbed him; it made him feel as if he was avoiding Callet. After a moment's consideration he went up the fire escape, to the landing outside the old man's room. This was the top of the fire escape. From there, an iron ladder completed the remaining distance to the roof. He pulled at it to test its solidity before grasping the rungs and climbing up. It curved over the parapet, on to the roof.

The parapet was a foot high; it enclosed two sides of the roof, facing north and east. On the west side, only a gutter divided the slates from the drop past five stories to the waste ground between the house and the church. The breeze was cold. He moved round the angle of the roof to shelter from it, then sat cautiously on the slates, his feet braced against the parapet. Towards Camden Town, the lights of the plastics factory that worked all night lit the sky. The exhilaration was still in him, relaxing into a sense of quiet and power. When the sound of a heavy lorry passed on the Kentish Town Road his mind moved ahead of it, through Whetstone and Barnet, to the north. The thoughts were controlled, clear-cut and deliberate. The feeling that drove them seemed to flow steadily and certainly. They moved towards an image of gratitude, of reverence, of affirmation; it became a cathedral, bigger than any known cathedral, symbol of the unseen. He thought: This has taken me five years. A vision of all knowledge, of human achievement in imagination and courage. Not the mystic's vision, but the philosopher's, freed from triviality and immediacy. I am the god who dwelleth in the eye, and I have come to give right and truth to Ra. But how many times? Half a dozen in five

180

years. And now stimulated by a sadistic queer and an infatuated girl. Nunne succeeds where Plotinus failed.

He began to laugh, his back jerking against the slates, his feet braced apart. It made him realize that he was cold. He began to wish that he had thought of bringing an overcoat.

Never make a yogi. Not enough patience. Or need the warmer climates. Intensity of life. Monastery in the Himalayas. An old man stared into the dawn, his face lined with strength of will, unimpressed by the five-thousand-foot drop into the valley. Isaiah or Michelangelo. In tense hands, he holds the world's will, beyond tragedy. A faint pencil line of light along the eastern horizon.

To change. To change. To what?

An image of Caroline came to him, and he felt a momentary distaste. The unseen, the imaginative adventure, was just what she did not represent. Like Kay, the girl from the Slade School, it was an idealism she offended. The warm, predatory body, the desire to be possessed. Her animal vitality conducted the tension away, like an earthing wire.

To change. But no physical change. Only a constant intensity of imagination that would require no cathedral symbol to sustain and remind. Isobel Gowdie, big-breasted farmer's wife, sweating and curving to the indrive of an abstract darkness, the warm secretions flowing to abet the entry of a formless evil. To escape the dullness of a Scottish farm by daylight, the time trap. Symbol of the unseen. The unseen being all you cannot see at the moment. Until the consciousness stretches to embrace all space and history. Osiris openeth the storm cloud in the body of heaven, and is unfettered himself; Horus is made strong happily each day. Why the time trap? Why the enclosure? Invisible bonds, non-existent

181

bonds, bonds that cannot be broken because they are non-existent. Human beings like blinkered horses.

The cold had penetrated the thin coat and trousers until he felt naked. He stretched and flexed his limbs, then blew into his cupped hands. The iron of the ladder numbed his fingers. He lowered himself back over the parapet, feeling with his feet for the rungs. Descending, he was afraid of the numbness in his fingers, aware now of the drop to the concrete flags below. He felt relieved as his feet touched the iron platform.

When he switched on the light, he saw that his hands were black with dust. There was a blur of grime on his cheek, where he had raised his hand to touch it. He went up to the kitchen, and found that the kettle was half full of hot water.

After he had washed, he set the alarm for eight o'clock. It was three-thirty. He was asleep almost as soon as he closed his eyes.

Chapter Seven

Pale December sunlight made him sweat as he cycled along Leadenhall Street. The traffic in the City was heavy. He was aware that it irritated drivers of cars when he was able to steer in the narrow lane between a line of stationary traffic and the pavement, and it pleased him to do it. When cycling, he felt that the driver of every car was a personal enemy.

The mental activity of the previous night had left a feeling of freshness, and he felt no irritation towards the traffic. When a woman stepped off the pavement in front of him, forcing him to brake sharply, he only smiled at her and shook his head in remonstrance; he guessed her to be a foreigner from the fact that she was looking left instead of right.

It was shortly after nine-thirty when he stopped in Aldgate High Street. He leaned the bicycle against the wall outside the Lyons Corner House, and locked the back wheel. The self-service bar was almost empty. He bought tea and two toasted buns, and sat at a table near the window. A middle-aged woman wearing a pink smock collected dirty cups off the table. He returned her smile, and felt as he did so a sense of anticipation that was like convalescence. The whole café with its food smells, the workman opposite reading the *Daily Express*, the heavy traffic in the street outside, all touched some mechanism of nostalgia in him. It felt like waking from a long sleep. He took the leather-bound notebook from his pocket, and wrote in it: 'Whitechapel, 1 December. I qualify as a modern Faust. Shut up in a room, thinking too much.

Enter Austin Mephistopheles, twisting the waxed ends of his moustache . . . But who is Gretchen?'

He stopped writing, reflecting that Caroline or Gertrude might easily see the notebook. He had been about to elaborate the question. Instead, he wrote: 'Like Mephistopheles, Austin sells me love or life. My side of the bargain is still obscure.'

On the opposite side of the road a barrel organ began to play, tinnily, each note jangling like a rusty can dropped from a height. It aroused in him a memory that was also a sense of smell and colour. For a moment, it eluded him, then returned: the City office, the smell of ledgers, and the French tobacco of the belligerent Scottish clerk who lived at Southend. The last time he had heard it played, *Mon cœur s'ouvre à ta voix*, had been on the Thursday afternoon, five years before, when he had walked out of the office without giving notice, the solicitor's letter carefully folded in his wallet, and had stepped into the traffic and sunlight of Bishopsgate, still dazed by the feeling of relief.

The memory reconstructed itself with a detail of sense and feeling that he found surprising; it revived the hot afternoon smell of dust and motor exhaust, and the damp smell of the entry below the office where he kept his bicycle. For a moment, he considered walking through Houndsditch to look at the office building again, then dismissed the idea, recalling the boredom and self-contempt that had accumulated there over a year.

Almost immediately the sense of reconciliation disappeared. He had remembered the pink cheeks and the wispy blond moustache of the Scottish clerk, and the memory stirred shame and anger. The Scotsman had professed a violent anti-Semitism: he referred to Hampstead and Golders Green as Abrahamstead and Goldstein's Green. His arguments with Sorme had always finished with mutual declarations of contempt, leaving behind a taste of futility. These arguments, and an abortive affair with the office girl, were all that stood out in Sorme's memory of the year in the office. The girl's name was Marilyn; she was plump, not particularly attractive, and came from Stepney Green. But she was given to wearing semi-transparent dresses, with very little underneath them. When she bent over the filing cabinet, the outline of her pants showed clearly through the fabric, and the three clerks stared surreptitiously until she straightened up. Finally, he invited her out to the theatre and took her drinking afterwards. Later the same evening, in the Victoria Park, he knew with certainty that he did not want to possess her, that his desire had been an illusion born of boredom and the sexy innuendo of office conversation. She had probably assumed it was chivalry that had made him gently pull down her skirt after she had raised it. He was glad, three days later, to leave the office without seeing her, and contemptuous of himself for being glad.

The recollection left him feeling uncomfortable and ashamed. He finished the toasted buns and went out.

He walked the bicycle along the pavement as far as Middlesex Street, then mounted and rode slowly towards Bishopsgate. He dismissed the memories, and thought deliberately of Caroline and Gertrude; immediately he began to feel better. In Widegate Street he stared with interest at a pregnant woman who pushed a battered pram loaded with washing, and felt the release of some inner tension of smell and colour, a renewal of the excitement. He turned into Spitalfields Market and dismounted; it was impossible to ride among the people who crowded the narrow space between parked lorries and the market building. Almost immediately a man in shirtsleeves swung a net-bag of cabbage off a lorry, missing Sorme's head by a fraction. The man grinned, saying: Watch yer loaf! Sorme grinned back, halting for a moment to avoid a trolley loaded with potato sacks. The inner warmth was like being drunk, but without the sense of limitation.

On the corner of Brushfield Street, he stopped to consult the London atlas he carried in his saddlebag. The traffic in Commercial Street was an unbroken stream, filling the air with vibrations and the smell of diesel exhausts.

The pavement of Durward Street was barely two feet wide; the roofs, windowsills and kerbstones formed a perspective of unbroken parallel lines from one end of the road to the other. The street was deserted.

He stopped before number twelve. The brown paint on the front door had been weathered into scales.

He stood there, in front of the window, hoping to hear some movement from inside the house that would relieve his hesitation. Now he was on the point of knocking, he remembered Nunne's comments about Glasp, and the warning of the Hungarian priest. He tried to think of the words with which he would introduce himself. Finally, he rapped loudly, and waited.

A window opened above his head. He stood back to look, hoping it would be Glasp. It was the window of the house next door. A woman asked him:

Did you want Mrs Greenberg, or the lodger?

A man called Glasp, Sorme said. He felt embarrassed, as if some guilty secret was being exposed to the whole street.

The lodger. He won't be long, the woman said. He usually goes out about this time for breakfast. I don't know which caff he goes to.

It doesn't matter. I'll call back later.

The window slammed again. He noticed the curtains of

186

the house opposite stir as someone looked out at him. He cycled back along the street, irritated with himself, and with the woman next door for not minding her own business. Her effect had been to make him feel an intruder.

At the end of the street, he dismounted, and leaned the bicycle against the wall, under the *No Entry* sign. The idea of looking for Glasp in the local cafés did not appeal to him. He looked at his watch, and decided to take a walk round the neighbourhood. It had been a long time since he walked round Whitechapel, thinking of the Jack the Ripper murders. Now, while the mood of receptivity was still on him, the prospect pleased him. He locked the bicycle, binding the chain twice around the wheel.

Opposite the end of Durward Street was the shell of a theatre, with broken rafters and fire-blackened walls exposed. He stood, staring across at it, experiencing a desire to climb the wooden fence that hid the lower storey, to pick his way across the rotten floorboards, and smell the odour of damp and decay that came from heaps of rubble. It was almost a physical craving. It puzzled him. Things were happening inside him that he found difficult to understand. It felt as if his nerves had been disconnected, then reconnected in a different order, generating new appetites and a new sensibility. He turned and walked along Vallance Road, away from the main road. He picked his way carefully across the bomb site, taking care to avoid treading on rusty barrel-hoops. Across the street, an empty school building looked as desolate as the ruined theatre; on its walls, whitewashed letters two feet high stated: Union will get rid of the Reds. At both ends of the inscription was a symbol of a lightning bolt in a circle. He crossed the road past the school, on to another strip of waste ground bordered by empty houses and stumps of broken walls, and paused for a moment to look in the windowless aperture of a disintegrating building. The floor was covered with rubble, old newspapers nibbled by mice, a torn pink brassière. A narrow stairway, still intact, curved around the opposite wall. As he looked, a mouse ran out from among the newspapers, and disappeared into a hole in the skirting board. Someone had pointed out this house to him before; in 1943, the body of a Finnish sailor had been found on the upper floor by some children playing hide-and-seek; he had been robbed and left to die, battered by a brick swung in a silk stocking.

The house next door was still occupied; the front door stood open, and the smell of frying sausages came from it. Outside the door, a baby lay asleep in a pram.

He wandered, without aim, through the littered streets. In Hanbury Street, the new blocks of flats and the children's playground looked incongruous. He stopped again outside the barber's shop at number 29. In the yard behind the shop, the third of the Ripper's killings had taken place. He had once seen a photograph of it, taken immediately after the murders; it looked completely unchanged by the intervening seventy years. The barber looked up from shaving a customer as Sorme paused by the door. He said:

Hello. Long time no see.

Sorme said: How are you?

Fine. Never see you in here for haircuts these days.

I don't live around here now.

At the end of Hanbury Street he found himself facing Spitalfields Market again. As he passed the Wren church, an old man came out of the public lavatory, muttering:

Tanner for a cup o' tea?

Sorme fumbled in his pocket, turning his eyes away from the dewdrop that hung on the end of the man's nose. The clawed, dry-skinned hand took the two threepenny pieces; the man glanced around quickly to see if any policeman had observed him. His hand rested on Sorme's sleeve. Uncertain of what was being demanded of him, Sorme looked into the watery blue eyes. The man's voice was an indistinguishable mumble; he pointed to his feet, on which he wore grubby plimsolls. Sorme assumed he was asking for more money, and started to grope for loose change. He stopped when he caught the words:

. . . lived here for close on seventy years.

Seventy years?

That's right. Near seventy years . . . I been 'ere.

He brushed at his nose with the cuff of his overcoat, and dislodged the transparent drop. Another formed immediately. Sorme averted his eyes. The overcoat was so long that its hem dragged on the pavement. He said politely:

You don't look that old.

Oh yers. Seventy-three, and worked every day of my life till I 'ad the trouble.

Sorme realized that the man was not drunk; he was talking to dispel loneliness, or perhaps out of gratitude for the sixpence. His words were scarcely distinguishable. Sorme said:

You must have been alive at the time of the Jack the Ripper murders.

Eh? Jack the Ripper? Yers. I can tell you something about that. He done his last murder over there . . .

The bent hand gestured in the direction of the market building. Sorme said:

Miller's Court?

That's right. Over there, it used to be. Before they built the market. Used to be Dorset Street. I know, 'cause I used to do a paper round at the time.

Sorme said with surprise:

How old were you?

'Ow old? Lemme see . . .

The watery eyes concentrated. The transparent drop fell on to the pavement. He said finally:

Why, I was ten at the time, just ten.

Sorme calculated quickly. Eighteen eighty-eight to nineteen fifty-six – sixty-eight years. He said:

And you say you're seventy-three?

That's right. Seventy-three. Seventy-four next April. And I used to take the mornin' papers to Miller's Court. Then one mornin' I goes there, and there's a crowd round the door. And a copper says: She won't want no more papers 'ere, sonny. Don't you go bringin' any more papers 'ere. An that's 'ow I know she'd been murdered. That was Jack the Ripper.

Sorme looked at his watch, saying:

Amazing! Well, I must go now. Goodbye . . .

The old man raised a hand in salute as he turned away. Sorme turned into Fournier Street, thinking: Either he's five years older than he thinks, or he's lying. He walked hurriedly now, taking the shortest route back to the place where he had left the bicycle.

He unlocked the wheel, unwinding the chain from around it, swearing when he got grease from the spokes on his fingers. He wiped them clean on his handkerchief, then walked the bicycle back along Durward Street. Up to the point where the street divided it was a one-way street, and a policeman stood on the opposite corner.

Before he had advanced more than a few yards into Durward Street, he noticed the old woman who came towards him from the other end of the street. She was carrying a half loaf of bread under her arm, clutched against a baggy cardigan of purple wool. She stopped, and inserted a key in a door. He rested his right foot on the pedal of the bicycle and scooted the dozen or so yards between them, arriving behind her as she pushed open the door. He said: Excuse me . . .

She went on into the house, without looking round. He guessed her to be deaf, and reached out to touch her shoulder. She turned, looking startled. He said loudly:

Does Mr Glasp live here, please?

The tired, red-rimmed eyes looked blankly at him. He repeated the question. She turned and waved her hand towards the stairs, with a gesture of complete indifference. She said:

Yes. 'E's in. Go on up.

He felt doubtful, looking into the dark room that smelt of age and Victorian furniture. He shouted: Upstairs?

But she had turned away, and was already half way across the room, leaving him to close the door behind him. At the other side of the room, she said over her shoulder:

'E might be asleep.

Sorme went cautiously up the stairs, leaning forward and groping, feeling bare wooden boards, partly covered with worn linoleum. He stumbled near the top, and swore softly. The landing was in complete darkness. There was a strong smell of paraffin. As he stood there, peering into the dark, a door on his right opened. A man's voice said:

Hello. Who is it?

He said: Mr Glasp?

That's right. The voice had a faint Yorkshire accent.

My name is Gerard Sorme. I saw some of your work yesterday, and wanted to meet you.

You a painter?

No, a writer.

You'd better come on in, the voice said ungraciously. I haven't much time.

I won't keep you long . . .

He felt slightly bewildered; he was unprepared for

coming face to face with Glasp so suddenly. He would have liked to be allowed a few minutes to decide what to say. Glasp's tone led him to feel that the meeting would be short.

Glasp said: Take a seat.

The room was large. It seemed to have been made by knocking down a wall, and running two rooms into one. It had an irregular L-shape, and could be entered by two doors, one in each arm of the L. The only furniture was an old-fashioned single bed with brass rails, a stool and a small table. There were many canvases leaning around the walls. In front of the window stood an easel of the type used in schoolrooms, with another canvas on it. Sorme sat on the stool, near the window, in a position from which he could see the whole room. A black paraffin stove was burning at the side of the stool; automatically he warmed his hands over it.

Glasp said: Well, what can I do for you?

His tone was blunt and irritable. He stood, leaning against the end of the bed, a tall, bony man with a mop of shaggy red hair and an unshaven chin. His blue polo-necked sweater was stiff with paint-stains.

Sorme said apologetically: Look here, I know it's rather an imposition just to come and introduce myself to you like this. But if you feel I'm wasting your time just say so, and I'll go.

Glasp looked surprised, but in no way disarmed; he said ponderously:

How do I know whether you're wasting my time until I know what you want?

Feeling at a disadvantage, Sorme said:

I don't want anything except to meet you. I saw two of your canvases yesterday and liked them.

Glasp said, with a touch of sarcasm:

I expect you have a busy time. If you go and call on every painter when you take a fancy to one of his pictures.

Sorme declined to be offended by his tone. He said:

In this case, 'like' is the wrong word. I thought the pictures completely extraordinary.

Still Glasp's face registered no pleasure; if anything, a shade of mistrust passed over it. He said:

May I ask where you saw them?

In a basement flat belonging to Austin Nunne . . .

Oh, you're a friend of Austin's, are you?

There was no mistaking the tone of sarcasm now.

Yes.

A patron of the arts, so to speak?

No, Sorme said steadily, controlling the irritation. I don't buy pictures. I can't afford to. I just thought I'd like to meet you.

He made his voice level, preparing to stand up and walk out of the room. He was beginning to resent Glasp's tone, and was annoyed with himself for placing himself in a position where Glasp could regard him as an intruder.

Glasp picked up a blue-and-white-striped mug from the floor, and began to sip from it. He sat on the edge of the bed, saying:

Well, I'll be candid with you. I live here because I don't like meeting people. Also, of course, because it's cheap. But mainly because I don't like people much . . .

Why?

Why don't I like people? For the same reason I don't like the smell of rum or China tea, I expect.

Sorme was trying hard to sum him up. The masked resentment in Glasp's tone inclined him to regard him as a paranoiac. His inclination to walk out was curbed only by a dislike of feeling completely defeated. He decided to make another effort. Smiling with deliberate amiability, he said:

As a matter of fact, both Austin and Father Rakosi advised me not to call on you.

Why?

They seemed to have the idea you'd be rude.

Glasp grunted, and took another swallow from the mug. Sorme stood up. He said:

Well, you've a perfect right to be left to yourself. I'll leave you.

Glasp was staring into the mug, which he held between both hands in his lap. He did not move. He said:

What did you want to see me about?

Sorme felt again the inadequacy of his reasons. He said:

I thought you might be able to tell me something about Austin.

Glasp looked up at him; he said grinning:

Why, do you want to blackmail him?

No.

You queer?

No.

Then why?

His manner was no longer pointedly hostile; it was detached and noncommittal. Sorme sensed that his curiosity was aroused. He said reasonably:

Look here, you're making things rather deliberately awkward for me, aren't you? I liked your canvases. I wanted to meet you. I also knew you'd been a friend of Austin's and Austin also interests me. But if you hate meeting people, and you don't feel like discussing Austin, just say so. I can go.

Glasp looked at him; his expression was speculative and cool, like that of a man about to buy something which he wishes to devalue.

He reached out and took a palette from the table and

began to clean it with a table knife. Without raising his face from it, he said:

I can't tell you much about Austin. I never knew him well, and never liked him much. Why does he interest you . . . if you're not queer?

For the same reason that you do, I suppose.

What have I got in common with Austin?

Sorme felt the need to say something convincing, and could think of nothing to say. He plunged with the first words that came into his head:

From your canvases, I should say . . . a certain quality of fanaticism.

He saw at once that he had said the right thing. Glasp said:

And you think Austin is a fanatic? He never struck me that way, I must say.

It's difficult to explain. I don't know him well enough yet. But I suspect it's there.

And why does it interest you?

That's also difficult to explain. I always liked the idea of living alone. I used to think about entering a monastery . . .

Glasp interrupted him: You're not a Catholic?

No.

And why didn't you go through with the monastery idea?

I saw no point. Besides I wasn't sure that I'd enjoy being a monk. I doubt whether the aims of a community of monks would be the same as mine.

And what were yours?

Sorme looked at him, and felt himself relaxing under the unconcealed interest that Glasp showed. He said:

I don't know . . . I suppose I wanted to see visions.

Glasp stood up. He said: And what happened?

Nothing much. For a year I read Plotinus and St Francis

de Sales and the rest . . . but I felt something was missing. I began to feel my imagination had gone dead. I began to think I needed sex and human intercourse. So I made a few friends, and got involved with a couple of girls for a very short time. It didn't help much. I didn't want that either. I began to think I'd simply lost all desire to stay alive. I felt sick of books, and sick of people . . .

I know the feeling, Glasp said.

He had begun to squeeze tubes of paint on to the palette. He took a brush from the jam jar that stood on the windowsill, and began to paint. He said quietly:

I've been through all this myself. There's only one remedy. . . Work.

He waved the brush at Sorme. Sorme said:

That's OK if you know what you want to do. I didn't.

You say *didn't*. Do you feel different now?

Well . . . yes. I met Austin a week ago – barely that. In many ways, I feel sorry for him. He's like me too. But . . . I can't explain. But suddenly, I begin to feel that something important's happening to me. A sort of daylight's coming through.

Glasp said:

But why Austin? I think that's what you literary gents call an anticlimax!

Sorme said: I don't know. He strikes me as being oddly like me . . .

Glasp said: Does he? There was disbelief in his voice.

Yes. Did you ever go to that flat of his in Queen's Gate?

I didn't know he had a flat in Queen's Gate.

I went yesterday. It surprised me. It looked like something out of Edgar Allan Poe. Black velvet curtains. A cabinet of liqueurs. The work of de Sade and Masoch. And your pictures . . .

Glasp said with surprise: So that's where you saw them? Well . . .

He was smiling as he went on painting. He said:

This is a new side to Austin's character. Glasp and de Sade, eh? The two paintings he bought from me . . .

He had some Japanese prints signed OG as well.

They're Korean. I copied them from a set in the British Museum.

He painted silently for a moment, then stood back to look at the effect. He said, without looking at Sorme:

All the same, I don't see much in common in your tastes . . .

No. But . . . there's a similarity of aim. Except . . .

Except what?

I sometimes wonder if it's just a matter of enterprise. I don't share his tastes, but I admire the wish to experiment. It seems a good thing in itself . . .

You mean chasing little boys?

No, I wasn't thinking of that. I was thinking of the sadism.

Glasp stopped painting to stare at him.

Is he? I didn't know that.

Didn't you? I thought you knew him very well.

No. Glasp went on painting. Not well at all, apparently. How did you find out?

He told me so. Father Carruthers knows about it too.

What sort of practices?

Glasp's Yorkshire accent suddenly became more noticeable. His attention seemed to be focused on the canvas. Sorme said:

I don't know. Nothing spectacular, I suppose. Probably wallops his boy friends.

In the other room, a kettle that stood on a gas ring began to send up a jet of steam; the water bubbled out on to the bare floorboards. Sorme went over to it and lifted it off the gas ring. Glasp said:

Cup o' tea?

Please.

Glasp laid the palette on the table, and replaced the brushes in the jam jar.

What I don't understand is this idea of yours that you're like Austin. From what you tell me, you don't seem to have anything in common.

No? I think there's a lot in common. We're both dissatisfied. We're both experimenters. Only he seems to have carried his experiments rather further than I've ever dreamed of.

Glasp was washing out an aluminium teapot at the sink in the other room. He said:

No? You mean you'd like to wallop your girl friends?

Sorme said, laughing: No. I'm sure I wouldn't. All the same . . .

And why did you want to meet me? Did you think I might be another?

Another what?

Bloke that goes in for experiments?

I thought you might be.

Glasp said, smiling: I suppose you're right. Where do we go from there?

Nowhere, probably, Sorme said. He took the mug of tea and spooned sugar into it. He noticed that when Glasp smiled his forehead twitched and contracted; it seemed to be an involuntary nervous spasm. Glasp saw him noticing it. To distract his attention, Sorme said:

You have big hands. Like Austin.

Glasp sugared his tea and stirred it. His hands were large and ugly, with big knuckles; they looked faintly grimy, networked with lines of paint dust that had sunk into the pores. He said *Les mains de Troppmann*.

198

Who?

Troppmann. Don't you know about him? Jean Baptiste Troppmann, the multiple killer.

No. Who did he kill?

A whole family. About eight people.

What on earth for?

Money. He made a few hundred francs out of it. He had enormous hands. They still call big hands '*mains de Troppmann*' in some parts of France. I expect it ran in his family, and the surname came from it. Too much hand.

Was he a sadist?

I don't think so. Just homosexual, with an obsession about making money.

The tea was hot and strong. Glasp stood his on the windowsill, and went on painting. Sorme asked him:

Are you interested in murder?

Sometimes.

When?

Glasp said, with an odd smile: Crime runs in our family . . . in a sense.

Sorme said, grinning:

You come from a famous line of burglars?

Not quite. He grinned back at Sorme over the teamug; his forehead twitched again. As far as I know, our connection with it was always indirect. I had a great aunt who was the last victim of Jack the Ripper. My mother once had a meal with Landru in Paris. And my great-grandfather knew Charley Peace.

Did your mother know it was Landru?

No. She knew nothing about him. He said he was an engineer named Cuchet, and tried to get her to come away with him for the weekend. She recognized his photograph a few months later when he was arrested. She said he'd behaved like a perfect gentleman . . .

Amazing!

Some people are attracted by crime. Others seem to attract it. My family attract it. You notice that, as soon as I settle in Whitechapel, a crime wave begins? That's in the family tradition.

Sorme looked at him closely. He sensed an underlying seriousness. For the first time, he was aware of an element of strain in Glasp; it came out also in the twitching forehead. He asked:

Are you serious about the aunt who was a victim of Jack the Ripper?

Quite serious. The last victim.

The woman who was killed in the room in Miller's Court?

No. There was another one. She was killed under a lamp-post in Castle Alley. That was Great-aunt Sally McKenzie. I don't know much about her except she seems to have been the black sheep of the family.

I've never heard of that one . . .

He began to wonder whether Glasp was inventing the whole story. He said, smiling:

You seem to come from a family of victims.

That's right. All victims. Unconscious masochists. Except me. I'm a conscious masochist.

Are you?

Glasp smiled at his look of surprise. He said:

Not in Austin's sense. I don't go in for that.

Sorme moved the stool closer to the wall, so that he could lean back on it as he watched Glasp. There was something jerky and emphatic in the way Glasp painted, an intentness in his concentration on the canvas, that made Sorme think of a fencer. He said:

I won't stay here talking any longer. It's probably just putting you off your work.

That's all right, Glasp said.

Sorme watched him, unspeaking for about five minutes. He said:

Would you mind if I had a look at some of the paintings in there?

Again he sensed Glasp's hesitation. He was on the point of saying: It doesn't matter . . . when Glasp said:

Go ahead. But don't talk about them.

All right.

He went into the other room and looked at the canvases leaning against the walls. The first thing that struck him was that their colours were harsher than in the canvases he had seen in Nunne's flat. The greens and blues, the dream-technique that showed the influence of Chagall, had disappeared. Here the drawing was crude and violent; it accentuated the discordance of the primary colours that seemed to have been applied straight from the tube. Most of them were nature studies: trees, a clump of irises, a wall overgrown with lichens; there was a painting of iron railings, with a street lamp that was painted without romanticism, or even an attempt at atmosphere. The canvases occupied the whole of one wall of the room.

On the far side of the fireplace, in a wide recess, hung an enormous, half finished canvas. It was at least four times as big as anything else in the room, being about six feet deep by four broad. At first glance he took it to be a Crucifixion. It showed a man nailed to a cross, and suspended from an open window. The cross appeared to be supported by several chains, and a pulley was visible through the window. One of the man's hands, pierced by a nail, hung by his side.

Sorme repressed the temptation to ask what it represented. He stood back, staring at it. As he stood there, he heard Glasp leave his painting and go out of the room.

The painting of the crucified man was high on the wall.

Below it, leaning in the recess, were a number of canvases, stacked against one another. The topmost one showed the enormous frightened face of a boy. Behind his head, in the top left-hand corner, stood a chest of drawers, with three drawers pulled out, and what looked like some pink female undergarment hanging from the top drawer. From behind the boy's head protruded a bare arm, as of someone lying face downward on the floor. Sorme pulled the canvas forward, and glanced at the one behind it. This seemed to be in Glasp's earlier manner. It was a beautifully delicate painting of a naked girl. She looked about ten years old. She was standing in front of a fireplace, holding out a handkerchief to dry in both hands. Her arms and legs were thin, and the whole body had an air of undernourishment, yet Glasp had managed to utilize her thinness, to blend it with the orange firelight and the blue shadows of the room, to convey a sense of gentleness and nostalgia. Sorme found it curiously moving; he would have liked to take it from among the other canvases and stand it where he could study it better. Before he had decided to do this he heard the noise of a lavatory cistern flushing next door. He pulled the painting forward and glanced at the one behind it. It was another still life, with harsh colours and angular drawing. He let the canvases fall back into place, and turned to look at a study of a cornfield that leaned against the wall next to the sink. Glasp came back into the other room. He said:

Well?

You've certainly changed your manner, haven't you?

I hope so. Do you like these?

Very much. They're quite violently impressive. You ought to have an exhibition.

Can't be bothered. They're all bloody crooks. It's all string pulling and arsehole-crawling.

Glasp came over and stood beside him. Sorme said:

What's this?

He pointed to the crucified man.

That's Matthew Lovatt. Classic case of attempted suicide.

When?

Oh. I'm not sure when. He was a shoemaker of Geneva some time in the eighteenth century. He got an obsession about wanting to die on a cross, like Christ. He made three attempts, all failures. The third time, he fixed up a sort of pulley in his bedroom, which overlooked the market place, and attached the cross so it could be lowered out of the window. His main problem was how to nail himself to the cross. He could nail his feet, and one of his hands, but the other hand puzzled him. He finally solved it by boring a hole in the cross, and piercing one of his hands with a nail beforehand. He then used the pierced hand to wield the hammer to nail his feet and the other hand. Having done that, he released the pulley, and let the cross shoot out of the window, over the market place. Unfortunately, he was too weak by that time to insert the nail in the hole he'd bored for it – so he hung there.

Glasp gestured at the canvas, where the naked man hung like a deflated Petrouchka. Sorme said:

Did he die?

No. They got him down, and he lived to be eighty or so. Never made the attempt again, either.

Will you finish it?

Oh yes. When I have time . . .

What about this one?

He pointed to the face of the boy.

Glasp said, shrugging:

I don't like that. It was supposed to be Heirens, the Chicago killer.

I've never heard of him. Who was he?

A seventeen-year-old boy. He used to climb in through windows and steal women's underwear. When the women interrupted him, he killed them. On the wall, over one victim, he scrawled in lipstick: For God's sake catch me before I kill again.

Sorme pulled a face. He said:

It's a pretty ghastly subject for a painting. Don't *you* think it's a little morbid?

Of course. The condition itself is morbid.

He turned and went back into the other room. Sorme said: What about the canvases behind this one? May I look?

Glasp turned round; he said sharply:

No. I'd rather you didn't. I don't like them.

Sorme followed him. His tea was still on the stool, half finished. He drank it in one draught. He felt that it was awkward to try and express his admiration for Glasp's paintings; Glasp had so obviously conditioned himself not to care about praise or blame. He said finally:

Thanks for letting me see them.

That's OK.

Uncertain what to add, Sorme allowed his eyes to wander around the room. They stopped at a reproduction of Van Gogh hung over the bed. It was hung in a position where he had not been able to see it from his place on the stool.

You admire Van Gogh?

Glasp said: Yes.

He turned round and looked at the reproduction. It was badly lit, being on the same wall as the window, opposite the door.

Glasp said: That's my idea of a great painting.

Why do you think so?

For the same reason that my Matthew Lovatt and William Heirens are failures. That thing's more than a

204

painting – it's the tragedy of Van Gogh observing his own tragedy. In my pictures, you need to know all about Lovatt and Heirens to get the full impact of the painting . . . it's literary painting. In *that*, it's all there. You don't need to know that Van Gogh cut off his own ear. The title's enough: Self-portrait, the man with his ear cut off. That's what painting should be. That's why my painting's so lousy. That picture of Corbière leading a pig on a ribbon . . . you saw it, didn't you? Austin liked it. He would . . .

Sorme interrupted him:

I don't agree. I think you're being unfair to yourself. Your Corbière picture has a terrific impact even if you've never heard of Corbière. The same goes for your Lovatt and Heirens.

Glasp broke in before he could go on; his voice was impatient:

Thanks. I'm glad you like them . . .

Sorme decided to drop the subject.

Look here, I'll leave you. Thanks for putting up with me.

Glasp said mechanically: Not at all.

Sorme went to the door. He said:

Why not come over and have a meal with me? I'd like a chance to talk to you.

As he spoke, he was certain Glasp would refuse. But Glasp said:

Thanks, I'd like to. Where do you live?

Camden Town. Change at Moorgate from here. Could you make it this week?

I suppose so.

What's today? . . . Wednesday. Tomorrow or Friday would be fine.

Glasp stopped painting. He said, after a pause:

Yes, that's all right. Which day?

Friday? I'll give you my address.

He sat on the bed to write in his notebook, drawing a map to show the route from Kentish Town Underground to his lodging. He tore it out, and left it on the pillow. As an afterthought, he added his phone number.

Make it around six, if that's OK by you, then?

OK, Glasp said. He did not look up from his painting.

The stairway was completely black. He groped his way to the stairhead cautiously. The smell of paraffin was strong on the stairs; he discovered why when he stepped in a pool of it on the floorboards, and almost pitched down the stairs.

The uniformed man at the door of the Reading Room smiled and nodded as he went past. He loosened his collar and unbuttoned his jacket; cycling had made him warm. A woman wearing what looked like Victorian bathing costume was walking in front of him. She pushed through the door and allowed it to swing in his face. He caught it with his foot.

The grey-suited, studious-looking man who stood inside the information counter smiled at him:

Hello there. It's a long time since I saw you.

Hi, Ronnie. How's it go?

The woman looked sharply over her shoulder, as if she suspected them of talking about her. Sorme followed her with his eyes, then commented:

The old witch seems to be in a filthy temper. She tried to knock me out with the door.

Yes. She's been like it for two days. Somebody started a quarrel with her the other day about occupying two desks, and she hit him with her umbrella. She's been glaring at everybody ever since.

Sorme said, chuckling: I wish I'd seen it!

Where have you been recently?

Oh, changing my lodging, and various other things. But

look here, Ronnie, can you help me? I want to consult some books on sadism.

Rather a jump from mystical theology, isn't it?

Sorme said cautiously:

It's just an idea for my novel. Thought I'd introduce a sadist.

I see. Well, there's the obvious stuff – Krafft-Ebing and Stekel and that kind of thing. How's that?

It's a beginning. Surely there must be lots of others?

Oh yes. But a lot of it would be in foreign languages in medical journals. You'd have to consult the bibliography in one of the standard works – Bloch or somebody . . . Have a look in the subject catalogue under psychology. Would you like me to have a look?

Please. These damn catalogues confuse me. I'll go and find a seat.

He left his raincoat over the back of a chair, and placed two reference books on the table to prevent anyone from taking it. In the downstairs lavatory he washed his hands and face in hot water, and returned to the Reading Room feeling cooler. There was no one behind the information desk, but on his own table he found a pile of catalogues with slips of paper stuck in to mark the places. He spent a further quarter of an hour tracking down the books in the author catalogues, and making out request tickets for them. He handed them in, then took his raincoat and left the Museum. He was beginning to feel hungry again.

In a pub in the Charing Cross Road he ate a beef sandwich and drank a pint of bitter. It was still only a quarter to one. He had no expectation of his books arriving before two o'clock. He spent the next hour wandering around the secondhand bookshops, and bought finally a copy of the first volume of *The World as Will and Idea*. It was an old copy, with a badly torn binding. He felt pleased with himself as he walked back to the Museum; he had wanted it for years, but had been deterred by the price of new volumes.

The books had arrived when he came back. The Reading Room was crowded now the lunch hour was over. It felt more hot and stuffy than before. He removed his raincoat and jacket and settled down to looking through the ten volumes that formed a rampart between his own desk and that of the man sitting on his right.

An hour later, the warmth was making him sleepy. He pushed away the volume on the Düsseldorf murders and stretched his arms and legs. He decided to go down to the lavatory and wash his face again.

As soon as he stood up he saw Nunne. He was walking towards the central desk, carrying a pile of books. Sorme stood there and watched him as he pushed the books across the counter to the assistant. At that moment, as if feeling Sorme's eyes, he turned round. Immediately he grinned and waved. Sorme waved back, and went over to him.

Gerard! What on earth are you doing here?

Reading.

How extraordinary! How long have you been here?

Since twelve-thirty.

So have I. How lovely to see you. Are you ready to leave yet? Let's go and have some tea.

Sorme was about to agree, then remembered the books. If he handed them in while Nunne was with him, Nunne would be certain to see the titles. He had no wish to let Nunne learn of his curiosity. He said:

Well . . . no, not just yet. I'd like to finish my book.

What is it?

A life of St Teresa of Lisieux. I want to finish it today. Look, why don't I meet you in about half an hour somewhere?

Sorry – I have to see an editor before five. What are you doing this evening?

Nothing.

Then shall I call around for you about seven? We can go and have a drink.

All right. That's fine.

He returned to his books feeling slightly guilty. There was something almost childlike about Nunne. The spontaneous way in which he had accepted Sorme intensified the guilt. Sorme was charmed and flattered by it, and ruled out the possibility that it might be purely homosexual. He found it difficult to go on reading about Kürten without feeling, illogically, that he was betraying Nunne. He read on for another quarter of an hour, then returned the books to the counter. He folded the request tickets and put them in his wallet. On his way out of the Reading Room, the librarian said:

You off, Gerard?

Hello, Ronnie. Thanks for the catalogues.

You found the books you wanted?

He said, grimacing:

Yes, thanks. I found them pretty repulsive.

I'm not surprised. Do you still intend to use a sadist in your novel?

I think so. But I don't think I'll model him on any of those people. They all seem to be subhuman.

What else did you expect?

He walked the bicycle down Coptic Street, looking into the teashops he passed in the hope of seeing Nunne. Finally, he leaned it against the plate-glass window of the Lyons Corner House and glanced inside. Nunne was not there either. For some reason he felt irritated with himself; his meeting with Nunne left him with a feeling of anticipation. The idea of cycling back to his lodging seemed an anticlimax. He turned into Bloomsbury Street, trying to imagine his room, to evoke its atmosphere and appearance, in order to decide whether he wanted to return there. He decided abruptly that he didn't. Then he remembered Miss Quincey's invitation to call on her. It was half past three; still early enough to drop in for tea. At Camden Town station he crossed the traffic lights instead of turning right for Kentish Town. Half way up Haverstock Hill he dismounted and pushed the bicycle. He felt too hot, too irritated by traffic, to exert himself to the extent of pedalling further.

At the corner of the Vale of Health he stared after the girl who was walking away from him, up the hill; there was something familiar about her. He pulled the three-speed lever into bottom gear and cycled after her. Before he was ten yards behind her he was certain of his recognition. He called:

Hi, Caroline!

She turned round.

Hello, there! Gerard! What are you doing here?

I was going to call on Gertrude.

She's not in. I've just been.

What are *you* doing here?

I'm staying overnight. I just took the afternoon off. You *do* look hot.

He outbreathed deeply, and balanced the bicycle against the kerbstone.

I am. Bloody hot. Where are you going to now?

To have a cup of tea in the café. Are you any good at climbing?

Fairly. Why?

Because you could climb over Aunt Gertrude's back gate and see if her spare key's there. She usually keeps it in the gardening shed.

All right. Let's go and see.

He took her hand as they walked into the Vale of Health; she immediately detached it.

You hadn't better. Aunt might come up behind us in the car.

Would it matter?

Not to me. But there's no need for her to know more than she has to.

He glanced at her, struck by a note of hardness and common sense in her voice. She kissed her lips at him, smiling.

He leaned his bicycle against the wall of the house. She pointed to the tall wooden fence with a gate in it.

Can you climb it?

I expect so.

He leaned the bicycle against the fence and stood on the crossbar. He was able to swing himself astride the gate, and clamber down into the back garden. She called:

Is the gardening shed locked?

He tried the door.

No.

Good. Open up.

He unbolted the gate for her. She went into the shed, and emerged a moment later with a key. Sorme looked around the back garden, it was the first time he had seen it in daylight. There were tall hedges on either side and a concrete path that wound across a lawn to some apple trees at the far end. In the centre of each lawn were two big circular flower beds. He said:

Will she mind? I mean, will she mind us breaking in like this?

Oh no. She's expecting me, anyway. Come on in.

She unlocked the back door. He said:

She's damn' lucky to have such a place.

Why don't you try proposing to her? You might move in.

Don't be silly.

He removed his raincoat and hung it at the bottom of the stairs. She was filling the kettle and setting it on the gas. She said:

I'm not. I would if I was a man.

Sorme came behind her, and slid his arms around her waist.

I wouldn't mind if you lived here.

She leaned her head back, and let him kiss her mouth. He allowed his hands to rest against her, feeling the flatness of her thighs and the hard shapes of suspenders against them. She said:

Ooh, stop it! We ought to behave.

Why?

Aunt might come.

All right.

He stepped away from her, aware of a tenseness in his stomach at the warmth of the contact. She said softly:

I don't want you to stop.

Neither do I.

He pulled off his jacket, feeling suddenly tired. He said:

I'm going to wash. I feel a wreck.

In the bathroom, he stripped off his pullover and shirt, and washed his chest and neck with warm water. He leaned against the wall and yawned deeply. In the bedroom next door he could hear sounds as Caroline moved around. His shirt was damp with sweat. He tucked it into his trousers, then combed his hair, beginning to feel slightly better. He had washed his face with an almost dry sponge. Looking at it closely in the mirror, he saw he needed a shave.

Her bedroom door stood open. He said:

What are you doing?

Changing.

212

Can I come in?

She was wearing a flowered cotton dress. He stood behind her as she combed her hair, seated in front of the mirror.

Do you keep your clothes here?

Some of them. Old ones mostly.

This doesn't look old.

He leaned over her and allowed his lips to brush her ear. He said:

I should have come in a few minutes sooner.

She smiled at him from the mirror, then stood up. He tried to put his arms around her. She pushed them away.

No. Let's go down.

Why?

Aunt might come.

We'd hear the car.

The kettle should be boiling.

He turned her round and pulled her closer. She was wearing no shoes, and he had to bend to kiss her. She put both arms around his neck. If he had straightened up, she would have swung six inches off the floor. He felt the warmth of the out-thrust underlip, then the yielding as her lips parted. Her body was bent back in his arms. He said:

You're too short.

She said, laughing:

You're too tall.

He pressed her waist close to him and lifted her off the ground.

I'd get a stiff neck if I had to keep bending down there!

He carried her two steps backwards, then lowered her against the bed. The backs of her knees pressed on the edge, and she allowed herself to be released on to it. She said plaintively:

Do behave yourself. She might come.

He lifted her legs and pushed them across the eiderdown, then lay down beside her and kissed her again. He felt the same excitement and tension as on the previous evening, and a sense of repetition. He also recognized instinctively that she was not as excited as he was, and kissed her more firmly, caressing her left breast with his free hand. She stopped resisting, and allowed him to lie half way across her. When he stopped kissing her, she said:

You *are* naughty. We oughtn't . . .

He stopped the words by kissing her, and felt her tense under his weight, then relaxed and lay beside her, his face against the pillow. She said pleadingly:

It isn't the right place. Let me come and visit you. It's no good here.

He said: All right. The hoarseness of his voice surprised him. He cleared his throat, and looked at her face. Her chin looked sore, and he remembered that he needed a shave. She was lying with her cheek on her right arm, making no attempt to move, although he was no longer holding her. The wide hem of her skirt spread behind her across the counterpane. He slipped his left arm underneath her neck and pulled her to him again. She could feel his excitement, and he was aware of the beating of her heart as he kissed her. His right hand pressed into the back of her thigh, then moved up to her buttock, and felt the smoothness of her knickers against his fingertips. She said:

Please not now, Gerard . . .

They both heard the noise of the car simultaneously. He said, groaning:

Oh, Christ, just my luck.

She sat up on the edge of the bed, pulling down her dress. She glanced in the mirror and switched at her hair with her fingers. She looked at the expression of gloom and ferocity on his face, and bent to kiss him.

Come on. Get up. Let me tidy the bed.

He rolled off unwillingly, muttering. She said, laughing:

Stop scowling and go and make the tea.

They heard the sound of a car door slamming. He said:

I can't. I'm ready to rape the first girl I see. Even Gertrude.

I expect she'd be delighted!

She ran out of the bedroom and down the stairs. He went into the bathroom, and sat on the edge of the lavatory seat, staring at his feet. The excitement began to die out of his shoulders and thighs. He heard a key inserted in the front door, then the door opened. Caroline's voice called:

Hello, Aunt.

Miss Quincey said:

Hello, dear. How did you get in?

Gerard got the back door key.

Gerard . . .?

The voices retreated into the kitchen. He looked at himself in the mirror, and combed his hair. Then, to supply a reason for his presence upstairs, he pulled the lavatory chain. He made sure that his clothes were adjusted, then went downstairs.

Caroline was alone in the kitchen, pouring water into the teapot. When he looked enquiringly at her, she pointed towards the door. He went into the other room and found Miss Quincey taking several books out of a briefcase and arranging them in the bookcase. She said brightly:

Hello, Gerard. What brought you here?

I was hoping we could have some tea together.

Was it important?

215

No . . . I've been at the British Museum this afternoon. I got tired of reading and thought I'd like to see you.

She finished arranging the books, and straightened up.

That was sweet of you. You should have rung. How long have you been here?

Oh, five minutes. I met Caroline at the end of the street . . .

She smiled at him.

Well, you'll have to come over some other afternoon. Would you like to stay for supper tonight?

What about your meeting?

You needn't come if you don't want to. You could take Caroline for a walk on the Heath. It'll be over by nine.

No. I'd like to, but I'm seeing Austin . . . Anyway, we couldn't really talk much, could we? . . .

She said cheerfully:

No. I expect you're right.

She placed her hand on his arm and squeezed it as she went past, smiling at him. He wondered what had made her so good tempered. The slight sense of guilt about Caroline made him feel that, whatever the reason, he was exceptionally lucky.

When he heard her speaking to Caroline in the kitchen, he was glad he was seeing Austin later. It gave him no excuse to stay. With the two women together, in the same room he experienced a draining sense of self-division, a feeling of being victimized.

Chapter Eight

For heaven's sake, not so much whisky! You'll have me pie-eyed before we get to this club.

Drink what you can, Nunne said. He handed Sorme a tumbler half full of whisky. He said:

Now. Food. Let's see what we have in the fridge.

May I come and look at your kitchen?

He followed Nunne out of the room, and stood in the doorway of the kitchen, watching him take food out of the refrigerator and place it on a trolley. He said:

It's bloody big. Big enough for four kitchens.

It belonged to my uncle. He liked giving large dinners prepared by several cooks. It's really rather large for me. But I like a lot of space when I'm cooking.

The kitchen gave the impression that it had been installed as a showroom, or transferred immediately from the Ideal Homes Exhibition. The rack of glass plates and dishes, the rows of saucepans, even the enormous deal table in the middle of the room, looked as if they had never been used. The white enamelled bench next to the gas stoves had half a dozen electrical gadgets clamped to its edge. The pattern of yellow and white check that covered the walls was repeated in marble shades on the floor. Sorme said:

Don't you ever have girls trying to marry you to get in on this?

It has happened. Not recently, though. I don't let girls see it any more. Do you like asparagus?

I don't think I've ever had any.

Really? Then here is where you start.

What does Gertrude think of this place?

She sometimes comes and uses it. When she wants to cook something really exotic. It has timing gadgets fixed to everything . . . Catch!

He gave the trolley a sudden push and sent it shooting towards Sorme. Sorme said, laughing:

Fool!

He caught it before it hit the wall. It contained a dish of asparagus spears, and a cold chicken with one leg missing. There was a glass jug of mayonnaise that looked as if it was frozen solid. He said:

What would you have done if I'd missed it?

Taken you out for supper. Would you take it in there? I'm buttering bread. Help yourself. Plates and things underneath. I'll bring the salad.

Back in the dining-room, he pulled a wing off the chicken, and cut several slices, leaving the leg for Austin. He piled asparagus on his plate, and spooned the almost solid mayonnaise beside it. He propped a book against the cushion and began to read. From the kitchen came the sound of a cork shooting out of a bottle.

Nunne came up beside him as he read, and piled salad on to his plate.

I've found some champagne.

Good. But I've still got all that whisky.

Drink that later.

Sorme was forced to stop reading as the plate wobbled and almost fell off his knees. Nunne said:

Hold on. I'll give you a tray.

After looking around vaguely for a moment, he said:

Can't find a tray. Use this.

He pulled a large, thin book out of the case, and handed it to Sorme. Sorme asked:

What is it?

He opened it, and discovered sheets of music, written

218

with a pencil, and curious symbols drawn between the lines.

Do you recognize it?

No. I can't read music.

It's not just music. It's the original manuscript of Nijinsky's *Rite of Spring*. Those funny signs are a choreography he invented himself. That's his handwriting across the top.

Where did you get it?

From a collector.

Sorme began to eat again. He left the manuscript volume open on the cushions beside him. Nunne said, smiling:

Can't you bring yourself to eat off it?

It's a funny sensation. To know he wrote this with his own hand.

That writing in green ink on the cover is Stravinsky's handwriting.

Yes?

I say, you're not eating those asparagus spears whole!

Aren't I supposed to?

No! You eat down to the tough part. Like me.

Oh, I see. Thanks.

He reached out for his champagne glass. He said:

To Vaslav.

He emptied it in one draught. A sensation of warmth and delight coursed through him like a faint electric shock. Nunne repeated: To Vaslav, and drank, Sorme said:

I suppose it must be rather fun to be rich.

Nunne grimaced:

Better than being poor. But it doesn't guarantee anything.

No?

219

He laughed, feeling that the pleasure had to find some expression. Nunne said curiously:

What is it?

I was hungry.

He would not tell Nunne the real reason: that he felt suddenly reconciled to his own existence, able to weigh it, summarize it, and feel only gratitude. It was a sensation he would have been glad to convey to Nunne, feeling grateful to him for being the cause of his insight. But saying it would have meant nothing. Nunne stood up and poured more champagne into both glasses. He said:

I'm surprised you get so enthusiastic about Nijinsky. You never saw him dance.

Sorme shrugged.

It's not that. There's something else. The independence. A sort of pure vitality.

I'm surprised you don't prefer someone like D.H. Lawrence, who expresses it far more clearly.

No. I can't stick Lawrence. He seems to me to stand for a diluted version of what Nijinsky stood for. He always gives me a feeling that people matter too much to him. They nag him, and he doesn't like them much. Anyway, he was all wrong about sex.

I'm afraid I just can't agree. I admire him very much.

All right. Let's not argue about it. Tell me something. Why is Gertrude so fond of you?

I'm afraid I don't know. I just don't know. We've known one another so long . . .

He swallowed the last of the chicken leg, and placed the bone carefully on the side of his plate. He said, with apparent irrelevance:

I'm delighted you get on so well with her.

She's sweet. But all this religious stuff worries me.

Don't let it worry you. She likes you.

Do you think she's ever had *any* experience with men?

Probably very little. Why? Do you find her attractive?

Sorme admitted: She's the type that attracts me. Slim. Good figure.

Well, don't, please don't take her to bed. It wouldn't be good for her.

Why?

Because she takes everything too seriously. If she wants a man at this late date, she ought to marry.

Sorme said gloomily:

I dare say you're right.

He was sorry he had mentioned the subject; he was not sure yet whether he seriously wanted an affair with Gertrude Quincey, and to speak of it seemed premature. As if he guessed Sorme's thought, Nunne said:

Don't worry! I don't really suspect your intentions towards Gertrude. Anyway, she's a little old for you. And that's not the real reason you like seeing her, is it?

Sorme looked at him with interest:

No, it's not. What do *you* think my reason is?

Something to do with her beliefs. You can't make out whether she's dishonest.

That's pretty good guessing. But it's not just Gertrude . . . it's me. I want to know where I differ from her. You know . . . I'd need to have a nervous breakdown, or be brainwashed or something, before I could swallow all that stuff about the Bible being the last word on everything . . . I just don't understand it. I mean . . . was she brought up to believe it? Is that it? She seems quite intelligent in other ways. You know what I mean? If she put on a powdered wig and claimed to be Madame de Pompadour it'd puzzle me less . . . I could understand someone with an obsession having strange ideas. But she seems perfectly balanced. She's not an Oliver Glasp . . .

Oliver? Do you know Oliver?

221

Sorme stopped, feeling, for a moment, that he had given something away: he recovered immediately, saying:

Yes. I went to call on him today.

Nunne was obviously astonished.

What on earth for?

What you told me of him made me curious to meet him. And I liked his canvases. Father Rakosi gave me his address.

Nunne regarded him with amusement:

You really are odd! Why didn't you mention it to me?

I intended to. It wasn't supposed to be a secret.

And what did you say to each other?

Not much. I thought he was going to be rude to begin with. He growled like a dog . . .

That sounds like Oliver!

Then we talked about . . . oh, religion, asceticism. And finally about murder . . .

That also sounds like Oliver!

Why? Is it one of his favourite subjects?

Oh yes. Quite his favourite.

Why, I wonder?

I don't know. He has a thing about pain and suffering. He lets it drive him a little haywire occasionally. Broods on it too much. When I first knew him, he had some theory . . . let me think . . . oh yes . . . an idea that – life is a preparation for eternal torment. He had it all worked out. The body acts as a sort of buffer against pain, but in spite of that we suffer all the time. And when we're freed from the body, there'd be nothing to keep off the pain . . . just eternal pain. From which he deduced that everyone ought to make himself suffer all the time . . . as a sort of practice for eternity. I think he used to wear a shirt studded with tintacks.

Really? I never suspected that.

But he's not entirely a crank, Oliver. I really believe he has a sort of second sight.

Are you serious?

Quite. His family are Irish, you know.

I thought he came from Yorkshire?

Lancashire. Liverpool Irish. I don't think he's ever been in Ireland. But someone once told me – Father Carruthers, I think – that Oliver's grandmother was a famous witch-cum-holy woman in County Clare . . . mediumship, second sight, the lot. And Oliver shows signs of the same thing occasionally.

How?

Promise you won't repeat this to him?

I promise.

Well, he hadn't been sleeping properly – and had awful nightmares. One morning he told his landlady: A man called Thomas is going to be murdered on the Common tonight. She thought he was off his rocker. Well, that night, a man called Thomas *was* waylaid on the common – for his wallet – but they hit him too hard and killed him. Oliver had dreamed it exactly as it happened.

Sorme felt the hair prickling on his scalp. He said: Christ!

And Oliver couldn't sleep the next night either – he still had dreams. Luckily, his landlady sent him to see a doctor, who sent him to a psychiatrist. Father Carruthers found the money, and he went into a private mental home for a while. That cured him. But the fact remains, he dreamed of the murder before it happened.

Are you sure he dreamed it *before* it happened? I mean, is there any proof of that? Did he try to contact the police or anything?

Not as far as I know. What could he have done? Clapham Common's pretty enormous – and there are thousands of men called Thomas in London.

Who told you all this? Oliver himself?

No. Father Carruthers.

Nunne divided the last of the champagne between their glasses. He said:

Now, how about fruit? Would you like a peach? Or some ice cream?

Neither, thanks. That was delicious.

You haven't finished your whisky.

I haven't started it!

Nunne glanced at the clock.

Half past ten. It's still a little early for the Balalaika. We shouldn't get there till about half past eleven. Would you mind if I make a few phone calls now?

Certainly. Am I in the way?

No. I'll use the bedroom extension. Look, help yourself to more whisky if you need it. I shan't be long . . .

He disappeared into the bedroom. Sorme yawned and stretched. He was already feeling a little drunk. He waited until he heard the phone bell tinkle as Nunne lifted it from its rest, then poured most of his whisky back into the decanter. He had been waiting ever since Nunne poured it for an opportunity. He sat down again, holding the glass, which now contained only a quarter of an inch of spirit. Feeling curiously dreamy, almost bodiless, he started to look through the Nijinsky manuscript.

He opened his eyes when the car crossed the Edgware Road, then closed them. Nunne said:

You remember Socrates in the *Symposium*? When all the practised drinkers were under the table, he stayed awake, discoursing on tragedy. Nietzsche loathed him, yet there was something of the superman in him. Are you asleep?

No.

Don't fall asleep. We've arrived.

Nunne had become livelier over the past hour. In spite of his resolve not to drink, Sorme had accepted another whisky, and had listened while Nunne talked of his father and became steadily drunker. The effects of his crowded day were beginning to make themselves felt. The night air helped to revive him.

The car turned off into a narrow street, and halted between the gates of a factory and a row of dingy houses. Sorme reached for the door handle. Nunne said:

Hold on. I'm going to back on to that waste ground.

Fragments of broken glass reflected the reversing light. The car bumped on to the pavement. From behind the wall came slow coughs of a shunted train; red coals reflected on the smoke. Sorme slammed the door, and staggered. Nunne gripped his elbow:

Steady, child! *Avanti!*

He raised his cane to shoulder level, pointing.

How far is it?

A ten-minute walk. It'll waken you up. C'mon, boy.

Sorme said, grinning:

You make me sound like an Alsatian dog.

Unintentional. Have you ever been to a brothel before?

Is that what this place is?

More or less. Don't worry. They're quite civilized.

Is that a man over there?

It would seem so.

The man lay across the pavement, his head in the gutter. He lay quite still. When they crossed the road towards him, he stirred.

Nunne said: Are you all right?

He prodded the buttocks with his cane. The man said thickly:

Amori. Goawayfergrizake.

It's after closing time, you know. Time you went home.

The man raised himself to his knees, and crawled across

the pavement. He sat down heavily, banging his head against the wall. He said:

Amori. Goway. Sleep.

By all means, Nunne said.

He stepped over the outstretched legs. He said:

Virgil guides Dante into the second circle. *Dove il sol tace*. Where the sun keeps its trap shut.

Sorme said grinning:

Not Virgil. Mephistopheles.

What charming ideas you do have! I'd like to wear red tights.

The man behind the door asked: Members?

I am, Nunne said.

Got your card?

Nonsense, Sam. You know me.

Sorry. No admission after midnight without a card.

I never had a card.

Nunne leaned forward, and whispered something in the man's ear. The man's eyes dropped to the wallet, which Nunne tapped with the head of his cane. He glanced at Sorme.

Is he all right?

Of course. As sober as I am.

Ten bob each. Member and guest. Sign the book for 'im. The stairs were narrow. Sorme was reminded of innumerable coffee bars in Soho and Chelsea. The notice on the door said: The Balalaika Club. Members Only. There was a drawing of a banjo underneath.

Sorme's first impression was of a large room crowded with men and women. The lights were shaded with pink paper. On a raised platform a quartet of Negroes began to play their instruments; the music was jerky, low-pitched, unsoothing to the nerves. A tall man in a dinner jacket hurried to meet them. He said:

Good evening, Mr Nunne. And how are you?

Fine, thank you, Mitzi. Lot in tonight.

Ah, yes. We've been very busy. This is your table, sir.

He led them across the dance floor to a table in the corner. Nunne pulled the table back for Sorme, saying:

You go inside, Gerard.

The man asked: What can I order you to drink?

More champagne, I think. Don't you, Gerard?

Sorme said: Anything for me. He would have preferred soda-water, but did not like to ask.

Champagne, please, Mitzi.

While Nunne ordered, Sorme had a chance to look around. He could see nothing unusual in the appearance of the room, or in the people who danced. No one seemed to be drunk. A few feet away from him a man dressed in evening clothes was kissing a girl, pressing her head back against the wall. One of his hands, partly concealed by the long tablecloth, lay on her thigh. She broke away from him, saying in a deep masculine voice:

Lay off, will yer?

Sorme looked away quickly. He found Nunne's eyes regarding him with amusement.

How do you like it, Gerard?

I haven't had much chance yet.

Listen, Gerard, why don't we get away? Right out of England? To some other country.

You suggested that the other night.

Did I? And what did you say?

I can't remember. But it's impracticable.

Why?

For several reasons. To begin with, I haven't any money.

I know that! I didn't expect you to pay!

That's even more impracticable!

Why?

Oh . . . I couldn't take your money. Secondly, I don't

227

want to waste time gallivanting round the world. I'd rather stay in London and work.

You could work on board ship. There'd be plenty of time. We could go to India . . .

It was South America the other day!

No, India. Let's make it India. You know, Gerard, I'd like to go into a Buddhist monastery for a while . . . You could work there!

I'd rather be in London.

But why? You admitted to me the other day that you're bored here.

I was. That's quite true.

Aren't you still?

Well, that's the odd thing, you see, Austin. Ever since I met you I've been feeling better . . . I've been getting a sort of sense of purpose.

But you'll be bored again if I go to India!

You don't understand.

Well, explain to me . . .

Sorme made an effort to push back his drunkenness. His thoughts were clear, but he anticipated the effort that would be involved in speaking them without slurring most of the words.

You see, it's like this, Austin. Before I met you, I used to feel . . . no, that's not what I mean. What I mean is . . . I used to feel purposeless. See? I used to live from day to day . . . Why? Because I was alive, and it's easier to live than do anything else, once you're alive. It wasn't always like that. But you know, when I was at work I used to think that the one thing I wanted was to be free. Free to work and do as I like. Sometimes, in the evenings, I'd read a book, or listen to a symphony concert, and when it was time to go to bed I'd feel so excited and . . . well, so certain of what I wanted to do with my life, that I couldn't sleep, I just couldn't sleep. Well, I thought that

228

if I didn't have to work all day, I could really do everything I'd ever wanted to. You see? I could read those books and listen to those symphonies at ten in the morning, and be happy and excited before midday, and then write like a madman for the rest of the day, while the inspiration lasted. That's what I thought I'd do . . .

But it wasn't like that, was it?

No, it wasn't. I've told you what it was like. I got to the stage of living like an animal – just eating and sleeping, and feeling a contempt for myself cover me like soot. I knew that if I'd got enough money I'd spend all my days buying books and gramophone records – or probably, like you, going to hear Sartre lecture in Paris, hear Callas sing in Milan.

Touché, dear boy, Austin murmured.

Well . . . enough of that. I think I'd just forgotten to live. I let myself slip into a state of sloppiness and boredom, that's all. And since I've met you I've begun to recover the old sense of purpose. Oh, it's not anything very clear. It's just a sense of excitement, like being on the point of discovering something. But it's genuine all right. And you started it, but it's nothing to do with you personally.

Oh, I see . . .

Don't take that personally. I'd be very sorry if you went away . . .

Nunne said gloomily:

Be careful. One of these days, you might be glad to run away from those glimpses of purpose.

Why?

Nunne seemed suddenly sober. He stared at the table-cloth. He said:

It depends what you pay for them . . . Is anything the matter? You look rather pale.

I'm feeling a little sick. It's this heat, I think.

229

Can I get you anything? Try an angostura. I always have one when I feel sick.

No, thanks. I think I might go outside . . .

There's a door next to the lavatory. It will take you into a backyard. Have a sit down out there.

Sorme said: Thanks.

The dancing stopped, and he stood up, hoping to get an unobstructed passage to the door. Unfortunately, the music started again immediately. Nunne said:

Listen, Gerard. If you feel sick, go up the fire escape, and into the second door on the left. You'll find a bathroom.

Thanks, Austin.

He pushed his way to the door, feeling the sweat standing out on his face. The night air was cold. He felt better in the yard. It was as if something flat and alive, something with legs, turned itself slowly in the pit of his stomach.

The yard seemed completely black when he came out. He found the fire escape, and sat down on the bottom step. As he sat there, he heard a movement in the far corner of the yard, and whispering. He felt too sick to worry, leaning his cheek against the cold iron of the rail.

On the other side of the wall a train whistled and released steam, startling him. Drops of water fell on his face. The sky was clear, full of stars. On the other side of the door the music sounded exhausted and inconsequent.

Someone crossed the yard towards him. A man's voice said:

Listen, would you mind going away?

A face was thrust close to him; the breath smelt of tobacco and garlic. It was too much for him. He jumped to his feet and turned his back away from the man as the first heave came. He was sick, his head pressed against the wall, tasting simultaneously champagne, whisky and asparagus. He felt a kind of incredulity, wondering how he could ever have swallowed these things, things that now seemed wholly revolting, that he could not imagine himself at any time finding pleasant. The stupidity of drinking champagne when he had no desire to drink also overwhelmed him. He heard the man recross the yard, and say:

Oh, Christ, he's sick. Let's get out.

Footsteps crossed the yard. Another male voice said:

Let's go somewhere else.

They went through the door. He felt a smouldering loathing of them for being there at all, and a deep relief when they were gone. He lurched across to the fire escape and sat down again, glad of the cold that now came through his clothing. His stomach still twitched as he tried to forget it. He spat, and wiped the sweat off his face with his hands. He knew it was coming again, and wished it would all come at once and get it over with, and realized the extent to which his stomach rebelled at the quantity of alcohol. When it came to a head, he stood up and leaned over the rail, the heat rising in waves from his stomach like fever. He stood there for several minutes, coughing and trying to make it subside, thinking: Never again, never again, feeling the tears cold on his eyelashes. Finally, he sat down again. The sweat chilled on his neck and belly. He heard someone outside in the passageway, and was afraid they were coming into the yard. No one came, but the thought worried him. He stood up, trying to remember the instructions Austin had given him to find the bathroom. The door at the top of the first flight of stairs was locked. He climbed slowly up the next flight, stopping once to stare out over the railway siding that was now visible. The door stood open; he went through into a lighted passageway. The door of the bathroom stood open. He switched on the light, and locked himself in. He crossed to the lavatory and sat on the pan, leaning his back against the pipe. He felt like sitting there for the rest of the night. The heat was still rising from his body. The room smelt of primroses, and he disliked this. The twitching of his stomach made his breathing convulsive. He sat there for about a quarter of an hour, with no desire to move, staring at the threefold greaseline in the cracked enamel surface of the bath. Then it came again, and he knelt on the floor, vomiting into the lavatory, now bringing up nothing but small quantities of a bitter liquid, which he spat against the pattern of blue flowers that decorated the inside of the pan. He thought: Christ what have I done to my stomach, that it does this to me? His knees began to hurt, and he pulled over a bathmat covered with rubber nipples, and slid it under his shins. When the sickness subsided he pulled the chain and stretched out on the floor, resting his head on the mat. Someone tried the bathroom door, then went away. He lay still for another ten minutes, and came close to falling into a doze.

Nunne's voice called: Gerard, are you in there?

Yes.

Are you all right?

No. He grinned to himself.

May I come in?

He pulled himself slowly to his feet, wishing Nunne would go away, and unlocked the door. Nunne came in.

Are you all right?

Sorme said thickly:

I have been sick three times. I suspect I am going to be sick three times more.

He sat on the edge of the bath.

Would you like me to drive you home?

I just want to stay here – that's all. For a while.

Poor Gerard! I'm terribly sorry. You do look ill.

232

Sorme thought with fury: Bloody stupid comment. He said: Just let me alone for a while, please.

All right. Look, I've got an idea. I'll be back soon. Lock the door again.

Sorme leaned forward and locked the door behind him. He sat down on the floor, and buried his face in his hands. He noticed that his hands were dirty, probably with dust from the fire escape, and realized that he must have transferred a great deal of it to his face. He felt no desire to stand up and find out by inspecting his face in a mirror. The room was cold, and a draught came from under the door. He was glad of it. He was afraid he was going to be sick again; his stomach lurched threateningly when he thought inadvertently of food.

Nunne called:

It's me. May I come in?

He opened the door again, getting a glimpse, as he did so, of his face in the shaving mirror. He looked like a coalminer. The tears had cut paths through the dirt.

Listen, Gerard, I've fixed up so that you can sleep here. They've got an empty room. Do you feel like coming up now?

I'd better wash my face.

Don't worry. There'll be a washbasin in your room. Come on.

Sorme followed him up a flight of stairs. He said:

You shouldn't have bothered. I'll be all right in half an hour. I could go home.

No need. It's all fixed.

Nunne turned round, and added in a lower voice:

I'm staying too, anyway.

Sorme did not answer. He was thinking: Nowhere near me, I hope. As if Nunne guessed his thought, he added:

I'll be in the room below you. So knock the floor if you want anything.

Sorme felt suddenly ashamed for the dislike he was beginning to feel. He said: Thanks.

It was better in the dark. After half an hour the sickness subsided, and left him feeling completely rested. It was a curious silence, compounded of exhaustion and strength. He was glad to lie there in the big double bed, hearing faintly shreds of music, tinny and far off. There was a window in the roof above his head, although no starlight penetrated the dusty glass. In spite of the tiredness, the sense of interior power that had been with him all day was still there. There was also a sense of unconnectedness, as if nothing that had ever happened to him had really happened. He thought vaguely: Good title for a book: things do not happen. He felt that even the prospect of his own death would leave him unmoved, certain that nothing final and irrevocable could happen. When he thought of Austin he felt pity, thinking: too involved. He will never be free. He doesn't realize that things don't happen, that nobody is really himself, that man is God in a box.

The bedclothes were thin and light, but he was not cold. He slept for a little, but woke again, feeling that it was somehow a pity to sleep and waste the feeling of certainty. A few seconds later he slept again anyway, and dreamed of Nunne: Nunne was standing on the rooftop of a house in Berkeley Square, and shrieking like Petrouchka at the night sky. He woke abruptly, deeply aware of Nunne, feeling his presence in the room. There was no one. Nunne had stood there, his arms flailing, shouting something at the sky; below, the crowds watched his protesting silhouette; many shouted, urging him to jump. But Nunne would not jump; Sorme was certain of it, and the certainty made him glad. In the empty house below, he hurried up uncarpeted stairs, hoping to reach the roof before it happened, feeling a happy excitement, certain now that there would be a light of prophecy over London, from Islington to Marylebone, from Primrose Hill to St John's Wood, and hanging like a red sun over Kensington Gardens. Nunne wouldn't jump. He would stand there, Austin, Vaslav, Petrouchka, above the rooftops. But he was not in an empty house. He was in a brothel, lying in an attic room. And Austin was there.

He was standing by the window, staring out. In the faint dawnlight, the big naked body looked like a marble statue. The shoulders were broad; rounded muscle, a dancer's shoulders.

Sorme could not see his eyes. They would be stone eyes, not closed, immobile in the half light, nor like the eyes of the priest, grey in the ugly gargoyle's face. When he closed his own eyes he saw the dancer, the big body, moving without effort through the air, slowly, unresisted, then coming to earth, as silent as a shadow. It was very clear. The face, slim and muscular, bending over him, a chaplet of rose leaves woven into the hair, a faun's face, the brown animal eyes smiling at him, beyond good and evil.

Cold the dawnlight on marble roofs, more real than the jazz. You're gonna miss me, honey. Glass corridors leading nowhere.

And then the leap, violent as the sun on ice, beyond the bed floating without noise, on, through the open window.

The excitement rose in him like a fire. The rose, bloodblack in the silver light, now reddening in the dawn that blows over Paddington's rooftops. Ending. A rose thrown from an open window, curving high over London's waking rooftops, then falling, its petals loosening, into the grey soiled waters of the Thames.

He wanted to say it, with the full shock of amazement: So that's who you are!

Certain now, as never before, the identification complete.

It was still there as he woke up, the joy and surprise of the discovery, fading as he looked around the lightening room. He said aloud: Vaslav.

Part Two

Chapter One

His room felt cold, and somehow unoccupied. He lit the gas under the kettle, and lay down on the bed, his eyes closed. It was a quarter past seven; it had taken him just over an hour to walk from Paddington. He felt weak and tired, but curiously at peace. He wondered whether Nunne would find the note he had left on the pillow; he had seen no one as he left the house.

In the room underneath a radio was playing. He heard a man's voice call: What have you done with the plug off my electric razor? The sky outside the window was heavy with rain clouds and dawn. It was the first time for many months that he had been awake so early, and the sensation brought a certain freshness with it, and the thought of charladies in the Mile End Road catching City buses and of men in overalls carrying lunch tins. The rain clouds hung low, like smoke.

He made tea and sat on the bed to drink it, covering his knees with the eiderdown. The room was chilly, even with the gas fire burning. He read till he heard the eight o'clock pips from the radio below.

He met the German girl on his way back from the bathroom. She said:

There's a letter on the table for you.

Oh, thanks.

The neat handwriting on the envelope was strange to him, but he recognized the heading on the notepaper. The typed message read:

There is something I would like to talk to you about.

Could you ring me when you receive this, please? Gertrude Quincey.

The first-floor tenant, carrying a briefcase, pushed past him, saying irritably: Excuse me. Sorme moved automatically, staring at the two lines of type, frowning with the effort to guess what Miss Quincey could want. He pulled a handful of change out of his pocket, and found four pennies. As the number began to ring, he experienced a sudden misgiving about the earliness of the hour.

A woman's voice said: Hello?

Gertrude?

Who is it?

Gerard Sorme.

Hello, Gerard! This is Caroline.

Hello, sweet. What are you doing there?

Having breakfast right at this moment.

Where's your aunt?

In the garden. Hold on a moment and I'll get her . . .

Wait. Don't go yet. When am I going to see you?

That's up to you.

Could you make it tomorrow night?

I . . . Here comes Aunt Gertrude.

He heard her say:

It's Gerard, Aunt.

Miss Quincey's voice said:

Hello, Gerard.

I've just got your letter.

Yes. I'm glad you rang. When will you be free to come over? Her voice was as detached as a receptionist's making an appointment.

When you like . . . more or less.

Could you come today for lunch?

I expect so. Is it anything very important?

I'll explain when I see you.

All right. See you then. By the way . . .

Yes?

Will there be anyone else there?

No.

Ah . . . well, see you later. Bye-bye.

He hung up, feeling slightly foolish. He had half suspected it might be to meet some Jehovah's Witness colleague.

The girl came past him, carrying an armful of sheets. She said: You're up early today.

I'm reforming. The clean, healthy life.

He locked the door of his room behind him, and lay on the bed. He felt suddenly very tired. The idea of lunch with Miss Quincey did not appeal to him, nor the thought that Oliver Glasp was coming for supper. He would have to buy food and wine, to go to the bank, to sweep and tidy his room.

Still thinking about it, he fell asleep.

When he woke up, it was half past twelve. For a moment he could not think what time it was, or what he was doing there. His head was still thick with sleep. When he remembered the lunch appointment he felt no inclination to get up. Finally, he sat on the edge of the bed and ran his fingers through his hair. The gas fire still burned; the room was airless. Sitting there, he noticed something white sticking under the door. He crossed the room, walking heavily, like a drunken man, and picked it up. On the back of a torn Woodbine packet someone had written: Miss Denbigh phoned. She will come tomorrow evening.

In the bathroom he plunged his face into a bowl of cold water and blew vigorously, to clear his head. He stripped to the waist and washed, then changed his shirt and trousers and hurried out of the house. It was five minutes to one. He felt light-headed, as if he had just risen from a six weeks' spell in a hospital bed. He resented the daylight

241

and the noise of traffic. Something inside him wanted to shrink into a tight ball. At the bank he withdrew five pounds, but only after the cashier had pointed out that he had forgotten to sign the cheque.

He rang her doorbell with a sharp jab of his thumb, feeling unreasonably irritated with her for laying claim to his time. As soon as he saw her the tension disappeared. She smiled happily at him:

Hello, Gerard. I've just rung your lodgings to see if you'd forgotten to come.

I'm awfully sorry. I fell asleep and didn't wake up till half an hour ago.

That's all right. Take your coat off. Are you on your bicycle? Sit down. A glass of sherry?

No, thanks. I think I'd better lay off it for today.

Why?

I feel fragile. I was up late last night.

With Austin?

Yes.

He wondered about the meaning of the look she gave him. She said:

Well, sit down, anyhow. I'll bring you some soup in a moment.

The radio was relaying a concert. He closed his eyes, listening to the Mozart concerto, and wished he was at home and in bed. He remembered Caroline, but the thought of having her in his room gave him no pleasure. It only brought the reflection that he would have to change the sheets on his bed, which would mean cycling to the laundry. His thoughts switched to Nunne, and his dream of the night before; it seemed meaningless. He felt irritated with them all, with Miss Quincey, Austin, Caroline, Glasp. He thought, with closed eyes: What have I to do with the bloody fools? The resentment brought a longing for solitude, and a vague wish for some intenser form of existence.

Soup?

Thanks. Aren't you eating?

In a moment. I've had my soup. Do you want a tray?

No, thanks. I'll go to the table.

The first mouthful of tomato soup brought a keen pleasure that made him want to laugh. His stomach relaxed with gratitude, and an inner peace passed over him like a wind, giving a sense of some secret glimpsed and recognized. Miss Quincey asked:

Do you mind coming to eat in the kitchen? When you've finished your soup, of course.

Thanks.

The kitchen was warm; the windows were obscured by a mist of condensed steam. The concert was still audible through an extension loudspeaker above the table.

I hope you like kidneys? It's kidney pie.

He swallowed the first mouthful, and found it good. He said:

When are you going to tell me why you wanted me to come?

Afterwards.

He looked at her, hearing the hurried note of a repressed anxiety in her voice. He said:

All right.

She ate without raising her eyes. The brown woollen dress she was wearing moulded itself to her figure, and had the effect of making him aware that her face seemed older than her body. She looked up suddenly and caught him staring at her. She said critically:

You don't look at all well.

I feel all right.

It was true; there was only still the fatigue, a desire to

243

close his eyes and retreat from the necessity of focusing his attention.

Where were you last night?

At some club . . .

What club?

Just a night club.

You shouldn't let Austin drag you to clubs.

No.

He suffers from a permanent state of boredom. You ought to know that.

I expect you're right.

A voice from the loudspeaker announced that the last item on the programme would be the Prokofiev Fifth Symphony. Sorme said:

Good. My favourite symphony. Will it go up louder?

He wanted an excuse for finishing the meal without further talk. Miss Quincey obediently reached out and turned up the volume, then ate without speaking. He experienced a sudden flash of affection for her, looking at her averted face, feeling an intuition that she would be easy to hurt.

When he finished eating, she asked: Fruit?

No, thanks. I'm full. I enjoyed it.

Good.

He tried to frame some compliment about her cooking, but gave up the effort. Watching her fill the kettle, he reflected gloomily that her cooking had given her a right to lecture him. It would also be impossible, after such a meal, to refuse to attend at least one of her Bible classes. He had come to the conclusion that this was what she wanted to talk to him about.

Would you like to listen to the music in the other room? I'll bring in coffee in a moment.

When she came in twenty mmutes later he was asleep in front of the electric fire. On the radio someone was giving a talk on gardening. He woke up as she switched it off. The noise of rain on the windows became audible; the wind was blowing it in flurries. He said ruefully:

I'm afraid I'm a rotten guest. I can hardly keep awake.

He sugared the coffee from the bowl she held out.

What happened last night?

Oh, I drank too much . . . and got sick.

Is that all?

He glanced at her in surprise.

Yes. What else did you think?

I don't know.

He could not see her face clearly as she sat down; the half light of the December afternoon filled the room with shadows. He watched her, waiting for her to speak, and finding it difficult to keep his eyelids from dropping. The silence lengthened. She asked finally:

Do you mind if I ask some rather frank questions?

No. Go ahead.

He could feel rather than see her hesitation. A suspicion took shape, and sparked across his mind.

How well do you know Austin?

He said honestly: I don't know. Why?

She began to stir her coffee quickly and nervously, now staring into his face. He said:

What is it you think I ought to know about Austin?

When she spoke, her voice was slightly breathless. It made him feel as if she was looking down from a height that frightened her.

Do you . . . know why Austin has never married?

He sat up in the chair, the suspicion expanding into a startled incredulity. He answered quickly:

I expect he doesn't like girls.

He watched her, now completely awake, sensing what was about to come, and feeling no desire to help her. He

245

wanted to see how she would manage it. She asked, after a silence:

Do you understand me?

I'm not sure. What are you asking me?

I . . . it's very difficult for me . . .

Well, how about coming right out with it? Who's been talking to you about Austin?

You mustn't mention this to him.

No.

Well . . . Brother Robbins.

What on earth does he know?

She seemed glad to be back on solid ground again.

He has to do a lot of social work – door to door. And when he met Austin for the first time – two weeks ago – he thought he'd seen him somewhere. He didn't tell me at the time, but he made enquiries . . .

Yes.

. . . and found that Austin is quite well known in certain circles that are . . . known to the police.

Criminals?

Oh no!

Irritated into impatience, Sorme said bluntly:

You mean homosexuals?

She said weakly:

Yes.

Your Brother Robbins sounds like a silly gossip, Sorme said curtly.

Oh no. He thought I ought . . .

Her voice tailed off; the effort to get it all out had made it tremble noticeably. She asked finally:

It is true, then?

Yes.

And you've known all the time?

Most of it. But what does it matter?

She was looking at him steadily now, and he could

sense the confusion of feelings that was trying to find expression. He said:

Let me answer the question that's in your mind. I'm not homosexual myself.

She said, blushing:

I knew that.

Did you? How?

I . . . you . . .

It made him wonder suddenly if she had noticed his speculative looks at her figure. But she went on, with a kind of hopelessness in her voice:

Perhaps I didn't know. I just assumed.

His hostility dissolved in the face of her bewilderment. He would have liked to put his arms around her. He said:

Look here, there's no sense in getting excited about it. I've known about it since I first met Austin, but it didn't worry me. After all, it's his own business. I like him because . . . well, we're both writers, we've got a lot in common. And . . . he's a nice person.

But . . . don't you think it *matters*?

Do you mean, do I think it's wicked? No, not especially. I'm glad I'm not homosexual myself, but after all it's a matter of taste. I know that some people seem to be homosexual out of sheer worthlessness. But others seem to be born like it . . .

He was remembering, as he talked, the impatience that he'd felt last time he had been here, his irritation in the face of her self-assurance. Now the self-assurance had collapsed, and he felt no better about it. The reversal was too complete.

Are people really born like it?

Of course! Didn't you know?

No, I . . . I never met anyone like it before. Do you think Austin was *always* like that?

247

I should think it likely. I don't know him well enough. What sort of a child was he? Was he a mother's pet?

Oh yes, very much. But why?

Oh, it could have something to do with it.

He began to talk, as detachedly as possible, about statistics of homosexuality, factors of childhood influence, of sex hormones, trying to see her face in the half light. She listened without interrupting. When he paused, waiting for her to speak, she asked abruptly:

Could he be cured?

I don't know. It's rather late. Probably he doesn't want to be cured. Besides, that's not necessarily Austin's real problem. He accepts it, yet something still worries him.

What do you think?

I don't know. Many homosexuals lead quite ordinary lives. They sometimes settle down with a boy friend, and live like any married couple.

Don't people notice?

Sometimes. But there's nothing very strange about two men sharing a flat.

But you think Austin feels guilty about it?

No. There's just something about him that makes him nervous and restless. I don't know what it is. Something torments him. Whatever it is, it drives him into this lone-wolf attitude. I don't think he could ever live with anyone.

She said with astonishment:

I should hope not! What would his poor parents think?

He said, smiling:

That's another question I can't answer. I can only tell you what any doctor or psychiatrist would tell you – that it's not necessarily a matter of moral turpitude.

She said hesitantly:

The Bible forbids it . . .

No doubt it does. The Bible forbids fornication and a lot of other things that go on all the time.

That doesn't make them right!

No, you're right; it doesn't. But men and women *can* get married and legalize it. Homosexuals can't. So what can be done?

She sat, staring into the red bars of the fire. The only sound in the room was the drumming of rain. Sorme stared out into the garden; from where he was sitting he could see his bicycle, covered with the yellow cycling cape. Under the dead sky the lawn, sprinkled with rotting leaves, looked as forbidding as a no-man's-land. The darkness and rain aroused in him a sensation of comfort. Looking at Miss Quincey, he considered the possibility of kissing her, just to see how she would react. She gave him the impression that she was confronting a problem that she was incapable of grasping, and that now nothing would surprise her. She asked:

Couldn't we persuade him to see a psychiatrist? Just on the off-chance of getting a cure?

You could try.

I wonder if his parents suspect? But no, they couldn't . . .

They might.

She was almost talking to herself; he replied only for the sake of politeness. She said:

He was always a strange child. He had a cruel streak.

Sorme asked with interest:

Did he? How?

Not real cruelty; just a sort of impulsive thing . . .

How?

He once pushed the gardener's boy off the roof of the shed, and broke his arm. And he had a curious dislike of dolls.

Was he often cruel?

Not often, no. But he had a sort of . . . dark side to his character. He'd go into sulks for days on end and refuse

249

to be coaxed out of them. He could never keep toys for more than a few hours – he had to break them. And he didn't get on with other children because he sometimes tried to hurt them or break their toys. It was the same kind of thing as his dislike of dolls.

Whose dolls?

Any little girl's. He once smashed a beautiful doll that belonged to his cousin Jane – an enormous doll that came from Austria. He smashed it with a hammer. He broke all my dolls . . .

You played with dolls? Sorme asked, smiling.

Not then. But I had dolls that lay around in some old cupboard. Austin discovered them and tore them to pieces.

He sounds quite a delinquent!

Oh no! He wasn't like that all the time. It was just occasionally – a demon seemed to get into him. And when that happened, he became a different person.

But why do you think he smashed dolls?

I don't know. He gets bored so easily. And when he gets bored, I think he has an impulse to do something violent. He's quite capable of asking you to pack a bag and go off to the other side of the world with him . . .

He has!

What did you say?

I refused. I've other things to do.

Good. You must be *very* firm with him. You could be a good influence on him . . . if you don't let him lead you along his own paths.

He won't lead me any further than I want to go!

She seemed to read another threat in this. She asked doubtfully:

Don't you think it might be better if you stopped seeing him?

What should I do instead? Come and see you?

He said it teasingly; to his surprise, she answered with gravity:

You could if you wanted to.

He stared at her, trying hard to see the expression on her face. He said:

I'd enjoy that.

But what are we going to do about Austin?

I don't understand you. There's nothing we can do. Anyway, I'm afraid I ought to go now.

Right now? It's still raining.

I . . . I wanted to get a bath. I feel like a haystack. And I've got to cook supper for someone later. Excuse me.

He stood up and went out of the room.

As he came out of the bathroom, she called:

By the way, Gerard?

Yes?

Wouldn't you rather have a bath here?

No, really, thanks . . .

Her suggestion embarrassed him for some reason.

Is it easy to get a bath where you live? Is there always hot water?

There's a geyser – you put a bob in it . . .

When he thought of the bathroom, with its door panelled in brown glass and the deep, old-fashioned bath that could be filled with infinite slowness from the temperamental water heater, he began to feel that Miss Quincey's suggestion had much to be said for it. She said:

It sounds ridiculously troublesome. It would be so much easier here.

Would it be any trouble?

None whatever.

Well – in that case, thank you . . .

As he undressed, he imagined that Gertrude Quincey had become his mistress, and that he was living here. For some reason, it was very easy to imagine. Except, of

251

course, for Caroline . . . Caroline was a problem. He thought about it as he released himself cautiously into the warm water. Five years of celibacy, of partial boredom, of the unsuccessful attempt to harvest his own solitude. Then abruptly involvement, too many people, and two potential mistresses. Caroline offered herself with curious frankness. It was the kind of thing one imagined might happen in daydreams; when it happened, it was almost impossible to resist. Yet in many ways Gertrude was the more attractive of the two. The challenge was greater.

He helped himself to bath salts from the row on the windowsill; they smelt of lemon. As he replaced the jar, he heard a sound of singing. He listened carefully, and realized it was Miss Quincey. A moment later she stopped. He sat there, straining his ears to catch the sound above the noise of water refilling the hot tank. It was difficult to imagine Miss Quincey singing to herself, especially after their conversation.

As he dried himself, he could hear her moving about in the room next door. This was the room Caroline slept in. He combed his wet hair, humming a theme from the Prokofiev symphony, and wondered how he could get to know more about Gertrude Quincey.

He opened the door and stepped out on to the landing. He could hear her now in the room at the end of the passageway. He moved towards it, treading softly on the thick carpet.

She said: Oh, you startled me!

Sorry.

How do you feel now?

Fine. Much better.

She finished spreading the counterpane, and pulled it into position. As she turned, he seized her around the waist and lifted her off the ground, doing a single turn with her before setting her down. He said:

I should bath more often.

The feeling of her body excited him. Her cheeks were flushed. She said:

I'm glad you feel better.

He found it difficult not to reach out for her again. Before he could make up his mind, she went out of the door, saying:

Come along. You shouldn't be in here.

Why not?

Because it's my bedroom.

That's no reason.

She said: People wouldn't like it.

He followed her down the stairs.

People won't know, will they? And it's none of their business, anyway.

Perhaps not.

She went ahead of him into the kitchen. He had begun to feel as if he was pursuing her, so he restrained himself from following her, and went instead into the sitting-room. There he sat trying to read a newspaper, while his thoughts recurred constantly to the feeling of holding her, and to the fact that she had made no protest. The uncertainty made him restless; he began to feel annoyed with himself. A moment later she opened the hatch between the kitchen and the sitting-room, asking:

Would you like a cup of tea before you go?

Er . . . thanks. What are you doing now?

Washing up.

Can I help?

No, thank you. There's almost nothing.

He went into the kitchen, and found her at the sink, wearing a plastic apron. She said:

You needn't have come . . .

No?

253

He came up behind her, and put his arms around her waist from behind, saying:

I wanted to. After that superb meal . . .

Stop it, Gerard!

She made no attempt to push his arms away. He lowered his face until his chin rested against the top of her head.

Do you object?

Of course I object. Do stop it, please.

He released her, and picked up a tea towel.

Does it make you angry to be touched?

No . . . but it's rather pointless, isn't it?

Her tone was not encouraging, but he had already made his decision. He said cheerfully:

Oh, I don't know. I must admit I enjoy it.

Don't be silly.

Why silly?

Just because I invite you to lunch you don't have to flirt with me.

He took the last fork from her, and dried it.

Tell me, Gertrude . . . These Jehovah's Witnesses who come here . . . don't they ever flirt with you? I mean the men, of course.

They're mostly married.

Hmmm. What about this artistic set?

What artistic set?

Austin told me you have a lot of arty-crafty people around. She looked at him with surprise:

I don't know what he's talking about. I know one or two people in Hampstead – a retired colonel, a publisher's reader.

He suspected that she was trying to keep the conversation deliberately casual. The kettle was already boiling; she started to make tea. He asked:

And do you object to being flirted with?

Don't be silly.

That's no answer.

She snapped suddenly:

No, I don't mind. But it's rather pointless, isn't it?

I don't know.

He was sitting on the edge of the table. As she turned he tried to take hold of her again. She twisted away and pushed his arms down.

Do stop it, Gerard! I really don't know what's making you behave like this.

He said, laughing:

Half an hour ago you thought I might be homosexual!

I didn't! That's untrue! I never thought so for a single moment.

Good. So long as I'm sure.

She poured milk from the bottle into the jug with an indignant jerk of her wrist. The milk shot over the rim of the jug and splashed on the tray. She said:

Oh really, Gerard!

He was on the point of saying 'It's your own fault!' when she turned on him suddenly. To his surprise, he saw she was on the point of tears. She said:

Do *please* stop it!

All right . . . I'm sorry. I didn't mean to upset you.

He had started to suspect that she was secretly enjoying his attempts to flirt with her; her distress bewildered him. He turned and went into the other room, and dropped on to the settee. Her attitude was not entirely a disadvantage. At least it helped in some ways to destroy the formality that had made him so irritable last time he came. He picked up the newspaper and tried to concentrate. The article he began to read stated that people use three times as many facial muscles frowning as in smiling, and that therefore one saves energy by smiling. He folded the paper and hurled it at the armchair opposite and scowled into the bars of the fire, wondering what to say to her when she came in. She was a long time bringing the tea. He began to wonder if she wanted him to go without seeing her. A moment later she came in, pushing the trolley.

I'm sorry I've been so long.

He said automatically: You haven't.

He watched her pouring the tea without speaking. When she handed him his cup, he said:

I really don't understand you.

She sugared her own tea without looking at him.

I don't understand *you*!

You really find it repellent to be touched?

Of course I don't! It's just that . . . it's silly to start behaving like that.

Like what? he said, determined to be uncooperative.

I'd rather talk . . . as we did the other night . . . about sensible things.

He said reasonably: I like talking with you too.

Then let's go on like that!

But I also like touching you. It gives me pleasure.

He could feel her uncertainty, and he pressed the advantage. He leaned forward, smiling at her, and said:

Even the other night, when we were talking, I kept thinking how pleasant it'd be to put my arms round your waist.

She dropped her eyes to the cup.

But why?

Because I find you very attractive.

She looked into his face seriously; her impatience had vanished. She said:

But it's silly, Gerard!

Why?

Because . . . What could come of it?

He shrugged: I don't know.

Nothing. Nothing at all. I'd like to be your friend – but you're a great deal younger than I am . . .

He decided abruptly to force the issue.

You'd like me to stop coming here?

No, of course I wouldn't! I like to talk to you. I think . . . I think that you're a serious person and you're searching for something . . . and I'd like to help you find it. Because I'm older than you and . . . I've been through it myself . . . and I *could* help you . . . But we ought to be serious about it.

He said, shrugging:

In that case, there's not much more to say.

Why?

He finished drinking his tea. He felt that the conversation had reached its natural conclusion, and that there was no point in going on. He said bluntly and dogmatically:

I've been alone for five years now. I can go on being alone for another five, or for another fifty if it comes to that. I don't need helping and never have. I like seeing you, but if you're going to start drawing lines and setting limits, I'd rather chuck it all.

He set his cup back on the tray. She asked:

More?

He looked at his watch, saying:

No, thanks. I'd better go.

She said quietly: Let's not quarrel.

All right.

It made no difference to his feeling of having reached an end. She said:

Have another cup of tea.

All right.

She poured it, and handed it to him. He drank it in silence. She began to speak, hesitantly:

I know you've been alone. I don't want to . . . try to

257

interfere. You've got so used to the feeling of having to fight the battle alone that you've become suspicious of other people. You've become hardened to them. But I know you're not really hard . . . I know you've a lot of sensitivity . . . Perhaps you're really afraid of being hurt . . .

Her tendency to use phrases like 'searching for something' and 'fight the battle' made him wince inwardly, and increased his impatience. He began to wonder if she saw his attempts to flirt with her as some kind of complicated defence against her. He interrupted her:

My desire to steer clear of your Jehovah's Witnesses isn't a fear of being hurt. It's a fear of being bored.

For a moment, he wondered if he'd gone too far. But her face showed no sign of offence. She said reasonably:

I haven't tried to make you meet them, have I?

No. That's true.

He stood up.

I'm afraid I'll *have* to go.

Her face was troubled as she looked at him; he could tell that she was trying to gauge how far he was impatient with her. She said hesitantly:

You *do* understand, don't you?

Yes, I understand.

You won't speak to Austin . . .?

No.

She followed him out into the hall. He buttoned his raincoat and belted it, then extracted the beret from the pocket. The silence hung between them, the silence in which there would normally have been thanks and disclaimers, vague arrangements to meet again. The situation seemed so full of latent comedy, of which she was completely unaware, that he found it difficult not to smile. As he opened the door, she said: Goodbye, Gerard.

Bye-bye.

He turned to her, took her by the waist, and pulled her to him. He felt her stiffen for a moment, then give way. She moved her face slightly so that his lips touched her cheek. He held them there for a moment, feeling the warmth of triumph stir, then released her. He turned away from her and went out of the door without looking back. He walked cautiously across the wet lawn in case he slipped and spoiled the exit.

As the bicycle free-wheeled down East Heath Road, he experienced a pure elation. He said aloud: You bloody fool. It's time you grew up!

The church clock chimed four as he passed the Chalk Farm Underground. The sight of the grocer's shops reminded him that he still had to buy food for Glasp. He bought a half pound of gammon and four tins of vegetables, and packed them in his saddlebag. As he was about to ride off again he noticed the headline of the evening paper inside the station. He dropped twopence halfpenny into the tin and took one. The bold type read:

HAS KILLER MOVED TO GREENWICH?

Aware of the unease that moved his bowels, he leaned against the wall, reading it.

'The body of a young woman was found in a disused warehouse near Greenwich Reach this morning. Early this afternoon she was identified by her husband as Doris Elizabeth Marr, twenty-five-year-old housewife of Albury Street, Deptford. The husband, Reginald Marr, 26, who works nights in a Deptford laundry, told police that his wife had set out at ten last night to visit her mother in Woolwich . . .'

His eyes travelled to the bottom of the column: 'The people south of the river are asking themselves the question: Has the Whitechapel killer decided to move?'

A peculiarly unpleasant sensation touched him with

disgust: it was a hot, sticky feeling in the area of his stomach.

At Kentish Town station he bought the other two evening papers and stuffed them in a roll into his pocket. Somehow, the feeling of disgust affected the satisfaction he felt whenever he thought of Gertrude Quincey. He found it difficult to understand the sense of foreboding the news report produced.

Back in his room, he sat on the bed and read all three accounts of the murder carefully. One of them carried a full-length article with a diagram of the site of the murder; the writer asked how a married woman had been lured so far off her normal route from Deptford to Woolwich, and seemed inclined to doubt whether the murderer was the Whitechapel killer.

It was still only four-thirty; Glasp was not expected for another two hours. When he closed his eyes, the image of Gertrude Quincey's face came to him, the mouth soft, the eyes slightly frightened. It was the way a woman might look before she grasped the intention behind the violence of the man who intended to kill her. He tried hard to dismiss her face, and watched it re-form every time he closed his eyes. His whole body lurched with pity and repugnance; he reached out for the bookcase, and took the first book his fingers met; it was Merton's *Seven Story Mountain*. He started to read, but found it hard to concentrate. Finally, he laid the book on the floor, and dosed his eyes again.

There was nothing at first. The sleep was clear, without images. Then he began to see it: in the half darkness, in a warehouse, an animal like a crab; something flat with prehensile claws. He was aware of nothing else; only the crablike creature, moving silently into the half light; moving strangely, obliquely, but with intention, entirely itself, possessed by an urge that was its identity, entire unification of its being in one desire, one lust, a certainty. It was not a man; it was what was inside a man as he waited.

He heard someone knocking on the door downstairs as he peeled the potatoes. He called: Hello.

Glasp's voice said: Ah, I'm in the right place!

Good. Come on up. I'm just starting to cook supper.

Glasp stepped cautiously up the stairs, lowering his head as he came to the bend. Sorme finished slicing the potatoes, and poured them into the seething nut oil in the chip pan. Glasp picked up an old newspaper from the table and scanned the front page with perfunctory interest; he sat with his feet thrust out, his shoulders against the wall. His face looked as pale and unshaven as on the previous day. Sorme noticed that his socks were of different colours. He said:

I see that the Whitechapel murderer seems to have changed his field of activity . . .

What?

Haven't you seen the papers?

No.

A woman in Greenwich has been assaulted and killed. The police seem to think it's the same man . . .

Greenwich? Glasp said. I don't believe it. It can't be the same man.

Why not? What makes you think he's sticking to Spitalfields?

Glasp shrugged.

I don't know. But he's stuck pretty close so far, hasn't he?

Yes. But surely that's a good reason for moving? Whitechapel'll soon be too hot to hold him. What makes you think he'd want to stay there? Do you think he's looking for something in Whitechapel?

Glasp said:

Now, *I* don't know, do I? Your guess is as good as mine. I heard a bloke today who seemed to think it was the Fascists out to terrorize the Jews.

Where did you hear that?

Oh, some bloke up on a platform this morning. Communist.

But *were* any of the victims Jewish?

I dunno. I don't think so.

But you don't think this Greenwich murder is the same man?

Glasp said impatiently:

Oh now don't ask me! I don't know.

Sorme sensed that his impatience was not intended to be offensive, and he suppressed the twinge of irritation it produced. He had decided that the apparent rudeness in Glasp's manner was only the result of too much living alone. He said:

I hope he's caught. I'd like to find out who he is.

Glasp looked up at him; he said ironically: – I dare say a lot of people feel like that.

Like what?

They want him caught to satisfy their curiosity. Not because he's killing women.

Sorme said seriously:

I dare say you're right. After all, how can anyone really identify himself with an East End prostitute? Most people probably feel that the murderer needs as much pity as his victims. At least he's doing something that most men are capable of . . .

Do you think most men *are*?

I think so. We're still animals with sudden and violent appetites. I can't count the number of times I've passed a woman in the street and wished I could get her in the dark. Haven't you?

I suppose so. But that's a long way from rape. I'd like to see the man caught because he's a menace in the part where I live. Tomorrow it might be somebody I know.

Glasp's northern accent had become more noticeable. Something in his tone impressed Sorme with its seriousness. He said:

I suppose you're right. That's another reason for hoping he's moved to Greenwich.

What difference does it make? Wherever he moves, lives get wasted. People have to die, just because a man's something worse than a man, a dirty animal, something that only thinks of his own pleasure, with no moral sense.

Glasp's tone was so irritable and belligerent that Sorme decided to drop the subject. He made a mental note to raise it again later, when his guest was in a better mood. He said:

Well, let's hope he's caught soon. Shall we go downstairs? These chips'll take another ten minutes.

He opened the bottle of red wine and poured into two tumblers.

Glasp smacked his lips, saying:

This is good stuff. Very nice. What is it?

He picked up the bottle and looked at the label. Sorme said:

I like wine – when I can afford it.

You can say that again. I haven't been able to afford anything but Spanish hogwash for five years.

I'll leave you for a while. Look through my books. Or there are records there if you like music.

He opened the door, and walked into Caroline, who had her hand raised to knock. He said:

Hello, sweet! I didn't expect you.

I haven't come to stay; don't worry.

She was already in the room. Sorme said:

263

You two don't know one another, do you? Oliver Glasp. Caroline Denbigh.

Caroline said:

Oh, you're the famous Oliver Glasp! I've met you somewhere before, haven't I?

Glasp was staring at her, wearing an odd, sulky expression. He said:

I don't know.

The accent became broad, as deliberate as that of a Yorkshire comedian. Looking at Caroline, Sorme found it impossible to imagine why Glasp should seem displeased. She was wearing a fur coat, with a fur hood that almost covered her face. The face, under the fringe of blonde hair, was as pink and round as a doll's. He said:

Have a glass of wine, sweet?

Ooh, rather!

She pulled back the hood to take her first sip of wine. She was wearing black gloves. Sorme said:

I've got to go and cook some chips. Come on up to the kitchen with me.

When they were alone in the kitchen, she said:

I don't think he likes me much.

Oh, I don't know. His manner's always a bit gruff. He's all right when you get to know him.

Isn't it hot up here?

Take your coat off.

No, pet. I won't stay. I'm just on my way to rehearsal and I thought I'd come and say hello. It doesn't start till eight. I wanted to make sure you hadn't got any other women.

Where have you come from?

Aunt Gertrude's. I'm sleeping there tonight.

Oh yes. How is she?

She's all right. What did she want to see you about?

Austin.

Oh yes!

Why, what did you think . . .?

Oh, I don't know. She wants to get you into her Jehovah's Witnesses.

How do you know?

Oh, it's pretty obvious. What did she want to know about Austin?

She's found out he's queer. I think she wanted to know if I was.

And what did you say?

I tossed her vigorously on the bed and made her think I was a goat in disguise.

Don't be silly! What did you say?

Oh, nothing . . . I just tried to make her see that there'd be no point in giving Austin a lecture on the laws of Moses. She took it rather well, on the whole.

Tell me about it. In detail.

He gave her an account of his conversation with Miss Quincey while he fried the gammon, stopping at the point where he had a bath. She said:

She looked a bit upset when I came home. I wondered what had been going on!

What time was that?

Oh, about four.

He shook the chips in their wire basket until the brown ones came to the top, then immersed them again in the boiling fat. He said:

Does she know you're here?

No. I've got a feeling she'd be jealous.

Why? Do you think she's after me?

I shouldn't think so!

Why, then?

Because she discovered you before I did. I think she wants you for her Bible class.

Hmmm.

She had laid her coat over the kitchen chair. She was wearing a plain red dress, with a band of fur round the neck. He bent and kissed her, and felt the coldness of her lips which gave way immediately to the inside of her mouth. The familiar reaction of desire came over him; as she stood against him, he cupped her buttocks in his hands and strained her thighs tight against him. He said, laughing: Bed?

Not now. There's someone in your room!

There won't be tomorrow night.

You'll have to wait till tomorrow then, won't you?

He experienced a lurch of delight at her frankness. He said:

You could come back later tonight . . .

I couldn't. Aunt Gertrude'd get suspicious. Then I'd have to go home to Wimbledon every night . . .

The saucepan lid began to jar softly as the steam forced it open. He released her with regret and turned back to the cooking. She said:

You know, I've met that man somewhere before . . .

Where?

I don't know. Let me think. St Martin's . . . St Martin's . . .

The Art School?

No, I . . . It's something to . . . Ah, I remember. The amusement arcade. In the Charing Cross Road. That's where I saw him.

That doesn't sound like Oliver!

Yes, it was. I'm sure. He was with a little girl, and he started a row about one of the machines – it didn't work, or something. He was wearing a dirty old duffle coat.

What was the girl like?

I don't know. I didn't really notice her. Quite a little girl – about ten or eleven, I'd say.

Attractive?

What, at that age! You don't think he likes them *that* young, do you?

I shouldn't think so. But I saw a painting he did of a little girl – might be the same one.

He turned and peered down the stairs, wondering if their voices were audible to Glasp, and decided not. She asked;

What's the time, Gerard?

Ten past seven.

I'd better be off.

Wouldn't you like some supper?

No, thanks. I've had tea.

He took the warm plates from under the grill and used the fish slice to put the bacon on them; he shook the fat out of the chips, and poured them from the wire basket on to the plates. Caroline said approvingly:

Mmmmm! You're quite a good cook. If we ever got married, you'd be useful.

He asked:

Do you want to get married?

She rubbed her head against his shoulder.

I wouldn't mind being married to you.

What! On less than a week's acquaintance?

As he turned to face her, she put both her arms round his neck; she said softly, defensively:

I don't need to know you for a long time. I know what you're like already.

Do you? What am I like?

Well, you're good tempered . . . and one day you'll make a huge success.

Hmm. I dunno about the good temper.

She pulled his face down to her. When he had kissed her, she said:

Shall I tell you something? I decided to make a beeline

267

for you the first time I met you at Aunt Gertrude's. I shouldn't really tell you that, should I?

Why not?

It might make you feel chased.

I am chaste.

Not that chaste, silly! I mean it might make you feel you're *being* chased.

I'm that too.

I know you are. Does it worry you?

Not in the least. Look, sweet, I've got to take Oliver his dinner. Come and have some more wine.

No. I haven't finished this yet. Anyway, I don't want to go in there again. I'll say goodbye now. Don't come down.

As he kissed her, she pressed herself against him. He was certain she was aware of the rising need in him, yet her body clung to him, infusing its warmth. When she had gone he inhaled deeply, then expelled the air in a long sigh. He felt an ache across his chest and back, as if someone had beaten him with some padded object. The desire throbbed in him, subsiding.

Glasp was sitting on the bed, reading one of the *Notable British Trials*. He began to eat quickly, ravenously. After swallowing two mouthfuls, he said, in an oddly throaty voice:

Oaaaaah! I was bloody hungry!

Sorme said smiling: Good.

He was too preoccupied with the thought of Caroline to feel any inclination to talk. They ate in silence for ten minutes, and Sorme refilled both glasses. Glasp put his empty plate on the floor, and attracted his attention with a growl like an animal.

You said you hadn't heard about that last murder of the Ripper?

That's right.

It's here.

Glasp swallowed, cleared his throat, then read:

'In the early morning of the 18th of July 1889 an unknown woman was murdered in Castle Alley, White-chapel, her injuries being similar to those sustained by the earlier victims. At 12.15 on the morning of the murder a police constable had entered the alley and partaken of a frugal supper under a lamp. At 12.25 he left the alley to speak to another constable who was engaged on the same beat. Returning at 12.50 he found the body of a woman under a lamp where he had previously stood. The ground beneath the body was quite dry, although the clothing of the woman was wet. A shower of rain had fallen at 12.40. The murder was therefore committed between 12.25 and 12.40, when the rain commenced to fall . . .'

I didn't see that, Sorme said. What book is it?

The trial of George Chapman.

Ah yes. I found that in the room when I moved in last Saturday. But doesn't it say the woman wasn't identified?

She was. It was my Great-aunt Sally. Sally McKenzie.

The wine bottle was almost empty; Sorme opened a second one. Glasp relaxed against the wall, stretching his legs on the bed and yawning. He said:

That was good. You're bloody lucky, you know, Gerard.

Why?

Oh, enough money to do as you like.

Haven't you?

Blimey no! My slender income comes from a bloody shark of a dealer who sucks me dry!

Does he take all your paintings?

No. Only the things he thinks he can sell. Like street scenes, and pretty-pretty landscapes.

You make a living from it. That's something.

Not much.

269

Anyway, why should my few hundred a year make me lucky? The only lucky man's the man who can create. I've been stuck on the same book for five years.

Why don't you finish it?

I can't. I keep trying. There's something missing.

What?

Oh . . . the inspiration, I expect.

Is that all?

Sorme looked at him. It was obvious that Glasp's mood had mellowed considerably with the meal. He said:

No, that's not all. I've got other problems too.

Such as?

Sorme said, smiling:

I don't know that I can explain them to you without your flying off the handle.

Eh? Glasp said. Me? What do you mean?

Oh . . . such as when we were discussing the White-chapel murders earlier this evening.

Oh, that's different . . .

Not entirely. Because I can see certain aspects of myself reflected in the murderer. Can't you?

No. Anyway, what's that got to do with finishing your book?

All right. I'll try to explain. I ask myself: Why does a man commit a sex crime? I know it's partly sheer weakness . . . But that doesn't answer it. I read in a newspaper the other day that seventy per cent of the sex crimes in the States are committed by teenagers. Why is that, do you think?

Glasp shrugged:

Because they've less self-control at that age.

Not only that. Because they think they're going to get more than they really ever get. I once read a case of a youth who was driving a lorry, and passed a girl on a lonely road. He turned the lorry round, knocked her down, and raped her in the back of his lorry. Then he dumped her body down a well and blew in the well with dynamite. They caught him eventually and electrocuted him.

He paused, to give Glasp a chance to comment. Seeing that Sorme was looking at him, Glasp said:

Well, it served him right, didn't it?

Yes, but that isn't what strikes me about it. What impressed me is the stupidity of it, the waste, the pathos. Try to put yourself in his place . . . Can you do that?

I expect so.

Supposing he'd got away with it. What would *you* feel afterwards, looking back on it . . . even if you weren't afraid of detection? Wouldn't it be the stupid gap between your motive and what you actually got out of it? He sees a desirable girl on a lonely road. Suddenly, she represents for him all the taboos and frustrations of his adolescence. He feels he *ought* to be allowed to possess her. You remember how, in Greek mythology, Zeus went around raping everybody – changed himself into a swan, a dove, a bull? He gave his sister Demeter a daughter, then raped the daughter too . . . Do you see what I mean? Well, he feels just that . . . the god's prerogative. He revolts against his limitations, he turns the lorry around . . . But he's not a god, and he lives in a state with laws, and the laws condemn him to death.

Glasp had begun to grin as Sorme talked. He interrupted:

And he's not as intelligent as you seem to think either. Do you think he had any thoughts about Zeus and Leda when he turned his lorry round?

No. I'm trying to get at his feelings, even if he couldn't express them . . .

I know. But it's not true. He's probably a bloody bullnecked yokel who thinks of nothing but how many women he can screw behind the dance hall on a Saturday night. When he rapes the girl, he doesn't feel any pity for knocking her down. He doesn't feel that, if he'd really wanted her, he could easily have made her acquaintance and seduced her without killing her. Her life doesn't mean anything to him, or the feelings of her family. It's all that balanced against one stupid lust, and he lets the lust win. Can you feel any sympathy after that?

I agree; you're right. But it's still not the whole truth. Listen to me. One day I was cycling along the Embankment when I saw a girl and a soldier looking at the river. It was a windy day, and suddenly her dress blew right over her head. And I tell you, I experienced a sensation like a kick in the stomach. For weeks afterwards, I got into a fever every time I thought of it.

Glasp interrupted:

Sounds like ordinary sexual frustration!

I know. But what would have satisfied it? I suppose, if the girl had been alone, I might have made her acquaintance. I might have finally persuaded her to come to bed. But that wouldn't satisfy it. It's something far more violent and instantaneous than a desire for an affair. It's a sudden longing for far more freedom than we possess. It's an insight into freedom – that's the reason it's so overpowering. What's more, it hasn't much to do with ordinary lust. I once had a girl friend . . . when I lived in a basement off the Marylebone Road. Well, one Sunday I made love to her more times than I would have thought possible – until I felt like a wet dish rag. I got a feeling that I'd never want a woman again in all my life, that I'd emptied myself completely. Then I walked out of my front door to get the milk, and a girl came walking past overhead in a wide skirt that swayed open and showed me her legs and thighs. And, you know, I could have carried her off to bed whooping! I was astonished to realize that I hadn't exhausted my desire. I'd just exhausted my desire for a particular girl. My appetite for women generally was untouched.

Glasp was frowning. He had not touched his wine since Sorme refilled the glass. He said:

I don't understand what you're trying to prove. I don't see what you mean about an insight into freedom.

I can't explain easily. But it has that effect. It's a sort of vision of more life. It makes you feel as if you've been robbed of the powers of a god. It's as if we *are* gods, as if we're really free, but no one realizes it. And it comes back to us occasionally through sex.

Glasp murmured: D. H. Lawrence and all that.

No, not just that. It's not just the sexual orgasm that counts. I've got a friend -- a journalist -- who's as indefatigable as Casanova at trying to seduce women. But he doesn't actually enjoy going to bed with them. That part bores him. He just needs to feel the conquest, to feel that he *can* go to bed if he wants to. I can't explain it . . . but I feel as if we *ought* to be gods, as if the freedom of the gods ought to belong to us naturally, but something's taken it away.

Glasp said, smiling: You'll make a good Catholic yet.

I doubt it. I just feel that our slavery to sex is just a need to regain something that is *naturally* ours. It would be an internal condition of tremendous intensity. There wouldn't be any more sex crime then. It'd be a state of such inner power that other people would be superfluous. The need for a woman is only the need to regain that intensity for a moment . . .

Glasp held up his hand to silence him. Sorme asked:
What is it?
Someone calling, Glasp said.
Sorme got up and went to the door. He heard the girl's voice shouting:

Telephone! Mr Sorme.

He called: Thank you.

He hurried downstairs, experiencing the warm sense of wellbeing that came from food and wine. The receiver was on the hall table. He said:

Hello?

Gerard? This is Austin.

Hello, Austin! How are you?

Very well, thanks. What are you doing now?

I've just finished supper . . .

Are you free?

No. Oliver Glasp's here.

Oh . . .

Sorme could hear the disappointment in his voice. Wondering if it was dislike of Glasp, he asked:

What is it?

Nothing. When is he going?

Oh . . . in a couple of hours. He's only just arrived.

Oh.

Why? Did you want me to come over?

Well, I did, rather. Can't you get rid of him?

Not really. Not without being impolite. You know how touchy he is. Is it anything important?

No. I'd just like to see you. Could you come in a couple of hours?

Sorme said, sighing:

No, Austin. I'm dog-tired, and I've been falling asleep all day. When he goes I want to sleep.

I won't keep you up all night, I promise.

On the point of yielding, Sorme thought of the prospect of getting to Albany Street, and felt a sudden certainty that he didn't want to go. He said:

It's not that. I'm really fagged out. I wouldn't be good company if I came.

Nunne said, with scarcely concealed irritation:

Oh, all right!

Let's make it tomorrow, or some time.

I'll ring you again.

The line went dead. Sorme hung on for a moment, wondering if they had been cut off. He replaced the phone, and returned upstairs. He said:

That was Austin.

Glasp said:

Oh yes. What did he want?

Just to know how I felt. We had a late night last night.

Did he want to see you now?

He suggested it. I told him I couldn't.

Glasp was bending over the case of records. He said:

I think you'll find Mr Nunne rather a demanding person before you've finished . . .

Yes?

Glasp was sitting on the end of the bed; he had all the records spread over the counterpane. He said:

Like all weak men, he has to use his friends as crutches.

You think he's weak?

Don't you?

I'm . . . not sure.

You'll find out, Glasp said.

He selected one of the records, saying:

Unless you'd like to go on talking, what about some Mozart?

Certainly. More wine?

No, thank you. And then, if you're agreeable, let us adjourn to the nearest pub, where I can repay some of your hospitality with a little brandy . . .

You don't have to do that.

Nevertheless, I'd like to.

Glasp was affecting a curiously pedantic and stately manner of speaking. Sorme said, laughing:

That's OK by me.

He put on the record, then relaxed in the armchair, closing his eyes. The events of the past twenty-four hours revolved round him as he listened; he felt as if they had happened to someone else.

The night was icy cold. As he came out of the Kentish Town tube, he wrapped his scarf closer round his throat, and buttoned the raincoat under his chin. Glasp had seemed completely drunk when he caught the train, but he had refused Sorme's offer to go as far as Moorgate with him. He felt warm inside, and pleasantly tired, but not drunk.

As he was half way up the first flight of stairs, the phone began to ring. He turned and retraced his steps. The door from the basement opened, and he called:

It's OK, Carlotte. I'll answer it.

The voice said: Could I speak to Mr Sorme, please?

Speaking!

Gerard? I didn't recognize your voice! This is Bill.

Hello, old boy. Where are you?

I've just come on to the paper for the night. We're going out to do a news story on this Greenwich murder. Would you like to come?

What sort of a story?

Oh, you know the sort of thing . . . We go around with the police patrol and take photographs. Interested?

Well . . . I dunno. I would be, but I'm deadly sleepy. I didn't get into bed till eight this morning . . .

All right. Well skip it then. We'd got a spare seat in the car if you wanted to come. You know the photographer, Ted Billings?

Oh yes. Well look here, thanks a lot for asking me, and any other night I'd be delighted . . . But I really am all in. But listen, Bill. If anything important crops up, let me know. I'd be quite interested to be on the spot. It's just that I'm so sleepy at the moment . . .

OK, old boy. Don't worry. I'll call you some other night. Just thought you might like to come. See you later.

As he undressed he regretted being so tired. He would have enjoyed accompanying Payne on the story. He even wondered whether the thought of it might not keep him awake.

As soon as he climbed into bed, he knew better. A tide of warmth caressed him. He chewed and swallowed the last of an alkaline tablet he had taken as a precaution against a hangover, and pressed his face closer into the pillow. The thought of Caroline passed through his mind, arousing a feeling of pleasure that arose partly from the memory of asking her to stay the night, and the realization that, even if she had accepted, he would have been incapable of making love. It was also anticipation.

He woke up and stared at the door. For a moment he was uncertain whether it was not the climax of some dream that had wakened him so abruptly. As he listened, he heard a murmur of a voice. He peered at the luminous dial of his watch in the dark: it looked like six o'dock. He turned over, and buried his face in the sheet. A moment later he heard footsteps on the stairs. He raised his head, listening. Someone knocked on his door. He called:

Yes?

The door opened slightly. A man's voice said:

Someone on the phone for you. You're Mr Sorme, aren't you?

Yes . . . thanks. My God . . . what an hour! I'm awfully sorry . . .

He pulled on his dressing-gown, and went outside. The man was going downstairs ahead of him. He was saying:

Phone's right opposite my door. He woke me up.

I'm really terribly sorry . . .

He was thinking: F – that bloody Austin!

He said: I can't tell you how sorry I am . . .

Chap said it was an emergency . . .

He went towards the phone, thinking: I'll tell him he'll get me chucked out if he goes on like this . . . Six o'clock . . . bloody fool.

He snatched up the phone, and restrained an impulse to shout into it. He said, controlling his voice:

Hello?

Hello, Gerard. This is Bill Payne.

Bill! What do you want?

You told me to ring you if anything happened. There's been a double murder in Whitechapel . . .

His hair stirred, as if he had received an electric shock. For a moment he let the phone drop to his side, and heard Payne's voice talking in the distance. After a moment, he raised it again, and heard the voice:

. . . that was an hour ago. So, if you want to get over you'd better come right away.

Where is it?

Mitre Street. It's on the left near Aldgate station. There's a little café about two doors away from the station. I'll meet you in there.

He said – OK. I'll be with you as soon as I can get over.

He replaced the phone and sat on the edge of the table. The cold made no difference. It seemed that the beating of his heart must be audible to everyone in the house.

Chapter Two

In spite of two pairs of gloves, his hands were numb before he reached Holborn; he pulled off the left-hand glove and rode with the hand in his trouser pocket, pressed into the hollow of his thigh. The streets of the City were deserted. The cold had wakened him, yet he felt an internal exhaustion that was almost a luxury, as if all his emotions had been short-circuited. It made him feel strangely free. Before he arrived at the end of Leadenhall Street he had forgotten his reason for riding out so early. The sight of an old man, crouched in a bus shelter, covered with an overcoat, started a train of thought on the difficulty of human life, and on the human tendency to increase its difficulty by useless movement. The thought that, in three hours' time, these streets would be crowded with people who possessed no motive beyond the working day, no deep certainties to counter-balance the confusion, made him grateful for the silence of the streets, and the inner silence of his own exhaustion.

He recognized Payne, standing by the entrance to the Underground. He was lighting a cigarette and stamping to warm his feet. Sorme called: Hi, Bill!

Hello, Gerard. Glad you made it.

Sorme leaned the bicycle against the wall and groped in the saddlebag for its chain.

I thought you were going to wait in the café?

I've only been out here a minute. I wanted a breath of air. You leaving your bike here?

I expect so. It'll be OK.

Good. Come on, then.

Where is this place?

Mitre Square. It's on the other side of Houndsditch.

What happened?

Don't know yet. Another woman found. And, half an hour before, they found another one over in Berner Street . . . that's on the other side of the Commercial Road.

The killer's been having a gala night!

This'll cause some trouble, you see, Gerard. It'll be the biggest manhunt England's ever seen. The police daren't let him get away with another.

Have you seen the bodies?

I got a look at the one in Mitre Square. The other one's been taken away.

What time was it found?

This one? Only about an hour ago. We were just on our way back to the office when we got the flash. We got here before anyone else got on the scene.

Thanks for ringing me.

That's OK. This kind of thing can be very useful to a writer. As a matter of fact, it's the first murder I've ever been engaged on so closely. But it's fantastic, you know, Gerard. He must have killed the woman in Berner Street, and then come straight on down here, and killed again within fifteen minutes.

Have you phoned your story through?

Of course! We nearly got a scoop. First on the scene, photographs and everything.

Sorme had a sense of speaking in an excited babble; there were a dozen questions he wanted to ask, but they crowded one another out of his mind. He said:

Tell me about it in detail. Tell me exactly what happened.

I can't. We don't know the full story ourselves yet.

I mean – tell me what's been happening to *you* all night.

In a moment. We're nearly there.

How was she killed?

This one? Throat cut. But she'd been mutilated pretty badly.

How?

Her face slashed and stabbed all over.

Christ!

Payne said shortly: Made me feel pretty sick.

They turned into a narrow street; looking up at the sign, Sorme saw its name – Duke Street. Payne said:

Ugh! They've started to crowd already.

In the faint light, they could see people crowded half way up the street. Payne said:

We'd better go round the other way. There's only a narrow alley leading into the square from this side.

Sorme asked: What do you think will happen now? It's bound to cause a panic.

There's no telling. I've got a suspicion the Government wants the papers to keep the murders in the headlines to distract attention from the international situation.

That's an interesting idea! You think it might be the Foreign Office behind the murders?

Wouldn't be surprised! They say it's full of sexual perverts . . . not the kind that are interested in women, though.

They turned off Aldgate again, and into the street that ran parallel with Duke Street. It was a narrow street, and the crowd blocked it from pavement to pavement.

Payne said resignedly:

You won't see much, I'm afraid. You should have come with me last night.

Fear and excitement stirred his intestines. The street was silent; its stillness produced an atmosphere of tension and foreboding. As they came nearer, he realized that people were talking to one another in low voices, standing in groups. One of the largest groups was made up of photographers with flashlight cameras. Payne approached these. He asked:

Anything happened, Ted?

A short, plump man with a red face said:

Hello. Back again? No – nothing yet.

His hands were thrust deep into the pockets of a heavy overcoat. Outside this, knotted around his neck, he wore a woollen scarf with bands of colour like a school scarf.

Macmurdo here yet?

Yes. Came ten minutes ago. He's in there.

He nodded towards the rope barrier that separated the street from the square. Get a picture?

Yes. He didn't like it.

About time he got used to it! one of the photographers said. He spat into the gutter.

Sorme approached the barrier. It was not difficult to get close; the crowd was not packed tightly. There was nothing to see. On the left-hand side of the square was a tall warehouse, labelled 'Kearley and Tonge'. The only exit from the square seemed to be a narrow alleyway in the far right-hand corner. The police were crowded in this corner; two of them were doing something with a tape measure, crouched on the pavement. Between the legs of the police, Sorme could see the body, covered with a cloth.

Somewhere on the far side of the square a woman began to howl; it was not a scream, but a harsh cry from the throat. The people standing near Sorme began to take an interest. One of them said:

'Ello! Somebody recognized her?

A woman answered: No. Nobody's been near it.

The howling stopped suddenly. Payne came over to him.

Any idea what it was, Gerard?

No. It came from the alley over there.

Payne approached one of the policemen standing by the rope barrier; he held out his Press card, asking:

Can I go across?

No. I'm afraid you can't, sir. My orders is to let no one across. Not till the pathologist comes.

Is that what they're waiting for?

That's right.

Who is it? Simpson?

I dunno, sir. All I know is, 'e's being a ruddy long time.

Another policeman came over from the group in the corner. Payne asked him:

Any idea what the yelling was about?

The policeman, a middle-aged sergeant, said indifferently:

Just some woman havin' 'ysterics.

One of the men standing near the barrier pressed forward belligerently. He said:

I should bladdy well think so too. What are you blokes doin' for your wage packets, I'd like to know?

A fat woman, wearing a shawl over her head, said:

Now, Bert, don't start gettin' nasty. They're doin' their best.

The man said dogmatically:

I'm not nasty. I got a right as a taxpayer to know why the police haven't done nothing, 'aven't I?

The sergeant seemed unperturbed.

Another journalist had pushed up behind Sorme. He asked: Any idea who she is yet, Sergeant?

Not yet.

Well, why do they keep on gettin' murdered, that's what I want to know?

A tall, skinny man had taken up the argument from

283

behind the woman in the shawl; his voice was nervous and high-pitched. The sergeant looked at him slowly, then shrugged:

That's what we all want to know.

He turned, and began to walk back towards the body. The man called after him:

And that's what you buggers are paid for – to find out!

Payne said in Sorme's ear:

There's a lot of feeling against the police.

I'm not surprised.

Payne began to edge out of the crowd. He said:

Come on. There's nothing to see.

A heavily built man with a blond moustache came up behind Payne, and clapped him on the shoulder. Payne said:

Hello, Tom! Only just arrived?

The big man chuckled:

Not likely. I was here before you were awake.

You weren't, you know! We were first on the scene. We were already in Whitechapel when the alarm came.

Were you? In that case, I apologize.

That's all right, old boy. Ask me any questions you like. I charge a small fee, of course.

Payne turned to Sorme, saying:

You don't know Tom Mozely, do you, Gerard? This is Gerard Sorme, Tom.

Is he on the *Chronicle* too?

No. Gerard's a writer . . .

Mozely interrupted:

By the way – did you hear that woman shrieking?

Yes. What was it?

Somebody started a rumour that the police had found a crowbar with blood on it, and this woman just started to yell. I was standing a few yards from her . . . made my hair stand on end.

284

Have they found a crowbar?

No. It was just a rumour. Did you see the other body?

Yes. We were there when the news of this one arrived.

Is it true she'd been bashed over the head?

Yes. Looked like just one blow.

Hmmm . . . Doesn't sound like our bloke, does it?

I don't know. He was probably interrupted.

Sorme said:

What happened?

Before Payne could reply, someone began to call:

Make way there!

An ambulance was nosing into the barrier. Flashlight cameras began to explode, revealing the square for a moment as if by lightning. Payne said:

It looks like Starr.

Who?

The pathologist.

Sorme looked with interest at the square-shouldered man, with the good-tempered face of a farmer, who was pushing his way into the square. Payne immediately pushed after him, grasping Sorme by the sleeve. The constable stopped them, replacing the rope; whereupon the crowd re-formed in packed ranks across the entrance to the square. Payne said:

I wanted to get a place to watch this.

What happens now?

Nothing much. They just shift the body. Look at the faces of some of these people.

Sorme looked cautiously around him and saw set, unemotional faces. There was none of the curiosity or morbid excitement he had expected. He whispered:

They look pretty grim.

Payne nodded briefly, staring across the square. The police formed a circle around the body, and the patholo-gist knelt beside it. His examination was brief; he dictated something to a girl, who scribbled on a notepad. He stood up and made a sign to the ambulance men, who carried a grey metal shell and placed it beside the body. Their legs masked it as they lifted it; Sorme could see only the torn hem of a skirt that trailed on the ground as the body swung into the shell. A moment later the doors of the ambulance closed behind it, and the engine started. The policeman removed the rope again, saying: Make way there.

The crowd began to break up. From the warehouse across the square an old man emerged carrying a bucket and a sweeping brush; he splashed water on the pavement where the body had lain, and scrubbed at it with the brush. The ambulance moved slowly out of the square. A sudden feeling of chill passed down Sorme's back, making him shiver. He turned away, past the window of the small shop, meeting briefly the cardboard smile of a girl in a toothpaste advertisement. For a moment, he experienced an intuition of the state of mind of the murderer, the revolt against the abstract blandishments, the timeless grimaces, the wooden benedictions that preside over railway carriages and roadside hoardings.

Payne said:

Let's go and get some tea.

Good idea, Mozely said.

Coming, Gerard?

Yes.

You look all in. Tired still?

A little.

A group of photographers walked in front of them. The sky was light now. He allowed himself to lag behind both groups, anxious to concentrate on the insight until it faded, aware of his inability to express it in words. He was hungry: in the café he would eat. How could any insight survive the unending tides of the blood, the body's seasons? The struggle was lost in advance.

Payne said:

You sit down, Gerard. I'll bring the teas over.

I want something to eat too.

All right. I'll get it. Cheese roll?

He sat beside Mozely at a corner table; the reporter was making shorthand notes on a pad. The photographers were occupying a table near the window. He felt tired, discouraged by the prospect of the ride back to Camden Town. Mozely looked up at him suddenly:

What did you think of it?

Of what?

The way everybody reacted?

They all seemed pretty subdued, I must say.

That's the word. Subdued.

Payne sat down opposite them. He said:

Can you wonder? This makes six murders in a few months. They're beginning to wonder how many more.

Do you think it's the fault of the police?

What can they do? They can only follow up every clue and keep hoping he'll slip up.

Happened in the Cummins case, Mozely said.

What was that? Sorme asked.

During the war. He was a sexual maniac. He killed four women – mostly prostitutes – in the Soho area. Finally, someone interrupted him while he was strangling a girl in a doorway in the Haymarket. He ran off and left his gasmask case behind, so they got him . . . But the interesting thing is this. When he was interrupted in the last case, he promptly went off and found another girl in Paddington, and tried to kill her too. She got away as well.

Payne said:

287

That was before my time. Anyway, do you really think this bloke's a sexual maniac?

Mozely said, shrugging:

He's a maniac of some sort; that's a dead cert.

Sorme ate the cheese roll hungrily; when he had finished it, he crossed to the counter and bought another. When he returned to the table, Payne was saying:

. . . and he saw someone bending over the body. He shouted Is there anything wrong? And the man said: Yes. I think she's dead. Go and get a copper, quick! When the man got back five minutes later, the man had gone – there was only this woman.

What's this? Sorme asked.

The first murder last night.

Do they think the man was the murderer?

I don't know. It sounds likely.

Mozely said:

They'll soon find out when they discover how long she'd been dead.

Sorme said:

Could the man describe the bloke who sent him for the policeman?

No. It was in the dark, and he says he didn't go within ten yards. I shouldn't be surprised if he wasn't afraid of bumping into the murderer!

How was she killed?

A blow on the head. It must have been a tremendous blow with a bar of some kind.

And the other woman had her throat cut? He certainly varies his methods!

Sorme asked:

Do you think it sounds like the Greenwich killer?

Mozely shook his head.

I doubt it. You know what it sounds like, don't you?

Payne interrupted:

As if the killer got a bit fed-up about the headlines asking if he'd moved south of the river?

Exactly.

The three of them drank their tea in silence.

Mozely said finally:

What I can't understand is this. He must have got blood on his clothes after that second murder. And he *must* have passed a policeman as he was getting away. The place was alive with them. How did he do it?

He could have had a car parked near the scene of the murder, Sorme said.

Too dangerous. The police take the number of every car parked around here at night. The risk would be too great.

Payne said:

Whoever he is, he either has amazing courage or he's insane.

Insane, Mozely said.

But he must be after something in Whitechapel . . . either that, or he lives here. Or why should he stick to this area?

He's not after anything, Mozely said. How could he be? He doesn't seem to pick his victims. He just takes anybody who comes along. Have you come across this Leather Apron idea?

No. What's that?

Oh, a lot of people think it's a chap called Leather Apron. Nobody seems to know who he is or what he does, except that he's a foreigner, and terrorizes some of the whores around here.

Payne asked:

Have you mentioned him in your story?

Yes. I don't think it'll come to anything, but I heard his name mentioned half a dozen times this morning.

Did you ask any questions?

Of course. No luck. He seems to be just a name.

It might be worth following up, Payne said.

Have you heard this story about the foreign crime experts? They say there are several on the case now.

Sorme said:

I've heard about that. There's some German . . . I forget his name . . .

Mozely said: By the way, did you read that letter in *The Times* yesterday?

No.

Very interesting. Apparently there were several murders at a place called Bochum in Germany after the war – just like these. The man apparently wrote a letter to the police saying he'd kill six more women, then stop. The murders stopped immediately after his letter.

And they never caught him?

No.

Payne laughed softly:

I heard a theory the murderer was a Turk who killed several women in Istanbul. They'd need a special branch of the United Nations to follow up all the stories!

Sorme finished drinking his tea, staring at the crumbs left on his plate; he was trying to imagine what he would do if he met the murderer on a dark night in Whitechapel. He imagined him as a thin man, middle-aged and bald-headed, with bloodless lips, and the eyes of a fanatic. The thought that, at that moment, somewhere in London, the murderer was free, perhaps drinking tea beside some woman in a café, or hanging on a strap in the Underground, produced a lurching sensation of the stomach.

Mozely stood up suddenly. He said:

Oh well, back to work! You coming yet, Bill?

No. I'll have another cup of tea first.

Sorme stood up, pushing his chair forward, to allow Mozely to pass, Mozely said:

Thanks, old man. Well, bye-bye. If you get any line on Leather Apron, you might let me know . . .

I will, Payne said. You just go back to your office and have a good sleep. Leave it to Payne.

As Mozely went out, Payne crossed to the counter, saying,

More tea for you, Gerard?

Please. But let me get them.

No! I get it off expenses.

He brought the teas in their thick cups and set them on the dull surface of scratched plastic. He stretched and yawned.

I must go back and get some sleep. How you feeling, Gerard?

Half dead.

Are you sorry I got you out of bed so early?

No! I'm glad you did. It was interesting . . .

Why?

Anything that gives you a sense of reality is interesting. Somehow, I'd never realized these murders really happened. Why do you think somebody does something like this, Bill?

That depends. It depends on who he is. If he's a university professor, the reasons will be different from if he's a drunken navvy or a sex-crazed teenager . . .

Sorme said: Whoever he is, he's alive somewhere in London at this moment . . . and has friends who probably don't even suspect . . .

Abruptly, as he passed Smithfield Market, he decided to visit Father Carruthers. It was a fortuitous decision, taken with no definite motive that he was aware of.

The Hungarian priest opened the door. Sorme had anticipated that his hour of calling might seem unusual, but Father Rakosi showed no surprise; he had been seated in the depressingly cold waiting-room for only a few moments when the priest returned.

Father Carruthers will see you now.

Thank you. I'm sorry to disturb you.

He received a curiously shy smile in return.

Father Carruthers was standing by the bookcase, wearing a red quilted dressing-gown; standing, he seemed small, almost dwarf-like. He looked better than last time Sorme had called.

Ah, Gerard. How are you?

Well, thanks. You look better.

I feel better this morning . . . Well, this is rather an early hour for you to call. Is anything wrong?

Nothing special, father. I've been in Whitechapel since seven o'clock.

Why?

A journalist friend called me. You've heard about this double murder?

No. What has happened?

He lowered himself into the deep armchair, his knees towards the coal fire that filled the room with oppressive heat. Sorme said:

Two women were murdered in the night – within half an hour of one another.

And why have you been to Whitechapel?

Sorme recognized the relevancy of the question. He said uncomfortably:

Oh . . . simply because my friend happened to call me up . . . It's interesting for a writer . . .

He knew, as he said it, that it was untrue; he also felt a curious certainty that the priest knew it too. But the ugly, silenus face showed no sign of disbelief. The priest only said:

You look tired.

I am.

There was a knock at the door. The priest called: Hello?

A short, white-haired man looked into the room. His eyes wandered from Father Carruthers to Sorme.

Good morning, Larry. Am I interrupting?

His voice was deep and resonant; the accent was distinctly German. The priest said:

Hello, Franz. No, you're not interrupting. Come in.

The German came into the room, closing the door carefully behind him. He took the priest's right hand in both his own, and shook it gravely, asking:

Well, and how is my friend this morning? You look better.

I feel better today, thank you. Franz, let me introduce you to Gerard Sorme. This is Professor Stein of Düsseldorf.

Stein turned to Sorme, and made a slight bow. The keen, old man's face was square and clean-cut; above the jutting chin, the line of the lips was tight and straight, and the eyes were as hard and clear as blue glass. The shock of white hair combined with the features to give the face an impression of great power; it seemed incongruous on the short, plump body. Sorme shook his hand, and found himself also bowing slightly in return. Stein said:

I hope I am not interrupting a conversation?

Not at all. I'm just a casual caller.

Like myself then, Stein said. He smiled charmingly at Sorme, and began struggling out of his overcoat. As Sorme helped him, he said:

It's abominably hot in here, Larry. I'm sure it can't be good for you. Ah . . . thank you, sir.

His German accent made the colloquial English sound quaint. Sorme placed the coat on the bed. Stein said:

With your permission, Larry, I shall sit by my coat. I have no wish to be toasted.

The window's open, the priest said mildly.

Stein produced a handkerchief and blew his nose with a loud, trumpeting noise. He then opened a snuffbox and offered it in turn to the priest and to Sorme. Sorme said:

No, thanks.

He watched with secret amusement as the two men snuffed the brown powder with the air of connoisseurs. The priest brushed a few spots off the front of his dressing-gown. He said:

Well, Franz, have you been rooting around White-chapel too?

Stein looked surprised.

You've heard already? I didn't realize that you read the journals.

I don't. Our friend Gerard has been there.

Stein looked at Sorme: he asked, frowning: You live there?

No, I don't, Sorme said. I just . . . went there when I heard about the murders.

You must have heard very early!

I did. A journalist friend rang me at six this morning. Excuse my asking, but are you connected with the investigation?

I . . . er . . . I am connected with them . . . in a sense. I am a pathologist as well as a doctor of psychology. But tell me, why did you wish to – er – visit the scene of the crimes?

Sorme felt himself colouring; he was aware of the priest's eyes as he answered:

I'm a writer. It's an interesting experience.

Most certainly it is, Stein said emphatically. Such experience is invaluable to a writer. Heinrich Mann made just that remark within my hearing once . . . that very few serious writers have written of murder with authenticity – Zola excepted, perhaps. You know *Thérèse Raquin*?

I'm afraid not.

Stein turned to the priest, saying:

But these murders are really terrible! You talk of human wickedness, my friend, but if you had thirty years, as I have, dealing with crime and violence, you would speak only of human sickness.

Sorme waited for the priest to reply; when he only smiled, Sorme asked:

Do you suppose this man is insane?

Stein turned his piercing eyes on Sorme.

How can we know, until he is caught? The murders prove only one thing – that his condition is pathological.

The priest asked: Do you think the police are any nearer to catching him?

Who can tell? They have received two letters written by a man who claims to be the murderer. That may help.

Sorme said with interest: Have they? Has this been made public yet?

Today, I think. I personally think they are practical jokes.

What did they say?

Oh . . . they jeer at the police for failing to catch him, and promise more murders. The latest was delivered this morning, a few hours after the second murder.

That sounds like the murderer.

Why? Anyone living in Whitechapel could have written the letter in the available time. Even you. You were told of the murder at six o'clock, you say? The letter was posted at Scotland Yard at about seven o'clock.

Sorme said smiling: I see your point. But what I really meant was that it sounds like the murderer to write to the police.

Why do you say that?

Yesterday the newspapers were asking if he'd moved to Greenwich. Last night, he commits a double murder in

Whitechapel. He sounds like a man with a sense of being in the public eye!

Stein said, smiling: That is true. Nevertheless, I suspect a practical joker.

For any particular reason? Sorme asked. He spoke with a cautious politeness, aware that he was in a privileged position in being able to question Stein, and anxious not to appear morbidly curious. Stein interlaced his fingers, and stared gravely at his knees; he appeared to find Sorme's questions perfectly natural.

To begin with, the pathological killer is not often a boaster. You see, his crimes are often due to an overpowering impulse, and when the impulse disappears he may become a completely different person. In Germany we have a name for this type of crime. We call it *Lustmord* – joy murder. Motiveless joy murder. And the joy-murderer is not often proud of the impulse that turns him into a wild animal periodically. You see?

The priest said softly:

But if I remember rightly, your friend Kürten wrote to the police.

That is true. But not to boast – only to draw attention to a body. And then perhaps you remember the case of the Chicago murderer – I forget his name – who wrote above one of his victims: Stop me before I kill again.

Heirens, Sorme murmured.

Ah, you know the case! Well, you see, that is the schizophrenic murderer.

He turned to the priest, and an almost mischievous smile passed across his face. He said:

Now you see, Larry, why I had to become a psychiatrist rather than a priest. How could I prescribe penances for sins when I am not sure that the man who performs the penance is the same man who commits the sins? That is a problem you can't answer me.

The priest said, smiling.

We also recognize your split personality in the Church you know, Franz. But we talk of sin and remorse instead. It all comes to the same thing . . .

Stein chuckled throatily. It was obvious that he enjoyed luring the priest into discussions. He said:

No, no, Larry. It is not the same thing at all. When you prescribe a penance, you assume the man who committed the sin is the same as the one who will do penance. But what if they are two different people, eh? What about that?

The priest said quietly:

I wouldn't prescribe a penance for such a man.

No? Stein said, raising his bushy eyebrows. And what would you do?

Try to help him, just as you would.

And how can you help him, if your only way of describing his condition is in concepts like sin?

The priest said:

I need only two concepts to understand his condition – spirit and matter.

Stein said, smiling: Not even God and the devil?

Not even God and the devil.

Then tell me, sir, how you would explain a man like Kürten in these terms?

I'd have to think about it . . .

Ah! You said that last time we argued!

He turned to Sorme and winked, saying:

He is a very difficult fellow to argue with. All these Dominicans are the same . . . When you get them in a corner, they demand time to think!

The priest's expression remained mild and thoughtful. He said slowly:

Very well, if you want me to try to explain . . . I would express it this way. Man knows himself as body, and what

297

he knows of spirit comes through grace. The poet would call it inspiration. But the spirit bloweth where it listeth. Man has no control over his inspiration. If a piece of music or a poem has moved him once, he can never be certain that it will happen again. But man hates to think that he has no control over the spirit. It would discourage him too much. He likes to believe that he can summon the spirit by some ordinary act. Instead of striving to prepare himself for it through discipline and prayer, he tries to summon it arbitrarily through some physical act – drinking Düsseldorf beer, for instance . . .

Stein said, chuckling:

Which is the way all good Düsseldorfers summon the spirit, since our *Dunkelbier* is the best in Germany.

The priest laughed with him, and for a moment Sorme had a curious impression that he was listening to an argument between two undergraduates instead of two men in their late sixties. He shrank deeper into his armchair, wanting them to forget his presence. The priest stopped laughing first, and Sorme had a glimpse of the tiredness that always lay behind his eyes. Stein also became grave again. He said:

Very well. But what has this to do with the murderer?

It has to do with sex. For sex is the favourite human device for summoning the spirit. And since it is also God's gift of procreation, it nearly always works . . . unlike music and poetry.

Or beer, Stein said.

Quite. But even sex is not infallible. And man hates to think that he has no power over the spirit. The more his physical methods fail him, the more voraciously he pursues them. His attempts to summon the spirit become more and more frenzied. If he is a drinker, he drinks more, until he has more alcohol than blood in his veins. If he is a sensualist, he invents sexual perversions.

Ah, Stein said.

There are many other ways, of course – the lust for money and power, for instance. All depend upon man's refusal to face the fact that the spirit bloweth where it listeth, that no physical act can be guaranteed to summon it . . .

Sorme had forgotten his resolution to keep silent. He said:

But is there *no* certain way of summoning it, father?

The priest went on looking at Stein as he answered:

None. The best we can do is to train ourselves in patience. When the priest invokes the descent of the spirit in the Mass, he does not expect to see it or feel it; he accepts by faith that the wine has become the blood of our Lord, the bread His flesh. The priest knows that all he can do is wait. The business of religion is to teach men patience. As soon as man loses patience, he loses all he has . . .

So! Stein said. What am I to tell my patient who feels an urge to rape a child? To have patience?

The priest said, with unexpected sharpness:

What else? Why does he want to rape the child? Can you explain it?

Stein shrugged:

It usually springs from a feeling of insecurity. Or boredom. Many of my patients have complained that they feel a perpetual sense of injustice – that they have a right to lead more interesting lives. A sexually frustrated man will try to express his sense of injustice in sexual murder.

The priest had begun to look tired; his voice had become low and monotonous:

Religion teaches that all men are equal in the sight of God, that the beggar is no better off than the king, that all men die and are subject to the same miseries. If a man felt that, how could he feel a desire to rape a child?

Stein said: True. But a man would need to be a philosopher to feel that, and most psychopaths are not philosophers . . .

The priest said quietly: He would need to be a philosopher . . . or a Christian.

Stein stood up. He said: Perhaps you are right, my friend. But I think we should leave you. I think we are beginning to tire you a little.

Sorme could not help smiling at the injustice of the 'we'.

The priest said: It is kind of you to come and see me.

Stein said, smiling: I like seeing you.

He turned to Sorme, and said: We have known one another for nearly fifty years.

Sorme said politely: Really?

So! Stein said. We leave you to your meditations.

The priest said: You must come in again, Gerard.

Thank you, father. I'd like to.

Have you seen Austin since you came here last?

Yes. Quite a lot. I'd like to talk about him some time, father . . . By the way, father . . .

He glanced uncomfortably at Stein before formulating the question, then went on:

Does . . . Mrs Nunne know about . . . Austin?

The priest took his meaning immediately. He said quickly:

No. Why?

I wondered. His aunt – a Jehovah's Witness – found out through some busybody friend of hers. But I don't think she'd mention it to his parents.

Stein had put on his overcoat, and was standing by the door. The powerful face was beaded with perspiration; it was obvious he found the room oppressive. Sorme said:

Well, goodbye, father . . .

300

Goodbye, Gerard. Goodbye, Franz. I hope you'll come again next time you pass by. Both of you.

Auf Wiedersehen, Larry. I shall certainly come.

Sorme followed the short, broad-shouldered figure down the stairs. Stein said over his shoulder:

I could see he was becoming tired. He tires very easily.

Quite.

They let themselves out of the front door. Sorme said: Well, goodbye, Professor. I hope we shall meet again.

You are not walking this way?

No. This is my bicycle.

Ah. I see. Very sensible. Well . . . perhaps you would care to join me in a cup of coffee?

Sorme said: I'd be delighted!

It surprised him that the German should ask. While he had been in the priest's room, he had been certain that Stein regarded him as a superfluous third. He felt suddenly friendly towards the little man. He replaced the bicycle clips in his pocket, and walked beside Stein along Rosebery Avenue, and into the Farringdon Road. As they walked, Stein explained:

Larry and I studied together in Rome forty years ago. At that time I was to become a Jesuit. Imagine me!

What happened?

I discovered the writings of Freud, and changed my mind!

The German gave a throaty chuckle.

Didn't you have to study medicine, though?

I did. My parents preferred that I become a doctor rather than a priest, so we had no disagreement. I left Rome, and went to Vienna to seek out Freud . . .

The café was empty; a woman was cleaning the stone floor with a mop and a bucket. She stood the mop in the corner, and dried her hands on her apron to serve them coffee. Stein produced a packet of Manikin cigars, and offered it to Sorme. He lit one, and leaned back in his chair, puffing meditatively until the coffee arrived. As the woman leaned between them he looked across at Sorme, and asked suddenly:

How is Austin nowadays?

Taken unawares, Sorme said with surprise:

You know Austin?

I . . . know him slightly. But I know a great deal of him.

With instant certainty, Sorme knew that this was the reason Stein had asked him for coffee. He said:

Oh, he's very well, thanks.

He poured the jug of cream into his coffee, and left the next move to Stein.

You are a close friend of his?

Sorme looked into the ice-blue eyes, and wondered at the defensiveness that rose in him.

I know him fairly well. He interests me greatly . . .

Stein smiled suddenly. Leaning forward, he said quietly:

You do not have to be alarmed. I know about him through Larry. I know that he is a sadist.

Why are you interested, if you don't mind my asking?

Not at all. You do not have to repeat any of this to him . . .

No.

He was in Düsseldorf for a time, and he was known to the police. Nothing serious, of course, but I came to know of it through my connection with the police.

Stein leaned back, and drew deeply on his cigar. He gave the impression that the subject had suddenly ceased to interest him. Sorme drank his coffee, allowing the silence to lengthen. He was wondering whether Stein was to be trusted, and what Stein thought he might be able to tell him about Nunne. Stein caught his eye and smiled, as if they were two passengers in a railway carriage who happened to be facing one another. Sorme said:

Professor, I'd like you to answer me a question, if you would . . . Has Austin any reason to be afraid of the police?

Stein answered promptly:

As far as I know, no. Can *you* think of any?

No. But then I'm neither a homosexual nor a sadist.

I see. But tell me, why are you Austin's friend if you have so little in common with him?

I happen to like him . . .

Quite. There is nothing strange about that. How long have you known him?

Sorme said, smiling: Precisely a week.

Sorme could almost see the disappointment and loss of interest. Stein stubbed out the cigar and emptied his coffee cup. He said:

You should talk to Larry about Austin. He knows him better than I do. But allow me to presume to offer you a piece of advice. You may believe you can have a relationship with Austin in which his homosexuality and sadism are unimportant. But don't take this for granted. He may surprise you.

Sorme said: Thanks, I won't.

Stein looked at him steadily for a moment, the bushy eyebrows drawn together. Then he said briefly:

Good.

He stood up, and dropped a half-crown on the counter. The woman said: Thank you, sir.

Outside again, in the dull light of the Farringdon Road, Stein said:

Larry is a remarkable man. But he will not live a great deal longer. If you like him, you should see him as much as you can.

I will. I like him very much although I've known him for less than a week.

Really? You are a person who makes many acquaintances?

No. I'm not.

No? Well . . . I must say goodbye. Or rather, *auf Wiedersehen*. We shall meet again.

Sorme shook the outstretched hand; the grip was strong. He stood there, watching Stein walk in the direction of the Embankment, the white head thrown back.

He locked the door of his room, and lit the gas fire; his hands and feet were numb. The knees of his trousers were wet; it had begun to rain as he passed St Pancras. He removed the trousers and shirt, and slipped on his dressing-gown, then filled the kettle with water and set it on the gas. He sat with his legs stretched out to the fire, too sleepy to read, surprised at the inner silence that took possession of him as he stared at the red-hot fire. It was complete concentration and certainty. His tongue probed his teeth, found a hollow that needed filling, and sucked at it. But there was no sense of urgency, no guilty feeling about his procrastination. He reached out for the book on the table – it was *The Trial of John Watson Laurie* – and began to read the introduction. After reading a few pages, he dropped it on the floor. The story of the Arran murder seemed commonplace and boring compared with the Whitechapel crimes. The kettle boiled; he made tea, and got into bed to drink it, turning the gas fire low, now feeling completely warmed and relaxed. As he drank, he felt a temptation to write in his journal, to try to record the insight that was growing inside him. Only the fear of destroying it by trying to intellectualize it restrained him. When he had finished the tea he placed the cup on the chair and sat staring at the opposite wall, not fully aware of it, but knowing that he had achieved the state of creativity that had eluded him for the past year. It seemed ironical, almost funny. He was in his own room; the door was locked, in case Carlotte came to summon him to the phone; she would then assume he was out. He felt suddenly as if the world had contracted within the confines of his four walls, and there were no more doubts. What he had achieved was only a certainty of his own existence, it was a recovery of subjectivity. He thought: the man who possesses his subjectivity possesses everything; and knew it to be true. But it was difficult to keep awake. The insight brought a sense of acceptance, of affirmation, that tempted him to lie down and close his eyes. He was at once lying on a hillside above the sea, lulled to sleep by sunlight and insects, and standing on the walls of the palace at Mycenae, watching the soldiers drilling in the courtyard. All poetry and philosophy were contained in the certainty.

To defeat the drowsiness, he switched on the gramophone, and put a record of Sibelius on the turntable. The first notes of the symphony intensified the insight, an awareness of his past. The sensation reminded him of his dream of Nunne in the brothel, and Nunne made him think of Nijinsky. It was all that Nijinsky had ever meant to him, concentrated into one emotion. It was belief; belief in himself, and in life, and in God. He felt like saying: I accept life. I accept everything.

He thought, with a kind of blank wonderment: I have recovered it. I have recovered my subjectivity. If I could live like this all the time, I'd never doubt again.

Unreality. Unreality is loss of subjectivity. For five years I have lived in an unreal city. Now it is *my* city.

It was becoming more difficult to bear the insight. He made a mental act of turning from it, closing his perceptions. A sort of cool darkness supervened. As the first

305

movement of the symphony came to an end, he reached out and turned it off, then lay down.

Before sleeping, he set the alarm for half past four, remembering Caroline. He felt exhausted and purified, and the thought of seeing her was pleasant.

When he woke, the fire was out. The winter afternoon was already turning dark. It was not yet half past four. He reached out for the clock and pressed in the switch that would prevent the alarm from ringing, then got out of bed and switched on the light. He took the new trousers out of the wardrobe and put them on; the knees of the other pair were still damp. As he was transferring his money into the new ones, and searching for a shilling for the gas, he sneezed. It cleared his head. He filled a cup with cold water, drank it down without lowering it from his lips. It dissipated the last of the drowsiness. The mood of certainty had still not disappeared. He put on his jacket, took his heavy overcoat from the wardrobe, and went downstairs. There was a winter smell in the air, a mixture of smoke, coldness and dusk. He walked down Great College Street, past the lighted shop windows, and found it necessary to suppress a desire to run and laugh aloud.

When he let himself back into the room, it was a quarter to six. The shops had been crowded with late Friday shoppers, and hung with banners with the inscription 'Shop Early for Christmas'. He stood the two bottles of white wine on the windowsill, near the open window. For the next quarter of an hour he swept the room, dusted the books, and re-made the bed with clean sheets. He collected together the greasy plates, still unwashed from the supper of the previous night, and the cups and glasses and took these up to the kitchen. While the kettle boiled, he read the evening paper, sitting at the enamel-topped table. The front page dealt with the letters received by the police, and quoted both of them in full. There was a photograph of one of them with the caption: Do you recognize this writing? The writing itself was an illiterate scrawl, with two blots, but no visible fingerprints. The first letter read:

Dear Boss, So the police are looking high and low for me are they? They'll have to look bloody hard to find old kiddo, because he's allergic to flatties. But he'll keep you all entertained with more saucy work if you don't try to rush him. Next time, he'll clip off the ladies' ears and send them to you. I'm not a commie, so don't let the sods take credit for my risks. your faithful servant: Leather Apron. P.S. Please keep this letter back til I can do some more work.

The second letter was shorter:

Dear Boss, I was not kidding when I promised some more work. Got interupted on both jobs, so couldn't get the ears. Will send later. I got some of the real red stuff to write this but it went thick. Thanks for keeping back my first letter, your faithful servant: Leather Apron.

The report stated that both letters were written in red ink, and that both were free from fingerprints.

Hello, Gerard!

The voice from the bottom of the stairs startled him. As she came up, he said:

Blimey, sweet, you nearly gave me heart failure!

Sorry.

He put his arms round the heavy overcoat and kissed her, then lifted the large collar and pressed it against her ears, kissing her cold nose and eyelids. She said:

Mmm! You need a shave!

I know. I'm just about to have one.

Can I help you cook?

No thank you, sweet. You can go and sit in front of the fire and play yourself some music.

As her lips brushed past his cheek, she whispered:

I don't have to go home tonight. I've told mummy I'm staying at an all-night party.

Good.

She asked: Why are you smiling?

At what Gertrude'd think if she found out . . .

The neon lights at Camden Town gave him a sense of well-being. He walked with his arm around her, and was suspicious of the pleasure he took in feeling her next to him. He could never cease to be conscious of her inexperience, of the fact that she was nearly ten years his junior.

She said: Darling, I feel horribly drunk.

That's all right. You can sleep it off.

Will your landlady mind, do you think?

She won't know. Nobody need know if you leave fairly late.

He felt a kind of pity for her. Her inexperience made her offer herself with no reservations; it was pleasant and a little frightening.

He opened the front door softly, and sent her in first. As they were mounting the first flight of steps, the telephone started to ring. He said, groaning:

Oh, Christ, if that's Austin I'll have kittens . . . Go on up to my room, sweet. I'll answer it.

He said: Hello?

Could I speak to Carlotte, please?

I'll get her for you.

He called into the basement: Carlotte! He went back up the stairs, muttering underneath his breath: Thank God!

She was lying on the bed, still wearing her overcoat. She said:

Oh, sweet, I feel so drunk . . .

Well, sit up! It makes you feel drunker when you lie down.

Does it?

He collected the greasy plates off the table, and the two empty hock bottles, and took them to the kitchen. He scraped the plates into the wastebin, then placed them in the bowl. He felt too sleepy to go to the bathroom for hot water.

When he got back to the room she was in bed. He felt disappointed; he had hoped to watch her undressing. Her clothes lay across the chair. She lay with her back to him, her face buried in the pillow. He smiled at the blonde head that was almost completely concealed by the sheets; there was something endearing and childlike in her complete lack of any attempt at feminine mystery. Within a few seconds he was in bed beside her, his bare arms encountering the nakedness of her shoulders with a physical shock.

He had been right in supposing her sleepiness would not withstand the strangeness of sleeping with a man for the first time. She turned over immediately, and put her arms around his neck. Exultation bubbled up in him; he remembered the frustration on the boat, and later on her bed at Gertrude Quincey's, and his suspicion that something might prevent him from ever feeling her naked body beside him in bed. It was not true, and the realization seemed to involve some more general truth that he was too excited to examine. A phrase from the Sibelius Third Symphony came into his head, and combined with the pleasure that rose in him as he touched her breast. They lay there in the dark, not speaking, only exploring one another's bodies. At that moment, he felt a desire to engulf her, to absorb her completely. She stopped him as he moved his weight across her.

Is it . . . will it be safe, sweet? I don't want a baby yet!

It'll be all right . . . don't worry . . .

He felt her tense under him. He said:

Bite my shoulder if it hurts. Don't worry.

Oh sweet . . . it . . . it hurts . . . oh, it *does* hurt. Stop it, please.

Her loins tensed, and she writhed away from him. He was not disappointed; on the contrary, he was delighted that he continued to want her, that he had not experienced the usual lurch of the stomach and paralysis of desire, the feeling that it had all been a mistake. He said gently:

Don't get so tense, sweet.

I can't help it. God, does it hurt all girls as much as this?

I expect so.

Have you ever . . . done it before?

Yes . . . but let's not talk about it.

I don't mind, really I don't. I wouldn't like you to be a virgin too.

She suddenly began to giggle.

God, imagine what it must be like when the man's a virgin too . . .!!!

They recognized that in the Middle Ages. You know about the *droit de seigneur*?

No. What is it?

I suspect it was to prevent women from having their first marital experience with an inexperienced husband. The lord of the manor – who was assumed to be an accomplished lover – would sleep with the wife of his tenant on the first night, and take her maidenhead.

Did they really do that?

He had been speaking with the deliberate intention of relaxing her, and he could feel the success of the attempt.

I'm not sure that the custom doesn't still exist in some countries.

He started to kiss her again, and felt her response immediately. As he started to move his weight, he said softly:

Try to help me this time. Relax.

I *do* try, really. I just can't help it. That's right, sweet: it's soothing. I'm sorry I'm not very good, Gerard.

Don't be silly.

I am. I suppose you'd much rather be in bed . . . ooh, sweet, careful . . . oh, it hurts. I . . .

She pressed her clenched teeth against his shoulder, then suddenly wriggled away.

I'm sorry, sweet . . . I can't. It hurts.

Lie still. Don't worry.

He heard a clock somewhere strike three, as he stared into the darkness. He suspected she had just fallen asleep; her breathing was quiet. He now felt no sexual excitement, and no sense of strangeness in her presence. He lay on his back, and remembered previous occasions like this, and the violence of unresolved feeling, forgotten the next morning, but revealing in its upsurge areas of himself that he had never explored. He remembered the girl on the Embankment whose dress had blown over her head, the fever of lust, and thought: perhaps that's all sex is . . . a fever. A cheat. If it had been Caroline, I'd have felt the same lust. Yet she lies here, and I take it calmly. Is it a confidence trick? Supposing I succeeded next time I tried. What would be the difference? She would be my 'mistress', that's all, a symbol of my domination, of success. But would there be any revelations as I made love to her? Would I feel curiously renewed, brushed by a sort of immortality? What about all the D.H. Lawrence stuff? No, he was a fool and a fraud. It *can* be good, but never that good. Never in its own right. Only as a part of your bigger

311

aims. The orgasm is just raw energy, light and heat. What makes it important are the ideals it illuminates.

She sat up suddenly. He asked:

What is it?

I want to go downstairs . . . I'll put my overcoat on . . .

Take my bicycle lamp. It's on the bookcase.

He stretched out in the bed. It was a wide single bed, big enough for two, but it was a luxurious sensation to have it to himself for a moment. The room was not dark. He could see the outline of her clothes on the chair. By reaching out his hand, he could feel the silkiness of the slip between his finger and thumb. It reminded him of a train journey from Liverpool to London; across the gangway sat two schoolgirls, both about fourteen, dressed for the holidays and travelling with large suitcases. One of them was exceptionally slim, and wore a brown tweed skirt; this had slipped about two inches above her knees, showing the elaborately embroidered hem of a nylon petticoat. Her stockings – obviously new for the occasion – were sheer hose. He suspected she was a little proud of the embroidered hem of the slip, for she made only two perfunctory attempts to pull down her skirt in the course of a four-hour journey. At first he had tried to ignore the sight, feeling slightly ashamed of the desire that rose in his throat. He tried staring out of the window, and allowed his imagination to toy with the idea of holding her in his arms. Finally, he had possessed her so completely in imagination that it caused a shock of surprise to look at her – and at the tantalizing area of embroidered nylon – and to realize she was still a stranger. Once she met his eyes, and looked away, blushing. What amazed him was that she still made no attempt to conceal the lacework that hinted at bedrooms and surrender. At Paddington, he seized his bags and rushed along the platform, possessed by a sudden conviction that she would catch the same bus, sit opposite him again for a further half hour, and print her image indestructibly in his brain. But he never saw her again.

If it had been she who was sleeping with him now, whose clothes lay on the chair beside the bed, no fulfilment could ever reproduce the intensity of travelling opposite her from Liverpool to London. It was somehow a cheat, a desire without an object.

Caroline came back into the room; her body was cool as it encountered his. He began to kiss her hard, delighting in the instantaneous reflex of desire that pressed her body against him. This time he made no sudden moves to alarm her, only caressing her as she lay by his side, kissing the hardening nipples. As her body recovered its warmth, her arms tightened around him; the tension in her muscles suggested that she was trying to force their bodies to interpenetrate by physical pressure. His own desire was lagging behind the excitement that constricted her breathing. He allowed himself to be led by her, moving across her, responding as her hands fumbled to adjust their position. He heard her breathe: 'Now', and knew it was successful, encountering warmth where before there had been only resistance. She moaned suddenly: Oh God, it hurts . . . He felt the sharpness of her teeth on his lower lips as the resistance of her loins disappeared. She said: Lie still . . . *still* . . .. Don't move.

He lay there, obediently, his face buried in the pillow, feeling her relax under him. He felt no sexual excitement; there had been no pleasure in the act; now he felt only the detached pleasure of an accomplishment. When he stirred, accidentally, she said instantly: Don't move!

Some time later he had begun to doze, lying in the same position, when she woke him by movements. He had relaxed completely; now, as he began to feel desire, she said: Oh God, it still hurts.

Never mind, sweet. It worked.

She said, in his ear: Yes. I'm not a virgin any more, am I? It's really worked. Oh . . . please stop moving, sweet. Please . . .

He felt her tense underneath him, concentrate on the pain; this time he ignored her, and kept on moving. When her hips began to move rhythmically, he knew it was all right. Abruptly, he knew it was not a cheat. What was happening now was realler than any of his thoughts about sex, more real than anything except pain: it was an intimation of the reason behind the tireless continuity of life. He felt astonished at his own stupidity for not realizing it before. He wanted to make a vow: to accept always, only accept, accept anything, embrace everything with the certainty that all things would yield like this, an engulfing pleasure. Her body was curved up to him, her teeth on his lips, her nails in his back. The light threatened to hurt him, to burn and shatter as it flooded from his loins and stomach and brain.

When their bodies were relaxed, still throbbing, like two cars standing by the roadside after a long race, he asked her: What happened, sweet?

I don't know. It hurt horribly. And I just concentrated – ever so hard – on the pain, just thought of nothing else. Then the pain went, and I was enjoying it.

Chapter Three

She insisted that he stay in bed while she made tea. The thought that she might be seen walking around in his dressing gown alarmed him, but her pleasure was so obvious that he could not bring himself to stop her. He sat up in bed, trying to read, but with only half his attention on the book, listening for the noise of Callet moving around in the next room or Carlotte cleaning the stairs. Caroline was in the bathroom. A few moments later she came out and mounted the stairs; at the same time he heard other footsteps on the lower flight. As she came into the room, he asked:

Who was it?

Who was what?

That.

The noise of footsteps passed his door, and went on up the next flight. She said:

I don't know. I didn't notice.

Probably Carlotte going to clean the old man's room. Unless it's a new tenant.

Footsteps sounded across the floor above them. He said:

You look sweet in that dressing-gown. It needs to be a foot shorter.

She sat on the edge of the bed and kissed him. Even without makeup, and with her hair uncombed, her face looked pink and childlike.

How do you feel this morning?

Sore. Otherwise fine.

Tired?

No. I'll get back into bed if you like!

He pulled her shoulders back on to the bed, and kissed her. There was a heavy thump from overhead. Sorme looked at the ceiling, saying:

Are you there, truepenny?

There was a grinding noise, as of an armchair being moved on castors. Caroline said:

I expect it's the girl tidying the room. Let me up. I'll make the tea.

He watched her as she stopped on the hearthrug, spooning tea into the two pint thermos, and tried to observe the emotions she aroused in him. He was glad he had slept with her; he was glad he knew her body now; but that was all. There was no deeper satisfaction, no assuaged hunger. It was something he could not define. It worried him. The experience had left almost nothing except a slight physical tiredness. He thought: What *do* I want anyway? What do all men want? The need is universal. Caroline . . .

She was getting dressed now, standing naked on the hearthrug in front of the gas fire, slipping into her clothes without self-consciousness. She is a natural mistress. Or wife. Same thing, I suppose. Wants a husband. Thinks she's in love.

But I don't want to be a husband. Nice little hubby, good dog.

I am too many people. Need to express myself. With her body under mine. How else? Watching the dawn rise over Yamdrok Tso or Sadiya. Why not Islington or the Welsh Harp?

> . . . from Islington to Marybone
> To Primrose Hill and Saint John's Wood,
> Were builded over with pillars of gold;
> And there Jerusalem's pillars stood.

Could never kill. Life delights in life. I have too much. Too comfortable. Need a battle to fight.

The press studs at the waist of her skirt engaged with a snap of metal. She poured tea into two mugs through a strainer. She said:

I wish we could go away somewhere. For a long time . . . It'd be nice to live together, wouldn't it?

He said, smiling: Why not? You could move in here.

What about your landlady? What about mummy and daddy? What about Aunt Gertrude? And what about Austin?

Well, what about Austin?

He'd be jealous.

I doubt it . . .

As he was about to take the tea from her, someone knocked on the door. He said softly:

Oh blimey!

He jumped out of bed, and snatched his dressing-gown from the back of the chair, afraid the door would open before he could reach it. He was tying the cord as he opened it; Carlotte said:

There's someone on the phone for you . . .

Oh, thanks . . .

She leaned towards him:

And I'm afraid . . .

She gestured with her head towards the stairs. He stared at her without comprehension.

What?

She said, in a conspiratorial hiss:

He is back!

Who? Not the old man?

She nodded. He was divided between indignant incredulity, and a fear that she might look into his room and see Caroline. He said:

Oh blimey . . . I'd better answer that phone . . .

317

She nodded sympathetically, smiling. Her smile was more friendly and intimate than he had known it before; it increased his alarm in case Caroline appeared behind him. He mumbled:

I'll get my slippers . . .

and closed the door. He raised his finger to his lips to signal Caroline to be silent, and found his slippers. He caught Carlotte half way down the stairs.

Does Mrs Miller know he's back?

Oh yes. She sent him.

She must be mad! Doesn't she care if he sets fire to the place?

The girl turned and looked at him; her eyes were curiously mocking. Her face distorted into a strange grimace that gave it a devilish appearance. She said softly:

`She has increased his rent!

Before he could reply, she had run down the flight of stairs into the basement, and left him staring at the phone that lay on the hall table.

Hello?

Hello, Gerard. Austin . . .

Oh hello. How are you?

I'm OK. Look, can you have lunch with me today?

I . . . yes, I expect so. Any special reason?

Yes. I want you to meet two friends of mine . . .

Who are they?

American writers.

Anyone I know?

Probably not. They're both young. I think you'll find them interesting. They belong to a group called the Chicago rebels. Can you get over here about midday? We'll have a drink, then go to Soho. OK?

OK. Thanks. By the way, I didn't say thanks for the other night . . .

For making you sick, you mean?

No, but . . . you were very sweet.

Not at all, old boy. See you later. OK?

He returned upstairs, feeling how totally unpredictable Nunne could be. The last time he had phoned he sounded like a spoiled child; now he sounded like a protective elder brother.

Who was it?

Austin.

Speak of the devil!

He wanted me to go for lunch. But if you're free for lunch, I can put him off . . .

No, don't worry, darling. I ought to be getting home, otherwise mummy and daddy might start trying to phone the friend I'm supposed to have stayed with last night!

He pulled her to him and kissed her. Her mouth tasted of warm tea. It was a luxury to feel her warmth pressed against him; a sensation like electricity ran through his chest and thighs. As she pressed herself closer, her left arm disengaged itself from his neck, and the hand groped inside the dressing-gown. He said thickly.

What a silly thing to do . . . getting dressed.

He pulled open the press studs at the waist of her skirt, and unzipped it. Helping her with the buttons at the back of the blouse, he noticed that his tea was untouched.

He made love very gently, aware of the tension in her, the fear of being hurt.

They lay side by side, looking at the ceiling. He said:

That old bleeder's back upstairs.

Are you sure?

Afraid so.

He raised on one elbow, and tasted his lukewarm tea. She said:

I'll make you some more.

Don't bother . . . You know, I think I'll ask Austin if

319

he doesn't know of a flat. His father owns half Marylebone. I don't think I can stand this old sod for another week. It'd wreck me.

Someone knocked on the door, startling him. He whispered to Caroline: Ssshh! and slipped out of bed, reaching for the gown.

He expected to see Carlotte. It was the old man. His eyes looked less watery; he was wearing a tweed suit that seemed to be of good quality, and a clean shirt. He smiled shyly:

I'm sorry to bother you, sir, but do you happen to have a match?

His voice was clear and firm. Sorme groped in the dressing-gown pocket, and handed him a box.

Thank you . . . but I won't take the box . . .

That's all right. It's nearly empty.

The old man smiled at him, as if they had some secret reason for liking one another, and dropped the matches in his pocket. He shuffled his feet uncomfortably. Sorme said:

I . . . hope you're . . . better now.

I am. Thank you.

As if Sorme's words had decided him, he turned and walked away. As Sorme started to close the door, he turned round, smiling apologetically.

Perhaps you'd like to see the morning paper?

He pulled a folded newspaper out of his pocket and handed it to Sorme, then disappeared hastily, as if afraid of having committed an indiscretion.

Sorme went back into the room, opening the paper. The headlines read:

HUSBAND ARRESTED FOR GREENWICH MURDER.

Who was it?

Him. He jerked his chin at the ceiling.

He sounded all right.

Oh, he does. He *is* all right till he gets drunk. Which he is for about twenty-three hours a day.

He stood at the table, reading the front page. She was dressing again. He said:

So he didn't move after all.

Who?

The Whitechapel killer.

As he was pulling on his shoes, she said suddenly:

You ought to buy a flat in Whitechapel. I bet the value of property's gone down since these murders.

That's a very clever remark, sweet.

Don't you think?

Why not? Or perhaps Austin and his father are in this together – Austin doing the murders and his father buying the property at cut prices.

She said, grimacing: But I shouldn't think Austin would murder women, would he?

I don't know. I'll ask him when I see him.

He arrived at Albany Street half an hour late. The doorman said:

Ah, Mr Nunne's waiting for you, sir. You haven't brought the other two gentlemen with you, then?

No. No sign of them?

They hadn't arrived five minutes ago, when Mr Nunne rang down.

Nunne opened the door. Sorme said immediately:

I'm sorry I'm late.

That's all right. They haven't arrived yet either. How are you, Gerard? You look tired.

Too much writing, I expect.

Whisky?

Thanks. By the way, Austin, I meant to ask you when we were alone . . . Do you know of any unfurnished flats or rooms around here?

For you?

Yes. I'm thinking of changing.

But my dear boy, you're *always* changing.

I know. Do you remember that old man I told you about?

Yes. Is he out of hospital?

Sorme nodded.

He arrived this morning. So I expect I'll get no sleep until he has another accident.

Nunne sat in the armchair, and lit a cigarette.

There are always ways and means, aren't there?

Seeing Sorme's puzzled look, he said:

We might arrange a little accident, don't you think?

Are you serious?

Quite. For instance . . . The buzzer sounded. Nunne crossed to the door. Alone for a moment, Sorme stared at the bars of the fire, and wondered what new aspect of his personality Nunne was preparing to spring on him. He heard a loud American voice say:

Hiya, man! Good to see ya.

They came into the room, followed by Nunne. Nunne said: That's Gerard Sorme. Gerard, this is Cal Teschmeyer and Rudi James.

The short, Italianate-looking man said affably:

Hiya, Gerard. How're ya?

His friend reached over the back of the chair, patted Sorme on the shoulder, and said in a deep, pleasant voice:

Glad t'meetcha, man.

He flopped into the armchair that Nunne had vacated, letting his arms fall limply over the sides. He had a long, hollow face, with three days' growth of blond stubble on the chin. Like his companion, he wore a leather jacket, with a brightly coloured shirt underneath. The Italian-looking man sat beside Sorme on the divan, saying:

What d'they call you – Jerry?

You can if you like.

Good. I'm Cal and he's Jimmy.

Nunne asked from the sideboard:

What will you have?

Any bourbon?

Yes.

Jimmy turned round in his chair, and peered into the drink cabinet. He whistled shrilly.

Hey, dig that crazy man! He's got a dozen bottles of the stuff in there! We struck lucky, son. Yoohoo!

He sprang up, loped over to Nunne, and seized a bottle with both hands, kissing it fondly. He said throatily:

Boy, am I glad to see you!

Cal asked Sorme:

You a writer?

Sorme said, shrugging: Nothing worth talking about. What do you write?

Novels. Jimmy there writes poetry. He founded his own school . . .

Aw, can it! Jimmy said.

. . . which our friend and sympathetic mentor Professor Trilling . . .

Sonofabitch! Jimmy shouted.

. . . referred to as the diarrhoea school of poetry!

He began to laugh; it was a high laugh that lurched and squeaked; somehow it reminded Sorme of an old car on a bumpy road. Jimmy said vengefully:

Yeah, and ya know what *Time* Magazine said about his last novel . . .?

Nunne handed him a tumbler half full of whisky. He seized it, sniffed it ecstatically, and poured it down his throat immediately. He said affectionately:

Aust'n, I love ya. Ya got what it takes.

He allowed Nunne to pour more whisky, saying with mock belligerence:

Who cares what the bastards say? Like Omar Khayyàm said, 'the dogs bark but the caravan rolls on'.

Nunne handed Cal a glass, asking gravely:

Have you boys been drinking already?

Oh, he's not drunk, Cal said. He's always like this. Ain't ya, daddy-o? He's been talking all night.

What about? Sorme asked.

Oh, God or something.

Jimmy asked: Where d'you keep your records?

In there.

Cal said: Somebody told him about Merejkovsky or something, how these Russians used to sit up all night, and when somebody yawned, they'd say . . .

Jimmy shouted: Hey, wait, lemme tell it. Listen! They'd argue all night, these guys, and when somebody suggested hitting the sack, do you know what they'd say? 'We can't sleep yet. *We haven't decided if God exists.*'

He gave a high whoop of delight, and turned back to the record cabinet. A moment later, he said with admiration:

Hey, man, get this! Miles Davis and Dizzy and – wow! – a whole album of Bird. Can we play some?

Nunne said cautiously:

Don't you think we should go and eat first? It's after one.

Just one, Jimmy said. Just one side of Bird. We can grease later.

Cal asked Sorme: Do you dig bop?

I . . .

Before he could answer, the gramophone drowned his voice. Jimmy lay back on the floor and kicked his feet in the air: he shouted: 'Bells, daddy-o!'

Cal leaned over, and shouted in Sorme's ear:

You a jazz fan?

I don't know much. I like Bix Beiderbecke.

Great! Cal shouted: He gestured at Jimmy. He don't. Thinks it's square stuff.

Sorme glanced cautiously at his watch, wondering how soon he could get away. The noise and strange language struck him as deliberate exhibitionism. He looked up, and caught Nunne regarding him with amused interest: the brown eyes were as soft as an animal's and as sardonic and caressing as a heathen god. For a moment Sorme felt again the curious awe and submission that he had felt before in Nunne's presence; the sense of being with someone of a different species. Nunne closed his eyes and relaxed in the chair.

As the record came to an end, Jimmy sat up. He said sadly:

That gone cat Charlie. He killed himself.

He looked across at Sorme, and Sorme was struck by his sincerity. He asked: What happened to him?

Cal said briefly: Booze and hop.

Little fat guy, Jimmy said. As sweet as they come, but temperamental. We used to know him, on the West coast.

Nunne switched off the gramophone. He said:

Let's go and eat. I'm ravenous.

Sorme followed them out of the room. Jimmy walked with a shambling gait that was almost ape-like. Sorme wondered what Cal meant by 'booze and hop': he presumed 'hop' was another word for 'bebop'; the idea of a short, fat man dancing himself to death struck him as curiously depressing.

The two Americans stopped talking during the meal; they ate voraciously, giving Sorme the impression they hadn't eaten for days. But when Nunne asked casually, Hungry? Cal said:

I ate a big breakfast. That always makes me eat like hell for the rest of the day.

They drank the wine like beer, in long pulls. Jimmy said abruptly:

Trouble with British writers, you don't kick enough.

Kick who? Sorme asked.

Anybody. F'rinstance – what you writing now?

A novel.

About what?

A sexual killer.

They looked impressed. Cal said:

That's a good subject. Why d'you want to write about it?

To make money.

Well, why not, Jimmy said. 'S a good reason.

He looked puzzled. Nunne said, smiling:

He's pulling your leg.

Jimmy smiled, broadly and candidly:

Oh yeah? Well, it's still a good reason. But seriously, you really writing about a sex killer?

Cal leaned forward.

Do you know any?

Certainly, Sorme said. Several. Me and Austin, to begin with. Perhaps you and Jimmy. I don't know.

He's right, Jimmy said unexpectedly. He's got you there, Cal. You don't need to know one. It could be anybody.

Is that what you're gettin' at? Cal asked.

Suppressing a strong desire to get up and leave, Sorme said:

No. Not really.

What, then?

He decided to make the best of it; after a moment's thought, he said:

I want to isolate the modern sense of dispossession. The sense of being left in the cold. Of not having enough of life. Do you know what I mean?

Do we! Cal said.

Jimmy said excitedly: Sure, I know what you mean. Like a guy I knew in S.F., spent most of his life in reformatories and gaols, and you couldn't hold him still. His favourite diversion was landing his girl friends with babies. That way he felt he was making the best of it. That boy wanted to eat and drink his freedom . . . anything for kicks; he had to keep moving, doing things, drinking, smoking tea, laying sweeties. That boy wanted a past to look back on next time he landed in gaol.

He turned to Nunne, saying:

Didj'ever read Thomas Wolfe? There was a dispossessed man for you . . . 'Scuse me, man, I just gotta go to the can. Where they keep it in this place?

Nunne directed him; they watched the two of them crossing the room together, talking excitedly, attracting attention from most other diners in the room. Nunne said:

What do you think of them?

They tire me out. I'd like to get home.

Really? You're being very antisocial today. And they like you. I can tell.

I like them. But they don't know how to make conversation. There's no attempt to get in tune. They just fire questions and comments at you like a machine-gun. And they seem to imagine that it's all getting them somewhere interesting. I couldn't resist talking about dispossession. They're about the worst examples I've ever seen.

You're being a little premature, you know. Cal has some rather interesting views on mysticism. He became a Mohammedan a few years ago . . . By the way, are you serious about writing this novel?

No. I invented it on the spur of the moment. You can't talk seriously about your work like that, at five seconds' notice.

Nunne said reprovingly:

You're not sufficiently interested in people, you know, Gerard. I've noticed it in you before.

Maybe, Sorme said noncommittally. The Americans were returning, Jimmy walking with the exaggerated ape-slouch, and still talking and gesturing. As soon as Jimmy sat down, he asked:

D'you ever try Yoga?

Not seriously, Sorme said.

Pity. You ought to try that. Cal used to practise it – the soofi method, it was called. I used to know a guy here in London who did it too . . . boy, he was really whacky, used to shoot himself full of coke, then sit like a screwball on his can for days.

Sorme began to scrape at the label of the empty wine bottle with his fingernail, wondering how to excuse himself quickly. He was feeling the beginning of a mental exhaustion that interfered with his digestion. Before he could invent a reason for leaving, he caught a name, and looked up quickly:

Did you say Glasp?

Yeah. You know him?

Oliver Glasp, the painter?

Jimmy said: I dunno whether this guy painted, and I can't remember his first name. But he was a real screwball.

It could be the same one, Sorme said. It's an unusual name.

Could be. This was five years ago. He was a bit of a pervert, too.

Was he? How?

Oh, he had a thing about little girls . . . always talking about them. We all reckoned he'd finish up in stir.

Could it be Oliver? Sorme asked Nunne.

328

I doubt it. By the way, Gerard, you ought to go soon if you're supposed to be taking a phone call at half past two.

Sorme looked at him with gratitude. He said:

Yes, I suppose I ought. I'm sorry to have to leave.

Let's meet again afterwards, Jimmy said. I'd like to talk some more about this dispossession idea.

I can't make it today, I'm afraid . . . but Austin could arrange it easily . . .

To his surprise, they both stood up and shook hands with polite formality when he left. He hurried out into Greek Street with a sense of relief. It had begun to rain.

He walked into the rain, his coat collar turned up, oblivious of the people who hurried past him on the narrow pavements. A Negro woman tried to accost him at the junction of Shaftesbury Avenue; he smiled vaguely at her and walked on. Something worried him; he wished Nunne was still there. On a sudden impulse, he turned into a phone box. The Hungarian priest answered the phone. Sorme gave his name and asked if Father Carruthers was free. A few minutes later, the priest returned, and said that Father Carruthers would be free until four o'clock. Sorme looked at his watch. It was after three. He said:

Thank you very much. I'll come over now.

On the bus, travelling down Holborn, he wondered what he wanted to say to the priest. It was some compulsion to unravel a knot; but his ideas about what he was unravelling were uncertain. He was balanced on the edge of an excitement that refused to be defined.

The Hungarian priest took him up, and left him at the end of the corridor. Father Carruthers was sitting in front of the fire, wearing a dressing-gown over pyjamas. Sorme was pleased by the warmth of his grip as he shook hands: he was secretly afraid of boring the old man.

I'm glad you came, Gerard. Sit down.

When Sorme was seated, and before he could speak further, the priest leaned forward, saying:

Did Stein ask you any questions yesterday?

Yes. We went and had a cup of coffee . . .

Who suggested that?

He did.

The priest looked grave.

And he asked you about Austin?

Why, yes. How did you know?

The priest ignored him. He was staring past Sorme's head out of the window. Something in his face kept Sorme silent; it was an expression he would never have associated with the priest, a mixture of power and concentration with detached regret, a summary. The silence lengthened. Glancing cautiously at his wristwatch, Sorme noticed it was almost twenty to four. The priest looked at him; he seemed to have come to a decision. He said quietly:

I think you are a reliable person, aren't you, Gerard?

I hope so, father.

The priest's tone was clear and businesslike.

In my profession, I am often obliged to make decisions that contravene the law – or, rather, ignore it. I have to work upon the assumption that individual souls are of value. The law judges a man by what he has done: I have to judge him by what he is. Do you understand?

Sorme nodded.

What I am going to tell you now will place us both in that position . . .

He was silent: Sorme waited, with a foreboding. He anticipated what the priest was going to say and prepared himself for it.

On Thursday night, Franz Stein received information from the Hamburg police that gave him reason to suppose that Austin might be the Whitechapel murderer.

He stopped. Sorme sat there, surprised by his own calm.

He asked finally:

Will they arrest him?

Not yet.

Why?

They have no evidence. It would be very difficult to find evidence at this stage. He is being watched all the time.

And is he . . . the killer?

He could be.

The questions piled up in him, obstructing one another like a cumulative accident on an arterial highway; he felt them escaping in the confusion. The priest watched him without speaking. Sorme said:

He's not insane. I'm certain he's not insane.

I don't know.

But . . . is it sense? Do you . . . do you know what the Hamburg report said?

Yes. He is well known to the prostitutes who cater for sadists. And he is suspected of murder.

Murder?

Of a young male prostitute. There is no definite evidence. He is one of a dozen suspects.

Sorme said with sudden indignation:

But hell, father . . .! That's no reason to suspect a man . . . of mass murder, I mean, is it? Is that all? Is there anything else?

No, that's all.

But in that case, it's not so serious. Austin might be one of a hundred suspects. And he has one great fact in his favour. He's queer. You say he's suspected of killing a *male* prostitute. Surely that . . .

Quite. The evidence is slim. But there is evidence. If Austin is the murderer . . . and it is just possible, after all

. . . if he is the killer, then he stands no chance of escaping detection now. The police are clever. They know there is no point in alarming him. If they had any evidence at all, they'd make an arrest. As it is, they will watch him to see if he provides evidence. If he drove to Whitechapel tonight and walked around the streets – even if he did nothing more – they might arrest him.

After a silence, Sorme asked:

Suppose he is the killer . . . what'd happen to him if they caught him?

The priest said softly, with precision:

They would hang him.

Are you sure, father?

Quite sure.

No chance of Broadmoor?

None whatever. Even if he was declared insane, he would be hanged. He has no past record of mental instability – no periods in asylums, or past convictions that might be interpreted as pathological. They would have to hang him, as they hanged Heath and Haigh and Christie – because the newspapers have headlined the murders until there is a widespread neurosis about them.

Sorme knew suddenly, without needing to ask, why the priest had confided in him. He felt an urgency of anger rising in him, a protest against the unreasonableness of it all, the stupidity and unfairness that was a force of nature, not a human failing, and was therefore somehow unchallengeable. He asked quietly.

What am I to do, father?

That is difficult. I want to ask you one thing: please do *not* tell Austin. There are other ways. If you see him often . . .

I've just had lunch with him!

Good. Well, there are ways. You might pretend to notice that you are being followed. You might invent

332

someone who has asked you questions about Austin. But if you tell him, and he is finally caught and tried for murder, then you are an accessory. Do you understand?

I see . . . You think he might tell?

He would, eventually. Sooner or later, he would feel the need to confess fully. I am assuming now that he might be the murderer.

Sorme said:

Father . . . I promise I won't tell him outright.

Good.

But . . . I dunno quite how to put it . . . have you *any* idea of whether it's likely . . . of whether Austin might be . . .?

The priest shrugged.

How can I tell? I haven't seen Austin for a long time.

His reply left Sorme baffled; he could feel himself become inarticulate as he tried to explain himself. He said:

But I don't think it's likely, you know! It's just not likely!

Why?

Because . . . well, because one's friends don't usually turn out to be murderers, I suppose.

The priest smiled.

Mine have.

Really?

On two occasions. However, that's beside the point. After all, it can hardly come as a surprise to you that Austin should be suspected. You have spoken to me about your own suspicions.

Yes . . . but I think I know him better since then. He's mixed up, I know. He's almost the original crazy mixed-up kid. But he's also gentle and good tempered and generous. These qualities just don't go with a killer.

The priest said:

And yet you showed no surprise when I told you of the Hamburg murder. Were you certain *that* was not Austin either?

I . . . I don't know. I don't think . . . it's likely. But . . . well, how can I tell? I don't know the circumstances. It's possible. A foreign city, an attempt to con him or rob him in the night . . . and Austin's enormously strong, I'd guess. It *could* happen and still not mean a thing . . .

And supposing it was not like that? Supposing it was ordinary sadistic murder? How would you feel about it then?

I don't know, but it wouldn't necessarily make any difference. I'd still want to know why before I decided. I mean I'd want to get inside Austin's skin and feel as he did when he . . . did it.

Why?

Because . . . you can't judge anything otherwise. Besides, it's not so hard to understand. Sometimes you don't really do things – another part of you does them, and you're only a spectator. I could put myself in the skin of a sadist all right.

Could you?

I . . . think so.

Have you ever caused suffering . . . physical suffering?

I suppose so. I used to kill chickens at Christmas when I was a boy. But I didn't particularly enjoy doing it. And I once drowned a mouse that I found in my waste bucket, and poured boiling water on it as it swam around. But that was because I was afraid it'd take hours to die. I wouldn't do that now.

Why?

It'd make me feel sick. Besides, there's an instinct in me that hates killing.

The priest said quietly and conclusively:

Then you could not place yourself in the mind of a sadist, could you?

That doesn't follow. A sadist's a sexual killer, isn't he? That makes it different. Most people can sympathize to some extent with a sex crime.

Can they?

I . . . think so. I can, anyway. I think many people have a permanent feeling of being sexually underprivileged. But I'd have to think about it. It's not easy.

Do you think of yourself as sexually underprivileged?

Yes, but that's only the negative side of it. I think it's a kind of vision . . . of complete fullness of life that underlies it. After all, the sexual impulse isn't so important. I sometimes wish I could outgrow sex altogether . . . I know that sounds odd, but it's true.

It doesn't sound at all odd, especially not to me. A man doesn't have to be a saint to rise above sex. A great many scientists and mathematicians have done it, and a large proportion of the philosophers.

I know, father, I know. But it's not as simple as that. You can't just decide to exchange sex for the life of the mind or whatever it is. I used to have a Freudian friend whose favourite phrase was 'Everybody's neurotic'. I used to think he was a fool, but I'm beginning to see his point. What's a neurosis, after all? It's a pocket of unfulfilled desire – *any* kind of desire. And human beings work on unfulfilled desires – there's nothing else.

Except habit.

Yes; but habit only keeps us living. Desire keeps us moving forward. And we all want to keep moving, so we all cultivate our desires. You know something, father. I've been so confused for the past five years because I didn't want enough. I thought I could live off Plato and Beethoven, and found I couldn't. But it's not because there's anything wrong with Plato or Beethoven. It's me

– I'm not ready for them. But don't you see, father, I shouldn't be aware of sexual problems if I hadn't tried to leave them behind. And I'm sure it's the same with Austin. If he's a sadist, it's because he's torn in two. *I* don't know Austin as a sadist. I know him as a rather generous dilettante who likes ballet and music and philosophy. I think it's the same with him as with me. You know, father, Shaw said we judge an artist by his highest moments and a criminal by his lowest. But what happens when a man's a mixture of the two? You can't sentence the criminal half to death and let the artist go free, can you? Especially when you know he wouldn't be a criminal if he wasn't an artist.

You think the criminal should be allowed to kill other human beings?

No, father. God forbid! I just think that . . .

He felt suddenly deflated. He finished lamely:

. . . it's more important to cure him than punish him.

I agree. The problem with Austin is whether he's curable . . .

He glanced at the clock on the mantelpiece. It was a quarter past four. Sorme said:

I'd better go. I'll try to find Austin.

Be careful, Gerard. You don't want to be sent to prison as an accessory.

No, father.

The priest said, smiling:

Not to mention me.

I promise.

Before you go . . . would you mind asking Father Rakosi if there's anyone waiting for me downstairs?

All right, father.

He met the Scotswoman as he opened the door. She said:

336

The man's gone. He waited ten minutes, then said he was going for a walk.

The priest said: Good. I'm tired. Could I have a cup of tea, Mrs Doughty?

Sorme went out into the rain and the falling dusk, feeling a stifled impatience with his sense of unreality. He felt as if he had just been acting in a play.

He half recognised the man who was approaching him across the road; a moment later, he saw it was Glasp.

Hi, Oliver! Where are you going to?

He sensed immediately a certain moroseness in Glasp's manner. Glasp said:

I was waiting for you.

There was a suggestion of a threat in his voice, that Sorme failed to understand.

How did you know I was here?

That woman told me. I was waiting to see Father Carruthers.

I see! That was you, was it? Well, what are you going to do now?

Glasp hesitated. Sorme looked at him closely, puzzled. Glasp said:

I didn't know you were a close friend of Father Carruthers.

I'm not. But I've seen him several times.

They stood on the edge of the pavement. Sorme laid a hand on Glasp's arm.

Come and have a cup of tea. We can't stand here in this downpour.

Glasp accompanied him into Farringdon Road without speaking. They walked to the café where Sorme had been with Stein. Glasp was wearing the most threadbare and shabby overcoat Sorme had ever seen, and it was soaked with rain. He was also hatless; his red hair clung to his skull and forehead in strands; the rain made it look deep brown.

The cafe was warm, and almost empty. They sat near the window, where the steamed surface was like a wall between them and the gathering dusk. In normal circumstances, Glasp's moroseness would have worried Sorme, but the excitement of his talk with the priest made him now indifferent to it. He drank his tea and thought about Nunne, wondering where he was now, trying to recollect any words or actions that might add weight to his suspicions.

He had almost emptied his cup before Glasp spoke:

What do you find to talk about with him?

With . . .? Oh, Father Carruthers. Oh . . . various things. Nothing that would interest you.

No?

I don't think so.

He had caught the suspicion in Glasp's face. He said:

Why? Did you suppose we were talking about you?

Weren't you?

No. Why on earth should we? You get some extraordinary ideas!

His tone was less restrained than his words; it implied: What makes you suppose we give a damn about you? Glasp coloured and drank a mouthful of tea in a gulp; Sorme immediately felt remorse. He said:

I've been talking over . . . some rather important subjects . . . I can't be more explicit.

Austin, Glasp said. It was not a question but a statement.

Yes.

Glasp said abruptly:

I'm sorry if I got the wrong idea. But . . . I've had one or two doses of people getting officious about me. And Father Carruthers used to be a member of the Reform Oliver Society.

338

Not at all. Are you going to see him now?

No. I won't go back.

Won't he wonder where you are?

It doesn't matter. He's probably glad to escape a session . . .

What are you doing now?

Going back home.

Why don't you come back with me? Have a meal and talk.

As he said it, he was almost certain Glasp would refuse. He was surprised to see Glasp hesitating, and the moment brought an intuition of his fundamental loneliness. Glasp said:

I've already had one meal with you.

There's not much, Sorme said. But there's enough for two, anyway. You may as well.

All right. Thanks.

The prospect of the ride in the Underground, with a change at Tottenham Court Road, so depressed him that he hailed a passing taxi as they came into Holborn. Glasp said:

You're picking up Austin's habits!

Sorme said: Never mind. I don't want to mess about in this rain.

He repressed his own sense of rashness by reflecting that Austin had paid for his lunch, and probably saved the price of the taxi.

He left Glasp to make the tea, and went downstairs to phone Nunne. There was no reply from the flat; the girl on the switchboard asked if she could take a message. Sorme declined, and returned to his room. The thought that the line might be tapped brought a sense of danger, and the realization that the call might easily be traced back to his own address. The memory of his hesitation, as he had waited for a reply, the uncertainty whether to warn Nunne that he had something urgent to tell him, constricted his throat with a sense of a close escape.

Glasp was not in the room when he returned. He drew the curtains, looking towards the lights of the Kentish Town Road, wondering if the police thought it worth while to keep a watch on him too. He sat in the armchair, and indulged in a fantasy in which he was arrested with Austin as an accessory before the fact. He imagined the Public Prosecutor describing his excursions with Nunne into Spitalfields, his acting as a decoy to lure a woman into some alleyway. He remembered suddenly that he had told Stein that his acquaintance with Nunne had been very short, and he was amused by the sense of relief that took him unaware. When Glasp came back into the room, he was startled, having completely forgotten about him. Glasp said:

Look here, what about skipping tea? Come and have a drink with me?

Sorme looked at the clock.

Well . . . all right. That's a good idea.

He could sense that Glasp was concerned about accepting his hospitality for a second time in three days; this worried him. He had no wish to make Glasp feel under obligation to him; accepting a drink from Glasp seemed an opportunity to disperse the awkwardness. He touched Glasp's overcoat, that hung on the back of the door, dripping water on the floor.

You'd better borrow my raincoat. We'll put this in the kitchen to dry.

That's all right. I've worn it wetter than that.

Yes, but . . . it'd better dry out. Come to think of it, I've got a plasic mac somewhere in here.

He rummaged in an unpacked cardboard box in the bottom of the wardrobe, and found the macintosh, tied in a tight parcel. Glasp sat huddled over the fire, his knees apart, steam rising from his trousers. He had combed his hair; it was slicked back in a glossy wave, looking brilliantined. He said:

That's one advantage of being a writer – it's easier to keep a small room warm. The only way to keep warm in that barn of mine is to stay in bed.

He looked strangely lugubrious in the plastic raincoat; it accentuated the stoop of his shoulders.

Looking at him, Sorme felt surprised that he had ever regarded Glasp as formidable; he seemed defenceless. But there was something alien about his stringy ugliness; it was impossible to feel protective about him.

They were the first in the bar. In the grate, a fire was beginning to burn through. Glasp sat close to it, drinking a pint of bitter. But when Sorme suggested a game of darts he accepted without hesitation, and scored a double with his first dart. Sorme was inclined to accept it as a fluke, but was soon compelled to revise his opinion; Glasp threw the darts slowly and clumsily, with a cobra-like motion of the hand, but with a startling accuracy. When they sat down again, he had beaten Sorme three times. Sorme said:

Where did you learn to play like that?

In my teens. I haven't played for years.

He emptied his pint, and banged it on the shelf. Sorme said: Another? Glasp looked surprised, and said: Oh, thanks. His mood had changed completely in twenty minutes, become relaxed and humorous. Sorme watched him emptying the second pint, and thought with amusement: When shall I ever learn? People are real. My mind likes creating patterns too much.

Glasp said: Perhaps I should have phoned the hostel.

He'll understand. Anyway, he was very tired.

Glasp nodded.

He's a good sort. I ought to see him more.

Sorme said: You said earlier that he used to be a member of the Oliver Reform Society? What exactly did you mean?

Glasp said, smiling:

You mean, what did they want to reform me from?

Well, yes.

Nothing serious. They used to think I'd be the new Chagall.

Didn't you?

It's not that. I just. . . don't like people having preconceived ideas about me . . . that I have to live up to. I'd rather be left alone.

Mmmmm. But what did you want to do when you were left alone?

That didn't matter.

Sorme said meditatively:

I know what you mean. But it's difficult, isn't it? You feel as if you want nothing except to be alone. Then your own weakness betrays you. You get involved in a different way – involved with boredom and loneliness. You know, I feel ashamed of the fact that I feel better now because of Austin. It's not a real superiority I feel over him. It's an illusion, pure chance.

Glasp asked:

Is it pure chance that you're not a sadist?

I . . . think so.

No. When you read your volume on the Arran murder, do you feel it's pure chance you're not the killer?

Sorme thought about it. He said:

No. Because I wouldn't murder a man for the sake of a few pounds as Laurie did.

You'd murder him for other reasons, though?

No, of course not. That's not what I meant. I don't

possess any of the instinct that could make me sympathize with a murderer. I don't think many people have. But everybody possesses a sexual urge. Why do you suppose the type of Sunday paper that specializes in sex crimes has such vast sales?

Glasp said:

Not sex crime alone. Any sort of crime. If you use that argument, you'll have to admit that the readers of Sunday papers have a suppressed desire to be footpads and blackmailers and kleptomaniacs.

All right. What's your conclusion?

Glasp did not reply immediately. The pub was beginning to fill up; a man was leaning across his shoulder to reach a pack of cards from the shelf. When the man was out of earshot, Glasp leaned forward. He said seriously:

I'll tell you. You're a fool to underrate yourself. You're nothing like Austin, or like Gertrude Quincey, or any of these other people you get mixed up with. They just waste your time.

Sorme grimaced and shrugged.

I suppose they do. But they've got some value, for all that.

Not for you. For you, they're just parasites.

Why parasites? It's the other way round. They give me meals, and I do nothing.

Except give them your blood.

Perhaps.

You do, Glasp said emphatically. Why don't you realize it? They don't belong to the same species as you.

Or you? Sorme said, smiling.

For a moment, he thought Glasp was offended; his look was hard and enquiring. Then he said:

Well, you answer that one.

Sorme restrained his pleasure at the implied compliment. He said:

A sort of Nietzschean master and slave morality, eh?

Why not, if it fits the facts? What's the point in imagining you're one of the mob if you're not? You're just a wolf pretending to be a sheep, that's all.

He emptied his glass. When Sorme tried to take it from him, he said: No, it's my turn. He crossed to the bar. Sorme stared at him. His glance fell on the plastic macintosh that lay over the chair, and he recalled Glasp standing in his room wearing it, his shoulders rounded, his face bloodless and alien, a man without vitality or direction. His veins were warmed by a secretion of excitement like anticipation, thinking: I wonder how many more there are in London? There might be enough to make a new age. Not Chicago rebels, but a generation with purpose. It's good to know Oliver. He's right about Austin. I'm sick of self-confessed weakness.

Glasp returned with two glasses. Sorme said:

What about finding something to eat?

All right. What about going up to see Gertrude?

Gertrude?

Why not?

Sorme stared at him in astonishment.

Are you serious?

Why not? It's only a ten-minute walk from here. We needn't stay. I'd like to say hello. It's a long time since I saw her.

All right. I know a pub in Hampstead where we could get something to eat.

Glasp emptied half of his pint in one draught. Sorme asked:

Did you and Gertrude ever quarrel?

No. Not really.

He stared into his glass; holding it between two palms, he looked like a clairvoyant gazing into a crystal ball. Then he went on:

I was pretty frank one night about her Jehovah's Witness stuff. I'm sorry now. She's all right. She's sweet.

I can't understand why she never married. She's not unattractive.

She got bitten once. Didn't you know?

I . . . I'd heard something about it. Caroline mentioned it.

Caroline? Oh, that blonde?

Sorme asked: Don't you approve of blondes?

Glasp said briefly: Not much.

Or sex of any kind?

That depends.

He emptied his glass, and stood up.

I'm going outside. You about ready to go?

Sorme had decided to phone her from Chalk Farm station, but a bus drew to a stop as they arrived, and they were on the lower deck, panting from the run, before he remembered. The sight of the Hampstead tube station brought a memory of Nunne. He said:

You know, Oliver, I'm worried about Austin.

Why.

He'll get himself into trouble.

That's his funeral.

Yes, but . . . the police suspect him of worse things than beating his boy friends.

How do you know?

Oh . . . I just happen to have found out.

They turned into Flask Walk; Glasp looked at him sideways as they passed under a lamp.

From Father Carruthers?

Yes.

How does he know?

I promised him not to let it go any further.

In that case, don't.

Sorme said: I suppose there's no harm in telling you. It

doesn't make any difference now. Carruthers has a German friend called Franz Stein – a police pathologist. He told Father Carruthers about a letter he'd received from the Hamburg police. Austin was suspected of killing a male prostitute.

He did, Glasp said.

What? How do you know? Are you sure?

Pretty sure.

How long have you known?

I didn't know until you just told me. But I know it's true.

How?

He was trying hard to see Glasp's face, wondering how seriously to take him. He felt a premonition of disappointment, a suspicion that Glasp might prove to be a charlatan. Glasp's tone was matter-of-fact; it puzzled him.

When I first knew Austin, I used to dream he was a murderer. I had one particularly vivid dream . . . I was walking behind two men by the side of a river. Suddenly one of them hit the other with a weapon of some kind, and pushed him into the river. It was night, and I couldn't see their faces, but I knew that one of them was Austin, and the man he killed was a tramp of some kind. I woke up immediately . . . A few hours later, Austin came to see me. As soon as I saw him, I decided it was all nonsense. He just didn't look like the man in my dream . . .

Are your dreams accurate?

No. More often they're wrong. I've got a morbid sort of mind. It picks up chance impressions and magnifies them. It's the same process that works in my painting. When I was a boy, I once dreamed that a boy in our class was killed in a train accident. For years I was convinced he'd die in a train. But he's a married man now . . .

But you still think Austin really killed this man?

I . . . think . . . When you said it, I remembered my dream. Suddenly, I was certain. You see, sometimes my dreams *are* accurate . . .

How do you account for that?

I don't try. It just happens sometimes.

They had arrived at the gates of Miss Quincey's driveway. Sorme could see a light in the sitting-room. He said:

Good. She's in, anyway. We'll have to talk about this when we come out.

Glasp said indifferently: All right.

I'd better try and contact Austin too. He ought to be warned.

Glasp looked at him as he opened the gate. He asked casually:

Ought he?

Chapter Four

Through the glass panel he saw the kitchen door was open; her voice was speaking to someone.

It looks as if she's got a visitor.

F – it, Glasp said. We should have rung.

Shall we go?

Miss Quincey came out of the kitchen. She called:

Is anybody there?

Sorme rang the bell. She said:

Gerard! Oh, hello, Oliver!

She stood there, looking with surprise from one to the other, holding the door. Sorme felt the awkwardness.

We . . . just thought we'd come in and say hello. We happened to be over this way . . .

I've got Brother Robbins here for supper. But come in . . .

Sorme said hastily:

Er, no . . . didn't realize it'd be inconvenient. We won't come in now . . . I don't want to interrupt . . .

She seemed to recover her self-possession.

That's all right. Come in for a few minutes, anyway. I'm making a cup of tea.

Sorme thought hard for some reason to get away; without looking at Glasp, he knew he was doing the same. Nothing occurred to him. He said lamely:

Well, thanks. But we won't stay long. We're meeting someone in half an hour . . .

Glasp followed him into the hall. He had not spoken so far. Miss Quincey said:

It's nice to see you again, Oliver. It's a very long time.

Take your coat off. Oliver, I think you've met Brother Robbins.

Brother Robbins heaved himself out of an easy chair, and advanced with an over-cordial smile. As Miss Quincey introduced them, he shook their hands with a tight, moist hand-clasp. Sorme found himself thinking: My God, Dale Carnegie standing for President; the fruity, slightly Cockney voice poured warmth and a smell of onions over him.

I've told you about Gerard, Miss Quincey said.

I'm most delighted to meet you, Brother Robbins said.

At first glance, he struck Sorme as a curious combination of a well-to-do grocer and a shady bookmaker. He was a foot shorter than Sorme, with a fleshy face and pot belly. His clothes looked slightly rumpled and grease-stained, but his shirt collar was immaculately starched, and an old school tie looked newly washed and ironed. Sorme conceived an immediate and keen dislike for him.

You're the young man who's thinking of joining us? Brother Robbins said.

Sorme looked with surprise at Miss Quincey. She interposed:

I don't think he's made up his mind yet!

Ah no. Quite.

Brother Robbins sat down again. Glasp stood there, looking sulky and out of place. Brother Robbins suddenly caught his eye, and said:

And I've heard you are too, Mr Gasp.

Glasp.

Ah . . . I beg your pardon. You paint, don't you?

Yes.

Miss Quincey said: Will you both have tea?

Er . . . no thanks, Sorme said. Not for me.

Nor me, Glasp said.

Sorme followed her into the kitchen. He said:

349

I think we'd better go . . .

All right. But stay a few minutes. You don't want poor Brother Robbins to think he has the plague.

All right.

Won't you have some tea?

We've been drinking beer.

Oh . . . I'm afraid I can't offer you beer. Not while Brother Robbins is here.

Would he disapprove?

Miss Quincey hesitated; she said:

Perhaps he wouldn't. I don't know. Do you *want* beer?

Sorme's inclination was to refuse; she had phrased the question in a way that made it difficult to accept. This irritated him, striking him as a challenge. He said:

I'd prefer it to tea.

Then perhaps you'd ask Oliver if he'd like beer.

Glasp was scowling at the carpet as he came in. Sorme said:

Gertrude says there's some beer if you'd prefer it.

Glasp shook his head.

No? I'm having beer.

He looked at Brother Robbins, and asked politely:

I hope you don't object.

Brother Robbins seemed to accept the question as natural, as if he was an old lady in a railway carriage being asked if she minds cigar smoke. He said genially:

Oh, not at all. Not in the least.

For you, Oliver?

Glasp said, with a bad grace:

OK.

Sorme returned in a few moments with two lager glasses of light ale, ice-cold from the refrigerator. He was thirsty after the walk up the hill, and drank as much as he could before his throat froze. Brother Robbins asked:

Do you two drink a lot?

350

Sorme sensed that Glasp was about to make a rude retort. He said hastily:

No, not a lot. We don't get together very often. Do you drink?

No. But not because I disapprove of it. I just don't like the taste.

Something in his manner stung Sorme to irritation. Brother Robbins was speaking with the elaborate courtesy of a prison visitor: he managed to imply that beer drinking was a particularly squalid vice which he was too broad-minded to condemn. Sorme emptied his glass defiantly and went into the kitchen for another bottle. Miss Quincey said, with a sort of horror:

You've drunk that already?

I was thirsty. May I?

He helped himself from the refrigerator. When he turned round, he met a worried and reproachful look; she seemed to suspect that he intended to start a drunken brawl. He said pointedly:

We'll go in a minute.

Oh no! Don't think that! I just don't want . . . Stay as long as you like.

Thanks.

He went back, taking the bottle.

Glasp was answering some question in an indistinguish-able mumble. Brother Robbins looked relieved to see Sorme again. He said:

Let me see – you were a Roman Catholic, weren't you?

No.

Church of England?

No. I'm an existentialist.

Yes? But er . . . I meant . . . religion.

I know. That's what *I* meant

Oh. I don't think I've come across that sect. Is it a new one?

Not really.

Who was the founder?

A Dane named Kierkegaard.

And do they believe in the redeeming power of Jesus Christ?

Kierkegaard did, certainly.

Ah, but did he also believe in Luther's justification by faith?

Oh no! He always attacked the established Church. He thought men ought to live like Christ instead of relying on the Church . . .

Good! Then he was on the right path! The trouble with most people today is that they don't realize the importance of obeying the laws of God. They think it's enough just to accept them. They don't seem to realize that the Bible has given us a strict code of conduct to cover every aspect of our lives.

Sorme nodded ponderously. His silence seemed to encourage Brother Robbins; he leaned forward, and switched on his Dale Carnegie smile again.

You ought to come to our Bible classes. I'm sure you'd enjoy them.

I'm sure I would, Sorme said insincerely.

Abruptly, Glasp spoke; he was sitting up and glowering belligerently at Brother Robbins.

Is it true you people expect the end of the world any day now?

Brother Robbins turned to Glasp, and smiled winningly, as if Glasp had just paid him a compliment.

It is. Not, of course, *any* day. The Book of the Revelation indicates that it will be within the next thirty years.

And that everyone in the world will be destroyed except the Jehovah's Witnesses?

The Bible tells us so.

Glasp gave a contemptuous grunt and relaxed into his chair. In spite of his dislike of Brother Robbins, Sorme immediately reacted in his favour. He said quickly:

Is all this in the Bible?

Certainly it is. The evidence is quite plain. The Bible says that the devil came down to earth in 1914, and that from that day forward, the world has belonged to him. And can you doubt it when you look around at the world? The threat of war everywhere, crime and evil reaching a new high level. Look at these murders in the East End. Look at what the Russians are doing in Hungary. Look at the H-bomb tests. The world has gone mad, because it belongs to the devil now. That is why the flock of Christ is persecuted. It is all just as the Bible predicted. The Apocalypse of St John makes it quite plain. It predicts that men will try to improve things, but it is too late. 'And he opened the pit of the abyss, and a smoke ascended out of the pit as the smoke of a great furnace, and the sun and the air were darkened by the smoke of the pit.'

He leaned forward to declaim the quotation. When he raised it to intone, his voice had a foghorn quality; it reminded Sorme of one of his uncles who used to recite 'The Boy Stood on the Burning Deck' at Christmas parties. Before he could comment, Brother Robbins had swept on:

Nothing can stop the dominion of evil in the world because the world belongs to the old evil one now. They might pass this Bill to stop hanging. They might persuade Russia to put an end to the Cold War. But nothing will stop the world from hurtling towards the Last Judgment.

He paused for a moment, passed a hand over his forehead. He wiped his damp fingers on the arm of the chair. Sorme said:

You sound pretty gloomy.

Out of the corner of his eye he saw Glasp smile. He

kept his own face stiff and grave in case Brother Robbins should feel he was being mocked.

Gloomy! No, I'm not gloomy. We are not pessimists. We go on joyfully, certain of eternal life. When the battle of Armageddon is over we shall all live on a paradise earth for ever.

This earth?

Certainly. This earth, but transfigured and made into a heaven.

But only after the battle's been won?

Of course.

Supposing your side doesn't win the battle?

That is impossible. God is all-powerful. We *must* win.

Sorme said: In that case, there's not much credit in winning, is there? It should be a walkover.

You don't understand, Brother Robbins said gravely.

Sorme saw the suspicion that flickered in his eyes for a moment. He said hastily:

Don't think I'm just heckling you. I'd like to know.

Then you should read your Bible. And I'm sure Sister Quincey would lend you some of our books and tracts.

Glasp said abruptly: We ought to go.

Brother Robbins turned a stern face on him. He said:

You should be more like your friend here and take a serious interest in serious questions. God is not mocked!

For a moment, Sorme thought Glasp intended to ignore the comment; he scowled and hunched his shoulders, his forehead wrinkling into creases. Then he said shortly:

I'd need to be a bloody moron to fall for that crap.

Miss Quincey came into the room as he spoke. She looked as if her worst fears had been confirmed, and as if she now expected Glasp to urinate on the carpet. She said:

Oliver! I shall have to ask you to go if you're rude!

Brother Robbins said equably:

354

No no, my dear. There's no point in doing that. If he doesn't believe, you won't make him believe by turning him away.

Then he ought to apologize. That wasn't polite.

Glasp said sullenly and sarcastically:

Oh no. It's not polite when I say what *I* think! It's OK for him to ram his opinions down everybody's throat. I'm damned if I don't believe it, but I'm not allowed any beliefs of my own. Just because he's got no sense of reality, I'm rude if I contradict him.

Miss Quincey took this unexpectedly well. She said:

It's you who lack a sense of reality, Oliver. Every great truth sounds fantastic. You think the truth has to be commonplace and ordinary, but you're wrong. It's you who are tied down by your sense of reality . . .

Sorme could see that Glasp was becoming more irritable and inarticulate as she spoke; he had a foreboding that Glasp would shout some obscenity and stamp out of the house. He intervened quickly:

I don't quite agree with you, Gertrude. I don't think Oliver rejects your beliefs because he prefers everyday reality. In fact, I think that every artist has the same kind of dreams – an earth turned into heaven, men made into immortals. On the other hand, it seems like wishful thinking to suppose it'll happen tomorrow week. We both believe that if you want to change the world into a paradise, you've got to do it yourself.

Brother Robbins had stood up as he spoke; now he extended his arms, as if inviting Sorme and Glasp to be embraced.

But my dear man, you're one of us. You want the same things. It's only a question of the means, and we can show you the way.

I agree it's a question of means, Sorme said cautiously. We ought to discuss it more fully some time.

They were all standing, looking at one another. Miss Quincey was obviously nervous about Glasp; as Sorme started to say: I'm afraid we'll have to . . . Brother Robbins interrupted with enthusiasm:

Why not now? I am always glad to discuss these things. Can anything be of greater importance?

We have to see someone, Sorme said, looking at his watch. But any other time I'd be glad . . .

To bridge an awkward lapse in the conversation he looked at Glasp, saying: Ready, Oliver?

Glasp muttered something, and turned his back on them. Sorme said:

Er . . . delighted to've met you. Goo'bye. 'Bye, Gertrude.

He hurried after Glasp, catching him up at the front door. Miss Quincey came after him, touching his shoulder. She said quickly:

Come back tomorrow, Gerard.

All right. I want to talk to you.

From the darkness outside Glasp called suddenly:

Goodnight, Gertrude.

She looked surprised, then called calmly:

Goodnight, Oliver.

She added quickly, to Sorme:

Ask him to come again – when I'm alone.

OK. Goodnight.

She had been keeping her voice low, her face close to him. Seeing that Brother Robbins and Glasp were both out of sight, Sorme bent quickly and kissed her. She stepped back a pace, looked quickly behind her towards the lounge, then said coolly: Goodnight.

She closed the door behind him; he went into the darkness, thinking: All women have a talent for intrigue.

Glasp was standing by the gates. Sorme said:

How d'you feel?

OK.

Gertrude told me to ask you to go back some time – when he's not there.

Glasp grunted. Sorme said:

Don't you like her either?

Oh, she's OK . . . Must be a bloody fool, though. Swallow that balls.

I wonder how far she does?

All the way, Glasp said with disgust.

They were passing the telephone kiosk at the end of Well Walk; Sorme said:

Do you mind if I try and phone Austin again?

No.

The telephonist's voice told him that Nunne was still not home, and asked if she could take a message, Sorme said:

No; it's not important. I just wanted to ask him to come to a party.

This evening?

Yes.

If you'd like to leave the address, I'll give it to him when he comes in.

After a moment's hesitation, Sorme gave his own address, reflecting that Glasp's presence gave him a reason for speaking of a party, in case he was ever forced to justify the call.

Not in yet? Glasp said:

No.

What are you going to do about him?

I don't know. Warn him in some way.

There's not much danger.

Why do you say that?

Because a crime committed a long time ago in Hamburg won't be easy to pin on him.

Sorme realized with surprise that Glasp had not yet

357

connected Nunne with the Whitechapel murders. For some reason, he had taken it for granted that Glasp knew. He rejected the idea of mentioning it now, remembering Glasp's outburst at supper a few nights before, and suspecting suddenly that Glasp was capable of betraying Nunne to the police. He said:

I hope you're right.

You worry more about Austin than he does about you.

Why? Do you think he dislikes me?

No. But he's the heartless type. He doesn't give a damn about anybody really.

On Haverstock Hill again, Sorme said:

What about another drink?

Good idea.

I know a pub.

The public bar was crowded; they went around to the saloon bar and found it less full.

Same again?

Please.

Grab those seats in the corner. I'll bring them over.

The episode at Gertrude Quincey's had destroyed the feeling of ease and the rising warmth; it began to return when he had drunk half the pint of bitter. Glasp said:

What were we talking about?

Austin.

Oh yes. Let's skip him. He doesn't matter.

All right.

Glasp was smiling, as if at some secret joke. Sorme looked at him enquiringly, raising his eyebrows. Glasp said:

What about Gertrude?

What about her?

You having an affair with her?

Oh, you saw that, did you?

You didn't try to hide it. With the light behind you.

Well, the answer's no. I like provoking her.

That was provocation, was it?

Pretty well. Just fun.

Am I being nosey?

No! There's nothing secret about it. It's a sort of joke.

You've done it before, like?

Well, yes. Just to provoke.

Glasp sipped at his beer; he had a manner of launching questions suddenly, as if hoping to take by surprise, and Sorme guessed another was coming. It came a moment later.

Do you want to sleep with her?

Sorme considered this carefully. In fact, the idea had ceased to interest him since sleeping with Caroline. He said carefully:

I don't *think* I do . . . I don't know.

Well, either you do or you don't.

No. It's not as simple as that. In a sense, I want to sleep with every woman indiscriminately, you know . . . When I hear about someone being given the freedom of the City of London, I sometimes think how nice it'd be if someone could grant you the freedom of all the women in the world. Just anybody. You produce an engraved scroll with a golden key on it, and say 'My name is Sorme; come back to my room . . .' Splendid idea.

Glasp said, laughing:

The sentiments of a sex maniac.

No. Not really!

No. I'm only joking.

But really, I think there's an element of truth there.

I'm sure there is.

Do you know those lines of Blake about the lion lying down with the lamb? Something about the golden age. That's the root of it, you know. We live in a fallen world, and we dream of a golden age when there was no such

359

thing as frustration. All men turned into gods because they can do what they like. That's why I find it hard to condemn Austin, no matter what he's done. There shouldn't be such a thing as sexual perversion . . . but then, maybe there shouldn't be such a thing as sex either. It's all part of a fall. You know Tolstoy's idea that nobody ought to have sex, except to beget children? That's logical. Either all sex is natural, or it's unnatural. There's no dividing line between normal sex and perversion.

He was aware as he spoke that it sounded illogical; Glasp was listening with his lower lip thrust out, an expression of distrust on his face. He made a conscious effort to sound more reasonable:

Put it like this. If I'm attracted by a girl, I know damn well it's not entirely a desire to sleep with her. If I'm curious to know what she's like in bed, it's more a desire to break down the barriers between human beings, not a desire to penetrate her. And if it gets to the point of bed, the chances are that I shan't want her any more. It's the same with Gertrude. There's something about that icy virgin attitude that provokes me. But I don't think it's a desire to have Gertrude for a mistress.

He observed an answering glow of sympathy in Glasp this time, but the need to catch his intuitions in words was too strong to allow him to stop and wait for Glasp's response. He felt a sense of complete wellbeing as he emptied his glass and set it down, leaning forward, aware of ideas straining to be expressed.

Have you ever been in a room with two women who've been your mistress? And when you look from one to the other, there's no *curiosity* about either. If either of them uncrosses her legs you don't bother to look to see how high the skirt goes. They form a small group, cut off from all the rest of womankind. You might desire them, but the curiosity's gone. Well, what I feel about Gertrude is curiosity, not desire. So I can't really say whether I want to sleep with her or not. Have another?

Glasp had finished his beer; he was looking around the room with an expression of distaste. He said:

Too many people. What about moving?

The room had been filling since they came in; now there were no seats left, and a group of people stood within a few feet of them, laughing noisily. Sorme said:

Most pubs in London'll be like this on a Saturday night. We could go back to my room.

What's the time? Eight o'clock. All right, if you like.

He filled the washbowl with hot water, then plunged his hands into it and leaned forward on them, suddenly tired. Through the half open door of the bathroom, he heard the phone ringing, and tensed automatically, waiting to be called. When the ringing stopped and no one shouted his name he dried his hands, thinking tiredly: People. How can I escape people? It was a sudden disgust, a reaction to the excitement of the afternoon and now the sensation of knowing Glasp with a sympathetic insight. It was the feeling of winning a game, the sensation of an increasing interior power, an energy for which he could find no immediate outlet.

Glasp was stretched in the armchair, his feet on the stool. On the turntable of the gramophone the first side of Prokoviev's Fifth Symphony was coming to an end. Two full quarts of beer stood on the table.

Shall I turn it over?

No. I'd rather talk.

Glasp held out the beer glass, tilting it as Sorme poured the brown ale. Sorme said:

You look pleased with yourself.

Do I?

There's a contented expression on your face.

Maybe, Glasp said.

Sorme relaxed in the other chair, raising his slippered feet on to the footstool; Glasp moved his own stockinged feet to make room. Sorme noted with interest that he was wearing a new pair of nylon socks. Glasp said:

Listen, Gerard. Has it struck you that Austin could be the Whitechapel killer?

Sorme kept his eyes fixed on his slippers, careful to show no surprise. He said finally:

Hmmmm. Perhaps. Not very likely, though.

You think not?

I don't think it's very likely. Seriously. Do you?

I think it's possible. We know Austin is a sadist. We suspect he killed someone in Hamburg.

Yes, but . . .

What?

We also know Austin. Can you look at him and connect him with the murders? I can't.

Glasp held his beer glass on a level with his nose and frowned at it.

Neither can I. That proves nothing. You know Austin is a sadist. Can you imagine him beating anyone with a whip?

No . . .

Yet he probably does.

Well, even so, these murders are heterosexual and he's queer. Why should he choose women?

Easier to pick up in Whitechapel.

All right. Second, why choose Whitechapel, where he's more likely to get caught every time he commits a crime? Why not move around London? And, third, why on earth should it be Austin, with several million other people living in London?

Glasp looked at him steadily.

You don't want it to be Austin, do you?

362

Sorme shrugged.

I don't know. I like Austin, but that wouldn't stop me from looking the facts in the face if they really pointed to him.

Glasp said: Anyway, you needn't worry. I wouldn't give him away to the police, even if I *knew* he did them.

No?

Anyway, you can bet they've got an eye on him now. If he's suspected of this Hamburg murder, he's a natural suspect for Whitechapel.

I suppose so. I don't understand the way these things work.

You don't understand sadism, anyway, do you?

Sorme asked curiously:

What makes you say that?

You're not the type.

No? What type am I?

Glasp said, shrugging:

You're like me. Not particularly interested in sex.

Blimey! Do you really think so?

Glasp grinned.

You think you are. But you're not. Try to understand what I mean. Austin's a sensualist. He's not a man of ideas. Nothing really interests him but what he can see and touch.

Oh, I dunno. I wouldn't say he has no ideas.

He hasn't. Perhaps he makes an effort because he's talking to you. If he ever got really used to you, he'd stop making the effort.

Yes, but . . . there's a kind of innocence about Austin. You don't understand.

Oh yes I do. There's a kind of innocence about sensuality. It doesn't have to leer and drool. But it just doesn't get off the ground. The most sensual man I ever knew was a collector of knives and daggers. He wrote several

363

monographs on the subject – known as the leading authority of Europe. Not an idea in his head, but the most amazing collection of facts about daggers.

Sorme said dubiously:

I see what you mean.

He was feeling vaguely hungry. From the cupboard he took a half loaf of bread, some Spanish onions, and a polythene bag containing Gruyère cheese. He said:

Help yourself if you're hungry.

He cut an irregular chunk of bread from the side of the loaf and plastered butter on it. Glasp said:

That's a good idea.

As he sawed at the loaf, he said:

Don't get the wrong ideas about Austin. He's no soulmate. He's all right, but if you get entangled with him, he'll suffocate you.

I know that. But I think you misjudge him. He misjudges you too.

Does he? What does he say about me?

Sorme hesitated, calculating the effect of complete frankness; a desire to provoke a reaction urged him to speak. He said casually:

Oh, he thinks you have some . . . sexual peculiarities.

Naturally, Glasp said contemptuously. He'd have to.

Sorme said, laughing:

Oh, I agree. They always want to pin it on other people . . .

What does he think . . . I'm addicted to? Men, boys or animals?

Neither. Little girls.

The effect was greater than he had anticipated. Glasp laid down the knife on the plate, staring incredulously.

He *what*?

Sorme ignored his excitement; he said:

Oh, you know what it's like . . .

He said that? Tell me exactly what he said.

As he spoke, Sorme heard someone outside his door; for a moment, he expected to see Nunne's face; then the key turned in the next room, and he heard the Frenchman open his own door. His heart pounding, he said quickly:

Oh, to do Austin justice, he was only reporting something he'd heard.

Are you sure?

Quite sure. Two Americans thought they'd known you in London several years ago. But after all, it might easily have been someone else. Or they might have said it for effect.

Glasp said slowly:

Well I'll be damned!

He emptied his beer glass, and refilled it; then sat hunched forward in the chair, staring into the fire. Something in the crouched tenseness of his body made Sorme aware that he was experiencing an inner upheaval that he was unwilling to show. Sorme's heart was still beating heavily from the noise outside the door. He said:

Look. Why don't we skip the subject? I'm sorry I told you.

But didn't he say any more than that?

Nothing.

Glasp said slowly:

These bloody queers amaze me.

Why?

They're interested in nothing but personalities. If I'd painted the greatest portrait since Rembrandt, it wouldn't interest him unless he thought I'd had an affair with the sitter.

This time, Sorme made no effort to contradict him. He glanced at his watch, wondering if he could suggest going out. The thought of Nunne arriving suddenly worried him. He said lightly:

I don't see why you let it bother you. I only told you to amuse you. I don't take Austin seriously.

Glasp looked at him, frowning.

But *why* did he say it? Where did he get the idea? You didn't tell him about that picture of a girl in my room?

No.

He felt acutely uncomfortable; he had seen the picture of the girl while Glasp was out of the room, and found the idea of lying about it disagreeable. He said:

I've told you, anyway. He got the idea from two Americans. I can vouch for it. I've met them.

Glasp shrugged irritably. He said:

Well, I don't give a damn, anyway. But I bet what you like he's seen me around with the girl in that picture, or been told about it.

Sorme said untruthfully:

I can't remember the picture, anyway. I doubt whether Austin knows about it.

Glasp subsided into silence, wolfing huge mouthfuls of bread with Spanish onion; the muscles of his jaw stood out as he chewed and swallowed. Somewhere below, a door slammed; again, Sorme wondered if Nunne had arrived. He said:

You know, I'm pretty sure you're wrong about Austin . . .

Glasp said:

Would you suppose I've got a taste for twelve-year-old girls?

I . . . well, I presume not. But quite honestly, it wouldn't particularly shock me if you had. Girls can often look quite adult at twelve.

Glasp said gloomily:

This one doesn't. She looks about nine.

Yes but. . . Look here, Oliver. I don't want to pry into your private life. Let's drop the subject, shall we?

Does it embarrass you?

No, but . . .

Well, it doesn't embarrass me either. I don't mind talking about it.

Sorme wondered if Glasp was slightly drunk: the assertiveness was blurred and heavy sounding. He said:

OK, if you want to, let's talk about it. Who is this girl, anyway?

Glasp emptied the quart flask of beer into his glass with deliberation, then screwed its cap on and placed it carefully on the floor. He said:

Her name's Christine.

To cover the awkwardness he was feeling, Sorme opened the second quart of beer and filled his glass. He felt a certain absurdity in the conversation; Glasp was, after all, under no compulsion to tell him about the girl; this seemed somehow the wrong moment and the wrong way in which to talk about her. He noticed that the gas fire was beginning to go out, and searched his small change for shillings, glad to have something to do, waiting for Glasp to go on. When he spoke finally, there was no trace of drunkenness in his voice. He said seriously:

You know, Gerard, it makes my blood boil when somebody like Austin gets nosey about my affairs. I never did anything to him, did I? I live on my own out there. I don't ask people to take notice of me. I avoid people because I don't enjoy playing the game. Do you know what I mean?

The social game, you mean?

I mean the personal game. You see . . .

Looking at him, Sorme could almost watch the words trying to force their way out; he found himself leaning forward, concentrating to help Glasp.

If you get involved with people, you've got to stick to the rules. It's like going to a public school or joining a posh club. If you want the advantages, you have to stick to the rules. Well, I'd rather not join the club. I'll do without the advantages. It's like exhibiting. If you exhibit your work, you put yourself at the mercy of a lot of half-witted bastards who don't know paint from shit. But it's no good complaining about not being understood. If you put your work on show it's like asking people to look at it. And if they make stupid comments, you've got nothing to complain about, because you asked them. Well, so I don't exhibit. Then if somebody makes a stupid comment about my work I've got a right to fetch him a backhander across the mouth and say: Shut your f – ing noise; nobody asked you.

It was coming now, and Glasp was talking like a machine, his face flushed, unaware of the breadcrumb stuck in the corner of his mouth. There was also a pleasure in his eyes, an astonishment that his feelings were really changing themselves into words and coming out.

It's the same with people. If you need people, you've got to persuade them to accept you on the level you want. It's OK for somebody like Picasso. Everybody accepts him, anyway, so he goes his own way. Do you see what I mean? But if you want to do good work, it costs more effort than it's worth to make them accept you . . .

I know just what you mean, Sorme said. It's happened to me many times. Just before I gave up work, I used to work in an office with a Scottish clerk who had a terrific chip on his shoulder. He knew I wanted to be a writer, and he used to enjoy getting at me – telling me I was a bloody intellectual and out of touch with reality.

You should have belted him one, Glasp said.

I felt like it. But what was the good? He'd just succeeded in getting under my skin. I think he had some sort of inferiority complex – he stuttered badly. But I had to put up with him because he sat next to me. I used to feel the same as you – a feeling of outrage that he should criticize me. I felt like saying: You're a bloody fool. I don't want to know you. Unfortunately, I couldn't help knowing him, and I couldn't help talking to him and working with him . . .

Glasp said bitterly:

Well, that's how I feel about Austin Nunne. Except that I *did* say to him 'You're a bloody fool. I don't want to know you.' And still I can't get away from his stupidities.

Sorme said: But wouldn't you feel differently if your work made you famous?

Of course. Because then I shouldn't have to argue with the fools. I could leave that to my admirers. Look at this man tonight – Brother whatsisname at Gertrude's. I could see he was a bloody fool and there was no point in exchanging two words with him. So I didn't. That's how it's supposed to be.

Sorme said guiltily:

You know, you're being a bit unfair to Austin about this matter of the girl. I'm pretty sure he doesn't know anything about her.

But you said he had . . .

Two Americans said it, Sorme said firmly. And they weren't sure it was you.

Glasp said irritably:

Austin's a fool, anyway.

Sorme said, smiling:

I wondered why you looked so fierce when I first introduced myself to you as a friend of Austin's.

It was about the worst thing you could say. But when I talked to you I found I liked you.

Thanks.

Shall I tell you why?

Sorme nodded. Glasp said:

369

You've got a job of your own to do. You don't waste time like Austin.

Sorme said, shrugging:

I waste too much.

Not like Austin. You know, something goes wrong with a man who wastes time. He starts to go rotten. You can almost smell him. Don't you feel that about Austin?

No. I don't feel he's very different from me.

You'll find out, Glasp said.

He sank deeper into the chair, bending his knees above the footstool, saying meditatively:

I'll introduce you to Christine some time. You'll like her. She's a talented child.

Does she paint?

A little. I'm trying to teach her. She has a lot of talent . . . more than me.

Seriously?

Seriously. I'm not talented; I have to work like hell for all my effects. She does it easily.

How old is she? Nine, did you say?

No, twelve. She looks nine, though.

How did you meet her?

In rather an odd way. One day, I was standing outside a bookshop in the Mile End Road looking through the sixpenny case, and this little girl stood at the side of me. She kept looking at an old leather covered autograph book – years old, the pages discoloured, but for some reason unused. And I could see she wanted this thing. When I looked inside it, I saw it was more expensive than the other books – not much – a shilling or one and six. And she kept putting it back and looking at other books, then taking out this thing again. I began to wonder if she intended to pinch it. But she didn't. She finally put it back, and walked off. Well, I'd found a couple of books I wanted, and I'd just sold some woodcuts to a shop, so I took the autograph book and bought it with the other two. Well, when I got outside she was already about half a mile away, so I ran after her, caught her up, and gave her the book.

Sorme asked, laughing:

What did she do?

She just took it, and stared at me. I felt a bit silly about buying it, so I turned and walked away. And that was that. Neither of us spoke.

What a strange thing to do!

Oh, I dunno. It was just an impulse, you know.

But how did you get to know her?

That happened later. I saw her a couple of times in the street, and guessed she must live near me. But I wasn't really curious, you know . . . Anyway, one day I was walking past the cinema in the Commercial Road – it was a Saturday afternoon and there was a queue of kids outside. And she came running out of the queue and said hello. Then she went belting back into the queue before I could say anything. Then about two days later I met her as I came out of a bread shop in Vallance Road, and she walked along with me. I felt a bit embarrassed – you know, I hate asking kids how old they are and what they do at school and all that stuff – I remember how it used to bore me when I was a kid. But it's difficult to think of much else to say. Anyway, she asked me what I did, and I said I was a painter. She said 'Oh!' not very interested – she thought I meant a painter and decorator. Then when I said I painted pictures she got very interested. I could almost see her building romantic daydreams about a real artist. Well, she had to go home that day, but I said I'd show her my pictures some time, and the next day I found her outside my house at about four in the afternoon, so I asked her in. She was funny. She looked both ways to see no one was watching, then dashed through the doorway like a jack rabbit. And I showed her my pictures, and gave her a cup of tea, and told her to come in any time she liked. She was obviously pretty shy . . . Well, the next Saturday afternoon, she turned up and insisted on watching me paint. Her parents thought she'd gone to the threepenny rush again . . . And that was how I got to know her.

She sounds charming, Sorme said. Was she really romantic about being an artist?

Oh yes. I found out that she'd developed a grand passion. I met her one day with some school friend, and she blushed like mad. And the following Saturday afternoon I started to pump her about it, and finally got her to admit that she'd told her friend that I'd asked her to marry me when she was sixteen!

Sorme said, laughing:

Well, why not?

Glasp shrugged:

Well, it's a possibility, I suppose – she has only three years to go. She's nearly thirteen.

Sorme said with astonishment:

Are you that interested?

I . . . You don't understand. You see, she comes from a big family – she's got seven brothers and sisters. They used to sleep four in a bed once. And her father's a warder in Brixton gaol – an absolutely bloody moron who spends all he can on booze. She's got an elder sister who's married. She married a Pole, and they live next door. And when the Pole comes home drunk and tries to beat his wife, she goes next door and sleeps with Christine and her other sister in a single bed . . . She sleeps down the other end. And I saw her mother once – a poor, wrecked old thing with terrific sagging breasts and no teeth. She can't be more than fifty, and she looks seventy. That's the sort of background she comes from. She wants to study at

372

art school – she's brilliant enough to get a scholarship – but her parents wouldn't even dream of it. Her mother told her that art students are no better than prostitutes. And, anyway, they want her to go to work when she leaves school and bring in a few shillings a week until she marries. Her family have lived in slums for generations. They don't *want* to do anything better.

That's stupid. Can't you persuade them?

Not a hope. Christine daren't even let them know she still sees me. I had a fight with her father once.

Blimey! How?

Glasp shrugged, then shook himself, grimacing, as if rejecting an unpleasant memory.

He's a drunk, a blustering stupid drunk. Christine's brother saw us in a café and told her parents. They gave her a thrashing and made her promise not to see me again. Luckily, we spotted the brother when he saw us, and I was able to warn Christine not to tell her parents everything – to say she'd only met me once or twice in the Whitechapel Art Gallery. Otherwise she might have told them about posing for me and had the skin beaten off her. Anyway, the next day I was passing a pub in Hanbury Street when her father came out and started to yell at me.

How did he recognize you?

Oh, he'd seen me around, and I'd seen him – they only live five hundred yards away, round the corner.

What was he shouting about?

Stupid lies . . . filthy lies. If a quarter of it had been true, he could have had me thrown in gaol for ten years. I didn't know what to do . . . I didn't want him to get Christine into any more trouble. So I tried soothing him. That only made him worse. He was half drunk. He grabbed my collar and started shouting in my face – shooting spit and beer all over me. I told him to let go and he just shouted louder. So I jerked my knee into his crotch, and hit him in the face.

Sorme exclaimed: Christ! He found it hard to imagine Glasp hitting anyone.

Then luckily a policeman came along and threatened to throw us both inside, so we broke it up and separated pretty quickly. The Whitechapel police don't stand much nonsense – they're a rough crowd. I half expected him to start telling the policeman I'd seduced his daughter, but he didn't. He just slunk off. I was pretty shaken.

Did he take it out on Christine?

No, that's the odd thing. She came round the next day and told me about it. She'd been in the kitchen when he came in, and he started to yell about taking her to a doctor to get evidence against me. Then her mother flew into a rage and threatened to leave him if he tried anything of the sort. And later her mother questioned her about me – wanted to know if anything had ever happened with me, and, of course, Christine denied it, and her mother believed her.

Sorme listened gravely, nodding, wondering how to phrase the question that was forming and anxious not to let it appear on his face. He said:

But even if he'd taken her, nothing would have come of it?

Nothing . . . except gossip, probably. That'd be bad enough. If it came out that she'd posed for me it might cause trouble.

Did she pose often?

Oh yes . . . I drew her the first time she came. But not in the nude, of course.

Then why should there be trouble?

Because later on she started posing naked for me.

Ah . . . that's difficult. Did she want to?

Oh yes. At first she was shy. Then one day she fell in

the brook in Victoria Park and got soaked. Her mother'd threatened to whip her if she played near water again, so she came around to me to get dry. She got into bed while I made a fire – it was a summer evening – and stayed there till her clothes were dry. Well, I persuaded her to pose sitting in front of the fire, and made a good sketch of her with the firelight behind her – one of the best things I ever did. After that she often posed.

Sorme said:

I can't help feeling you're playing with fire. Her father doesn't sound the kind who'd forget a quarrel.

Glasp said hopelessly:

I know. What can I do? Stop seeing her?

Well . . . that's up to you, of course. Would it make a big difference if you stopped seeing her for a few months – just to let things cool down?

Of course.

But you've done a lot for her. You've shown her a different way of life. She won't change now.

Glasp grimaced, shrugging:

I'm not so sure. Two of her sisters work in a hosiery factory. That's what her family want her to do. Besides, it's a pretty awful environment to fight against.

It must be a bit of a slum with seven kids.

It is. Sacking on the floor instead of mats, and boxes instead of chairs. And they're considered pretty well off because they live in a thirty-bob-a-week Council flat.

But as you say, she'll be sixteen in a few years' time, and you can take her out of it . . .

To what? My three pounds ten a week?

It'd be luxury after what she's been used to.

That's . . . not the point. It's not that I want to marry her. That'd only be a way of getting her legally outside her parents' grasp. That's what matters.

Sorme stretched in the chair, oppressed by the heat. He said slowly:

There could be other ways of doing that. Get someone to agree to act as guardian to her and send her to art school. Someone like Gertrude. If her parents could be persuaded . . .

Gertrude! Glasp said. That'd be out of the frying-pan into the fire!

Would it?

Glasp leaned forward, staring hard at Sorme; his forehead was twitching again, giving the thin face a slightly insane expression. He said:

You don't understand. I don't want someone else to get her. I don't want other people to keep getting in the way.

The intensity in his voice and the twitching forehead produced a curiously unpleasant impression on Sorme. He made his voice casual, saying:

Yes, I see your point. But you said you didn't particularly want to marry her.

And why should I? Glasp said; there was something strained and irritable about his vehemence. What would that give me, except a legal right to sleep with her?

Oh, a lot . . .

Glasp interrupted:

But I don't *want* to sleep with her. I don't even want to touch her. I'm not a bloody pervert. Don't you see? I just want her. I want her more than I've ever wanted anything . . .

He leaned back, his shoulders slumping; Sorme could almost feel the exhaustion that surrounded him like a grey air. He said soothingly:

That's OK. You've nothing to worry about, have you? You're not likely to lose her. And she's lucky she met you. What have you got to worry about?

Glasp said tiredly:

Not much. Not much at all.

Sorme stood up. He said:

Look here, I've got to go downstairs. Why don't we go
out and get a last drink before the pubs close?

Glasp's voice sounded dead.

I don't want another drink. It's time I went back,
anyway.

Just as you like . . .

Going down the stairs, he experienced a feeling of
revolt about Glasp and his problems, a sudden understanding that Glasp's mind was no more like his own than
Nunne's was, that his intellect was driven by emotions
working at steam-heat; the stuffy heat of the room seemed
like a physical counterpart of the climate of Glasp's mind.
He breathed deeply and gratefully the cold air of the
bathroom, smelling of damp plaster and escaping gas from
the Ascot, thinking irritably: He needs something to love
like the rest of us, but it couldn't be a kitten or a puppy
or even a woman, it had to be an under-age girl, so the
emotions can work up a nice pressure. And one day the
boiler bursts.

He was glad Glasp had decided to leave, his sudden
exhaustion had communicated itself to Sorme.

Across the waste ground he could see the light in his
room; it puzzled him. He could remember switching it
off. As he opened the front door, he thought suddenly:
Damnation, Austin, and was glad he had seen Glasp on
to the escalator at Camden Town Underground. Mounting the flight of stairs to his room, he saw the open door,
and the straw basket that leaned against the doorjamb. It
was full of empty beer bottles. He pushed open the door,
prepared to say: Hello, Austin.

The old man stood on the rug, his back to the fire, his

hands clasped behind his back. He wore a neat black suit with a collar and tie. He smiled apologetically at Sorme.

Sorme stood there, in the doorway, unwilling to advance into the room, feeling a choked rage rising in his throat. The old man smiled nervously. Sorme said:

What do you want?

I'm . . . very sorry to disturb you. I found your door open. . . . I . . . do hope I'm not intruding.

His politeness softened Sorme, but only to the extent of soothing the desire to be rude. He felt outraged by the invasion of his privacy. He said coldly:

I'd rather you didn't come into my room in my absence.

As he spoke, he made a mental note to lock the door and window whenever he went out.

The old man continued to smile, fidgeting with his hands in the region of the neatly buttoned waistcoat. He pointed at the empty beer bottle on the floor, and said:

I wonder if you require this?

Sorme stared at him blankly.

What?

Your bottle? Perhaps you have more in your cupboard? If you're anxious to get rid of them, I'd be glad to take them away.

Abruptly Sorme understood. He pulled open the cupboard and saw the empty pint bottles on the floor. He had no doubt that the old man had already looked. He said irritably:

Yes, do take them . . . There aren't many.

Ah, that's really very kind of you! Very kind.

The old man stooped and gathered up the three pint bottles, and the empty quart from the rug. Sorme watched him closely, wondering if he was drunk again. His speech had a clarity and precision it had lacked the last time Sorme had talked with him. He was wearing patent-leather shoes with a high polish. Sorme said:

378

I suppose you know that it's after ten-thirty. The pubs'll be closed.

The old man was standing by the door, inserting the bottles carefully in the straw bag. He looked up, frowning.

Ten-thirty? No.

He fumbled in the pocket of the waistcoat, then seemed to remember something. He said:

But . . . but my clock says nine-thirty.

I'm afraid it's wrong.

Oh dear . . .

He stood there, looking at Sorme, as if it lay in Sorme's power to solve his problem. For a moment, Sorme felt ashamed of the irritable satisfaction he had experienced in pointing out the time. He said:

I'm afraid you'll have to wait until tomorrow.

The old man said with dismay:

Oh no. I can't do that!

He came forward to the table again, and took a handful of money out of his pocket. He laid this on the corner of the table and began to count it. Sorme could see three half-crowns and some coppers. He said:

Look here, don't you think you'd better count that in your own room?

The old man glanced at him reproachfully, and went on counting. Then he looked up, and asked simply:

Can you lend me twenty-two and six?

No. I'm afraid I can't.

I'd return it.

I'm sure you would. Anyway, the pubs are all closed . . .

I know. But I know where I can buy gin. Are you sure you couldn't lend me twenty-two and six?

I'm afraid not.

The old man said tremulously:

Oh dear . . . I wonder if the French gentleman next door could?

He knocked on the door of Callet's room. It was impossible for Sorme to close his own door with the bag leaning against the jamb. He turned to the fireplace and made a face of despair at himself in the mirror. There was no reply from Callet's room. Sorme was certain he was inside; probably he had heard the old man's voice and decided to keep quiet. The old man knocked again. Sorme found the spectacle irritating; he went downstairs to the bathroom and locked the door. After a few moments, he heard the old man come downstairs. He flushed the toilet and went up again. Before going into his room, he removed the bag from the doorway, and leaned it against the wall outside. He locked his door, and flung himself into the armchair, thinking: I'll leave this bloody place and find somewhere else. That old swine ought to be in an institution.

As he listened, a knock sounded on the door. He started in his chair. He called: Who is it?

The old man's voice said: May I speak to you?

Sighing, he crossed to the door and unlocked it. The old man said:

I really *must* beg your pardon for intruding like this. I know it's unforgivable, but . . . I really must get twenty-two and six from somewhere.

Sorme said wearily:

I'm sorry, I can't help you.

The old man looked around, as if suspicious of an eavesdropper. His face took on a cunning expression. He advanced on Sorme, pushing him into the room, then said in a whisper:

I can tell you something that would interest you.

For a moment, Sorme was on the point of saying: I'm sure you couldn't, and pushing the old man out. He was prevented by an innate dislike of rudeness and a certainty that the old man would only begin knocking on the door again. The old man raised a finger at Sorme, and regarded him with a knowing, slightly reproachful expression. He said:

I'm not mistaken in supposing you are a man with a strong interest in religion?

Why?

Ah, you're suspicious, and quite rightly so. Not many people have a right to speak of religion. But I have. Now, let me tell you something that will surprise you. *I can open your third eye for you.*

He leaned forward and hissed the last sentence in Sorme's face and Sorme was able to observe that there was no alcohol on his breath. He retreated a step, and said:

I'm afraid I haven't got a third eye.

Aha! You think you haven't. You don't know. I thought you weren't one of the initiated. But you have honesty. You have honesty, or I wouldn't speak to you. Do you know what the third eye is?

He was speaking rapidly now, perhaps sensing Sorme's increasing desire to throw him out. Sorme shook his head.

Your third eye is your mystical eye. You have two eyes to show you appearances, but your mystical eye can show you into the heart of things. I see you have Blake and Boehme on your bookshelves. Well, they could see with the third eye. I can see with my third eye – at least, I could until I started to drink. It only requires a very simple operation to do it . . . if the subject is ready, of course. But I can sense you're ready. Now, wouldn't you like to have a third eye?

Sorme, interested in spite of himself, said dubiously: I suppose so.

Good, the old man said. Then we can arrange it. How

much would you consider the operation worth? Two pounds?

Sorme could not refrain from smiling. He said:

You want me to pay, do you?

The old man said simply: I need the money.

Sorme said: I'm afraid I haven't got it.

Really? It's a unique opportunity. I couldn't make the offer at any other time – for instance, on Monday, after the banks open. My price would be much higher then.

He was peering up into Sorme's face with a childlike anxiety; it was almost as if he was play-acting. Sorme knew he was not play-acting, and that the only alternative was that he was insane. But the realization caused him no alarm, or even excitement. He said apologetically:

I'm afraid I can't give you two pounds. I haven't two pounds to spare.

The old man said sadly:

Oh dear. Well, in that case . . .

He turned away from Sorme, staring at the doorknob. He said vaguely:

I wonder who could . . .?

He asked Sorme suddenly:

I suppose you don't happen to have a little gin hidden away?

I'm afraid not. Only some beer.

Mmmm. I haven't touched beer for years. But I suppose . . . in the absence of anything better. Well. Would you object if I drank a glass of your beer?

Sorme said:

Not at all. Take the bottle.

He snatched up the bottle from the table, and thrust it into the old man's hands. The old man took it dubiously. He said:

If you could lend me eight and ninepence I could buy a half bottle I suppose. But they wouldn't like it.

I'm sorry. I'm in the same position as you. I've no money to spare until I can go to the bank.

Oh. Well, in that case, I suppose I'd better have some beer. Have you a glass?

Sorme took a glass from the table and inverted it over the neck of the bottle. He said:

You might let me have the glass back some time.

Oh, I don't want to take it away.

He removed the glass, unscrewed the bottle, and carefully laid the stopper on the table. A feeling of comic resignation came over Sorme; he imagined Bill Payne in the room, watching with amusement and preparing an imitation of the old man's eager innocence and Sorme's baffled irritation. He sat down in the armchair, and stared at the old man as he poured beer. The old man caught his eye and smiled genially. He replaced the bottle on the table, screwed on the stopper, then came over and sat in the other armchair. He said:

Forgive me for not offering you some. But the bottle wasn't quite full to begin with, and I'm afraid I shan't have enough for myself. This is not selfishness, you understand, but ordinary self-preservation. Well, chin-chin, or whatever you young people say nowadays.

The military phrase sounded odd pattering over his lips. He drank the beer with an expression of distaste. When the glass was half empty, he lowered it, saying:

I'm afraid I wouldn't drink this by preference.

No, Sorme said. He took care not to sound interrogative, for fear of provoking another explanation. The old man said pleasantly:

I find you likeable. What can I tell you to amuse you?

Sorme said gruffly: Nothing, thanks.

Let me see. Weren't you interested in Jack the Ripper?

Sorme was unable to conceal his surprise. He said:

I suppose so. Why?

383

I knew it. I know a great deal about you . . .

Sorme wondered if Carlotte had mentioned the subject. He determined not to be drawn out any further. He said:

I'm not particularly interested.

No? All the same, I think I can tell you one or two things that would interest you. How old would you say I am?

He stared at Sorme so persistently that he found it difficult to ignore the question. He said finally:

Seventy, maybe.

The old man's eyes glittered with delight. He reached for the beer bottle.

Wrong again. I'm eighty-nine.

Sorme said unbelievingly: Yes?

I can show you my birth certificate to prove it. I have it somewhere . . .

He clapped a hand to his coat over his heart, then said:

I thought I had it. It must be in the drawer. But this is beside the point. I'm assuming you disbelieve me, whereas, in fact, I am sure you don't. Is that not so?

Yes, Sorme said.

Thank you, sir. A man prefers to be trusted. Well, there you are. Eighty-nine. Born on the twenty-third of August, eighteen sixty-seven. I may add that my father was in diplomatic service in Cracow, where he knew Zeromski. My mother was Polish. Well . . . the gentleman who is known to the Press as Jack the Ripper was a close friend of my father's. His name was Sergei Pedachenko, and he came from the same village as Grigory Efimovitch Rasputin. In fact, he was a relative by law of Grigory Efimovitch. Together they grew up in Pokrovskoe in Tobolsk, although Sergei Fyodorovitch was several years his senior . . .

As he reclined in the armchair, gesturing with his left hand as he talked, the old man made Sorme think of an actor in some Turgenev play. The words flowed out like a speech learned by heart. When the old man paused to empty his glass, Sorme found himself wanting him to go on. The old man talked as he refilled the glass:

Well, Grigory Efimovitch and Sergei Fyodorovitch belonged to one of the *raskolniki*, that is to say, a heretical sect, known as the Khlysty. And the Khlysty believed in salvation through sin. You understand? A fine theological point, as you will recognize. The more one sins, the more one can repent. A verbal sophistry, you say? Not at all. Consider that many a man who is inclined to saintliness suffers from boredom, a sense of futility. Consider that it is better to feel yourself a sinner than to feel as if you have no identity. This is admittedly a human weakness, that a man has to dramatize himself into an identity or suffer stagnation. You and I, sir, know that man is a god. And yet he can do nothing to make himself into a god unless circumstances are kind enough to give him an opportunity to behave like one.

Sorme found himself listening with increasing amazement; a sense of unreality came over him. A fantasy shaped itself in his head, that the old man was really an angel in disguise, sent to bring home to him a sense of his own immaturity. The old man could evidently see the effect he was creating; something like a smirk formed in his eyes as he talked. He raised his finger in admonition:

This is the paradox of our nature, the result of original sin. A tree can be itself by standing still. A man becomes himself only by making a bonfire of his potentialities. In the light of action, he sees his reality as it disappears in a new persona. And . . .

He paused to take a long drink, then said vaguely:

Where were we?

Jack the Ripper.

Ah yes. My friend Pedachenko. Well, to make it brief,

Sergei Fyodorovitch came to London to sin his way to salvation. He had read a book by Dostoevsky describing it as the most sordid capital in Europe. At the time, I was a boy of eighteen. He and I travelled together from Odessa. He brought with him an Austrian tailoress named Limberg, a woman of distinctly sadistic tendencies. They took rooms in Leman Street, and my friend embarked on his career of disembowelling. His mistress was always somewhere near carrying a cloak. When he had committed his crime, she would hand him the cloak: he would cover his bloodstained suit – he bought innumerable suits in the Petticoat Lane market – and together they would walk home arm in arm, like a respectable man and wife returning from a late evening with friends. On three occasions they were stopped by police when a mere glimpse of my friend's trousers would have given him to the hangman. On each occasion, they posed as a married couple and were allowed to proceed immediately. After his last murder, he sailed for America, where he became the proprietor of a brothel in New Orleans.

The old man emptied his second glass, and carefully filled it to the brim again, emptying the bottle.

Naturally, he was made very welcome on his return to Russia. He was appointed Archimandrite of the sect, and was generally regarded as something of a saint. He then began his career of repentance. His mistress Limberg had no taste for repentance and left Russia with another young man who hoped to emulate Sergei Fyodorovitch. My friend Pedachenko accompanied Grigory Efimovitch to St Petersburg, where he shared his extraordinary success for a number of years. They died within a year of one another – Rasputin in nineteen-sixteen, murdered by the bandit Yussupov, and Pedachenko in nineteen-seventeen, shot in the back by one of Kerensky's men.

The old man took a sip from the full glass, then stood up, holding it carefully. He said politely:

I shall now leave you, borrowing, if I may, your glass.

Sorme stared at him, unable to find words. The old man bowed slightly, saying gravely:

Goodnight.

He took the empty bottle, and went to the door. Sorme heard the bottle clink into the straw bag. A moment later, the old man returned, still holding the full glass. He said:

You are still certain you can't lend me eight and ninepence?

Sorme fumbled in his back pocket, and produced a crumpled ten-shilling note. He handed it to the old man without speaking. The old man bowed; he said formally:

Sir, you have saved my life. A thousand thanks.

He kissed the note, then backed out of the door. Sorme found his voice to say: Goodnight, as the door closed. The old man did not reply. He heard him mounting the next flight of stairs, the bottles clinking.

The tiredness had gone; he stood by the window, wondering what to do. A few minutes later, he heard the old man come downstairs again and go out of the house. After a moment's uncertainty, he went downstairs and rang Nunne's flat again. There was still no reply. He went and stood in the front doorway for a while, then returned to his room. It was too late to go back to Miss Quincey's and Caroline was on the other side of London. There was nothing for it but to go to bed.

He lay awake for two hours, thinking about the old man and about Austin. When he slept, the old man hovered in his dreams. Towards 2 A.M. he went downstairs to the bathroom, and washed his hands and face in hot water. After that, he slept. There was no sound coming from the old man's room.

He woke again in the cold dawn, dreaming that Gertrude Quincey lay pressed against him. While he kept his eyes closed, he could feel her body against his relaxed limbs, her arms round his neck. She stopped being there when he woke up fully, but the memory was as clear as a physical experience. He stared at the paleing sky; in the clear light of speculation, the desire disappeared; it was possible only through the blurred outlines of sleep.

The sense of wellbeing expanded in him, a knowledge of increasing power; for a moment he felt glad of the world and the existence of everything in it. Then he fell asleep thinking about Caroline.

Chapter Five

He was dreaming that Nunne had been condemned to death, and he was telling Stein that it was a monstrous stupidity, that Nunne was a man of genius, an irreplaceable loss to literature. But as he said it, he did not believe it. He knew it would be impossible to express his real reasons for defending Nunne to Stein or anybody else.

A noise woke him. He stared at the wall, and listened to a male voice in the room below singing a popular song. It sounded as if there were decorators at work in the room. He turned on to his back and stared at the sky through the window. It was marble-grey. He found himself wondering whether he would ever defend Austin if it came to a trial for murder. They would be wrong; Stein and the judges would be wrong; but there was no way of altering that. A good psychiatrist might have him declared insane; that would be the simplest solution; but Nunne was not insane.

He got out of bed to put the kettle on, turned the gas to medium and climbed back into bed. As he did so his eyes rested on the Nijinsky *Diary*, and something concentrated inside him. There was the image of a man walking along a treelined avenue at night, listening to sounds of music coming from a hotel lounge. In the man was an obsession with the superhuman, a desire to rise cleanly and naturally beyond human pettiness, maintaining the flight without uncertainty. For a moment he felt he understood Austin, received a clear insight into the disgust that became violence. He looked out at the grey sky, holding the knowledge firmly, thinking: Nothing matters but this power. No price is too high for it.

At the same time he heard footsteps on the stair, and guessed they were coming to his room. Carlotte's voice called: Mr Sorme!

Hello?

She opened the door.

Are you up yet? There's a gentleman to see you.

Who?

She shrugged.

I don't know. A German.

German?

He thought hard for a moment, then asked:

An old man?

Yes.

Ah. Ask him to come up, would you, please?

He pulled on a pair of trousers, and was tying his dressing-gown as Stein came into the room. Stein glanced at the rumpled bed, and smiled apologetically:

Am I too early?

Sorme shook his cold hand.

That's OK. I was awake. What did you want to talk to me about? Austin?

He was leading deliberately, unwilling to play a cat-and mouse game. Stein said:

Austin? No, not particularly. I am more interested in this old man above you.

For a moment, registering his surprise, Sorme believed him.

Why? You don't think *he's* the Whitechapel killer?

No. But he may know something. When he was in hospital, he shouted strange things in his sleep.

I'm sure he knows nothing, Sorme said decisively.

No?

I had a talk with him last night. He's as mad as a march

hare, but he doesn't know anything. How did you find out about him, anyway?

Stein shrugged expressively:

I happened to notice the address on Inspector Macmurdo's list of routine calls. I knew it was your address also. So I came on the off-chance that you might be able to tell me something.

To Sorme, watching him, the lie seemed transparent; but he remembered that Stein was unaware that Father Carruthers had spoken to him of Nunne. From Stein's viewpoint, there was no reason why Sorme should disbelieve him. He said:

I'll tell you what I can, but you ought to see him yourself. You'd see, he's cracked.

He raved about murder in the hospital.

Yes. But not these murders. The only Whitechapel crimes that interest him happened sixty years ago.

The Jack the Ripper murders?

Sorme said:

What on earth makes you interested in a man of that age? It must be obvious that he'd be incapable of a series of murders?

Stein said wearily:

Somewhere in London there is a killer. There is nothing to do but check every possibility.

I agree. But you're wasting your time with the old man. He's too old. And he's insane, anyway.

So is the killer.

You think so?

Stein said:

Yes, I think so.

The kettle began to simmer. Sorme said:

Sit down and have a cup of tea. You look tired.

Thank you. I am tired.

Don't you take a rest on Sundays?

Stein said, shrugging:

In a case like this, there is no time to rest.

He dropped into the armchair, placing his hat on the table. Sorme found himself feeling sorry for him. He spooned tea into the thermos flask and poured in the boiling water. As he turned off the gas ring he lit the fire. The room was warm from the burning gas; he removed the dressing-gown, and put on a shirt. He said:

Never mind. Maybe you'll catch him in the act some time.

Perhaps, Stein said. He contemplated the steam that rose from the flask, and then added:

He made another attempt last night.

What?

Sorme stared at him, wondering at the same time if Stein was trying to trap him in some way. Stein was not even looking at him. He asked:

What happened?

I don't know in detail. A woman was attacked in her room early this morning. Neighbours heard her screams and ran in. The man jumped out of the window and disappeared.

In Whitechapel?

Yes.

But what happened to the woman?

She was still unconscious at eight o'clock this morning. Her skull was fractured.

Will she live?

Probably. Luckily, the injuries have not affected the brain.

So you should get a description of the killer?

We hope so. But the room was in darkness.

Pouring the tea, Sorme thought: Poor Austin. There's nothing I can do now. Then he stopped himself, thinking: Why Austin? It may not be Austin.

Stein accepted the mug of tea, saying:

So you see why we are getting tired of it all.

I do. Never mind. With luck, you'll get a description.

Perhaps.

Stein relapsed into silence, drinking his tea.

You say you're sure he's insane, doctor?

I think so.

Sorme stopped himself on the point of asking: Insane enough to get sent to Broadmoor?

Instead, he asked:

Do you think all sexual killers are insane?

Why, no, assuredly not. Any more than a starving man who steals a loaf of bread is insane.

I see.

Stein looked at him and asked, smiling:

What are you thinking?

I'm wondering . . . if a murderer might not be saner than the average man.

How?

Sorme stared out of the window for a moment, then said:

For instance, in the days when sacrifices were offered in temples. The priests might have profounder insight into reality than most people. The killing was a symbol.

A symbol? Stein said unbelievingly.

Yes. A sort of rejection of the ordinary daylight. A deliberate turning away from daylight logic.

Stein said, frowning:

But a man who kills is under strain. He is not a philosopher. Someone knocked on the door. The girl called:

Telephone for Dr Stein.

Stein said wearily:

Again!

He made a tired gesture of disgust, and went out of the room.

Sorme finished drinking his tea, seated in the armchair.

Obscurely, he felt that something important was taking place, but he found it difficult to take it seriously. A sense of reality in him revolted against the complications of diplomacy and deception. Although he knew Nunne's life might be at stake, it was still impossible to feel completely involved. He tried to focus this sense of unreality, wondering how quickly Stein would interrupt him; after a moment, the feeling recreated itself briefly; he tried to verbalize it. What was at stake was murder – murder of a number of women. If they died, it was because they had no good reason to stay alive. The lives they lost were only half lives; consequently, the Whitechapel killer could only be half a murderer. And the killer himself was probably only half alive too. In that case, it was a case of quarter murder. Futility murdering stupidity and uselessness. Nietzsche had said that a whole nation was a detour to create a dozen great men . . .

Stein came back into the room. The tired look had gone. He said:

We have caught him.

Sorme sat up.

What!

Stein's eyes were alive with restrained excitement.

The murderer. He was caught an hour ago.

Sorme stared at him unbelievingly.

Who was it?

A Brixton labourer. He was the man who attacked the woman last night. His description was circulated, and a police car saw him trying to climb the dockyard wall. The woman identified him an hour ago.

Are you certain it's the murderer? Has he confessed?

No. In fact, he admits the attack last night, but says it was his first attempt.

Are the police quite sure it's the right man?

Quite sure. He had blacked his face with burnt cork.

They found a sponge smeared with burnt cork in his pocket.

Sorme said, smiling:

Well, congratulations. I hope you've found the right man.

Stein said shrugging:

He may not be. Murderers are imitative. In the Kürten case, an idiot was caught in the act of attempted rape, and confessed to the murders. Unfortunately, he was not the killer. I could cite many cases where a murder has been imitated by other murderers . . . All the same, we must hope.

Sorme said dubiously:

Brixton's a helluva way from Whitechapel.

Stein smiled.

This man was born and brought up in Whitechapel. Probably he knows Whitechapel better than Brixton. Besides, he may have motives of revenge against women in Whitechapel.

Stein lifted his teacup and emptied it. He said, smiling:

Now we shall see if your theories about the murderer's mentality are accurate.

He put the cup back on the table, and picked up his hat.

I thank you for the tea. I shall hope to see you again before I return to Germany.

I hope so. You – er – don't feel interested in the old boy upstairs now?

Stein said:

We shall remain interested, of course, until we are certain that this man is the murderer. But I intend to take a short rest now.

His smile was no longer tired. He said, politely:

I wish you good morning, and thank you.

Sorme shook his hand.

Don't mind if I don't come down?

Stein said firmly:

Not in the least. Goodbye.

Sorme listened to the steps descending the stairs, counting slowly up to fifty to make sure that Stein had left the house. Then he glanced in the mirror, caressed his unshaven chin with his fingers, and put on a jacket and overcoat.

Stein's visit left him with a feeling of suspicion; the news of the arrest had fallen out too neatly. It seemed prearranged. He turned off the gas fire, and made sure the window was fastened, then locked the door behind him.

Before he asked the question, he knew the answer would be negative. He stood, holding the receiver, contemplating with distaste the moisture that had condensed around the mouthpiece from the previous user. After a while, the girl returned:

The porter says that, as far as he knows, Mr Nunne didn't come back last night. I'll tell him you rang, shall I?

He walked along Camden High Street, uncertain what to do. A taxi cruised past, and for a moment he considered hailing it and going to the Kensington flat. Then the thought that Nunne might not be there either discouraged him. He stood, hesitating, at the corner of Crowndale Road, contemplating the boxes outside the post office. The sight of a bus labelled 'Farringdon Road' decided him; he jumped on to the platform before the lights changed. Relaxed on the upper deck, he noticed again the same sense of interior clarity that had come earlier in bed. A point of vitality stirred in him, imposing itself on the outline of St Pancras station, transforming the thought of trains into a sense of triumph.

The Hungarian priest was at the door of the hostel. He said immediately:

You want to see Father Carruthers?

If it's possible, please.

Yes? I don't know if he's resting.

It's very important.

The priest opened the door with a latchkey.

You will wait in there, please.

Thank you.

The formalities irritated him. He sank into the armchair beside the gas fire, then stood up again, tensing his shoulders with impatience. He glanced out of the door, and saw Robin Maunsell coming up the stairs. He withdrew his head immediately, wondering if Maunsell had seen him. The steps turned the corner, and went up the next flight. He smiled with relief. Almost immediately, the Hungarian priest came back.

Will you go up?

Thanks.

He pretended to be looking for his gloves on the armchair, to make sure Maunsell was out of sight. The priest said:

You have lost something?

Oh . . . no. They're here in my pocket . . .

He went up the stairs two at a time, at once impatient and cautious.

Father Carruthers said:

Good morning, Gerard. You're soon back.

Morning, father. Hope I'm not a nuisance.

The priest was in bed; he looked ill and tired. The fire in the grate was a mass of glowing coals; Sorme observed the contrast between the room temperature and the icy coldness of the priest's hand as he took it.

You're not a nuisance. But I'm afraid I'm not too well today. We shall have to make it brief.

OK, father. Briefly, then, Stein has just been to see me about Austin.

Was he quite frank with you?

Well, no. In fact, he hardly mentioned Austin at all. That's why I wanted to see you. He says the Whitechapel killer's been arrested.

When?

About an hour ago. The phone rang while he was with me. He claimed he'd come to talk about the old man in the room above . . . the one who tried to set the house on fire.

The priest said slowly:

I see. Well, what do you think?

I wonder if it's some sort of a trick.

Did he question you about Austin?

No. He hardly mentioned him.

But you believe he wasn't sincere about his reason for coming to see you?

No. I don't think the police really suspect the old man. He's too old. They might as well . . . they might as well suspect you. If you see what I mean . . .

Indeed, they might! Well, so you suppose they might still be interested in Austin?

Sorme said helplessly: I just don't know, father.

I'm inclined to feel they are. Have you seen him?

Well, that's another problem. Austin seems to have disappeared. He hasn't been home for twenty-four hours. Mind, he could be at the Kensington place.

Couldn't you phone?

He's not on the phone.

I see. And what about this man who has been arrested?

Some man who attacked a woman last night in White-chapel. A Brixton labourer. He'd blacked his face, apparently.

Ah, really?

Have you heard of him, father?

The priest said:

I have. And I'm afraid it sounds as if you're right.

Why?

Franz mentioned him to me a few days ago. He said that a man was frightening women in Whitechapel by jumping out of doorways with a black face. The police don't really believe he's the murderer. And Franz most certainly doesn't.

Why?

Because a man who jumps out of doorways and frightens women sounds a very different proposition from a murderer. He's a sadist of a sort, of course . . . but not the kind the police want.

But this man attacked a woman, father. He caused serious head injuries, according to Stein. It was in a room in Whitechapel, and he escaped by jumping through the window.

Indeed? Ah . . .

Sorme stirred uncomfortably on the edge of the bed. He unbuttoned his overcoat; the heat was making him sweat. The priest said finally:

If you are sure he attacked a woman . . . perhaps I am wrong.

Stein said he'd confessed to the attack, but not to the other murders.

I see. Then it sounds as if he was being quite sincere. If he was trying to deceive you, he wouldn't have admitted that the man had not confessed to the previous murders.

You mean he'd either tell me he had, or wouldn't mention it at all?

I'm afraid it sounds like that.

A shiver passed over the skin of Sorme's back. He said:

Why afraid, father? Do you think Austin's the murderer?

The priest said;

From my knowledge of Austin, it seems unlikely.

Why?

Because . . . I have known Austin since he was a child. I should say, I have been acquainted with him since he was a child. And his mother has talked to me about him a great deal. Do *you* think he could commit a murder?

The question took Sorme by surprise. After a hesitation, he said doubtfully:

That's not easy to answer. In the sense you mean, no. He's not a ruffian, he's not callous . . . But . . . I can't explain.

Try to explain, Gerard.

Sorme pulled off the overcoat, and dropped it on the bed, then unbuttoned the jacket. He wiped the sweat off his forehead. He said slowly:

You see, father, it's like this. I met him at the Diaghilev exhibition, you know . . .

Yes. What has that to do with it?

Quite a lot, actually. You didn't see it, did you? No. Well – it impressed me, because . . . it was like a fairy-tale. These old costumes, designs, soft music, scent – the same scent that Austin uses, incidentally – just like another world. Well, that's Austin's world, father, the world he *wants* to live in. He's not a very brilliant person. He wouldn't get much out of the writings of the saints or the Church fathers. But he wants to find an ideal world all the same . . . You remember, I told you the same thing about his basement flat?

Yes.

I think being alive exhausts him. He can't accept reality. I can understand him because I feel the same. The reality of the world batters him. It bullies him. So he wants to see it from some beautifully detached standpoint. That's why he's so theatrical. Instead of real slums, he wants a stage set that looks like slums. Instead of real despair and defeat, he wants tragic actors raving about it. He has to simplify everything . . .

I see your point. But this doesn't sound like the definition of a murderer to me.

He becomes the tragic actor himself, making a gesture of defiance. Don't you see, father. He dramatizes his own self-disgust. If he committed a murder, he wouldn't be a real murderer. He'd be a tragic actor playing Macbeth.

The priest said:

I'm afraid you overestimate his need for self-dramatization. I doubt whether it would extend to actual killing.

Sorme felt confused and involved, unable to capture the thread of insight. He said finally:

I dunno, father . . . It's all this feeling of wanting to impose yourself on the world. Murder's the ultimate taboo. In a certain mood, it could be a kind of suicide. I think that's how Austin feels. Unless he can dramatize it, the world seems unbearably alien. He wants to do something positive to justify his existence.

The priest's face clouded. He said:

I . . . see what you mean. All the same . . . I don't know. It doesn't strike me as likely.

No, and I agree, it's no final proof that Austin would commit murder . . .

You should see Austin . . . and perhaps you should warn him.

I thought you didn't want me to warn him?

Not openly, perhaps. On the other hand, it seems to me very probable that he is not guilty. In that case . . .

He broke off, staring at the eiderdown, his chin on his chest. Sorme was uncertain whether his attitude showed deep thought or simply fatigue. He stood up and crossed to the window, which was open about an inch at the top;

the faint current of cool air was a relief. As he waited, the priest went on:

What you say about Austin may be true for yourself. I could imagine a certain type of man who needs a sense of moral purpose, who feels the world to be meaningless . . .

Sorme interrupted:

Austin once said something like that to me. He said he felt futile or meaningless . . . no, unintended; that was the word.

Did he? What else did he say?

Oh . . . something about feeling he ought not to be alive. He said if there was any justice in the world he'd've broken his neck or something. Mind, he was in a pretty low state that evening.

Unintended. I must admit, you surprise me. But it bears out what you say. But, as I was about to say . . . I can imagine that a man might feel a need to enter the order of good and evil, to escape a sense of futility. And I can imagine him committing a crime merely to prove to himself that he is capable of evil, and therefore not entirely . . . unintended. But I have never in my life come across such a case – except, perhaps, in juvenile delinquents.

Sorme said, shrugging:

The way you put it, I agree it sounds unlikely. But I'm not talking about conscious motives. I'm just saying that *if* Austin was the killer, I could understand. I mean, take Oliver Glasp. . . . He's the same sort of person. I've seen a lot of Oliver over this past week, father, and I think I've got to know a lot about him. Well, I know he'd never suffer from any sort of strain if he believed in his own genius. He'd have a purpose then. As it is, he's got himself involved with some ten-year-old girl from a slum tenement. It gives him a sense of meaning from day to day, and that's what he needs to keep going. But he doesn't believe in his own reality enough to exist without something of the sort. Don't you see what I'm trying to say, father? Oliver needs people more than ideas – he's an emotional person. So when he's under strain, he gropes around for people. I need ideas more than people. When I rebel, it's a rebellion of ideas. But Austin's sensual as well as emotional. He needs a physical outlet for his rebellion – driving fast cars, flying an aeroplane. Doesn't it sound plausible?

He was carried away by the excitement of his own words; when he stopped, he experienced a feeling of guilt. Father Carruthers was listening with his head drooping, his eyes closed; he might have been asleep. Without opening his eyes, he said softly:

Yes, it sounds plausible.

Sorme said: I'm afraid I'm talking too much.

I'm sorry. I'd like to help you more. But I feel very tired.

Yes, absolutely, I'll go now.

Go and see Austin.

If I can find him!

Try at his Kensington flat. Take a taxi there.

All right. But I'll take a tube.

The priest said:

Open that top drawer behind you . . . no, the left one. There should be a plastic case there . . . Yes, thank you.

He opened the black wallet that Sorme had handed to him, and took out a pound note.

Take this and use it for a taxi.

No, really, father . . .

Take it. I have no use for money here – I spend my days in bed. Besides, you are doing an errand for me. I'd go if I could. Take it.

Sorme took the note unwillingly, and pushed it, folded, into his top pocket. He said:

Thank you, father. Shall I phone back to let you know?

No. If anything important happens, come back. But I shall sleep now.

All right, father. Thanks. I hope you get well soon.

Thank you, Gerard.

He let himself out of the front door. As he turned the corner, he met Robin Maunsell hurrying across the road. Maunsell said:

Well, Gerard, you're rather a stranger, aren't you? A stranger to me, I should say, because I hear that you're always popping in and out to Father Carruthers.

Sorme said embarrassedly:

How are you?

I'm very well. But what on earth's going on with you? Are the two of you planning a campaign to convert Austin Nunne?

Something like that, Sorme said, grinning.

Come in and have a cup of tea.

No, thanks, Robin. I'm just doing an errand for Father Carruthers.

Really? Are you coming back?

I expect so. Later in the day.

Well, I can see you're dying to go. Perhaps I'll see you later.

Sorme said untruthfully:

I'm just off for lunch. I'm pretty hungry. But I'll see you later . . .

All right.

As Sorme turned away, Maunsell said:

Give Austin my regards.

Sorme looked back in surprise, but Maunsell was already in the doorway.

He crossed Rosebery Avenue, walking towards Ludgate Circus, with the idea of finding a taxi in Holborn. His neck was still damp with sweat from the heat of the room, and his throat felt dry. For some reason, he felt no belief that Nunne would be in the Kensington flat. Nunne wouldn't be anywhere where he was known to go regularly if he was avoiding the police . . . The thought of the women's clothes came to him suddenly. At the time, Nunne's explanation had been inadequate. But his new suspicions provided no satisfactory hypothesis to explain them either.

In Fleet Street he turned into the bar of the first pub he saw. He ordered a pint of mild, and drank a half of it before the burning sensation went out of his throat. He grinned at the bartender, saying:

Ah, that's better.

From the next bar, someone called:

Cheerio, George!

Goodbye, Mr Payne.

Sorme said:

Was that Bill Payne?

Yes, sir.

He hurried to the door of the pub, and saw Payne on the point of crossing the road. He called:

Hi, Bill!

The noise of traffic drowned his voice; as Payne was about to step off the pavement, he jumped forward and touched his arm. Payne said:

Hello, Gerard! What are you doing here?

Having a drink. Come and join me.

In there? Where were you? I didn't see you.

The bartender said:

You're soon back!

Payne said, grinning:

I planted my friend here to give me an excuse. What are you having, Gerard?

I've got one, thanks. Have one with me. What is it?

Usual, please, George. Let's go in next door. This wood's icy to the arse.

A fire was burning in the lounge bar; Payne carried his glass to the table that stood near it. He said:

Have you heard the news?

About the arrest? Yes.

Payne said with surprise:

Where'd you hear it?

From a police pathologist.

Starr?

No, Stein – the German doctor I know on the case. He came around this morning to follow up the business of the old man. They phoned him while he was with me.

Did they? You mean they told him the hunt was off?

Oh no. Just that the man had been arrested. Stein admitted it might be the wrong man.

Why?

Well . . . surely it's obvious? He hasn't confessed to the murders . . .

Ah, then you haven't heard the latest. He's made a full confession since.

What! Confessed to what?

All the murders – except one of the women killed the other night.

Are you sure?

Quite sure. It came just before I left the office.

What did it say? Do you know the details?

Some of them. You know about the attack last night?

Yes.

Well, the police found charcoal marks on the woman's throat and hands. She was unconscious, of course. They started a fullscale murder hunt. He must have got into the dockyard somehow – down near Limehouse pier. And somebody spotted him as he tried to climb over the wall this morning. They say he's got a broken knee. He'd tried to clean the charcoal off his face, but there were still traces, and they found the sponge he'd been using in his pocket. They took him to Commercial Street police station and he denied the murders – although he admitted the attack last night. Then they took him to Scotland Yard, and he confessed the lot. So that's it!

Sorme found it difficult to conceal the cold feeling of relief that gave him a desire to laugh. He said:

So he's caught!

He's caught, Payne said.

Do they know anything about his motive?

No. But he's a bit of an idiot. Can't speak properly – has a hare lip – and he's been on probation for being involved in a robbery.

An idiot? That doesn't sound so good.

Why?

Stein told me that an idiot was arrested in the Düsseldorf case, and confessed to the murders. He wasn't the murderer.

I think the police must be fairly sure of themselves. They wouldn't announce his confession if they doubted it. Anyway, for the sake of the police I hope they've got the man.

So does everybody. But why did he wear charcoal last night? There was no sign of charcoal in the previous murders. And Stein told me they'd been after this bloke for a few weeks – he'd been jumping out of doorways and frightening women. That doesn't sound like the killer.

Payne said thoughtfully:

Perhaps you're right. That's a good point. I'll mention that to the chap who's doing the story. Anyway, why should he confess if he's not the killer?

Perhaps the police were rough with him. You said he'd got a broken knee. He wouldn't have much resistance, would he?

But the police wouldn't want him to confess if he wasn't the killer.

Sorme said, shrugging:

I don't know. It's only guesswork. I hope it's the right man. What's his name, by the way?

Oh . . . Bentley, Alfred Bentley. Lives in Brixton.

But he used to live in Whitechapel, Sorme said.

Did he? Are you sure?

That's what Stein told me.

I didn't know that. So he'd know the district well. Listen, Gerard, I'd better get back to the office. What's the name of this German, in case we want to contact him?

Stein. Franz Stein. And he's working with Macmurdo.

Right. Thanks a lot. I might ring you later. Let's meet for a drink.

All right. Be seeing you, Bill.

After Payne had gone, he finished his pint, staring into the fire. The excitement had been replaced by doubt. He replaced his glass on the counter, went into Fleet Street, and hailed a passing taxi.

When the taxi turned into Palace Gate, he asked the driver:

Would you mind waiting at the end of Canning Place? I shan't be long.

As he walked towards the house, he told himself he could return and dismiss the taxi if Nunne was in. He had no desire to encounter Vannet, and was afraid the taxi might attract his attention.

The area gate creaked open. The curtains behind the barred windows were drawn. He rang the bell and listened carefully. He could hear it ringing somewhere inside. There was no other sound. He rang again. After a wait of another half minute, he took an old envelope out of his pocket, scrawled a message on it and slipped it through the letterbox. Above his head, the front door opened. A man he had never seen before looked down at him. The man said:

Oh.

His head disappeared, and the front door closed again. Sorme decided to leave immediately, afraid that Vannet might appear. He felt better when the door of the taxi had closed behind him. He gave the driver his Camden Town address.

As he passed the telephone in the hall, he stopped and dialled Nunne's flat, knowing as he did so that it would be pointless. After a moment, the girl said:

I'm afraid there's still no reply, sir.

He groped through his pockets and found another four pennies. With his address book propped open on the coin box he dialled Caroline's number; a man's voice with a London accent answered.

'Old on a minute. I'll get 'er. 'Oo's it speakin'?

A moment later, Caroline's voice said:

Gerard! Hello, sweet!

Hello, pet. How are things?

Fine. What are you doing?

Nothing much. Have you heard the Whitechapel murderer's been caught?

Yes; it was on the radio just now. Isn't it exciting?

Terrific. How are you feeling?

Oh, all right, now. I've recovered.

Is anyone there with you?

No; daddy's gone upstairs.

When can you come over here again?

Not today, sweet, I'm afraid.

You doing something this evening?

No, but they don't like me to go into town on Sunday. They say I'm there too often. I could come tomorrow . . .

Good. Make it tomorrow night, then?

All right, darling. I'm longing to see you.

He went upstairs feeling curiously let down. The tension of the morning had aroused an anticipation in him. To spend the rest of the day alone seemed an anticlimax.

In his room he opened a tin of tomato soup, and ate it with bread and butter. He took a volume of Blake off the shelf and tried to read as he drank the hot soup. A few minutes later he returned the book to the shelf and took down *The Return of Sherlock Holmes*. This attempt was more successful; he read four stories before he became tired. It was now three o'clock. He remembered Miss Quincey's invitation, but felt no real desire to go there. He would have preferred spending the afternoon in bed with Caroline. He stretched and yawned, massaging his eyelids with his fingers, then stood up and looked out of the window. The day was grey and cold. He typed a note on a half sheet of quarto paper, then put on his coat and went downstairs, locking his door behind him. He propped the note against the telephone as he went out.

She looked pleased to see him.

Come and get warm. I've been expecting you.

Really? Why?

I just rang you up. The girl told me you'd left a telephone number, and when I asked for it it turned out to be mine?

He said, chuckling:

That must have been a pleasant surprise!

There was a coal fire burning in the sitting-room. The curtains were drawn, and the lamplight gave the room an atmosphere of warmth. He was suddenly glad he had come.

Where's Oliver today?

Oh . . . at home, I suppose. What did Brother Robbins think of him?

Oh . . . he thought he was a Communist. But he liked you.

Sorme said: Hmmm.

She asked, smiling:

You didn't like him much, did you?

Not much. Do you?

He's a very good man. He does a great deal of social work besides his work for us.

She saw Sorme's grimace as she said 'us', and coloured. She asked:

Why didn't you like Brother Robbins?

Sorme said:

I didn't dislike him particularly. But I can't imagine why you're mixed up with that bunch. I don't mind intelligently religious people. But anybody can see he's as crack-brained as a flat-earther.

She said, shrugging:

It's true he's not particularly intelligent. But he's kind-hearted, and that's the main thing.

I suppose so. But what's to stop you becoming a Catholic or a Baptist if that's all that matters? You'll find just as many kind people there, I expect.

I can tell you in one sentence. I can't stand churches.

No?

No. I don't know why. When I was a little girl, I used to be sick in church.

And is that the only reason you're a Jehovah's Witness?

Of course not. But it's the reason that I wasn't a member of any other congregation before I became a Witness.

But surely the Witnesses have a sort of a church – Kingdom Hall, or whatever they call it?

Yes.

Don't you go there?

Not often. Twice a year perhaps I go to prayer meetings

at the houses of other members – and of course I hold them here.

Sorme looked at her face, lit by the flames, and became aware of her as a different personality; she seemed younger, and also weaker. A kind of understanding was forming in him.

But you didn't feel the same aversion for the Bible?

Oh no. At least, I did as a girl. Or I should say, I was indifferent to it. I could never understand why they had to say 'art' instead of 'are' and things like that. And once I got slapped by my nurse when she thought I was making fun of the Bible. I wanted to know why it was always talking about people 'arising'. 'He arose and went to the land of Uz.' I said it made it sound as if the ancient Hebrews were sitting down all the time, and it was quite an event when they stood up.

Sorme said, laughing:

You sound as if you had quite a sense of humour!

No. I was serious.

The telephone began to ring. She went out to answer it, and called a moment later:

It's for you.

He said:

Good. That'll be Austin.

No, it's Oliver.

Oliver!

He went to the phone and said:

Hello, Oliver.

Glasp's voice sounded muffled.

Listen, Gerard, can you help me? I'm in trouble.

What sort of trouble?

I'm in Commercial Street police station. I'm under arrest.

What the hell for?

412

Oh . . . it's about Christine. Her father's laid a complaint against me.

What's the charge?

Seducing a minor.

But . . . but that's insane! I mean . . . they can't have any evidence. They've only got to examine her to find it's nonsense.

Glasp said:

I know, but in the meantime I'm in gaol. And Christine's run away, so I shall probably be stuck here till they find her.

Blimey! What a bloody nuisance. Can't something be done?

Yes. You could get me out if you could lend me the twenty-five pounds bail. Or if you couldn't, I'm pretty sure Father Carruthers would.

Right. Just hold on. I'll be right over with the money. See you in an hour. Twenty-five pounds.

Thanks a lot, Gerard. I don't want to spend longer in this dump than I have to.

Miss Quincey came out of the kitchen, saying:

Twenty-five pounds? What does he want that for?

She was carrying a tea tray with a teapot on it.

Bail. He's in the Whitechapel police station.

What on earth for?

He's charged with seducing a minor. Have you got twenty-five pounds in cash here?

No . . . Seducing a minor?

It's nonsense, of course. Actually, it's some little girl he's taken an interest in. He thinks she has artistic talent. Her father's a habitual drunk and he's trying to cause trouble. The charge'll collapse as soon as she's been examined by a doctor . . . I wonder if the police would take a cheque?

I . . . I know someone who'd probably cash one. But

413

how preposterous! Oliver really ought to be a little careful. Do you have to go immediately? Come and have a cup of tea first.

He followed her into the sitting-room. She said:

Have you got twenty-five pounds?

Well . . . not really. But Oliver thinks Father Carruthers could lend it to him.

The Catholic priest? But I doubt whether he'd have that much money in cash. I'd better lend it to him, I think.

That'd be very sweet of you. You'd get it back, of course.

I know someone who lives near here who could probably cash a cheque. But how silly of Oliver!

While he drank the tea, he outlined what Glasp had told him the night before. She listened gravely; when he spoke of the child posing she commented:

That was stupid!

He said:

I can understand Oliver's motive. He's a lonely person. He needs people.

She stood up.

I'm going to phone a solicitor friend of mine. He usually keeps some spare cash in the house for emergencies like this.

He drank another cup of tea while she phoned. She was speaking for a long time. He built up the fire, squatting on the rug, thinking: Why do all my friends seem to get involved in violence? And why do I loathe violence so much? Is it cowardice or laziness?

She said:

I've talked to my friend about it. I'm afraid Oliver is in rather a bad position. Even if the girl is still a virgin, they can accuse him of attempted rape. In that case, it all depends on the child's word. If there was any suggestion that he made advances to her while she was posing, he'd almost certainly go to prison.

Sorme shrugged, concealing his misgivings. He said:

That's all right. From what Oliver told me there couldn't be the faintest breath of such an idea.

I hope you're right. If you go down to Hampstead Heath station you'll find this solicitor's address just opposite. His name is Pettiford. I'll write his address down for you. He'll give you the twenty-five pounds. Will you come back here afterwards?

All right.

Here's the address. Go down East Heath Road as far as South End Green, and you can't miss it.

Glasp looked dishevelled and exhausted. He came into the office escorted by a policeman. He said:

Thank God you're here, Gerard.

Sorme was surprised by the warmth and gratitude of his smile. He said:

Sorry I'm late.

He asked the sergeant:

Can we go now?

Yers. But your friend'll have to stay where we can contact him. Otherwise you might lose your money.

Thank you, Sorme said automatically.

As they left the police station, a man approached them. Sorme noticed that Glasp shrank away nervously. The man thrust a sheet of paper into Sorme's hand, saying:

Take one.

Thank you.

One for your friend.

Sorme glanced at the duplicated sheet of foolscap as they crossed the road. It was headed: Justice for the people of Whitechapel? The message was short:

'The man who may be the killer of six women is now in

415

the hands of the police. The idle rich and the dirty bourgeoisie hope that he will be declared insane, and they will pay "trick cyclists" to try to defeat the ends of justice. But it is the people of Whitechapel who have suffered, and the people of Whitechapel who should have the last say. Bentley should hang! If we stand firm, all the psychiatrists in the world won't get him off. Forewarned is forearmed!'

Sorme said:

What a bloody odd farrago! Why on earth should the idle rich want him declared insane?

Glasp screwed his sheet up and dropped it into the gutter, shrugging irritably. He said:

The world's full of people who should be behind bars – in a zoo ! They're no better than animals.

Sorme dropped his own sheet of paper into a wastebin attached to the railings of the Wren church.

What do you intend to do now, Oliver? Gertrude says you can go and stay there if you like.

Glasp said sarcastically:

That's very kind of her.

She lent me the money.

Did she? Did you have to tell her about it?

I'm afraid I did . . .

Glasp shrugged ill-naturedly.

So long as she doesn't stick her Come-to-Jesus pals on to me.

But where do you intend to go now?

Where do you think? Back home.

And . . . would you rather I . . . left you now?

Why? Glasp said with surprise. He laughed suddenly, and laid his hand on Sorme's shoulder for a moment.

Sorry if I seem irritable. It's the bloody police, and that swine of a father . . . I'd take great pleasure in killing the bastard. When this is all over I'm going to consult a solicitor and see if I can't sue him for defamation of character . . .

How long have you been there?

In the police station? Since about nine this morning. Then they got hold of some senior copper to see about bail. You remember I told you about the fight I had with her father? Well, the same policeman was there today. So it lent colour to my story about his grudge.

But where's Christine?

I don't know. I haven't seen the father. I only gather that Christine's not to be found. She's probably hiding somewhere.

When did all this blow up?

Last night, I suppose.

But why? You told me he'd threatened to take her to a doctor before, and it had all blown over.

You can't tell with people like that. He's a drunk. Perhaps he had a quarrel with his wife, or somebody told him they'd seen Christine leaving my place. It could be anything.

You know he could accuse you of attempted seduction, even if the doctor reports she's still a virgin?

Glasp said:

So what? They've only got to ask Christine.

But . . . you didn't tell them about the posing?

No.

Do you think they know?

I don't expect so. Why should they? She wouldn't tell them.

But supposing she got upset and frightened? Children do, you know.

What if she did? So long as she told the truth, I've nothing to worry about.

No . . . I suppose so. You really need a solicitor.

I don't see why. It'll all be settled when they examine her.

When did she run away?

This morning. She's a silly kid . . . Last night her father told her he was going to take her to see a doctor this morning. Her mother's away, I think. So she slipped out early this morning. Naturally, he thinks she's got something to hide. So he went to the police.

But how could they arrest you without any evidence?

Because he laid a complaint. I think he told them she'd admitted something.

What! You mean that you'd . . .

Quite. He was probably drunk when he asked her.

Perhaps he hurt her and made her shout anything to get away.

Sorme was surprised at the detachment in Glasp's voice; there was none of the rage he expected.

But in that case . . . you might be able to charge him with false accusation later. You ought to get a solicitor.

Glasp said, shrugging:

And pay him with bottle tops?

It wouldn't cost much. And I'm sure Father Carruthers or Gertrude would lend you the money . . .

I'll think about it, Glasp said.

Sorme felt he was trying to keep him quiet. He said:

All right. That's up to you.

They had arrived at Glasp's address in Durward Street. As he started to insert the key the door opened. Sorme had the impression that the old woman must have been hiding behind it. She said:

Oh, it's you. I thought you were in gaol.

Glasp leaned forward, and shouted in her ear:

No. It's all right now.

Oh, it's all right, is it? Why have they let you out?

I can't explain now, Glasp bellowed. He pushed into

the front room and closed the front door behind them. The old woman shouted:

I can't have this sort of thing in my house. I'm only an old woman all on my own, but I can't have that sort of thing in my house.

Have the police been here? Glasp shouted.

The police? Yes, they've been here. You'll have to go. I can't have it . . .

Glasp turned to Sorme, saying quietly:

Go on upstairs while I explain to this bloody old cow . . .

As Sorme went up the uncarpeted stairs, smelling the familiar paraffin odour, he heard the old woman shouting:

I've never had trouble with the police before . . .

Glasp shouted back:

It's not my fault. I can explain . . .

He let himself into Glasp's room and closed the door. It was damp and cold. He found matches on the window-sill, and lit the oil stove and the gas ring. He found Glasp's kettle, filled it with water, and set it on the gas. A few minutes later Glasp came in. He said:

Those f – ing cops have been in here searching the place.

What? But surely they can't do that without a warrant? Did they have a warrant?

No. They just asked the old woman's permission. It's her house.

But it's your room. I'm sure they're not allowed to do that. You ought to get a solicitor.

Glasp sank on to the stool, warming his hands above the oil stove. He said gloomily:

The old bugger wants me to move out. That bloody father of Christine's! . . . I'd like to kill him. Why can contemptible animals like that make such a mess of my life!

419

Never mind. It's just a farce . . . But why should they search your room? What would they expect to find?

Christine, of course.

Oh yes.

Glasp said bitterly:

Or maybe her body. I don't think they put anything past me.

He began to wander round the room, peering at canvases. He said suddenly:

Oh, Christ!

What is it?

This portrait of Christine . . . I'd forgotten it.

Sorme remembered in time that he was not supposed to have seen the picture. He crossed to Glasp, and looked at the portrait of the underfed child. Glasp had pulled several canvases forward to expose it; they leaned against his shin.

Do you think they saw it?

I don't know.

I doubt it. Why should they? If they were looking for her they wouldn't examine your pictures.

Glasp opened a cupboard and took out a large folder made of brown paper. He laid this on the bed and opened it. Sorme deliberately refrained from showing curiosity, although he caught a glimpse of a sketch of a naked child. He asked:

Is there any sign that they've seen it?

Glasp peered closely at the pages.

Not as far as I can see. But I wouldn't expect the police to leave fingermarks.

Glasp closed the album with an exclamation of disgust. He dropped on to the edge of the bed and sighed. His big hands hung loosely between his knees. He said between his teeth:

F – ing swine.

The kettle began to simmer. Sorme emptied the teapot into the sink and rinsed it with warm water. He found the tea on the shelf, in a packet with the top screwed round. While he made it, Glasp began to go around the room systematically, looking for signs of disturbance. He said at last:

They're bloody clever. They've left no traces.

Have some tea.

Glasp lay down on the bed, pushing the folder aside, and closed his eyes. With his bony face upturned to the ceiling, and the big hands resting limply on the coverlet, he looked like a corpse. Sorme said quietly:

Poor Oliver. I know just how it feels. Why can't things be simple and straightforward?

Glasp's chest heaved with a kind of laugh that was little more than an expulsion of breath. He said:

No, you're wrong. I don't want things simple. That's not me. I don't know what I want. If my life was simple, I'd be like a fish out of water. I once knew an actress like that. She had to manufacture complications in her life. All her love affairs had to be messy. If they went wrong, she was all right. If they went right, she felt there was something wrong.

I think you're doing yourself an injustice, Oliver.

Glasp sat up, saying tiredly:

Thank God for my friends. They never let me think the worst of myself.

Sorme noticed the bundle of wood that lay in the fire grate.

You ought to get yourself some coal, Oliver. You need a fire in here.

There is coal. It's outside the door. I was just making a fire when the police arrived.

Let me make one for you.

Glasp said:

421

Thanks, Gerard.

He took a gulp of the tea, then lay down on the bed again, his eyes closed. Sorme found a coal scuttle outside the door and a bucket containing ashes. He laid the fire and started it with paraffin; in a few minutes the flames were roaring up the chimney. He crouched over it. The cold of the room had penetrated his overcoat. Glasp was lying in his shirtsleeves, the collar unbuttoned.

Aren't you cold there, Oliver?

I . . . suppose I am.

Glasp seemed fascinated by the flames. He crossed the room and sat on the stool, leaning forward, the teacup between his hands.

It's good of you to bother with me like this, Gerard.

Not in the least.

I'd have been fixed if you hadn't come today.

That's OK. You'd do the same for me.

The paraffin flames began to die down, but the wood was burning well. Outside, the afternoon was turning dark. Seated in the wooden chair, Sorme reflected how dismally uncomfortable Glasp's room was. Glasp said:

I never made many friends.

Sorme said, shrugging:

Nor me.

What's the good of friends if they don't understand the problems that worry you? You've got to be able to talk to them. You, for instance . . . I could talk to you five minutes after I first met you. That's unusual.

Thanks.

Sorme felt slightly awkward about the compliment; he said:

I've got a theory about people. You and I are completely different types. I think too much, you feel too much. I lay too much emphasis on the mind, and you lay too much on the heart. Now some people lay too much

422

on the body . . . Austin, for instance. When he gets repressed, he needs a physical outlet.

And what about you?

Oh, me. I try to think my way out of problems. I try to get detached from them. I don't like strong emotions much – I suspect them. That's why I don't feel too good at the moment about Austin.

Why? You don't feel any strong emotions about him, do you?

No. But he's stopped me from stagnating. I've become so absorbed in his problems that I've become quite detached from my own problems. That's all right . . . but it's not the right way to solve problems.

No? Why not?

As he spoke, Sorme became aware that his ideas reflected on Glasp; he repressed the misgiving, certain that Glasp would understand, anyway. He said:

I think it's a kind of weakness to get too involved in other people's lives. I once knew a girl who was the sort of person everybody told their troubles to. She gave the impression of being a very cool and calm sort of person, and people felt she was strong and sympathetic. When I got to know her pretty well, I found she had no ideas, no beliefs, no real self-confidence – in fact, she was a complete mess inside. She kept herself happy by worrying about other people's problems. She *liked* unhappy people – I suppose they made her feel superior. . . . And when I meet people like Gertrude who go in for social work and converting people, I wonder if they're not doing the same thing.

Glasp said:

Does it matter?

Yes, it does. It matters if people are made of marshmallow. Very few people are real inside. They need people and distractions as a cripple needs crutches. Look at me. Two weeks ago I felt completely lost. I didn't like leaving my room because the street made me feel as if I didn't exist. London made me feel like an insect, and when I got back to my own room and tried to write I still felt like an insect. Then what happens? I go to this Diaghilev exhibition and meet Austin. And immediately I stop being an insect. But that's the *wrong* reason.

What does it matter what the reason is?

But it *does* matter. I should have outgrown Austin's world a long time ago. I only went to the Diaghilev exhibition out of a sentimental feeling about Nijinsky. Normally, I can't stick ballet. Last time I went to the ballet, it nearly gave me diarrhoea . . . a lot of bloody prancing queers and posturing women. I had to come out half way through. And yet that's Austin's world. He's a romantic. He's not real inside either. He needs unreality to stop him from feeling an insect.

Glasp said softly:

We all need something to lean on.

But we shouldn't. If a man could kill all his illusions, he'd become a god.

Or kill himself, Glasp said.

No . . . He'd be strong enough to live. People die because they don't know what life is.

Glasp said: Who does?

I do sometimes. Just occasionally. And I spend all my time trying to regain the insight.

And what was your insight like?

I . . . It was a feeling of acceptance. It happened once when I was on Hampstead Heath, looking down on London. I was thinking about all the lives and all the problems . . . and then suddenly I felt real. I saw other people's illusions, and my own illusions disappeared, and I felt real inside. I stopped wondering whether the world's ultimately good or evil. I felt that the world didn't matter a damn. What mattered was me, whether I saw it as good or evil. I suddenly felt as if I'd turned into a giant. I felt absurdly happy . .

Glasp said:

I've never felt like that.

No?

He controlled the excitement his own words had aroused in him, waiting for Glasp to speak, watching the face that leaned into the firelight. Glasp spoke in a low voice, without emphasis. He said:

That's not how I feel . . . I suppose I need other people, as you say. For instance, this stupid business is bad for me because it makes me think about myself. And Christine's good for me because she makes me think about other people. Not just about her. She makes me realize that hundreds – thousands – are living in complete misery, never having a chance to feel these things you're talking about. They don't feel like giants or gods, and they don't feel like insects either. They're just ordinary men and women, and most of their lives is suffering or boredom.

He stopped speaking, and drank the remainder of the tea from his mug, then set it down on the green tiles that reflected the flames. The toe of his worn-out shoe pushed a fragment of smoking coal into the grate. He said:

That's my vision . . . if it is a vision.

Sorme looked at him silently, realizing the gulf that separated their ways of feeling, and understanding the futility of words. The coal collapsed over the burnt wood, sending up sparks. Glasp said abruptly:

What about going out for a meal? Are you hungry?

Do you know anywhere around here?

I know a place where we can get sausage, egg and chips for two bob.

Sorme said, standing up:

Good. Let's go.

Chapter Six

Sorry I'm so late.

Come in. Where have you been? Have you eaten?

Yes, thanks. I ate this afternoon with Oliver. I stayed and talked to him. He was pretty shaken up.

The fire was still burning in the sitting-room. The hands of the electric clock showed ten-fifteen. She touched his hand, and said:

Oh dear, you *are* cold. Come and get warm. Would you like a drink?

No, thanks. I've been drinking with Oliver.

He sat opposite the fire, and stretched out his legs towards it. Miss Quincey started to build it up with small nuggets of coal, using a glove that lay across the fender.

Is he all right now?

Yes. He's calmer, at any rate.

Have they examined the child yet?

No. That's the trouble. She's disappeared. When we got back to Oliver's room, the police had been there already. Oliver says they probably suspect him of murdering her to keep her quiet!

How silly!

Oh yes. He wasn't really serious. They probably suspected him of hiding her. Anyway, she's a little fool to run away like this. It makes it look worse for Oliver – as if she's got something to be afraid of. When we came out of the café Oliver saw one of her schoolfriends and persuaded her to go and call for Christine – to see if she'd come back. She hadn't, of course, and then he started to get really upset.

I'm not surprised, with a murderer at large in Whitechapel.

Haven't you heard? He's been caught.

No. When?

Don't you listen to the radio? He was arrested this morning. At least a man was arrested, and apparently he confessed later.

Good! Thank heavens for that.

I'm not so sure it's an advantage for Oliver. If the Whitechapel police had still got the murders to worry about, they might pay less attention to a drunken prison warder.

Quite. But where does Oliver think the child might be hiding?

Oh, anywhere. She only disappeared this morning. She might have spent the morning in Petticoat Lane market, or in the docks. She's probably back home now – unless she's staying overnight with a friend. Or she may go to Oliver's.

I hope so. I wouldn't like to think of her wandering around on a night like this.

As if to emphasize the words, there was a sound of rain on the window. Sorme went to the window and peered out; nothing was visible in the darkness.

Have you left your bicycle outside?

No. I came by train.

It's just as well. Would you like something to eat? I'm just having something myself.

Thanks.

He leaned against the refrigerator, watching her slice a joint of ham. The wine he had drunk with Glasp had made him feel sleepy. He asked her:

Have you heard from Austin recently?

No, not for several days.

I don't know where he's gone to. I've been trying to contact him for the last two days.

He may be at the Leatherhead cottage. He often goes there for weekends.

Ah, of course!

She glanced at him doubtfully.

Have you . . . have you spoken to him since you talked to me . . .

She left the sentence unfinished. Sorme said:

I had lunch with him on Saturday.

Yes.

She sounded uninterested. He took the plate with sandwiches, and went back into the other room. The rain was now beating steadily on the windows. He unfolded the paper napkin, and helped himself to a sandwich, then looked at her, smiling. She said:

I've been thinking about Austin ever since the other night. It seems a pity that he hasn't any close relatives who could . . . talk to him about it. There's no one who knows him well enough to be quite open with him.

What could they do, anyway?

She lowered her sandwich instead of biting it, regarding him steadily. She said:

They might persuade him to see a doctor.

That's true. On the other hand, he might feel they just didn't understand, and tell them to go to hell.

That wouldn't matter. If someone is dying of a disease, you don't ask them if they want to be cured.

Austin's not dying. And I don't think homosexuality qualifies as a disease.

He could sense a frustration growing up in her; her eyes flickered with irritation.

But he *ought* to have a chance to lead a normal existence. He'll inherit a great deal of money and property. He should have a son to pass it on to. He should have a chance to marry and settle down.

He said patiently:

I can see your point. But I doubt whether Austin wants to settle down. And I can't imagine him as a husband! Besides, why should you want to alter his life? He isn't unhappy – at least, not for that reason. What would you say if Austin suddenly wanted you to see a doctor to cure you of religion?

Oh, don't be silly, Gerard!

But if it's so important to marry and settle down, why aren't you married?

Her face coloured; for a moment, he expected a snub. She swallowed the remains of a sandwich, and said in a level voice:

That isn't the same thing at all.

Looking at her face, he felt a curious impulse of tenderness; she was right; it was not the same thing at all. The idea of being frank with her about Austin came to him, but he dismissed it immediately. Instead he said:

All right . . . If you like, I'll talk to Austin about it – tactfully. But I doubt whether it would have an effect.

A kind of hopelessness came into her eyes. She said:

Perhaps you're right. Perhaps it isn't my business. I'm fond of Austin. He's the only person in the family that I ever cared for much.

He said gently:

You can't take the responsibility for other people, you know. The best you can do is to offer help when it's needed.

But supposing Austin needs help?

Don't you see, Gertrude, you can only help when you understand fully? Your temperament's too different from Austin's to do any good.

Why do you say that? Do you suppose I've never felt like Austin?

He said:

429

I don't know. Have you?

I've wanted to let all my impulses loose. I suppose most people have. Austin's been lucky. He's always had the money to go where he likes and do what he likes, and no one has tried to interfere with him. In another sense he's been unlucky, because he's had too much freedom. But he's really a *good* person. He could never destroy the good in him, no matter what he did.

You're probably right. But don't you see? The fact that you've wanted to let your own impulses loose doesn't mean you understand Austin's impulses.

Do *you* understand them?

I . . . don't know. I think perhaps I do.

Then explain them to me.

He stared into the fire, feeling no desire to talk. The evening with Glasp had tired him. Aware of the persistence of her eyes, he said finally:

It's a feeling of being at a total loose end . . . having no sense of purpose or motive – a feeling of being disinherited. As if your existence was meaningless. And then sometimes you get a glimpse of an insight – a feeling that human existence *is* meaningless, but that you've got to give it meaning. And then you suddenly feel that you've got to stop living like a bad actor in a second-rate play. Somehow, you've got to start living properly. Well, human existence is mostly taboos, laws and rules. So the first thing to do – if you want to start living all the way down – is to break the laws and rules. That's the way you feel about it. And it just depends which laws and rules you feel like breaking. A man with a neurosis about being socially underprivileged might try to rob a bank or throw a bomb at the House of Lords. But most men suffer from a feeling of being sexually underprivileged, so it's more likely to break out in that direction . . .

He checked the impulse to say more. She waited for him to go on; then, after a moment, said sadly:

He doesn't realize there are other ways of . . . living fully. I wish I could teach him.

The resignation in her voice stirred an obscure pity in him; he found himself wishing she was sitting beside him on the settee, where he could touch her. Immediately, he felt a distrust of his own impulse, remembering the last time he had tried to touch her. He stood up, saying:

I'm afraid I'd better go . . . Excuse me a moment.

In the bathroom, he opened the window and looked out towards the Heath; the rain fell steadily. Drops of water ran down his face. The washbasin was half full of clothes soaking in soapy water; he leaned over the bath and washed his hands under the hot tap. He sat on the edge of the bath to dry his hands, taking pleasure in the warmth and softness of the towel, surprised by the curious happiness that rose in him, the feeling of expectancy.

She was still sitting in front of the fire. Something in her pose, the crossed knees, the shoe that hung loosely on the small foot, made her seem very young. He said:

What time does the train go from Hampstead?

I'm not sure. They go earlier on Sundays. It might have gone by now.

I'd better hurry.

You can't go yet. You'll be soaked. Hadn't you better stay here?

He asked with surprise:

All night, you mean?

You . . . could if you wanted to.

What about your reputation with the neighbours?

She looked away from his smile:

It's none of their business, is it?

Well . . . thanks very much. Where would I sleep?

Down here. Or in Caroline's room. I'm afraid you'll

have to make do with Caroline's sheets if you sleep in there . . .

That's fine. I don't mind at all.

I put them on last time she came here. They ought to be clean. Would you rather sleep upstairs?

I don't mind. Whichever is least trouble . . .

I'll go and turn the fire on.

He felt she was glad to get out of the room. He wondered if the thought of offering him Caroline's bed had suddenly struck her with embarrassment, recognizing its meaning as a symbol of vicarious intimacy. After a moment's hesitation, he followed her upstairs.

She was changing the pillow-case as he came into the room; the bedclothes were pulled back to air. The bars of the electric fire were warming to redness. He picked up a nylon nightdress that had slipped down the bottom of the bed, asking:

Is this Caroline's?

She snatched it from him, and dropped it into a drawer.

No. It's one of mine that she borrowed.

She went out of the room, saying:

I'll get you a hot-water bottle.

He looked down at the photograph of Caroline, and experienced a feeling that was not unlike guilt. With surprise, he realized he was a little in love with Caroline. It was an unexpected recognition; the feeling seemed to have developed retrospectively since he had last seen her. At the time, he had been aware of nothing but a certain amused tenderness, and the gratitude that is a response to a woman's offer of her body.

Miss Quincey came in while he was still looking at it. She asked:

Do you like Caroline?

Of course. She's very sweet.

She dropped the hot-water bottle into the bed and adjusted the sheets. She said suddenly:

I'd forgotten that I'd left the washbasin next door half full of clothes. I was starting to wash them when you arrived. So I'd better finish them now. Do you want to go to bed yet?

Er . . . no, not especially. Why?

I think I shall go soon. I'm rather tired.

He followed her out of the room, sensing a tension in her. He wondered if she was regretting asking him to stay. She asked:

Would you like some hot chocolate before I go to bed? I shall make some for myself.

Thanks. I'd like some.

She went into the bedroom; he heard the lock click. He stared at the door, shaking his head. Her changes of mood baffled him. He went downstairs slowly, toying with the idea of leaving, then abandoned it; she had already prepared the room.

In the sitting-room, he helped himself to a sweet martini, and lay down on the settee, unlacing his shoes. He ate the remaining ham sandwich, and stared at the moving shadows on the ceiling. He remembered Miss Quincey's face as she had talked about Austin, and experienced again a protective warmth. He thought with amusement: This family has a talent for inspiring affection. But they are all weak: Austin, Caroline, Gertrude. They need people.

Strange, the element of love that has nothing to do with sex. I feel it for Austin, for Caroline. For Gertrude too. Less, perhaps, for Gertrude. Why is it supposed to be impossible to love more than one person?

Still thinking about it, he fell into a light doze, lulled by the sound of running water from overhead.

He woke up suddenly and half sat up. A moment later

Gertrude Quincey came into the room, carrying a cup and saucer. She was wearing a blue dressing-gown, belted at the waist, and carpet slippers. Her hair was hanging loosely down her back; there was more of it than he realized. Without makeup, her face looked pale.

What time is it?

After midnight.

I've been asleep.

I know. I came in just now. I'm going to bed.

Wait. Don't go yet.

She had set the cup down beside the settee. He reached out and took her hand before she could move away, and pulled it gently.

It felt cold and slim. As she sat down, he raised it to his lips and kissed it. She made no movement to resist.

You're cold.

I know. I always get cold after a bath.

He tried to pull her down beside him, his hand on her waist. She resisted for a moment, then stood up. She said:

I've left my chocolate outside.

He listened as she went into the kitchen, then returned carrying her own cup. As she sat down beside him again, he felt a shock of pleasure. He had been certain she would sit in the armchair. He said:

Put your feet on.

No.

Please.

No, Gerard.

He pulled at her waist, causing her to overbalance; as her body rested against him, he repeated:

Please.

She swung her feet up beside him, tugging at the bottom of the dressing-gown. Immediately, he pulled her closer and bent to kiss her. Her face turned away, and his lips met her neck. The flesh was cold. He made no attempt to force her, glad to feel her pressed against him, the coldness warming against his face. He kissed her ear and the side of her face, stroking the long hair with his free hand. She shivered against him, then seemed to die. Her eyes were closed. He reached out for the car rug that hung over the back of the settee, and pulled it over them, then lay beside her, closing his eyes, the satisfaction running through him in a faint tremor. In the darkness behind his closed lids he forgot she lay beside him, feeling a total evacuation of thoughts and impulses that left nothing but his body's comfort. She had made no movement; only her breathing indicated she was alive. He was already half asleep when she stirred. She sat up, saying:

We'd better drink this.

He forced himself into a sitting position and took the cup from her. He drank it propped on one elbow, his shoulder against the cushion. It was lukewarm, and he drank it quickly. Neither spoke. As she took his cup, he lay down again; a moment later, she joined him. This time, she made no attempt to avoid his mouth as he kissed her. The thin lips excited him; he pressed them open slightly, breathing deeply. She was completely passive. His rising excitement brought a reaction of caution; he relaxed deliberately, and lay beside her again, pulling her against him. His left palm was flat against her back, enjoying the sensuous feel of the jaeger fabric that enclosed her body. The pleasure was a tension in him that resisted time; it was enough to feel her there. For a moment, his consciousness expanded and became complete, aware of his past, present and future as a unity, beyond self-doubt. When he looked at her face he knew she was not thinking, was deliberately refusing to think. He lay there watching the fire sink lower, and the hand of the electric clock moving from half past twelve to one o'clock. Although she made no movement, he knew she was not asleep. He began to feel the desire to sleep in himself. He said softly:

Let's go to bed.

For a moment she lay still, then stirred and pulled her legs clear of the blanket. He let her go out of the room first, then stood up and stretched. The empty cups were on the rug; he picked them up and placed them on the table. Then he went out of the living-room, turning off the light. As he passed Caroline's room, he went in and turned off the electric fire.

Her door was closed. It opened when he pushed it; the room was in darkness. From the bed, her voice said:

Please go away, Gerard.

He said gently:

Don't be silly.

He undressed in the darkness, and climbed into bed beside her. She was wearing a thin nightgown, like the one he had seen in Caroline's room; its contact with his naked flesh was a shock that destroyed his calm. His hand felt the curve of her thigh, over the buttock; he began to kiss her. When she pulled away, he said:

Wouldn't you have been disappointed if I'd slept in Caroline's room?

Her voice was a whisper, as if afraid of being overheard:

I didn't want this to happen. I didn't think when I invited you . . .

I know you didn't. But just now, when I came up? Did you still want me to sleep in Caroline's bed?

I . . . don't know.

He recognized the voice of a woman refusing to think. He started to take the nightdress off.

No, please. You mustn't.

Let me take it off. I want you naked.

You . . . can't. It's never happened before.

All right, I won't. But let me take it off.

She moved her body to allow him to free it, and he dropped it on to the floor. As he felt her body against him he knew nothing could stop it. In spite of her fear and his promise it would happen, and their bodies knew it. He felt her yielding, becoming passive against him, as he moved.

The dawn was showing through the curtains. He looked at her through the grey light and saw her eyes were open.

How do you feel, sweet?

Still alive.

Why, did you think it would kill you?

For a while, yes.

He kissed her, and experienced a pressure of tenderness that took him by surprise. He looked down at her face, the hair spread loosely against the pillow. He said:

It's a funny thing . . .

What?

I think . . . I'm a little in love with you.

She said: Good.

Her arms closed around him, pressing him against her; he kissed her cheek, and the hair above her ear. He said:

It's so silly, sweet. What are we going to do?

What do you want to do?

Stay like this for six months. Just like this.

You can't. You'd get cramp.

I know. And you'd get tired. And I'd lose my hair. What do you want to do?

She kissed his ear, caressing the stubble on his jaw with her left hand.

Whatever you want to do.

Don't you feel . . . guilty about . . . what's happened?

What do you think Brother Robbins'd say?

I don't care.

He let her warmth draw him down, feeling the tenderness that was a kind of annihilation. It was like kissing her for the first time. The night had made her into a different person. He said into her ear:

It's a funny thing . . . it's never been like this before.

Hasn't it? How is it different?

It . . . feels as though I'm in love with you.

Good.

You keep saying 'good'. Is it all that good?

She nodded, her face against his hair, her body moving gently. He said:

You know, Thomas Mann said the words of the marriage service are nonsense: These two shall be one flesh. Because sex depends on strangeness, on curiosity. But it's not true. Two people *can* become one flesh . . .

You ought to stop philosophizing, Gerard.

He said, laughing:

I expect you're right.

He lay beside her, his arm around her shoulders, looking at the ceiling.

Tell me something, sweet.

What?

Why didn't it ever happen before? To you, I mean.

I don't know. It just didn't.

Didn't you ever want it to?

It wasn't that. It was . . . Oh, let's not talk about it now.

All right.

It's not that I don't want you to know. But not now.

All right.

I'll tell you some time. It's not that I want to hide anything.

No. You wouldn't have anything to hide, anyway. You're not the type.

Neither are you.

He said:

Hmm. I don't know about that. There *are* one or two embarrassing episodes . . .

They wouldn't worry me.

I'm not so sure. One of them would.

Why?

Oh, never mind . . .

Does it concern me? If it doesn't, I don't want to know.

Well, it does, in a way.

She lay perfectly still. She asked:

It's not Austin, is it?

Austin? Why should . . .? You don't think . . . *No!* Is that what you mean?

I'm sorry. I know it's silly.

He kissed her face, laughing.

Poor sweet! You think you've got a sexual gymnast?

No. I didn't think that. But how can it concern me if it isn't Austin?

She pulled away to look at his face. She said suddenly:

It isn't Caroline, is it?

He found it difficult to answer immediately. She repeated: Is it?

I'm afraid it is.

Oh Gerard! But . . . you only met her a week ago.

I know.

But . . . what happened? Surely . . . it can't have developed far in a week?

We have, haven't we?

Do you mean . . .? *Have* you?

I'm afraid I have.

But when? And how? How did it happen?

He pulled away from her, propping himself on his elbow, where he could see her face. He said tiredly:

My sweet, it's no good asking me how it happens. She's a pretty girl. On the first evening I took her out, she told me she'd like me to become her lover . . . I didn't object. I suppose it's very wicked, but I didn't feel like being virtuous . . .

She lay there, looking at him. Her eyes seemed unusually large, and her lips very full. She asked:

Are you in love with her?

He gave the answer she wanted:

No.

Is she in love with you?

I don't suppose so. She may be infatuated with me. But next week it'll be some actor or writer.

She said slowly:

I don't know quite what to say . . . So, you're Caroline's lover as well as mine?

I *was* Caroline's lover, technically speaking.

And you've decided not to be any more?

He said firmly:

Now listen, sweet. Let's get this clear. I've told you this because it's no good keeping it a secret. Anyway, I'd rather you knew. If you want to throw me out and tell me never to come back . . . well, I'd expect it. Would you rather I hadn't told you?

No. I suppose I'd have to know eventually. But what do you want me to do now?

He lay down again, pulling the blanket over his shoulder.

I don't know, sweet. You'd better think about it.

He stared out of the window, then at the dressing-table that was clearly visible in the dawn light. After a moment, she said:

I don't understand Caroline. Does she often do things like this?

No. At least, she hasn't . . . gone quite so far.

But . . . she *asked* you to become her lover?

Don't put all the blame on her. It takes two to climb

into bed. Anyway, there's no point in making excuses. I'm afraid it's happened now.

When she did not reply, he turned over and looked at her; immediately, he had to restrain an impulse to put his arms round her. He said:

Well . . . am I thrown out?

Do you want to be?

No.

She smiled at him; it was sad and brief.

Then I don't suppose you are.

He leaned over and kissed her eyelid, and tasted the salt on the lashes. He said:

Poor sweet. I'm sorry, I really am. But . . . what are we going to do?

About what?

Well, about Caroline. I'm supposed to see her tonight. And, anyway, what ought I to do about her? I shall have to stop seeing her. But you can see the difficulties.

Do you *want* to stop seeing her?

Yes.

She laughed suddenly.

You really are silly. Why on earth did it have to be my niece?

I'm sorry, sweet, I really am . . .

Supposing you changed your room? Moved up to Hampstead? I know a room . . .

I couldn't do that. It'd seem like cowardice. The only alternative I can think of is to write to her and say I've gone abroad.

Why not? You could go to Paris or Rome for a few weeks. She'll find somebody else while you're away.

Oh, I wouldn't really go abroad. I couldn't afford that. But I could go home for a few months – to Yorkshire. I wouldn't feel so bad if I'd really gone far away.

She said hesitantly.

If you like . . . we *could* go to Paris. For Christmas and the New Year. And even then, we needn't come back here. I know a cottage in the Lake District . . .

He bent over her and kissed her.

Don't be silly. I wouldn't take your money.

Why not? If you were married to me you'd take it . . .

She stopped suddenly. For a moment, he hardly noticed; her nearness was sending excitement through him, radiating from the hand that could feel the smoothness of her thigh. He said:

Do you want me to marry you?

She shook her head.

I don't care. I want to do whatever you want to . . .

You're sweet . . . But that's no answer.

But we *can* leave London, Gerard. Why can't we do that?

He resisted the impulse to embrace her again, moving his body away from her. He said:

I'll tell you the main reason, sweet. I couldn't walk out on Austin.

What has Austin go to do with it?

I . . . can't explain.

But . . . I don't understand. Is Austin in some sort of trouble?

He looked at her puzzled face, and felt again her basic uncertainty of him. He said:

Listen, sweet, let's get up and make some coffee. And I'll try to explain to you. But let me think about it for a while.

Without speaking, she slipped out of the bed; he stared with admiration at the slim, firm body as she moved across the room. She snatched the dressing-gown from the hook on the door, and bent to switch on the electric fire. Then he was alone, listening to the rain that had started to drum gently on the windows.

He rolled over, and felt the warm area left by her body; it evoked a feeling of warmth and pity. He threw back the bedclothes and stepped on to the carpet. The air was cold; he pulled on his shirt hurriedly, standing near the fire, thinking: Am I in love with her? Is it possible after one night?

He belted his trousers, then stopped, warming his hands and knees. That's the trouble with being self-divided. You can never tell. I feel as if I'm in love with her now. What about tomorrow?

Caroline. She's sweet, but it's not the same. She's bound to know about Gertrude eventually. Anyway, it wouldn't be wise to tie up with Gertrude permanently. In ten years' time, she'll be nearly fifty; I still under forty.

He stared at the photograph of her on the dressing-table; she was in nurse's uniform, and looked about ten years younger. The eyes had the same expression he had noticed earlier in bed; they were wise and somehow startled. He thought: But I'm in love with her. Right now. Even if it only lasts until tomorrow.

The kitchen felt warm; the coffee percolator was bubbling on the stove, He bent over her and kissed her forehead. Her skin was clear and healthy; he was glad of that. He said:

You look like Lorelei with your hair down your back.

I don't feel like Lorelei.

She laughed, and ran her fingers through her hair.

How do you feel?

Strange. I'm not used to sitting in my dressing-gown in front of a man.

That's OK. You look superb. You look even better naked.

No. I don't.

He pulled back the dressing-gown, and kissed the tip of her breast.

443

You do. You've got a wonderful body. Like . . . a young girl.

He stopped himself on the point of saying: Like a sixteen-year-old. But she noticed the hesitation, and smiled at him, her eyes suddenly mischievous. He said, laughing:

I think you're a thought reader.

I don't have to be . . . with you.

He said:

Don't you really care . . . about Caroline?

Of course I care. I'd rather it hadn't happened. But it's no use wishing it hadn't happened. And anyway . . . it's in the past now, isn't it?

He put his arm around her waist, and pulled her to him as she went past. He said:

Yes. And I don't care.

She placed a coffee cup in front of him, and poured hot milk into it, catching the skin in a strainer.

But what about Austin?

Ah yes . . . Austin.

He waited until she was seated opposite, pouring the coffee.

Well, I'm afraid Austin's likely to be in trouble with the police.

Why? What has he done?

He spooned sugar into the cup, staring at the tablecloth. It was difficult to express it gently.

Well . . . you remember you told me once that he liked smashing dolls as a child?

Yes.

Why do you think he did that?

I . . . don't know. A lot of boys don't like dolls. They think they're silly. It's a sort of expression of contempt.

Perhaps. But, you see, Austin also has periodic urges to break things. Or hurt things. It's called sadism.

Sadism!

Her coffee slopped into the saucer. She set the cup down, staring at him. He said quickly:

Oh, don't get upset. It may not be as bad as you think. But the point is . . . well, that he's known to the police as a sadist.

But how? Why?

He said, shrugging:

Because he probably mixes with people who don't mind being beaten for money. And these people are known to the police. Anyway, to cut it short, he'd be an automatic suspect in a case like these recent Whitechapel murders. So would thousands of others, of course.

But . . . the man's been arrested, you said.

I know. And if he's the right man, there's an end of it. But he may not be.

I . . . don't understand. Austin wouldn't harm anyone. He *couldn't* be a murderer. Could he?

I know. I agree. But he's got himself into a rather nasty position. If he was sensible, he'd leave the country for a year. I don't know what kind of trouble he's in. I think that perhaps he's being blackmailed.

What makes you think that?

He told her in detail about the phone call from Switzerland, the basement flat and the night club. Watching her face, he found himself admiring her. After the first shock her face became calm, and she listened quietly, drinking her coffee. When he mentioned Stein and the Hamburg incident, she interrupted:

But that's stupid: he went into a monastery in Germany! Surely they don't think . . .

My sweet, it's not Austin they suspect in particular. As Stein pointed out, the police have to check on thousands of suspects in a case like this. Stein was involved in the

Kürten murder case in Düsseldorf, and the police interviewed a fantastic number of people over three years – I forget the figure, but it was something like half a million. And there's probably a great deal more sadism about today than you realize. What do you suppose happened to all the guards in places like Belsen and Auschwitz? They weren't all tried as war criminals – or even five per cent of them. I've talked to men who went through the German prison camps – men in the French Resistance – and I gather it happened everywhere. They weren't all sadists, of course. But movements like Nazism incubate sadism. Whereas in England it breaks out as the occasional sex crime or act of violence.

He was being deliberately abstract to reassure her, sensing that her fear was fear of the unknown, the unexplainable. She said:

But surely . . . it's not like that with Austin? He's just not that kind of a person.

Sorme said:

Ah, you may be right there. It's rather difficult to explain. There are probably two types of sadism.

He crossed to the kitchen window, and rubbed away the steam; the sight of the trees in the rain brought a sensation of happiness.

I think that with some people sadism is just an expression of animalism. They feel no responsibility to other people. Psychopathic criminals. But I think it *could* be just an expression of conflict.

How?

He did not look round; he had no desire to see her face and feel her need to be convinced. He said:

For example, I find that *I'm* tending to grow up sexually. You know there's an old Army saying: A standing tool has no conscience. I suppose that's where men differ from women. Sex is a raw, physical appetite

446

for them as well as a way of expressing love. It's the sense of life-purpose in a man, the need to turn every attractive woman into a mother of his children. Whereas, for a woman, sexual intercourse is a climax of lovemaking, an expression of tenderness, not an end in itself. Well, I find myself reacting to sex like a woman. If the most beautiful girl in London climbed into my bed and said, 'Come and get me', I'd fail. I can't make love like a machine.

She said, with a touch of irony:

I'm glad to hear it.

But that's only because the sense of purpose in me is becoming stronger, and therefore more selective. Don't you see? An animal mates and produces children instinctively. And a great many human beings do the same. But in some men there's a need to feel more conscious about it all. They oppose the instinct that ties them to a particular woman. Their sexual desire isn't directed at a particular woman, but at *all* women. Individual women excite such a man less than the idea of women in general. And that's the dangerous point where he could become the sexual criminal. His sense of purpose is higher than that of most men, but his instincts are still an animal's. If he can grow beyond that stage, he'll go back to the need for one person, and the sense of purpose passes beyond sex. It can become sublimated in a need to become an artist, a philosopher, a social reformer. But until that happens he's caught between two stools. His sense of purpose makes a fanatic of him, and his appetites can't soar above sex. Do you understand me?

I . . . think so. But . . . I don't see how it could lead to hurting people. If it's a higher kind of purpose . . .

Because of the conflict. The man begins to detest himself, and the disgust expresses itself as cruelty. Only in some people, of course. In others – Oliver, for instance

– the disgust would turn against himself. He might try to hurt himself. Or simply turn to drink or drugs.

Even so . . . a man who kills can't feel this sense of purpose you talk about.

Why? Don't forget, it's an attempt to resolve a conflict. Let me give you an example. One of the major feelings sexual intercourse arouses in me is a sense of my own inadequacy. For a few seconds, my memories are all intensified, my vision widens. And then it disappears. And I realize that my chief enemy is my own body. I live in the present all the time. And time dilutes my memory. I learn something today, and by tomorrow it's been washed away like footprints on a sandy beach. The present closes me in. Well, if I was a different type of person I might identify this frustration with sex. The resistance of the physical world might enrage me. I see a pretty twelve-year-old-girl in the street and know I can never satisfy the desire she arouses. The physical world frustrates me and my own body betrays me. And one night, I meet the girl in a lonely street and try to rape her. She struggles, and I strangle her. Do you see what I mean? The crime becomes a gesture of disgust, an act of defiance, but it could spring out of a deeper perception than most men possess . . . If I was a healthy farm labourer with a wife and ten kids, I might not feel that sense of inadequacy.

She shook her head.

I can see what you mean . . . but somehow I don't feel it. Although I think you're right about Austin. He *is* looking for something, and he isn't mature enough to know what it is. I know he's self-divided. But I can't imagine him hurting anyone.

Perhaps you're right. Perhaps he wouldn't.

But why do you want to see him now? Why do you want to stay in London? What can you do?

I don't know. I'd like to see him and talk to him. He doesn't know the police suspect him of the Hamburg murder.

Are you sure?

I think so.

Don't you think it might have been the police he was worried about when he rang you from Switzerland?

I don't know. He said it was 'rather an unpleasant man'. I assumed it was blackmail of some sort.

Didn't you ask him?

No. What could I do, except advise him to go to the police? And that doesn't seem the right thing to do at this juncture. But I think he ought to be persuaded to leave England now, while the going's good.

She looked into his face, biting her lip. She asked suddenly:

Do you think he could be the man who did these things in Whitechapel?

No. Of course not.

He said it immediately, allowing himself no time to think. But he knew it was not as simple as that. The Austin he knew and the Austin Gertrude knew were two different men. The Austin he had met in the Diaghilev exhibition was a man who was capable of inflicting pain. Later he had changed, but the change was a reaction to Sorme; it sprang from admiration. He remembered the expression on Nunne's face as he had looked at the photograph of the girl outside the Cinerama theatre. That was an Austin whom Gertrude had never met. He said:

All the same, I'd like to talk to him . . . frankly. He ought to be warned. Do you think he might be at Leatherhead?

Perhaps. We could go and see.

No. You musn't come. I'd have to be alone.

All right. But I could drive you down there.

When?

Today. But we'd better phone Albany Street first.

Good. That's fine. And could we go and see Oliver on the way? I'd like to make sure he's OK.

All right.

She stood up.

I'll go and get dressed.

He came to the door, and pulled her to him.

Poor darling. A lot's happened to you in twelve hours, hasn't it? How do you feel?

She smiled briefly.

Bewildered.

He tilted her face by tugging gently at her hair, and kissed her; her lips parted, and she relaxed against him. His hand moved inside the dressing-gown. He said softly:

Don't worry. It's going to be all right.

She shuddered suddenly, pressing against him; a sense of mystery and exaltation rose in him.

Chapter Seven

As the Consul backed out of the garage, he saw the two men walking down the drive. Looking in the driving mirror, Miss Quincey had not noticed them. He said:

You've got visitors.

Really. Who?

She continued to back the car until it was clear of the garage doors.

Two men. Do you know them?

She stopped the car and slipped it into neutral.

No . . .

She turned off the ignition.

Insurance salesmen, perhaps?

I don't think so . . .

They could be police.

The men had seen the car and were standing by the front door, looking across at them. Sorme said:

Listen. If they are police, for heaven's sake keep your wits about you. Don't tell them anything about Austin.

But . . . how do I explain your being here?

That's none of their damn business.

She got out of the car and went across the lawn, saying:

Would you close the garage doors, please?

He was glad to see she was calm as she approached them. He closed the doors and slipped in the lock, then stood by the car, watching her as she inserted her key in the front door and led them into the house. He hesitated about following her; if they were police, he would prefer to stay in the background. He stared up at the sky; it was blue and pale after the downpour; the December sunlight was warm.

She called his name. She was standing in the doorway, beckoning to him. As he crossed the soggy lawn, she came to meet him. She said quickly:

They want to see you too.

Are they police?

Yes. They seem to know who you are.

There was no trace of nervousness in her voice. He said, smiling:

That's OK. We've nothing to worry about.

They went into the house. The two men were in the sitting-room, standing in the centre of the rug; the bigger of the two was cracking the joints of his fingers. Something in the large, red face and the receding hair reminded Sorme of Brother Robbins. The big man said:

Mr Gerard Sorme?

That's right.

We are police officers. My name is Macmurdo – Inspector Macmurdo. This is Detective-Sergeant James. I believe you're a friend of a Mr Nunne?

He spoke slowly, with the formality of a beadle making an announcement; he had a slight Scottish accent.

That's right, Sorme said. He bent down and switched on the electric fire. As he did so, he thought he saw the detective-sergeant noticing his familiarity with the house, then thought with irritation: It's none of his business, anyway.

Miss Quincey said:

Won't you sit down?

No, ma'am, we won't do that. We won't keep you a minute – I can see you're on your way out. We're simply trying to find Mr Nunne. Do you know where he is?

Austin? No . . . Have you tried his flat?

We have, ma'am. He hasn't been back for two days.

452

But why do you want him? What has he done wrong?

Macmurdo smiled.

There's no need to get upset, ma'am. Most of the people the police interview haven't done anything wrong. Mr Sorme, do you have any idea where we might contact Mr Nunne?

I'm afraid not. What about his parents' home?

No. He's not there. When did you last see him?

I . . . I think . . . on Saturday. I had lunch with him on Saturday.

Have you had any contact with him since?

No. I've tried to phone him at his flat several times.

I see. For any particular reason?

No. He's quite a close friend of mine.

You've no idea where he might be?

None at all. Miss Quincey might have more idea than me.

Miss Quincey shook her head.

I'm afraid not. But he often goes off for days without bothering to tell anyone.

Macmurdo asked Sorme:

Did he tell you he was likely to be going away for a few days?

No.

I see. Well, thank you very much. Sorry to have troubled you.

Miss Quincey said:

But can't you tell us what it's about? His family must be terrified . . . with the police making enquiries about him.

Why, ma'am? Have they any reason to feel worried about him?

Well . . . no. But when the police start to enquire . . . it would be hardly surprising if they were worried. Can't you give me some idea of whether it's serious?

Before Macmurdo could reply, Sorme said:

You're investigating the Whitechapel murders, aren't you?

Yes. How did you know?

I've seen your name in the papers.

Miss Quincey sat down. She said:

Murders? Is Austin involved in . . .?

Her voice trailed off. Watching her, Sorme was surprised and pleased; she was showing exactly the right degree of uncertainty. Macmurdo said soothingly:

We only want to ask him a few questions. He might be able to help us.

Sorme said:

I thought the murderer had been caught?

The Inspector and the sergeant exchanged glances. It was the sergeant who replied:

So did we, until last night.

Has there been another murder?

Macmurdo said: Yes.

He walked towards the door, followed by the sergeant. Miss Quincey said:

But what could Austin know about it?

Macmurdo said:

He may know nothing, ma'am. That's why we want to see him. If you hear from him, I'd be grateful if you'd let us know. You too, Mr Sorme. Good morning.

Miss Quincey sat, staring at him, until the door closed. They watched the two figures walking back up the drive. She said:

So . . . it looks as if it is Austin they're looking for?

I . . . don't know. If there was a murder last night . . . it's hardly surprising, is it? They'd want to question everybody even remotely connected with it. Besides, they can't be very suspicious of Austin, or they'd have asked

454

more questions. They didn't even ask me about the Kensington flat . . .

Do you think they know about it?

Surely they must. They aren't as slack as all that.

He stopped, staring out of the window; they heard the sound of a car engine starting. He said slowly:

I just . . . don't know. I don't know what to believe.

She said quietly:

If he's guilty, there's nothing we can do.

She went out of the room before the meaning of her words came home to him. He switched off the fire, and went out. He heard her bedroom door open; when he went in, she was powdering her nose at the dressing-table. He said:

Listen, Gertrude. Tell me something. Supposing he is guilty. Would you let them hang him?

She looked at him from the mirror; her face was surprised.

What could I do?

Wouldn't you even try to help him?

She turned around to stare at him.

You mean . . . if Austin had killed all those women?

As she said it, he saw the dawning of belief in her eyes. It was no longer a remote possibility, too improbable to consider. The shock was reflected back in him. It was the first time he had considered it as a simple matter of crime and punishment. He said:

I can't believe he's the killer. After all, he's homosexual. But I'm certain he knows something about it. All the evidence points that way.

But how? How can he?

He moves among perverts. There's a kind of freemasonry. Anyway, it might not be one man who's responsible. It could be several . . . a society, even.

You mean . . . a society for killing?

Well, it could be. There have been stranger things. The thugs of India were a religious society.

He could see her clutching at the idea; it was a way out. He sat on the edge of the bed, and sank deeply into it. She said:

You think Austin could be somehow involved . . .

He knew what she meant; 'involved' was a euphemism for 'misled', 'corrupted'. He said:

It's possible. Most of these sadistic ventures seem to be communal. Anyway, it's probable that he knows something about it.

She said:

We ought to find him. Do you think it's safe to go to Leatherhead?

We could try. Perhaps if we went to see Glasp on the way, they wouldn't bother to follow us. Anyway, they may not be interested.

As he spoke, he was remembering the fact that Macmurdo was in charge of the case, and that nothing was less likely. For a moment, he was assailed by a temptation to leave it alone. He recognized the same doubt in Miss Quincey's face. He said: We'd better find out about this other murder before we do anything. It may have no connection with the previous murders. Perhaps they've really got the killer . . .

She said:

If it *was* Austin, there'd be nothing we could do.

He looked at her, and recognized the incipient defeat in her eyes. He said quickly:

Maybe.

You don't think it is, do you?

He resisted the impulse to turn the question aside; it sprang from a desire to protect her, and the time for protecting her might be limited. He said deliberately:

My sweet, it's no use ignoring it. He *could* be the killer.

It *is* possible. I don't want to believe it. I don't want it to be true. My imagination won't face it. But if it is true, we'll have to face it.

He could follow the sequence of emotions in her eyes: incredulity, a sharpness like pain, then the transfer of attention from the meaning of his words to the expression on his face, less uncompromising than the words; and, finally, an adjustment, a hope. He said:

I don't know what to feel either. I don't know if I can condemn him. How do we know what's lawful and what's not? You assume sex is wicked because the Bible condemns fornication. But the experience makes it hard to believe. Last night, I could almost feel you trying to readjust your values – trying to make up your mind whether you were being sinful or not . . .

She said: Making love isn't the same as killing.

Again, he was surprised by the control she had acquired in a few hours, the ability to adjust to new facts.

That's true. Anyway, I'm not trying to defend the urge to kill. I'm only trying to understand it without oversimplifying it. For instance, couldn't you imagine a murder that comes out of a need to express your freedom?

She said patiently:

That wouldn't make any difference. Nobody has a right to express his freedom by killing someone.

I'm not talking about rights. I'm talking about the question of responsibility. Look, sweet, let's assume for a moment that Austin is the killer. How far would he be responsible for the murders? If your cat makes a mess on the carpet, you spank it and throw it outside – you hold it responsible. But if you know the cat's suffering from something she ate, you don't hold her responsible . . . you assume she couldn't help it. Well, isn't it the same with murder? How do you know the killer hasn't reached a degree of boredom and self-contempt and misery that make it almost impossible not to kill? It becomes an overpowering appetite to regain his freedom . . .

She shook her head.

I don't understand. What has it got to do with freedom?

Don't you see? A man can become the prisoner of his own self-contempt. Take the Christie case, for example. He's a weak-looking, inoffensive little man who suffers from sensitive nerves. He develops a sexual neurosis – you know they nicknamed him 'Can't-do-it Christie' in Leeds? Well, sex ought to be a freedom from your personality, and the sexual neurotic can never possess that freedom – except in sexual fantasies. And a point finally comes where the fantasies aren't enough. The imagination fails. Then he kills, and suddenly he has everything he wanted – a real woman lying at his feet. And for a moment, there's a supreme freedom, a feeling of contact with eternity – he *becomes* a fragment of eternity. Then the tragic return to earth – an unconscious woman lying at his feet. He used to gas them, you know. And a feeling: My God, what am I going to do when she wakes up? Then back to the world of nagging worries and pettiness – strangling her, hiding the body under the floorboards, worrying about the smell. Don't you see what I mean? Without the self-contempt, the exhaustion and pettiness, there'd be no murder. He kills for the same reason the saint practises meditation and the poet writes about nature. It's an escape from personality. And De Quincey becomes a drug-addict, and Poe becomes a drunk. Without the sensitivity, the escape wouldn't be necessary. They want a greater intensity of life, and the only gate left open is murder . . .

He looked at her with pity; she was listening, but without comprehension. When he stopped talking, she only stared past his head at the wallpaper. The insight overwhelmed him: she can never understand. She knows only categories and chapters from the Book of Kings. She can never know real good or evil; the knowledge would wreck her.

It was the answer to his interest in her; the insight brought disappointment and tenderness. A woman's world, a world of people. Without Kali, the insane mother, infinity of destructiveness and creativeness. He said:

We'd better go. It won't do any good to sit here.

He stood up. She rose automatically, and followed him to the door. At the top of the stairs he turned and kissed her; there was no response in her mouth. He went on down the stairs, thinking: I wonder if a woman exists who doesn't have her roots in limits and self-doubt? Probably not. But the search is not finished yet.

As they drove past Houndsditch, he said:

I wonder where the murder took place? We should have asked Macmurdo.

Why?

Oh . . . curiosity. Turn left at the traffic lights. Let's go up Commercial Street and see if we can find out.

How would you find out?

Oh, there'd be a crowd, probably. Morbid curiosity.

How revolting.

Any sign of being followed yet?

She glanced in the driving mirror.

I don't think so. I can't tell . . . There's too much traffic.

Turn off by the church across the road. No, hold on a minute. I think we've found it.

As they drew level with the church, he could see the crowd at the corner of Brushfield Street, opposite the market. He said:

Stop here for a minute.

He edged his way into the crowd, peering on tiptoe over their heads. The attention seemed to be focused around an entry a dozen yards along the street. The concrete platform of the marketplace was packed with men and women who stared at the small group of policemen outside the entrance. There was no ambulance.

He made his way back to the car. He said:

Nothing much visible. We'll have to get a midday paper.

A small man in stained white overalls edged out of the crowd, and walked past them. Sorme said:

Excuse me . . . What's happening? What are they all waiting for?

The man said: Doncher know? Another murder.

Sorme said, with simulated astonishment:

But I thought they'd caught him!

Everybody did. But it don't look like it, does it?

What happened? Do you know?

The man said:

Not much. They found her in a room. Cut to pieces.

He shrugged, then turned and walked away. Sorme got into the car. He asked:

Did you hear?

Yes. It sounds horrible.

Sorme said: He may be exaggerating. You know how rumours get around. What's the time now?

Half past nine.

We'll go back via Fleet Street. We'll catch the early editions in half an hour.

She revved the engine.

Where to now?

Let's call on Oliver.

As the car drove along Hanbury Street, he said:

I must say, this is quite a piece of luck for Oliver. They won't have much time to bother about him now. Anyway, they can't have taken the charge very seriously or they wouldn't have allowed him police bail . . . Right here. You'll have to go down to the Whitechapel Road. It's a one-way street.

At the end of Durward Street, he said:

Would you mind waiting here for about ten minutes? I'll try to be quick. But I doubt whether Oliver feels very sociable . . .

No. I quite understand. Don't worry.

The front door stood open. He rapped with his knuckles, calling into the room:

Anyone home?

There was no reply. He mounted the stairs cautiously, still blinded by sunlight, surrounded by the familiar smell of paraffin in the darkness. He groped his way to the door and knocked. Glasp's voice called:

Hello?

He opened the door and went in. Glasp was lying on the bed, fully clothed. Sorme said:

Hello. How are things?

All right, Glasp said. How did you get here?

Gertrude Quincey drove me in the car. She's waiting at the end of the street. I just came in to see how you are.

He sat on the stool near the oil stove. He said:

Have you heard anything?

They've dropped the charge.

Good! Congratulations! When did you hear?

A couple of hours ago.

Sorme said:

Well, what's the matter? You don't seem very cheerful about it. Why did they drop it? Has Christine turned up?

Yes.

Good. And have they examined her?

No.

Why not?

Glasp said tiredly:

Look, Gerard, do you mind not asking so many questions?

Sorme looked at him; he was staring at the ceiling. The silence lengthened. Sorme said:

OK. I'm going now. You're sure everything's all right?

Glasp looked at him, raising his head. He propped the pillow under his head, and heaved himself up slightly, resting his shoulders against the brass rails of the bed. He said:

She admitted she's not a virgin, anyway. But it was the cousin who lives with them. And he's admitted it too. So they dropped the charge.

Sorme said: Good lord!

Glasp shrugged, then dropped his head back on to the bed. Sorme said finally:

That must be quite a . . . shock. How do you feel about it?

Glasp's voice was level, without emotion:

She's not my daughter. Why should I worry?

Sorme stood up; he said, without conviction:

That's the sensible attitude to take. There's nothing very surprising in it. You don't feel annoyed, do you?

No.

And you'll keep on seeing her?

How can I? They wouldn't let her.

But . . . she'll want to keep on seeing you.

Perhaps.

Sorme stood at the door, hesitating to go out. Something about Glasp's listlessness irritated him. He said:

Surely it's nothing to worry about? This probably happened before you met her. You're giving her something she never had before. Surely this makes no difference?

Glasp turned his head to look at him. He said:

Look, Gerard, I don't know what I feel about it. I feel as if I've fallen down ten flights of stairs. I'm not even sure what I felt about her. Perhaps that's what I wanted all the time . . . I don't know. I just can't understand it. Why should she want to do it? I'd like to talk to her . . . She even said she'd marry me once. I know it's stupid. But I felt I understood her . . . and I just *don't* understand.

You probably understand her better than her parents – or this cousin. Anyway, you can't drop the girl just because of this. It's just the thing you're trying to save her from. The slum background . . .

Glasp said: Perhaps.

I'd better leave you. You'll feel better later. Shall I come over later?

If you like. Not today.

All right. Don't let it worry you. Goodbye, Oliver.

He closed the door quickly, glad to leave the room. Glasp's self-pity annoyed him; compared with the problem of Austin, it seemed trivial.

She was smoking a cigarette. She said:

You haven't been long.

No.

How is he?

He's all right. The police have dropped the case against him. So we can go and collect the bail money if you like . . .

Have they? Good. I was sure they would. Is he pleased?

The car started; she backed into Durward Street and turned. He said:

No. He irritates me. They discovered that the girl's not a virgin, but her cousin's responsible . . .

How appalling!

And he's working himself up into a state about it.

Why? Is he angry?

463

I don't know what he is. The man's a fool. Do you want to go to the police station to collect the money?

Not now. It can wait. I expect they'll be busy, anyway.

They turned again into the traffic of the Whitechapel Road, and drove towards the city. He sank into the seat, scowling out of the window. He said:

I thought Oliver was a talented artist. But now I'm beginning to wonder . . . He's too emotional. What does it matter whether the girl's a virgin or not? She's still the same girl.

Is he very upset?

I can't tell. I think he'd been building her up as a symbol of innocence and all that kind of thing. The world of adults exhausts him, so he turns to children. Then when he discovers the children are subject to the same kind of corruptions, he goes all gloomy and suicidal . . . At least Austin's a bit more grown up.

But why should it make any difference to him? I don't see the connection. He should be glad they've dropped the case.

He said irritably:

God knows. He's a typical romantic. I've come to the conclusion that the twentieth century's suffering from a romantic hangover. People like Oliver can't see straight. Everything has to be morbid to interest him . . . Oh, never mind. Maybe I'm being unfair. Turn down Fenchurch Street . . .

In Fleet Street, they stopped to buy an *Evening Standard*. The headline read: Search for Missing Parson Continues. He glanced down at the 'latest news' column; there was no mention of the murder. He tossed the newspaper into the back seat.

No good. Probably they didn't discover the body until late this morning. Let's go and have a quick drink. I need one.

The saloon bar was empty; it was the same room in which Sorme had spoken to Bill Payne on the previous day. He drank a pint of bitter ale while Gertrude Quincey examined a road atlas to determine the best route to Leatherhead. He noted with interest the ease with which she drank a double Scotch straight. The beer and the sunlight gave him a sense of wellbeing. Miss Quincey closed the atlas. He said:

Do you think it's worth going straight to Leatherhead? Wouldn't it be better to try the Kensington place first?

Do you think it's worth it?

Perhaps not. I doubt whether he'd stay in London if . . . if he knew anything about it.

All right.

He smiled at her.

How do you feel?

She touched her empty glass with the tip of her finger.

Better, thank you.

But . . . about all this?

She glanced around and saw that the barman was beyond the range of her voice.

Unreal. I can't believe it's serious. I feel somehow . . . as if you, and Austin, and the police, were practising some kind of elaborate confidence trick on me.

He said sympathetically:

I know. I feel the same. I think maybe all real murders are like this – unless you're directly involved. It's only in novels that the detective stumbles on clues and bodies all over the place. In real life the murders take place offstage, and it's all messy and unbelievable.

He finished his beer.

We'd better go. For all we know, the police may be there before us. Do Austin's family know the Leatherhead address?

Yes, of course.

I wonder if they gave it to Macmurdo?

Shall I ring and find out?

That might be an idea.

He watched her go out of the bar, and again felt surprise at the calm with which she accepted the situation. He ordered another half pint of beer, and stood at the bar to drink it, thinking: I shall never understand women. Are they all like that? One day she's a Jehovah's Witness and the next she's my mistress and an accessory after the fact. No sense of incongruity. The ancients were right. Widow of Ephesus, Helen of Troy. Maybe it's just lack of vitality.

She was away for a long time. She came back with the brisk casualness of a woman who has been out to powder her nose, and stood in front of him, waiting.

He said: Another drink?

No, thank you.

He finished his beer and they went outside.

Well?

No. His parents haven't heard from the police.

Are you sure? Did you ask them?

No. Not directly. I just asked where I could find Austin. They said he might be at Oxford with some friends. I said someone had sent a letter for him care of me, and that someone had been telephoning me to enquire after him.

Good! What did they say?

It was his mother . . . She said she couldn't understand it, and that as far as she knew he wasn't in any sort of trouble. I told her that I thought it might be a bookmaker or someone he owes money to . . .

He said with admiration:

You're a born intriguer!

She smiled briefly:

It looks as if no one has been making enquiries from her, then.

Strange. Why did Macmurdo tell us he had?

I don't think he did. He only said that Austin wasn't with his parents. Perhaps they've been keeping watch on them.

The car turned left, towards the Embankment. He said: This sounds pretty odd.

I didn't know whether to give them any kind of warning. It suddenly seemed ridiculous . . .

The best thing would be to find Austin. How long should it take us to Leatherhead?

About an hour, if the traffic isn't too bad.

Approaching Westminster Bridge, he checked his watch with Big Ben. The river looked like a sheet of rayon in the sunlight; it was difficult to believe in murder in the unexpected warmth.

She said:

Austin *is* here.

He sat up and stared at her. She had not spoken since they left Merton.

Where?

Here, in Leatherhead. That was his car outside the hotel.

Are you certain? I didn't see a red car.

It wasn't a red one. It was the grey MG.

He turned, peering out of the rear window. It was impossible to make out a parked car among the traffic.

Hadn't we better turn and make sure?

There's no need. I am sure. I recognized the number. It's one of his father's cars that he borrows sometimes.

But supposing he's in the hotel?

I don't think so. He'll probably be at the cottage. But I'll go back to the hotel while you go to the cottage.

But he wouldn't be allowed to park for long in the main street.

It isn't the main street – it was in the side street.

How far is the cottage?

About two miles on the other side.

Have you been there before?

Once. He took me for a trip in the aeroplane.

Sorme said:

I suppose he could be in Paris by this time.

I doubt it. He wouldn't leave his car outside a hotel if he intended to leave the country.

He looked at her with admiration.

You'd make a good detective!

She smiled without replying. The car turned left into a side lane with a signpost that said 'No Through Road'. After another five hundred yards, she turned left again, and braked to a stop.

You'll have to walk from here. I shan't be able to turn if I go any further.

Where is it?

Beyond those trees. When you reach the trees, you'll see the cottage. It stands on its own.

And what will you do?

I'll wait for twenty minutes.

OK. If I haven't returned by then, you'll know I've found Austin. Where will you be?

Back in the hotel. I'm afraid you'll have to walk back. It's called the Crown, and it's in the phone book in case you want to phone me.

That's fine. Bye-bye, sweet.

He leaned across and kissed her. The sensation was strange; since the police arrived he had ceased to feel like her lover. Her lips felt cold and tight.

He climbed over the stile, and heard the car backing into the lane. The clump of trees was a hundred yards away, on the edge of the field. Beyond them, he could see nothing but the sky. In spite of the sunlight, the earth of the ploughed field looked hard and frozen. He took the path that ran beside the hedge, and walked quickly, his hands in his pockets. After the heat of the car, the wind was cold.

There was a pond in the midst of the trees; its brown water looked lifeless; a broken tree jutted from the middle like an arm. Standing on its edge, he could see the cottage in the corner of the next field. He experienced a sense of depression and foreboding. He stood there for several minutes, hoping to see some sign of life. There was no smoke rising from the chimney. Two windows faced towards the pond, but their curtains appeared to be drawn.

It was cold among the trees. He glanced at his watch, and remembered that Miss Quincey would be waiting in the car. He set out briskly across the field, hurrying to reach the cottage. He was aware of a desire to find it empty, to hurry back to the waiting car and to London.

The gate of the small front garden stood open. The walls of the cottage had been whitewashed, but winter rain had cut charmels in it, leaving rust deposits from the corrugated iron roof. Outside the back door, a water butt was full to overflowing.

He banged the rusty knocker, calling: Austin!

When there was no movement from inside, he shouted: Is anybody home?

He was suddenly struck by the thought that the place might be under observation by the police. He turned and stared at the clump of trees he had just left, at the bare hedges, and the haystack covered with tarpaulin in the other corner of the field. As he looked, he heard a movement inside the door. He looked round, and found Nunne's eyes looking at him from the letter-slit under the knocker. He stared back, too startled for a moment to speak. The flap closed and a chain rattled; several bolts

469

moved back. The door opened, and Nunne stood there in his shirtsleeves. His face looked unshaven and exhausted. Sorme said:

Hello, Austin.

Nunne smiled unsteadily; a smell of whisky came to Sorme. He said:

Come in, dear boy. Childe Roland to the dark tower came . . .

Chapter Eight

It was as if they were meeting for the first time. In the past two days, Nunne had ceased to strike him as a reality. His relief expressed itself as a desire to laugh. He said:

It's good to see you, Austin!

Thank you, Gerard. Your face is also welcome.

The small kitchen smelt of damp; behind the door stood a Calor-gas cylinder with the seal intact. The sink, stove and washing machine were all obviously new. On the draining-board stood three empty whisky bottles.

Which way?

To your left.

The room looked like a smaller version of the Albany Street flat. The carpet was the same eggshell blue; the walls were distempered in cream and navy blue. It was stiflingly hot; a paraffin heater with a hemisphere of glowing wires burned in the grate; the room was lit by two paraffin lamps with tall chimneys. The room had an appearance of disorder; there was a great deal of cigarette ash on the carpet and shells of monkey-nuts. On the table were the remains of a meal, and two whisky bottles, both full. Nunne threw a newspaper and some books off a chair, and said:

Sit down.

Thanks. Mind if I take my coat off?

How did you get here?

Gertrude brought me.

Where is she?

She's gone back to the hotel.

Nunne dropped into an armchair, and picked up a glass from the table. He said:

Help yourself to whisky. Open a fresh bottle. Why did you decide to come?

Sorme tore the lead foil off a bottle of White Horse, and poured himself a large one. He said:

The police have been looking for you.

He squirted soda, then turned round. Nunne was smiling. The teeth looked yellow and fang-like. He said:

I see.

Sorme took off his jacket and dropped it over the back of a chair. He said:

Mind if I open a window?

Do. Where did they visit you?

At Gertrude's.

When?

This morning.

I see.

Nunne was still smiling. Sorme anticipated the question, and was prepared to answer truthfully. Instead, Nunne said:

How long will she wait for you?

All day, if necessary. Or I could phone her at the Crown.

Good. Perhaps we'll do that later. I can drive you back to town.

Sorme allowed no surprise to appear on his face. He said:

Good. You're going up today?

I expect I may as well . . . now you've come. Allow me a few hours to sober up.

He stretched in the chair, yawned, then emptied his glass.

So you've come all this way to warn me? That's rather sweet of you.

Thanks. It's nothing.

Nunne crossed to the table, and poured more whisky. He was drinking it straight. On his way back, he stopped by Sorme's chair and placed his hand on Sorme's head. He said:

I can't tell you how glad I am to see you, dear boy.

Sorme recognized the note of sincerity through the whisky. He said:

Thanks.

Nunne leaned on the back of the chair. He was still swaying slightly. He said:

You *are* a friend, aren't you, Gerard?

Sorme looked up at him, and felt again the sudden knowledge of affection. He said:

Yes. I'm a friend.

Nunne smiled down, then walked unsteadily to his chair. Sorme said:

But if you intend to sober up, you won't do it that way.

Nunne said slowly:

No. I think you are right. Yes. I don't wanna get stinko yet.

He returned to the window and emptied his glass outside. He said:

Unfortunately, I need something to drink once I start. No milk.

He went back into the kitchen. Sorme heard him say:

Don't suppose champagne'd improve things. Or Niersteiner. That leaves baby pol or lemonade.

He returned carrying three bottles of lemonade and an opener. He poured a bottle into his empty glass and tasted it. He said:

Ugh! How disgusting!

He set it down on the arm of the chair as if it were nitroglycerine, then seated himself carefully. He said:

Well, go ahead. What did the police want?

473

Just to know where you were.

I see. Did they say anything more?

No. But when I asked Macmurdo if he wasn't in charge of the Whitechapel murders, he said yes. And he told me there was another murder last night.

Nunne said indifferently:

And did he give you any details?

No.

What time was the body discovered?

Not till late, I think. It wasn't in the early editions of the evening papers.

Nunne reached over and pulled a footstool closer. He closed his eyes, and stretched out, his head dropping forward. He said:

Rather an awkward situation, isn't it, Gerard?

I don't know.

Nunne smiled, his eyes closed. In his attitude of complete abandonment to exhaustion he might have been asleep. He said:

For five hours I've been thinking about this problem. But the whisky was beginning to overcome me.

He opened his eyes suddenly and looked at Sorme.

What am I to do?

Sorme said:

I don't know. I don't quite understand your problem.

He moved his chair further back from the fire; the breeze from the window had lowered the temperature of the room, but it was still overpowering. Nunne stood up and crossed to the window again; Sorme could feel a restlessness and tension that the whisky had not released.

Are you sure you weren't followed down here?

I should say it's pretty unlikely. I kept a constant watch. Gertrude even turned the driving mirror towards me so I could watch out of the back window.

How much does Gertrude know?

About as much as I know.

Nunne ignored the challenge in his words. He drew the curtain back and returned to his chair.

I wouldn't like to be interrupted. God, I feel pretty sloshed . . . I could do with a cold shower and a rub down. Never mind I want to talk to you.

He drywashed his face with his hands, and pushed his hair back. He drank down half a glass of lemonade, then sat down, grimacing. He said:

As you gather, dear boy, I'm in quite a situation.

How bad is it?

I'm not sure. Did Macmurdo have a warrant for me?

The words brought a tightness to Sorme's chest. He said:

No. I don't think so.

Nunne sat sprawled in the chair; he stared at Sorme and let the silence lengthen. His eyes looked bloodshot and exhausted, but their expression was sardonic. He said finally:

Well, Gerard?

Sorme said nothing, shrugging. Nunne said:

You're still too polite to want to pry into my business. But you're rather committed to it now, aren't you? You've come all this way to warn me. Why *did* you come?

I . . . I suppose, to warn you. I've been trying to phone you all weekend.

I've been down here. But I'm grateful, Gerard, very grateful . . . What would you do if they arrest me?

Sorme said carefully:

You mean for the . . . murders?

Nunne said quietly: Yes.

Could they arrest you?

I don't know. Probably not. And even if they did, I think they'd be forced to release me.

Sorme emptied his glass. He had just drunk an amount

equivalent to four fingers of whisky, and felt totally unaffected. He was also aware how much of his calm he owed to the drink. He reached for the bottle and poured another. Nunne wrenched the cap off another lemonade bottle. Sorme asked:

What makes you assume you won't be arrested?

They've no evidence.

He stood up again and went to the window. He said:

I'd hate Macmurdo to crawl under that window with a tape-recorder. I'm afraid I'd better close it. I'll turn the fire off.

Sorme said:

Are you sure they've no evidence?

Fairly sure. Nothing that would be conclusive in a court of law.

Sorme said:

They'd try very hard. They badly need to make an arrest.

I know. And they might find some excuse for holding me while they wait for a confession. They might easily do that. Hoping I'd crack. I wouldn't.

No?

No. Have you ever noticed that most killers talk too much?

The word made Sorme's hand tighten around the glass; it was there now, between them, like an upturned playing-card. Nunne said:

Whiteway, the Teddington Towpath murderer. Neville Heath. And Peter Manuel. They talked their way to the scaffold.

Sorme said slowly:

You classify yourself with them?

Nunne looked at him seriously; his head made a hardly perceptible gesture of approval, as if he were a professor, and Sorme his most intelligent pupil. He said:

No. I don't. But they remain of interest. You don't confine your reading to Goethe and Dostoevsky, although you classify yourself with them rather than with your contemporaries. The problem is that most criminals are stupid ruffians. Manuel and Heath and the rest were contemptible. Kürten was more interesting. In a more enlightened country – Sweden, for instance – he wouldn't have been executed. He was deeply interested in his own impulses. He used to read Lombroso and Havelock Ellis. With the help of a panel of intelligent doctors he might have added a new domain to psychology.

All traces of the whisky had disappeared, except for the occasional slurring of vowels; there was a feverish brightness in his eyes as he talked. He said:

You know, Gerard, I've sat in judgment on myself many times. I'm not an animal. I'm a man. I *can* judge myself. If I was a writer or a poet, the human race might agree that I can add something to their knowledge. That means that I must be an identity. I can analyse my own impulses, even if I can't control them. If I could talk to other people about them I might even learn to control them. So why should I be condemned and executed like a mad dog? No one has the right. It would be murder.

Sorme said:

This is what you've been thinking about all morning?

No. Not entirely. But I've thought about it often enough . . .

He crossed to the window again and peered out, then opened it and drew the curtain aside for a moment. The room was full of the acid odour of paraffin fumes as the heater spluttered. Sorme said:

But what are you going to do now?

Ah, that is a problem. There's only one thing certain. I've got to stop.

But . . . do you think you'll get away with it?

477

Why not? If they've no evidence against me . . .

But if Macmurdo's looking for you he must have a pretty definite suspicion . . .

That is nothing. No one saw me last night . . .

Sorme said:

It *was* you last night?

For the first time, Nunne looked guilty. He said:

Yes.

Did you . . . know the woman?

Nunne sat down. He said:

Ah, if you want to talk about that . . . we shall have to start all over again.

Sorme said:

I don't want to talk about it particularly.

You see . . . that's my real problem. I can't stay in England. If I was certain I wanted to be cured . . .

Don't you?

Partly. But it's not like a disease. Surely you can understand that, Gerard?

I think I do . . .

Don't you see . . . to do *anything* worthwhile, you have to be willing to allow yourself to be carried away? You see, I was born like this. It was in my blood. Like your restlessness. I could never settle down to an ordinary life. When I was seventeen I used to pray that I might become a great artist. I used to stare at pictures by Van Gogh or Münch, and think: These men had strange impulses. I think Münch had visions of blood too. I used to think that if I was strong enough I could become a great artist . . .

He seemed to collapse suddenly, dropping his head again into his hands. Sorme felt an immense pity moving inside him, and a desire to reach across to him. Nunne said:

It was no good. I was too lucky. My family had too

much money. To do a thing like that, you need to feel alone.

Sorme said quietly: Poor Austin.

Nunne looked up, smiling; his eyes were red where he had been rubbing them.

No. I'm not poor Austin. I'm f – ing rich Austin. But you know, Gerard, I have a theory. Subconsciously, I've been trying to induce a state of crisis in my life. To get rid of the money and privilege. And now I've done it. The crisis is here. There's no way back now. Think, if I'd left the country yesterday, this poor devil from Brixton might have been sentenced for the murders and no one would have known.

Sorme said:

I'm not so sure. The police have been watching you. Father Carruthers told me to warn you. Stein told him.

Father Carruthers? Nunne said. Is there anybody in London who doesn't know?

I don't know whether he knows. I didn't know until I saw you. I couldn't believe it.

Nunne said:

You believe it now?

No. Not really. Oh, I accept your word for it · . . . but it's not real to me.

Nunne stretched out his hands on his thighs, and stared at them. He said:

But it's true . . .

Sorme said:

But why? Why do you have to do it?

Nunne looked at him; his eyes seemed strangely hooded, concealed. He said:

How do I know? The impulse goes back so far that I can't even trace it. Haven't you ever felt anything of the sort?

I . . . suppose so. When I was about six I had a nasty

tendency to beat up boys who were smaller than myself
. . . if there was something about them that irritated me.
I don't know whether that was sadism or just high
spirits . . .

Nunne said, smiling:

It sounds like authentic sadism.

But I could always understand the impulse at the time.
It wasn't like – well, being possessed by a demon or
something. It was *me* all right.

Of course. It always is.

But . . . you talked to me once about doing something
that made you feel as if you'd been changed into an
animal.

Did I? Perhaps I did. But that's only a histrionic way of
putting it. If you look at yourself objectively, of course
you feel like an animal. But it's never as weird as that.
You know some psychiatrist has a theory that the old
legends of vampires and werewolves arose out of cases of
sadism – split personality. I never felt like a werewolf.

How did you feel?

Nunne was staring at his hands again. He said slowly:

I can give you an idea. When I killed that coloured
prostitute I felt an immense exaltation. I felt like a
prophet cleansing the world, like Jesus throwing the
moneychangers out of the Temple. And when she was
lying on the ground, I had to suppress an urge to shout
and bring the whole street to look at her. I wanted to say:
Look, she's dead. She's an example to the world . . .

He looked up suddenly, and caught the look of fascinated horror on Sorme's face. Somehow, he was not the
same person; his face and eyes seemed darker; he
reminded Sorme of a gypsy he had known as a child. He
said sadly:

I know. You don't understand. You can't.

Sorme said:

480

No . . . I understand a little. Was she the first?

Nunne stared back at him; his eyes were bolder now, and somehow depthless.

No. But . . . I don't want to talk about that.

All right . . . What do you want to talk about?

The problem of what I'm going to do.

What do you want to do?

I don't know. You see . . . I've let this impulse grow stronger. And today I feel quite cleansed of it – as if it had gone for good. Perhaps it *has* gone for good.

The hope was there; Sorme could see it clearly. It would have been impossible to counterfeit. Sorme said quietly:

Because of last night?

Nunne nodded.

Because of last night. Do you know something, Gerard? Last night, for the first time, I felt suddenly disgusted with myself. It seemed stupid and pointless. And all the way back here I was thinking: If I'm caught this time, that's the last time. It won't happen again . . .

And do you mean that?

I think so. I don't know. You see, Gerard, I still want to do something else. I'm still certain I *could* do something good, something important. Don't you think so? It's the same urge – the need to let something out of yourself.

Sorme said:

Look, forgive me if this question's stupid. I'd like to ask it all the same. Supposing everything turns out as you want it to. Supposing you go back to London and the police don't arrest you and you start a new life. Wouldn't you ever think back on . . . the past? Would you feel it had been written off and closed?

I don't know. I think so.

You don't feel – well, pangs of conscience . . .?

481

What's the point? It's done now. And if the urge has gone for good, then it wasn't all meaningless . . .

But what about the women?

Nunne shrugged:

Pooh, a few prostitutes. Women who'd sold their lives, anyway. Do you know what the woman last night said to me? 'I suppose you might be Leather Apron.' She *knew* I might be.

I suppose she didn't believe it.

She knew it was possible. She just didn't care. If you'd found some loathsome worm in a meat pie, you'd stop eating that brand of meat pie, wouldn't you? And if you carried on eating them, it would prove you didn't really care.

Or that I was too hungry not to eat them.

No. These women aren't too poor to give it up. They could live better as shop assistants or hosiery workers. They just don't care.

But why kill them because they don't care?

Nunne said with a kind of exasperation:

I don't know. I don't know why I want to do it.

He made a movement of his hand towards his stomach:

It's something in here. I feel sometimes that I could take an emetic and get rid of it all. It's like periodic malaria. But try to understand, Gerard. *It's not just a disease*. It's an excitement. It's a kind of inverted creative impulse. I feel as if I'm serving something greater than myself. It's . . . it's like a need . . . to build.

He made a vague shape in the air with his two hands. He laughed suddenly, and it startled Sorme. It was an easy laugh; there was a gaiety in it.

You see, there's even a sort of dramatic impulse behind it, a playwright's desire for climaxes. Don't you see?

Sorme nodded. He said slowly:

You mean . . . the newspapers ask if the killer's moved

to Greenwich – and immediately, there's a double murder? And a man's arrested, and everybody heaves a sigh of relief. And there's another murder . . .

Nunne was suddenly serious.

In a way, yes. But Gerard . . . if only I could feel it had gone out of me. For good. This thing has driven me . . . for three years now.

Since Hamburg?

Nunne looked surprised.

Yes, Hamburg? How did you know?

Father Carruthers again. Stein told him.

Nunne said shortly:

I thought they suspected.

Wasn't it a man in Hamburg?

A youth. Male prostitute.

He was the first?

Nunne nodded.

And . . . why did you feel the need . . .?

Nunne said, shrugging:

Don't know. You wouldn't understand.

I might. Did you hate him?

No. On the contrary. I loved him . . . a little.

And why weren't you caught?

Because no one knew he'd been with me. He had a lot of clients.

But . . . what did you do with him?

Are you really interested?

Yes.

I'll tell you. I dumped him in a bath of ice-cold water – it was midwinter in Hamburg – and left him there for an hour. Then I carried him up three flights of stairs, and left him in the room of a man whom I knew to be away for the night. He came in at five in the morning and roused the hotel. Then a doctor examined the body, and decided from its temperature that he'd been killed at least eight

483

hours before. And I had an alibi up till two in the morning. So I was allowed to leave the hotel the next day. It was a pretty low dump, anyway, and that was its second murder in a month.

Wasn't it all pretty dangerous? You might have been seen taking him upstairs.

That's true. That was dangerous. And the man in the next room heard me running the bath water at three in the morning; he mentioned it to me the next day. Luckily, I'd taken great care not to wet the hair. But it was dreadfully dangerous.

Nunne was speaking with a certain pride; he might have been telling Sorme a fishing story. Sorme glanced at his watch; it was one-thirty. He had been there about an hour. In that time, Nunne's demeanour had changed completely. He no longer seemed drunk; he talked with a clinical precision; his voice was calm and cheerful. The whisky had affected Sorme; he was aware of being more than half drunk, while feeling no loss of his power to concentrate. He felt a curious acceptance of Nunne; it was no more strange that Nunne should be a murderer than that he should be a homosexual; or that Gertrude Quincey should be his mistress. Things altered; the world was a perpetual flux. There was no finality in space or time; only an immense, unmeasurable freedom.

Nunne said:

Tell me what you're thinking, Gerard?

That wouldn't be easy. I can begin to understand . . . but there are still some pieces missing.

Such as . . .?

Wouldn't you prefer to be . . . normal? Or . . .

Nunne interrupted quickly:

Of course I would. But don't overestimate my abnormality. I suppose a hangman's job is abnormal, but he treats it as a job all the same. So does a man in a slaughterhouse. I know a man who spent the war training teenage boys how to kill easily and silently. I've known Commandos who have killed more Germans than they can count. One of them always goes to Germany for his holidays and says he prefers the Germans to any other race in Europe.

Sorme said gloomily:

You mean murder's a part of the modern mentality?

Of *any* mentality, Gerard. Society has always been based on murder. It's no use trying to outlaw murder with laws and moral codes. It has to disappear of its own accord – men have to outgrow it. Don't you see what I mean? My Commando friend – he's a perfectly law-abiding citizen. But murder's still in his system. If there was another war, he'd kill again. He hasn't outgrown murder. It's only that he accepts the laws that forbid it. That isn't the way for a man to grow . . . You think I'm being a Jesuit?

Sorme said dubiously:

Not a Jesuit. But your defence wouldn't go down in any court of law . . .

I agree, Nunne said promptly. And I wouldn't expect it to. It's not really a defence. I don't disown what I've done. How can I? I don't even understand it. I was born like it.

I know . . . But what I don't understand is . . . well, why you should do it. I can understand everything but the act itself. I can understand the hatred and the disgust. I once wrote a story about a man who kills out of sheer boredom and the desire to do something positive. But . . . the reasons aren't so important. You don't kill reasons. You kill a human being.

Nunne said seriously:

That's true, in a way. But it isn't as rational as that. It's

485

a kind of irrational resentment, I suppose. Not about people, or even society, but just about . . . the world.

He was not looking at Sorme as he spoke. His face was averted, and Sorme could see mainly the top of his head, and the heavy black hair that had been newly washed. A speculation about the reason for this passed through his mind, and a feeling of a chill. The conversation suddenly became unreal; he made a mental effort to restore it to focus. He said:

I think I understand you. I've known that kind of disgust. About three months before I left the office for good, I went on a holiday in Kent, and had an experience of the same sort.

His face still averted, Nunne said:

What happened?

Oh . . . I'd been getting pretty sick of the office. It made me feel dead inside. Finally, the weekends weren't long enough to get it out of my system. I couldn't read poetry or listen to music. It was like being constipated. Well, I got a holiday and went to Kent for a week's hiking. And for the first two days I felt nothing at all, just a sort of deadness inside. And one day I went into a pub in a place called Marden and had a couple of pints. And as I came out, a sort of bubble seemed to burst inside me, and I started feeling things again. And I suddenly felt an overwhelming hatred for cities and offices and people and everything that calls itself civilization . . .

He was talking compulsively, glad to speak of himself and restore a feeling of normality to the situation:

Then I got an idea. I sat down at the side of the road and thought about it. I'd read somewhere that the Manichees thought the world was created by the devil, and everything to do with matter was evil. Well, it suddenly seemed to me that the forces behind the world weren't either good or evil, but something quite incomprehensible to human beings. And the only thing they want is movement, everlasting movement. That's the way I saw it suddenly. Human beings want peace, and they build their civilizations and make their laws to get peace. But the forces behind the world don't want peace. So they send down certain men whose business it is to keep the world in a turmoil – the Napoleons, Hitlers, Genghis Khans. And I call these men the Enemies, with a capital E. And I thought: I belong among the Enemies – that's why I detest this bloody civilization. And I suddenly began to feel better . . .

Nunne was looking at him now, and nodding his head slowly as he talked. He said, smiling:

Quite. You understand too. The force behind the world is neither good nor evil. Men are not big enough to know anything about good and evil. That's how I felt . . . the first time it ever happened in London. I'd been to see Father Carruthers and I came away feeling sick of everything. He obviously didn't know what I was talking about. And I walked along Charterhouse Street, and there was an extraordinary sunset over the rooftops. And suddenly I detested it all. Did you ever read that piece in Stein's book on Kürten, about how Kürten used to dream of blowing up the whole city with dynamite? That was how I felt.

He stopped abruptly, and twisted his fingers together. He bent both hands backwards, making the joints crack. His voice had begun to sound curiously thick as he talked. Sorme watched him closely, sensing the tightness that was coming up inside him. Nunne stood up suddenly and went to the table. He poured half an inch of whisky into the tumbler, and tossed it back. When he spoke again, his voice sounded choked:

I can't explain the feeling . . . but you understand.

Sorme said:

Yes, I understand.

He said it to reassure Nunne rather than because he understood.

Nunne stood with his back to him for a few seconds longer, holding the empy glass. He turned around and ran his fingers through Sorme's hair. He was smiling again. He said:

I wish you *did* understand, Gerard.

He sat down again; this time on the edge of the chair, his fists resting on his knees. Although the room was now becoming cool, his face was sweating. Sorme said:

I think I *do* understand, Austin. But . . . you know . . . you'll have to stop it. If you stop now, you might be safe. But if you don't . . . nothing can save you.

Nunne said: I know. That's the problem.

Sorme leaned forward. He said:

But do you understand it? You're alive now. In two months' time you might be waiting in the death cell. They'd hang you, Austin. They'd have to hang you. They wouldn't dare to commit you to a mental home. Get away while you can. Go to Switzerland. Find a good psychiatrist and pay him five thousand pounds and tell him everything. But don't stay in London.

Nunne looked up and smiled, but the exhaustion was back. He said:

I know you're right, Gerard.

He cleared his throat, and ran both hands through his hair. He began to button up his shirt.

I'm very grateful, Gerard . . .

Nonsense.

I don't deserve a friend like you.

Sorme said:

Don't be silly.

Nunne stood up.

I suppose we'd better go.

As he spoke, they heard the noise; it was the sound of some metal object being knocked over outside. For a moment, they stared at one another. Sorme glanced towards the window. He said quickly:

That could be the police.

As he spoke, there was a sound of knocking on the door. Nunne said:

I'm afraid you were followed.

I'm sorry . . .

It doesn't matter.

He opened the door leading to the hall. Sorme caught up with him and grasped his arm. He said quietly:

Don't give anything away.

Nunne turned and smiled at him. It was the calm, sardonic smile that Sorme associated with his first meeting with him, the total certainty of superiority. Nunne said:

Don't worry, dear boy. *You* be careful.

He went out to the door. A moment later, Sorme recognized Macmurdo's voice.

Mr Austin Nunne?

Yes. What can I do for you?

We'd like to speak to you, if we may. I am a police officer.

Certainly. Come in. I've been expecting you.

Sorme could almost see the eagerness on Macmurdo's face. A moment later, he came into the room, followed by the sergeant and Nunne. He was saying:

Indeed? Why?

Nunne said:

Because my friend here came especially to tell me to contact you.

Sorme was still sitting down. He nodded briefly at Macmurdo.

How do you do?

Macmurdo said:

489

I didn't expect to see you here. I thought you had no idea where Mr Nunne might be?

Sorme said pleasantly:

I hadn't. I've been looking systematically.

Macmurdo's disbelief was obvious. He said:

I see.

He turned to Nunne.

Mr Nunne, would you mind telling me where you were last night?

Certainly. I was here.

All night?

No. I went out for a breath of air . . . just a drive around.

At what time?

Oh . . . as a matter of fact, I don't know. After midnight. My portable radio gave out.

How long were you out?

Oh . . . about two hours, perhaps.

Where was your car parked?

In the lane outside.

When did you leave it outside the Crown Hotel in Leatherhead?

Nunne sat down on the edge of the table. His face was grave and concentrated.

This morning. I went in to buy a newspaper. And it was such a lovely day that I decided to walk back. I'd had some coffee . . .

Macmurdo interrupted belligerently:

You know why I'm asking these questions, don't you?

I think so, Nunne said.

Why?

You are investigating the Whitechapel murders. You want to clear me for your list of suspects.

Sorme could see Macmurdo's irritation growing with the confidence of Nunne's replies. The sergeant was standing by the door, watching with interest. Macmurdo said:

Do you mind if we look around the house?

Nunne asked smoothly:

Have you a warrant?

No. But we can soon get one.

Nunne said quickly:

Oh, not at all. Please do look, by all means.

The sergeant went out of the room. A moment later, Sorme heard more men coming in from outside. Macmurdo seated himself in the chair Nunne had vacated. He asked Sorme:

And may I ask how you got here?

By car. Miss Quincey – Austin's aunt – drove me down.

How did you know Mr Nunne was here?

Why, we had a long talk after you'd gone and tried to decide where he might be. Finally, she remembered this place . . .

Where is she now?

In the Crown Hotel.

For the first time, Sorme felt alarm. He felt no fear for himself or Nunne, but Gertrude was a different proposition. He felt a pang of regret for telling her about Nunne. But she knew very little. Even if she admitted . . .

A plainclothes policeman came into the room and beckoned to Macmurdo; Nunne's eyes met Sorme's for a moment as the Inspector went out of the room. A moment later, he came back.

Would you mind telling me, Mr Nunne, why the fireplace upstairs is full of warm ashes?

Nunne said, smiling:

Oh, of course. I started to make a fire in the bedroom. Then Gerard arrived and I forgot. You'll see the wood and coal in the room . . .

Did you put any wood on it?

No. I was rather cold. So I lit a grateful of paper and some oily rags. I was sitting there enjoying the blaze when Gerard arrived.

Where were the oily rags from?

Oh . . . the shed outside. The decorators left them.

Which explains the smell of paraffin?

Quite.

Macmurdo said:

Decorators use turpentine.

Nunne said, shrugging:

I'm afraid I'm not responsible for what the decorators leave behind. Why does it matter, anyway?

Macmurdo ignored the question. He said:

Why are you in your shirtsleeves if you were cold an hour ago?

Nunne said:

Because this room was very warm indeed an hour ago. As my friend here will tell you. You'll find my jacket and pullover on the bed upstairs.

And what had you been burning in the kitchen stove?

Oh . . . more rubbish. Newspapers mainly. I like lighting fires.

You hadn't been burning anything else . . . clothes, for instance?

Nunne said, with a touch of impatience:

You mean bloodstained clothes? Look, Inspector, you don't have to keep fencing with me. I'd like to help you. Just ask me what you like, and I'll answer you as accurately as I can.

Macmurdo repeated deliberately:

Were there any clothes?

No.

You know it's something we can easily verify? By analysing the ash?

Nunne said:

Good. I'm glad to hear that. That should save trouble.

Macmurdo said:

I see.

He leaned forward, as if peering at the paraffin heater. He turned to Nunne suddenly, and said:

What did you do with Millie Rogers?

Sorme's heart lurched unpleasantly; he could see that Nunne was taken by surprise. Nunne said:

I beg your pardon?

Macmurdo said:

You were seen speaking to a woman named Millie Rogers outside a club in Paddington. The Balalaika Club. She was heard to say that she would come home with you. She hasn't been seen since.

Nunne said coolly:

I haven't the faintest idea of what you are talking about, Inspector. And in case you didn't know, my tastes don't lie in that direction.

You deny knowing a woman of that name?

I most certainly do.

You deny speaking to her?

No. Not necessarily. I might quite easily have spoken to a woman of that type if she'd accosted me. So, I imagine, might thousands of other men.

How do you know she was of 'that type'?

Really, Inspector! You don't leave much room for doubt!

The detective-sergeant came back into the room. He was holding a red beret. Macmurdo took it from him. The sergeant said.

Found it in the wardrobe in the bedroom, sir.

Macmurdo asked Nunne:

Whose is it?

Nunne smiled; he said:

493

Believe it or not, Inspector, it belongs to my aunt. She left it here.

The lady who's waiting now in the Crown?

Yes.

She's been down here?

Once. I took her for a spin in my aeroplane.

Is that the lady who said she didn't know where you might be? Macmurdo asked, with a note of sarcasm.

It is.

And why do you suppose she didn't mention this place to me when I asked her this morning?

Sorme interrupted:

I can tell you that. She'd forgotten it. Besides, it was quite a shock to her to have policemen looking for her nephew.

Macmurdo stared at Sorme with hostility; for a moment, Sorme expected an irritable rebuke. Then the policeman turned away, shrugging, and handed the beret back to the sergeant. He said:

Take some samples of the ash, sergeant.

He turned back to Nunne.

Do you mind if I see your hands?

Nunne held out his hands without speaking. Macmurdo took them in his own, and turned them over. He said:

You've cleaned your nails today.

Of course. I clean my nails every day.

You seem to have been particularly thorough today.

No. Not particularly.

Macmurdo dropped Nunne's hands. Sorme could see he was disappointed; his mouth was beginning to tighten into a line that somehow gave him the appearance of a bulldog. But before Nunne could sit down again, he asked:

Do you possess a knife, Mr Nunne?

Nunne said:

494

Of course.

He felt in his trouser pocket, and produced a small penknife. Macmurdo said:

I don't mean that kind. Do you possess a larger knife – for example, a Scout's sheath knife?

No.

Have you ever possessed such a knife?

Not since I was a child.

You don't possess any kind of knife that might be used in a fight? A flick knife, for instance?

No . . . There are one or two sharp kitchen knives at my flat, I suppose . . . But nothing very dangerous.

The sergeant came back in. He said:

There's nothing much else, sir. I've got samples of the ash.

Macmurdo nodded. He said:

Mr Nunne, I'm afraid we shall have to take you back to the Yard for questioning.

Nunne said sighing:

All right. I suppose it's necessary.

Sorme asked:

What about me?

We shan't be requiring you immediately, Macmurdo said.

Nunne asked:

Do you mind if I go and get some warmer clothes on?

Macmurdo nodded. He said:

Sergeant!

The sergeant nodded, and followed Nunne out of the room. As soon as they were alone, Macmurdo sat in the chair facing Sorme; he leaned forward, and said carefully:

You realize that if we find anything against Mr Nunne, you'd be liable for a long term of imprisonment as an accessory after the fact?

Sorme said bluntly:

Look, Inspector, you're barking up the wrong tree. Austin's not a murderer, no matter what his other peculiarities may be.

Macmurdo said:

Are you sure?

Pretty sure.

Tell me, Mr Sorme, what were you two speaking about before I came?

All kinds of things. The Whitechapel murders, among others.

Did Mr Nunne give you any explanation of why he should be suspected?

Nothing I didn't know already.

And what did you know already?

That Austin has certain – sexual peculiarities. Enough to make him a natural suspect in a case like this.

That he is a sadist, in fact?

All right.

But you still think he couldn't bring himself to kill?

Sorme stared back levelly; he said:

He is also homosexual. The victims of these murders were women.

He might have a resentment against women.

Perhaps.

Macmurdo persisted:

Don't you agree?

I've seen no sign of it.

Nunne came back downstairs; he was buttoning an overcoat. He smiled at Sorme, and Sorme smiled back. They were both aware that Macmurdo was watching them closely for any exchange of signals. Nunne transferred his smile to Macmurdo, saying:

Ready, Inspector?

All right, Bob, Macmurdo said.

The sergeant led the way out of the house.

One of the plainclothes policemen went in front. Nunne and the detective-sergeant followed. The other policeman walked behind them; finally, Sorme and Macmurdo brought up the rear, walking ten yards behind the others. Sorme was aware that Macmurdo was trying to make Nunne nervous; it was like a game of chess. Nunne would worry about whether Sorme had given anything away, and now Sorme had been threatened with an accessory charge, he had his own reasons for fear. As they climbed over the stile, Sorme found himself wondering: If Austin gives himself away, can they make the accessory charge stick? Poor Austin – he's weakened himself by taking me into his confidence. I wonder if there's any basis for this stuff about Millie Rogers? The clothes in the basement flat. Do they know about the basement flat? Wish I could speak to Austin.

Macmurdo said:

I don't understand you.

Why not, Inspector?

You've only known Mr Nunne for a week. Even if he was convicted, there'd be no case against you. Why involve yourself?

Sorme said coldly:

It's the first time I knew I *was* involved.

You rushed down here this morning to warn him. You must have realized he might be the man we want.

Sorme said:

He happens to be a friend of mine. And you asked me to contact him yourself. If you hadn't come, he would have come to you. We were just leaving for London.

As he said it, he thought he saw an element of doubt in Macmurdo's eyes; suddenly, he was certain. Macmurdo had no final evidence on Nunne. It was all bluff and hope. There had been four murders in a week. The arrest of the Brixton man was a failure. Macmurdo had to make an arrest somehow. Relief contracted his skin like cold water. Macmurdo said:

You're a very loyal friend, Mr Sorme.

I hope so.

Two black cars were parked in the lane where Miss Quincey had set him down. Sorme asked:

Can you give me a lift back to the Crown?

We can. I want to see the lady there – Miss Quincey, is it?

Nunne was climbing into the first car; Sorme could see that Macmurdo had no intention of allowing them any contact. He called:

Austin?

Nunne turned round. Sorme said:

If you get away in time, let's meet for supper tonight.

Good idea, Gerard.

He waved as he climbed into the car. Sorme felt a sense of triumph. It had been done; contact had been made; Nunne knew that nothing was wrong. Sorme climbed into the back of the other car, and Macmurdo followed. Macmurdo said:

I doubt whether you'll make that supper date.

No? Why?

We may have a warrant for his arrest when we get back.

Really? Is that wise?

I think so, Macmurdo said sharply.

Sorme allowed the malice to come out; he said, smiling:

Another false arrest might only make things worse. My impression is that everyone's getting rather short-tempered with the police. Supposing you arrest Austin and there's another murder tomorrow night?

Macmurdo scowled; again Sorme was aware of the uncertainty, the fear of making a mistake, the fear of ridicule in the newspapers. Macmurdo said irritably:

That's my worry.

I know, Sorme said.

He relaxed on the cushions and looked out of the window. The car in front had already passed the hotel.

Macmurdo said:

Stop here a moment.

The car halted at the traffic lights. Sorme asked:

Shall I get out?

You'd better, Macmurdo said.

Aren't you coming in? I thought you wanted to see Miss Quincey.

Macmurdo said shortly:

That'll do later.

Sorme stepped out of the car and slammed the door as the lights changed. He stood for a moment, watching it disappear among the traffic, then crossed the road to the hotel.

Chapter Nine

The girl behind the enquiries desk directed him to the bar. Miss Quincey was sitting alone in a basket armchair, reading a copy of *Vogue*. She looked up as soon as he came into the room; her smile was spontaneous and warm. It was good to be back with her again. She said:

I'm glad you came. I was beginning to worry. Is everything all right?

She took his hand as he bent over her, releasing it almost immediately. He said.

Not too bad, sweet. I'll get a drink. Will you have another?

No thanks. This is my second. I've just had lunch.

He brought his pint of bitter back to her table, and pulled a chair close to hers. He said:

It's lucky the police didn't come in here with me. They arrived about an hour after me.

They found Austin?

Yes. But it's all right. Don't be alarmed. I think it's going to be OK.

She glanced around the empty bar, then asked in a whisper:

Is it Austin?

He said noncommittally:

I'll talk about it outside. You ready to leave?

She nodded. He tilted the beer glass and took a long draught, almost emptying it. She asked:

Where is Austin now?

On his way to Scotland Yard. For questioning.

Have they a warrant for him?

No. And I don't think they will have. I've arranged to meet him for supper tonight.

She sipped her gin and orange; her hand was trembling slightly. He said:

Don't worry. He's probably one of fifty suspects they've questioned today. It doesn't mean a thing.

This seemed to reassure her. He finished the beer, and stood up. The barman said: Good afternoon, sir! as they went out.

Where did you park the car?

Over in the car park.

Neither of them spoke until the car had begun to pull out of the Leatherhead traffic on the Epsom road. He said:

Remind me to contact Caroline when we get back. I'm supposed to meet her for supper.

She ignored the words, staring straight ahead through the windscreen. Then she asked:

What has happened to Austin?

For the first time, Sorme realized that he had not yet decided what to tell her. An instinctive desire to protect her made him say:

He'll be all right. He's in trouble, but not too much.

But . . . does he know about . . .?

The murders? He didn't tell me specifically. I think he was afraid to involve me, for my own sake. But I'm afraid he knows enough to get him into trouble. As an accessory . . .

Then he's not . . .

No. He's not the killer.

Are you sure?

Quite sure.

Thank God.

Her relief touched him, and made him feel guilty. She

started to laugh, leaning forward; the car swerved, then straightened out. She said:

You don't know what a nightmare this past few hours has been.

He said sympathetically:

I can guess, sweet.

But I knew it couldn't be true. I know Austin's often a little foolish . . . but he could never do that.

The families of most murderers probably feel like that, you know.

But he's not a murderer. You said you . . .

No, he's not. But he may be in pretty bad trouble.

But why? Surely they aren't interested in anyone else?

They are. This murder hunt has turned the underworld upside down. An awful amount of dirt has been stirred up.

But what has he *done*? It can't be as serious as all that? His father can pay lawyers . . .

I hope it won't get to that stage. If he's sensible, he'll stay out of England for six months. Look, sweet, could you stop at the Post Office in Epsom? I'd better send Caroline a telegram. Do you know the address of this place she's at?

The Scottish woman said:

He's asleep at the moment. Can you come back at six?

Sorme said:

I'm afraid this is urgent. It's something he'll want to know immediately. It may be a matter of life and death.

She looked unimpressed.

I'm sorry. I can't disturb him when he's asleep.

He repressed the irritation that made him want to push her out of the way. The Hungarian priest came out of the vault behind him, saying politely:

Excuse me.

502

Sorme said:

Look, father. I've got to see Father Carruthers. It's urgent.

The priest glanced from Sorme to the Scotswoman; he looked embarrassed and doubtful. He asked:

And he is asleep?

The woman said:

And he can't be disturbed.

Father Rakosi asked anxiously:

Is it important?

Sorme took two paces back from the door, coming close to the priest. He said in a low voice:

It's about the Whitechapel murders. He asked me to let him know immediately anything happened.

The priest glanced at the woman, then said apologetically:

I think you'd better wait inside. I will see if he is awake.

The woman turned without another word, and walked off. Sorme followed the priest into the dark interior that smelt of polish and tidiness. The priest said:

You wait here, please.

Sorme stood by the frosted-glass windows, swearing under his breath about the Scotswoman. It was not her refusal that irritated him, but her hostility and the desire to obstruct. He thought: How dare she be hostile to me, the bitch? She doesn't know me. What makes people turn nasty like that? Is *that* a form of sadism?

The idea interested him; he sat in the chair, thinking about it. Sadism is inflicting pain. Does petty-mindedness qualify as sadism? The choice of stupidity rather than intelligence? But how do I understand Austin's? Inverted love . . .

The priest came back, he said quietly:

He is awake.

He turned and walked into the next room. Sorme

503

hastened up the stairs and along the corridor, half expecting to be intercepted by the Scotswoman. The priest's door stood slightly ajar; he rapped with his knuckles and went in.

Father Carruthers was sitting up in bed, the plaid blanket wrapped around his shoulders; his face looked tired and dazed. The room was colder than usual; the window was open.

Hello, father.

The priest said:

What has been happening?

Sorme closed the door carefully, and sat on the edge of the bed. He said:

Austin has been taken to the police station for questioning. There was another murder last night.

I heard about the murder. What do they want with Austin?

He sat up, pulling his body into a more comfortable position; Sorme leaned forward and stopped the pillow from slipping until the priest had adjusted himself. He said:

They suspect him of the murders.

Have you spoken to him?

Yes, father. I was there when the police arrived.

Do you think he might be guilty?

Sorme hesitated, still rubbing the sleep out of his eyes, the priest seemed too old and tired to burden with a knowledge of pain. As he waited, the priest pulled the blanket tighter round his shoulders, and sank deeper into the pillows. He said:

I take it your hesitation means that he is?

Sorme said:

Yes, father.

I'm sorry, the priest said.

Before he could go on, someone tapped on the door. It was the Scotswoman. Without looking at Sorme, she said:

Father, there's another gentleman downstairs to see you. It's the German doctor . . .

The priest looked at Sorme:

Would you like to see him?

Sorme said:

I don't mind, father. I can go.

Would you send him up, please?

The woman closed the door quietly. Sorme said:

This is a little too much like a coincidence . . .

You don't have to speak to him.

I've nothing to hide, father. But . . . you won't mention Austin, will you?

No. But if you're certain Austin's guilty, I'm afraid there's nothing any of us can do.

I know, father. But I've only got his word for it. And I don't intend to tell anybody – beside you – that he's guilty.

If the police have evidence . . .

They haven't any evidence.

The priest said:

We shall soon find out.

As he spoke, Stein came into the room. He looked dapper and healthy, swinging an umbrella. He showed no surprise on seeing Sorme, but smiled pleasantly and nodded. He tossed the umbrella on to the armchair, and removed his overcoat, saying:

How are you, Larry? You look better. And Mr Sorme. I'm glad to see you here.

The priest said:

This is an unusual hour to call, Franz.

I know. I would not have dreamed of interrupting you . . . but I saw our young friend enter. I was in the vaults

505

when he arrived. I would like to speak to him . . . while he is with you.

Sorme asked:

How did you know I'd come?

I didn't, Stein said.

The priest said to Sorme:

Would you mind closing that window, please? And putting a little more coal on the fire?

Sorme crossed obediently to the window. The priest said:

Why do you want to speak to Gerard when I'm present, Franz?

Stein said:

I think he understands.

Sorme glanced at his face as he bent over the coal scuttle; the exhaustion of the previous day had vanished; he looked calm and sure of himself. Sorme said:

I'd rather you explained, doctor.

Very well. You know that your friend Austin is at present at Scotland Yard?

Yes.

You also know that he will probably stay at Scotland Yard until he goes to prison?

Sorme replaced the coal tongs on their hook. He asked: Why?

Stein leaned forward; he said deliberately:

You know why. Because he is the man the police want for the Whitechapel murders.

Sorme sat down again. He said: Are you sure?

Stein glanced quickly at the priest, as if suspecting that he was backing Sorme in the deception. He said:

I am sure. And I think you are sure also.

Sorme decided to bluff; he stared Stein directly in the eyes, and said:

506

What I don't understand is: Why tell me about it? What can I do?

Stein held his stare; his eyes became penetrating and aggressive.

You were with him this morning.

Yes.

He felt relaxed and indifferent, waiting for Stein to make the moves, unwilling to help. Stein must have sensed something of this in his calmness. He said impatiently:

I think you fail to understand your position.

Sorme shrugged:

What *is* my position?

I will tell you. A man named Austin Nunne has inherited sadistic tendencies from his father's side of the family. He is sent to see a psychiatrist, who places his case history on report. A year later, he is suspected of killing a youth in Hamburg. He returns to England and becomes known in certain circles as a man of peculiar tastes. Finally, he murders a series of East End prostitutes, killing with increasing frequency. A week before the police finally come into the open with him, he makes your acquaintance and becomes infatuated with you. You are not homosexual; his frustration leads to more murders. Do I make the position clear to you?

Sorme said levelly:

Quite. If Austin is the killer, then I'm indirectly responsible?

Stein shook his head.

I am not saying that you are responsible, indirectly or otherwise. What I am saying is that you can help the police if you want to.

How?

Tell them, in detail, about your contacts with him in the past week.

Sorme said, shrugging:

I'll do that, willingly. But they won't find anything of interest. To begin with, I believe you're wrong in thinking Austin's infatuated with me. He's been inclined to make me a sort of father confessor. But what he's confessed hasn't been murder.

No? Then what?

Stuff about being bored, useless, futile, and all the rest. Secondly, if his sexual tastes are very sinister, he's taken care not to let me find out. He gives me the impression of glossing over many things . . . things about his sex life. But then, he knows I don't share his tastes; perhaps he doesn't want to obtrude them on me.

Stein said:

But you agree with me that it seems very likely that he is the murderer?

I . . . I wouldn't go so far as to deny it. But I don't think it very likely.

And yet when you began to defend a murderer to me yesterday . . .

The priest interrupted suddenly:

Franz, wouldn't it be better if you took Gerard to some other room to ask him these questions? I can't help, and I'd rather not be involved.

Stein said, with concern:

I apologize if we tire you, Larry. We . . .

The priest interrupted:

You don't tire me. But I suspect you want me to act as a witness, and I don't want to act as a witness. I'm too old to start appearing in courtrooms, and I don't want policemen taking statements from me.

Stein said politely:

I'm sorry, Larry. But you are wrong. I shall not ask you to act as a witness. I want you here to support me. Your friend will listen to you . . .

The priest said:

I don't understand . . .

Stein said earnestly:

Let me explain. I think Mr Sorme here knows that Austin Nunne is the man we want. I think he has suspected it for several days. I think he feels he owes loyalty to his friend, and has invented excuses for murder. I want you to tell him: there can be no excuse for murder . . .

The priest said tiredly:

I don't understand. You say the police are certain that Austin is the murderer. In that case, it's up to them to find evidence or get a confession. But even if Austin had confessed openly to Gerard, I don't see that would be of any use in court. It would be an unsupported testimony. If Gerard can help you and he wants to, well and good. But don't ask me to interfere.

Sorme said:

Look, Doctor Stein, let me explain what I feel. If Austin's guilty, I don't want to help convict him. But if he's innocent, I don't want to help him escape. I don't see why I should be dragged in at all.

Stein stabbed his forefinger at Sorme; he said:

You don't want to be involved! And supposing Nunne was released tomorrow – what do you suppose would happen? He would kill again.

Sorme said:

You are assuming that he is the killer.

You *know* he is the killer.

All right. Suppose for a moment he is the killer. Why should he kill again? He'd be the first suspect in every sexual murder committed in London for the next ten years. He'll feel a constant watch being kept on him. Do you think he'd kill under those circumstances?

Stein smiled faintly, and leaned back in his chair. He

509

seemed to feel the conversation was getting somewhere at last.

All right. You are right. The police would watch him day and night, waiting for evidence. He would probably leave the country. Wherever he goes, the police know about him. He is really a man on the run. Sooner or later he will kill again. It is inevitable. Nervous tension, fear, a feeling of persecution. If he kills again, you will be responsible. Think carefully about this. He is your friend. But he is also a murderer. If he is convicted, he may be judged insane and sent to a criminal lunatic asylum. If he is released, he has two enemies to fight – his own impulse to kill, and the feeling of being constantly watched. Would he not be better in a mental home?

Stein spoke persuasively; Sorme was aware he was using all the force of his personality to charm. He began to regret that he had started to argue. It was difficult not to be persuaded. He averted his face, aware that his indecision was showing there. He shrugged, saying doubtfully:

I don't know.

Stein smiled suddenly.

Will you let me show you something?

Sorme glanced up at him.

What?

It would not take long.

Sorme looked at the priest. His eyes were closed; he seemed to be asleep. His white face had withdrawn from the situation. Sorme said:

All right. Where is it?

Stein stood up.

Wait here for me a moment, if you don't mind. I have a phone call to make. Then we can go.

He went out of the room. Sorme stood looking at the door, wondering if he was standing outside, listening.

After a moment, he went to the door and opened it softly.
There was no one in the passageway.

When he turned round again, the priest was looking at
him. He smiled embarrassedly saying:

I don't entirely trust him, father.

He is honest.

Is he? What do you think he wants to show me?

The body, perhaps. I don't know.

Sorme said, with disgust:

I hope not!

A strange excitement stirred his stomach and loins. He
sat in the chair Stein had vacated. He said:

I'm sorry to put you in this position, father.

It is your problem, Gerard.

But – you see how I feel? I can't betray Austin, no
matter what he's done. Even if what Stein says is true –
that Austin would be better off in Broadmoor . . .

You feel you owe him too much loyalty?

No, it's not that. I talked to him this morning. He's not
insane. He's like me – he has problems that need all his
efforts to solve them. He's a free man, father. And it's
only in this past week that I've come to realize the
meaning of freedom. You see, father, I'm certain of one
thing: Austin did whatever he did out of a need for
freedom. He told me this morning that he thinks he's
been subconsciously driving his life towards a state of
crisis. You heard what Stein said? He inherited sadism
from his father's side of the family. God knows what else
he inherited. He's had a life that's made him neurotic. He
feels he's in a prison and he has the courage to do
something desperate to smash his way out of it. I know
it's wrong to kill – but it's done now. It's in the past. If he
gets out of this, he'll know more about the meaning of
freedom. Don't you see? He's fighting a battle against

511

himself as well as against society. Why should I help society? I sympathize too much.

The priest said:

There may be some truth in that, Gerard. But don't identify yourself too closely with Austin.

But that's just it, father. I *can* identify myself with him. The judges who condemn him wouldn't understand. They've got to condemn him because society has to go on somehow. But I can't cooperate. This man Stein is persuasive. He's plausible. But so was Pontius Pilate. He belongs to the world. He doesn't understand . . .

The priest said softly:

Be careful, Gerard.

Why, father?

You think Austin is made of the stuff that saints and martyrs are made of – the holy obsession. You may be wrong. He may only be . . .

The door opened, and Stein came back into the room. He said:

I am sorry. I should have knocked. Am I interrupting?

The priest said:

No; come in, Franz.

Stein said:

If Mr Sorme is ready, we need not disturb you.

Sorme stood up.

I'm ready.

Stein said:

I may see you later, Larry. Try to get some sleep.

Thank you, Franz. And Gerard . . . if you want to come back, I shall be glad to see you.

Thanks, father.

Goodbye, Larry. I may be back.

In the taxi, Stein looked out of the window without speaking. Sorme asked him finally:

What makes you so certain that Austin's your man?

Stein turned to him, smiling.

His case report.

From the psychiatrist, you mean?

Yes.

What did it say?

A great many things. But one of them was this. When Austin was thirteen, he was expelled from his private school for being the ringleader in an affair of bullying that led to the death of a boy. He was not directly responsible – the boy died of brain fever – but Austin was guilty, nevertheless. Immediately afterwards, he experienced a religious conversion. He begged his family to send him to a monastery as a novice. They refused, but they engaged some kind of clergyman as his tutor.

Stein sat back, staring at Sorme from under the bushy eyebrows. The shadows in the taxi made his face look as if it had been cut out of rock. Sorme said doubtfully:

I don't quite understand.

No? Then perhaps you will understand this. After the murder of a male prostitute named Grans in a Hamburg rooming-house Austin entered an Alsace monastery, where he stayed for about three months. At the end of the period, a neighbouring haystack caught fire. Austin was among the monks who attempted to stop the fire from spreading. The next day he left the monastery and returned to England.

I . . . I don't see what the haystack has to do with it.

No? Peter Kürten was a pyromaniac. He liked setting fire to things – especially haystacks. The sight of fire acts as a stimulant to many sadists.

You're trying to tell me . . . that Austin's a kind of split personality who bounces from murder to religion?

I think it possible.

What else did the report say?

Nothing that would interest you.

Mother-fixation stuff?

Stein smiled.

Yes. Mother-fixation stuff.

The taxi stopped at the traffic lights outside Aldgate East station. Sorme said:

Are we going to the police station?

No. To the London Hospital.

Why?

Stein said:

I want you to see the woman who was killed last night.

Why?

You should understand what you are condoning.

Sorme started to speak then changed his mind. As the taxi passed the market stalls at the end of Vallance Road, he recognized Glasp buying something in a brown-paper bag. He turned and stared through the blue glass of the rear window, but another car blocked the view. He had thought he saw a young girl standing with Glasp. A moment later the taxi stopped outside the Whitechapel tube. Stein climbed out, and paid the driver. Sorme stood on the pavement, craning to catch another sight of Glasp. Stein said:

Are you ready?

Sorme said apologetically:

I thought I saw a friend . . .

They crossed the road with a crowd of pedestrians. A sense of coldness invaded Sorme's chest and diffused to his stomach. Noting the confidence in Stein's manner, he prepared himself for a shock that would unbalance him. A bloated face formed in his memory, the lips blackened, a scarf knotted tightly around the throat; it was a photograph he had seen in Nunne's volume of medical jurisprudence. Walking beside Stein across the grounds of the hospital, he found it difficult to suppress a feeling of

514

sickness; his heart was pounding unpleasantly, driving the fever from his throat and the lobes of his ears.

A uniformed policeman stood at the bottom of the concrete steps; he smiled at Stein and nodded. His greeting seemed somehow out of place there, like an executioner's formal: 'I hope everything has been satisfactory, sir?' Stein went ahead through the green door, holding it open for Sorme. The familiar iodoform smell came out to him, bringing an immediate comfort. Sorme heard his voice asking:

Why did they bring her here?

The pathologist wants to make a careful examination. The police mortuary is too far.

The room was empty; white gowns hung from the pegs on the wall. There were only two stone slabs in it. Both were covered with white cloths that concealed human outlines. Stein wasted no time on theatrical effects. He pulled back the sheet from the nearest slab, saying:

I want you to look at this.

Sorme moved closer to look. The first impression of horror disappeared immediately; it was produced by the sight of the hair clotted with blood. It was not a human being on the slab; he could feel only the slight, stomach-gripping disgust of the smell of a butcher's shop. Feeling the need to speak, he said:

This is what pathologists refer to as 'the remains'.

There was no resemblance to living humanity, although the human shape was plain enough. It was as impersonal as a half finished model in a sculptor's studio, or the face of the mummy in the stone coffin in the British Museum. The gashes in the face had removed any possibility of expression. He could have made an inventory, as precise and detached as a pathologist's report on a post-mortem. It was impossible to make the imaginative leap and envisage someone doing this to a living body. It was too dead; it had never been alive. After he had stared at it for about half a minute, it was already meaningless. He observed instead the thin plastic cover between the remains and the white sheet, protecting the sheet from bloodstains.

Stein said:

How do you feel?

I don't understand. What am I supposed to feel?

Stein said quietly:

At this time yesterday, you could have met this girl in the street.

Sorme looked at the broken flesh, and said:

I know you're right. But I can't believe it all the same.

He looked up, and met Stein's eyes; there was disappointment there. He said:

I know what you want me to say. That there's a tremendous difference between theoretical approval of a crime and the actual commission. I know that. But what's the difference?

He was about to say 'What's the difference whether I approve of Austin's crimes or not?', then stopped himself. Instead, he pointed to the other slab.

What's under there?

Stein said shortly:

A woman.

May I see?

Without waiting for permission, he lifted the sheet that covered the upper half of the body. He had half expected to find a detective making a note of their conversation. The sight of charred flesh was a shock. He asked:

What happened to him . . . her?

The sight of the breasts corrected his mistake. They might have been carved out of ebony.

She was burnt, Stein said. Her husband threw a paraffin lamp at her.

Why?

Stein shrugged:

I don't know why. They had a quarrel. Probably he was drunk.

Who was she?

I don't know. I only heard what they said when they brought her in this morning. She is a married woman with three children.

How old was she?

In her mid-twenties. Excuse me a moment. I shall return.

Certainly.

He was glad to be left alone. The sight of the corpse produced no revulsion or horror; only a recognition of humanity. He pulled back the sheet from the whole body, and stared at it. It was too obviously and recognizably the body of a young woman. Where the charred flesh came to an end, the skin was burnt and raw. Fragments of clothing still adhered to her legs and arms. The fascination was one of pity and kinship. It might have been Gertrude Quincey or Caroline. The flesh had once been caressed; the body had carried children. He felt the stirring of a consuming curiosity about her. Why was she dead? Who was she? There was an absurdity in her death. How could twenty-five years as a human being lead inevitably to a mortuary slab, the breasts and smooth belly carbonized out of relevance to life? The belly and thighs were well shaped. If she had been alive, sleeping, he would have felt the movement of desire: its failure symbolized the absurdity of her death.

Stein came back into the room. He came and stood beside Sorme, then pulled the sheet back over the body.

Sorme said:

You are a romantic.

He adjusted the sheet over the other slab. Sorme followed him to the door. Before he opened it, Stein said:

Think about it. Which is more important. Loyalty, or . . . that?

Sorme said gravely:

I agree with you. But . . . there's nothing I can do.

Stein's eyes, as hard as dry ice, were trying to bore into his own, to force an admission. He said:

If you wanted, you could do a great deal.

Sorme shrugged.

If I wanted.

Stein asked coldly:

What do you mean?

Sorme said:

Would you answer me a question, doctor?

Well?

Did you support Hitler during the war?

Stein was taken by surprise; the eyes went out of focus for a moment, then recovered. He said:

Yes. Like seventy million other Germans.

Sorme said:

But you were a member of the Party. You were also a doctor. You must have had some idea of what was happening in places like Auschwitz and Belsen.

The surprise was replaced by irritation, which was controlled immediately. Stein said stiffly:

I fail to understand the point you are trying to make.

Do you, doctor?

You are suggesting that if I condoned Hitler's crimes, I should also condone Austin's?

No. But I can't understand why you should regard them as so dissimilar.

Stein said, with a touch of harshness:

It is untrue that I condoned Belsen and Auschwitz. We heard rumours of them – many Germans did. But we preferred to disbelieve them. There was nothing we could have done in any case. Nevertheless, Hitler's crimes and Austin's *were* different. Hitler was a political idealist. He may have been wrong, but he was not a sadist. Sexual killers were executed in Nazi Germany as they were in England.

But *why* do you want to catch the Whitechapel killer?

Because I have a responsibility to society. And as a doctor I have a responsibility to humanity. Remember this: Even Hitler thought he was serving humanity by exterminating the Jews. The Whitechapel murderer kills to gratify a personal lust. He knows he is serving nobody but himself.

Sorme said mildly:

He manages to do a great deal less damage than Hitler.

That is beside the point.

Sorme said:

Then let me make my point quite clear. Father Carruthers told me you became a Nazi in nineteen thirty-three. You must have known about the methods Hitler was using – all Europe did. But you didn't feel a duty to have Hitler arrested, or even to leave the Party. Well, you tell me that if Austin is the killer, I ought to help to condemn him, as a matter of principle. I'd just like to know how your principles condone Hitler and condemn Austin. If I'm being impertinent, I apologize. But I'm afraid I can't follow your logic.

Stein said irritably:

What you say is absurd. It is untrue that I condoned the concentration camps. But even if I had, it would not be a reason for you to condone sexual murder.

Sorme said:

Perhaps I don't condone it. Perhaps I just happen to feel as you did about Hitler's methods – that I just don't want to do anything about it.

Stein turned away, shrugging. He said:

In that case, I hope you are prepared to face the consequences of being an accessory.

He walked out of the door before Sorme could answer. Sorme followed him down the steps, closing the door behind him. He was not sorry that Stein was annoyed; it saved further argument.

Half way across the yard he stopped, pretending to look for something in his pockets. Stein halted at the gates of the hospital and looked back; seeing that Sorme was ten paces behind him, he shrugged and walked on. When he was out of sight, Sorme followed slowly. In the Whitechapel Road, he peered into the crowd, and saw the German standing in front of a shop window, waiting. As the traffic lights changed to red, he hurried across the road with a crowd of pedestrians, then turned in the opposite direction from Stein, and walked quickly along the pavement. At the corner of Brady Street he looked back. Stein was no longer visible; a moment later, he caught a glimpse of him signalling a taxi to stop. He stood there watching, concealed by the corner, until the taxi started in the direction of the City. Then he walked along Brady Street and turned into Durward Street.

He rang the doorbell several times, then, suspecting it was out of order, rapped with his knuckles. After another wait, he tried pushing the door. It swung open, and he found himself looking into the face of Glasp's landlady. She said:

Oh, it's you. He's not here any more.

Not here? Sorme said. He remembered she was deaf, and leaned forward to ask: Where is he?

You needn't shout. He's left. Just gone.

Has he left any address?

No. He says he'll send it on.

What about his pictures?

They're still there – upstairs. He's says he'll collect them. I 'spect he doesn't want the police to know where he's gone to.

She turned her back on him, and closed the door.

For a moment, he felt an irritable rage at her rudeness, and had to restrain a desire to kick the door. He stood still, letting it subside, then stepped back into the roadway and looked up at Glasp's window, suspecting that Glasp might have instructed the woman to turn him away, and might be peering out to see if he had gone. There was no one visible; he turned away, and walked off towards Aldgate. He had only walked a few yards when someone behind him said:

Excuse me . . .

He found himself looking down into the face of a girl of about twelve years old. She was muffled in a brown overcoat, with the collar around her chin. She said:

Were you looking for Oliver Glasp?

Yes. Do you know where he is?

She shook her head.

No. I wanted to see him. Do you think he's really left?

He asked her curiously:

Are you Christine?

She nodded, and her face reddened. He looked down at her with increased interest. Her hair was short and boyish, but the face was undeniably delicate and attractive. It looked pink, as if she had been running, and the flush increased its attractiveness. The eyes were wide and brown in the oval face. Sorme said:

I saw him less than an hour ago just around the corner, so he can't be far away.

But his landlady says he's gone away.

It looks like it.

Where do you think he might have gone to?

That's more than I can guess.

521

Her eyes became troubled.

Why do you think he went?

Sorme felt suddenly guilty about the brevity of his replies; it was obvious that she suspected him of disliking her. He said:

Oliver's a strange man. I think he was pretty angry and upset. I saw him this morning, and he seemed miserable.

She lowered her eyes.

About me?

I think so.

He could read in her expression the curiosity about how much he knew. Her face was disturbingly open, reflecting her emotions quite clearly. He could understand suddenly why Glasp had been so upset at the notion that she was capable of deception. She asked:

Did he tell you about it?

Yes.

She shifted awkwardly from one foot to the other; he noticed that she was wearing ankle socks. A stirring of curtain over her shoulder attracted his attention; it was Glasp's landlady peering out of the window at them. Sorme said:

Which way are you walking?

She said miserably:

Any way.

Walk along here with me.

She fell into step beside him; they walked towards the ruined theatre at the other end of the street. Neither spoke while they were in Durward Street. She asked finally:

Do you think he'll come back?

I don't know. I hope so. But it might be a long time.

They stopped on the corner of Vallance Road. A kind of baffled indignation came into her eyes as she looked at him. She said:

But he *can't* just go like that. He'd say goodbye to me . . . wouldn't he?:

Sorme said awkwardly:

I expect he'll be back.

Perhaps . . . perhaps he thinks he can't see me.

Sorme fed the hope that came up to him in her face.

I expect that's the reason. Now your parents know . . .

But that's all right now! Mum had it out with dad and made him agree to let Oliver come round to visit us. She said she'd leave him if he didn't stop tormenting everybody . . .

Her face was pink again, this time with excitement. He noticed that she spoke carefully and well, but the indignation strengthened the London accent. He said soothingly:

Probably he'll write to you.

Do you think he will? If you see him, make him write to me. I don't want him to go away. It's silly. It's all right now. Tell him everything's all right, won't you?

If I see him, I'll tell him. But he might not get in touch with me either.

She said with exasperation:

Isn't he silly! Why does he want to run away like that?

He shrugged and started to make some vague reply. She interrupted:

Is he trying to get away from you too?

He smiled at her penetration.

I think he's trying to get away from everybody at the moment. He's in one of his moods.

Do they last long?

He felt no inclination to admit that he had had no previous experience of them. He said:

Oh, not too long. He's sure to get in touch with one of his friends sooner or later.

But that's not *me*. If he doesn't want to see me, it's no good . . .

But I'll make sure he contacts you.

She stared at him hopefully.

How?

Oh . . . I'll tell him to.

But he might not want to.

All right. I'll send you his address, and you can write to him yourself.

Will you? Would you do that? I'm sure it'd be all right if I could talk to him.

Give me your address.

He took out his notebook, and wrote it down as she dictated it. She asked:

Do you think you'll see him soon?

I don't know. I'm afraid it might not be for a long time.

Oh dear. I wish I knew why he's gone.

He said uncomfortably:

I think he was a bit hurt . . .

Her eyes regarded him doubtfully for a moment; then she said:

About Tommy . . . My cousin?

He nodded. She said:

I thought they'd tell him about that. But tell him it wasn't my fault. Please tell him that. Make him understand, won't you?

I'll try to.

Oh please . . . I meant to tell him about it.

He said hastily:

Oh, it wasn't just that. I think all the trouble with your father and the police worried him . . .

She was tapping the point of her shoe on the pavement, then swinging it in short arcs around the other foot. He said uncomfortably:

I'm afraid I'd better go . . .

She said sadly:

I suppose I might not see him again.

He felt a flash of something like jealousy, and pulled the belt on his raincoat tighter to shake off the feeling. He said:

No. You'll see him again.

But perhaps not for a long time.

He asked:

Will it make much difference to you?

She nodded seriously.

Of course. I liked talking to him. He knew such a lot . . . and he was nice. And I liked to go there.

She looked up at him, and added, with sudden candour:

I don't like my brothers and sisters much.

He thrust his hands deep into the raincoat pockets, smiling at her. He said:

You're lucky you haven't got into more trouble.

I know. But it's worth it. I don't mind getting into trouble . . . But I hate being bored.

He said:

If you get too bored, come and see me.

Immediately, he regretted the impulse that had made him say it, ashamed to have said it to the girl who was so important to Glasp. It was a feeling of betraying Glasp. The girl asked:

Are you a painter?

No.

What then?

A writer.

Do you live around here?

I'm afraid not. I live in Camden Town.

Is that a long way?

Not very far.

Oliver came for supper, didn't he?

That's right.

She said doubtfully:

I'd like to come. But I wouldn't have to let dad know.

He said, smiling:

I hope you're not in the habit of accepting invitations to visit strange men?

Oh no. But you're not strange.

Thank you. But you don't even know my name.

What is it?

Gerard.

Yes. I know about you. Oliver told me.

He scrawled his address and telephone number on a page of his notebook, and tore it out.

Look, take this. If you want to come, you can phone me. Do you know how to make a phone call?

She said, with a touch of scorn:

Of course.

She folded the paper carefully, and stowed lt away somewhere inside the coat. He said:

I'm afraid I'll have to go now. Goodbye, Christine.

Can I come on Saturday?

Well . . . if you want to. Perhaps I'd better meet you somewhere. Will you phone me before then?

All right.

Will you have money for the telephone?

She nodded vigorously. He said:

Don't be too upset about Oliver.

No.

Goodbye, Christine.

Goodbye.

He walked towards the Aldgate tube, thinking: What an extraordinary child. What am I going to do with her? Could take her to Gertrude's for tea, I suppose. Then get Gertrude to run her back in the car. My God, that damn' fool Oliver! . . .

His mind came back to Nunne with a sudden shock; for

the past ten minutes, he had completely forgotten about him. For a moment, his mind held simultaneously the face of the child, and the unrecognizable face of the woman in the morgue. Disgust lurched from his stomach like a vapour of stagnation, and was succeeded by a heavy sense of pity and sadness. He found himself saying aloud:

Poor Christine . . .

Chapter Ten

As he was about to insert his key in the front door, the telephone started to ring. He withdrew round the edge of the wall, where his shadow would not be visible against the glass. A moment later he heard Carlotte's voice saying:

Hello . . . No, he's not in. I've just been up to see. I'll tell him you rang. Yes, he'll ring you. Goodbye.

The bell tinkled as she hung up. He turned his key and went in. She was starting to write on the memo pad.

Oh, Mr Sorme. You just missed a telephone call.

He said: I know. I wanted to miss it.

Did you? It was Mr Nunne. He wouldn't leave a message.

If anybody rings again, will you say I'm out, please?

You don't want to speak to anybody?

That's right.

A lady rang a few minutes ago. She said you'd know who it was.

Oh, thanks . . .

And you want to speak to no one?

Please. If you don't mind.

Oh, I don't mind. What if somebody comes to the door?

I . . . I expect you'd better let them up. I'll say I've just come in. I'm pretty tired. I'm going to sleep now.

She smiled sympathetically.

All right. I'll tell them you are out.

She went downstairs. He found four pennies in his

pocket and dialled Miss Quincey. She answered immediately. She must have been standing close to the phone.

Gerard. Where have you been?

Oh, all over the place. I've only just got in.

Are you coming up here?

No, sweet. I'm pretty tired. I want to sleep.

You could sleep here. Shall I fetch you?

It's not that. I've got a lot to think about.

About Austin?

Yes. But don't say anything on the phone. I want a few hours alone to brood about it all.

Is Austin coming over?

No. He just rang, and the girl said I was out. I don't want to see him right now.

Why?

I'll explain later. I may give you a ring in a few hours. I'm deadly tired now.

All right. Have a sleep.

See you later, sweet.

His own room was strange to him; it seemed a long time since he had been in it. He filled the kettle and set it on the gas ring, then lit the gas fire. Overhead, the old man was playing gramophone records. He thought: Christ, he's started early. He glanced at the clock and realized it was not early; it was almost eight o'clock. He had eaten a meal at the workman's cafe in the Kentish Town Road before coming in. It was not true that he was tired; it was an excuse for not seeing Gertrude.

He cleared the table of its dirty cups and glasses, and covered it with a folded army blanket from the bed. This was to deaden the noise of the typewriter for the room underneath. He began to type immediately; when the kettle boiled, he turned the gas very low, and went on typing. He used quarto sheets from a folder labelled 'Notes'. In half an hour, he had filled three of them.

He stopped to read back; excitement was like alcohol in his blood. Before he reached the end of the three pages, someone knocked on the door. He called: Come in.

It was Gertrude Quincey. She said:

I'm sorry. Am I interrupting?

Politeness made him say:

Not at all. Come and sit down. What made you decide to come?

She sat on the other side of the table. She was wearing a coat of light, pale fur, the colour of a teddy bear, with the high collar turned up; for a moment, she reminded him of Caroline. She said:

I wanted to see you.

He asked, grinning:

Did you suspect I'd got Caroline here?

No.

Her deepened colour told him his guess was not completely inaccurate. He said:

Would you like a cup of tea?

Yes, please.

He turned the gas fire lower; the room was stifling. She removed her coat and dropped it on the bed. She was wearing a blue woollen skirt that he had not seen before; it looked well on her slim figure. He put his arms around her and kissed her on the forehead, saying:

Mmm. Delicious.

She disengaged herself and took hold of his wrists.

What are you going to do about Austin?

I don't know, sweet. That's why I wanted to be alone this evening.

I'm sorry . . .

I'll be back in a moment.

He carried the teapot and dirty cups upstairs on a tray, and washed them at the sink. When he came back a few minutes later, she had found a cloth and was dusting the bookshelves.

Doesn't anyone clean your room?

The girl's supposed to do it once a week.

That girl who let me in? She's not very efficient. There's enough fluff under the bed to stuff a mattress.

He removed the typewriter from the table, and threw the army blanket on the bed. She grimaced at the sight of the plastic cloth underneath, with its circular stains of tea and beer.

Have you a sponge?

I think there's one upstairs. But don't bother now.

I don't want to keep staring at them. Up here?

She went out of the room and up the stairs. He poured boiling water on to the tea, and turned off the gas. She returned a moment later with a damp cloth, and cleaned the marks from the cloth. Through the open door they heard the ringing of the telephone.

Do you think that's for you?

Perhaps. But I've told the girl to say I'm out.

Supposing it's Austin?

I don't want to see Austin. Not right now.

I see.

She took the cloth back up to the kitchen. Sorme poured the tea. She came back and closed the door carefully, sat down.

Why don't you want to see him?

Because . . . I've got a lot to think about.

She said quietly:

He is the man the police want, isn't he?

He met her eyes, and felt no inclination to lie about it.

If he is, he's still free.

I know. The radio said so tonight.

Said what?

531

That the police had interviewed two men at Scotland Yard and let them both go.

Mmm. Did it? That's interesting.

Is he the man they want?

He knew suddenly there was no point in keeping it from her. He nodded. She sighed deeply, turning away from him. He watched her closely. She asked finally:

You didn't intend to tell me?

I didn't want to upset you.

What do you intend to do now?

There's not much I can do.

Why did you change your mind about meeting him this evening?

He shrugged:

I wanted time to think.

Are you . . . deserting him?

He said:

Listen, sweet. I want you to try and understand this. For over a week now, I've suspected that Austin might be the Whitechapel killer. I didn't let it worry me. He interested me too much. I wanted to understand him, not condemn him. Well, I've only just begun to understand him. If I saw him now, I'd have to make him realize that I condemn him. And I'd rather not do that. I'd rather he went on thinking I'm a friend.

Have you ceased to be his friend?

That's not the question. I thought this morning that I understood him better than the police. Now I know I was wrong.

But Gerard . . . he's still a human being. He needs help. He needs friends. If he's guilty, he needs them more than ever.

He said:

This afternoon I went to look at the woman he killed.

532

She was in the morgue at the London Hospital. It made me understand some things I'd never realized before.

What?

He leaned forward across the table, speaking with deliberation:

There was something I hadn't realized about Austin. He's insane.

Her face went pale.

He's not. I'm sure he's not . . .

I don't mean he's completely dotty, like the old boy upstairs. But there's a part of his brain that's as rotten as a rotten apple. He's let it get that way. He's let himself go rotten. Do you know why he kills? Because he knows he's suffering from a mortal disease. He's like a man with paralysis who needs stronger and stronger stimulants. He doesn't care any more.

As he spoke, her face reflected first unbelief, then a kind of desperation.

But please, Gerard, don't you understand? If that's true, we've got to stick by him. He needs it more than ever.

What about your Bible? Thou shalt not kill?

But the New Testament speaks about love, not about punishment. The law will punish him enough.

What makes you think he'll be punished? He knows the police have got no evidence against him. They won't find bloodstains on his shoes, or anything like that. And he won't confess. He loves all this. He's glad the police have got on to his trail. He likes crossing swords with them. It's another stimulant. He knows they'll never have a shred of evidence against him unless they catch him in the act. There's only one thing that worries me . . .

What's that?

He was stupidly careless last weekend. He had to phone me from Switzerland to ask me to collect some woman's clothes from his Kensington flat. That sounds dangerously like a subconscious urge to be caught . . .

Whose clothes were they?

I don't know. The police mentioned some prostitute who was seen accosting him outside the Balalaika Club. Maybe she's buried under the floor in his Kensington place.

Her face drained of all blood; for a moment, he thought she was going to faint. He said:

Careful, sweet. Are you all right?

She nodded briefly, and moved from the chair to the bed. She sat on the edge, leaning against the wall.

Are you serious. . .?

No. Not really. I don't seriously think he killed the woman. He's too careful.

But whose clothes were they?

Probably some he bought from a secondhand shop for the purpose. He wanted to make me a confidant. If I'd gone to the police, it wouldn't have mattered – he'd probably have taken them to the shop where he bought them and made some excuse about not wanting some boy friend to discover the clothes in his flat. As it was, he was absurdly over-secretive. He didn't have to go to Switzerland. He suspected that I might be sympathetic. He needed someone he could be open with. He chose me. He could see I was full of theories about revolt and modern civilization and the rest and he thought I'd make the perfect confidant – provided I didn't get too close to the reality. Unfortunately, Professor Stein – the German doctor – got the idea of showing me the body. Even then, it was almost a failure. The woman was too much of a mess to strike me as human. I'd still have come away without understanding. But there was another body in the place – a woman who'd been burnt to death. Suddenly, I realized what it meant – death by violence. Do you realize what it means? It's a complete negation of all our impulses. It means we've got no future. But we've got to believe in the future. And it's not just a question of my future – it's the future of the human race. If life can just be ended like that – snuffed out – then all the talk about the dignity of man's an illusion. It might be you or me. I suddenly understood something that I've seen once or twice but never grasped. If the world's good, it's because somehow life's all one thing. That's the meaning of sanity – everything's a unity, not just life but even water and stones. And that's why Austin's insane. Do you realize: he needs other people, but he doesn't really believe they exist? Life's meaningless to him. He's a man without a future. He can take life because he doesn't attach any value to his own. He might as well be dead.

She was shaking her head as he talked.

You're wrong. He's not as bad as that. He's always been spoilt and selfish, but there's a lot of good in him . . .

Try to understand, sweet. He's insane. The best thing that could happen to him now would be to go to Broadmoor.

But . . . what are you going to do? Tell the police?

No. I can't do that. He trusted me.

Why did he trust you?

He knew I felt as he does about a lot of things. You see, I didn't realize then that he was mad. I thought he wanted to express revolt against the way things are nowadays. I thought it was a kind of escape from personality. You know . . . things keep getting more organized. Everybody's encouraged to fit into the machine. But the more they try to take away freedom, the more it expresses itself in violence. The more they talk about law and society, the more the crime rate increases. People let themselves be manipulated to a certain degree – by the politicians and the advertisers – but a resentment builds up. And sex crime and juvenile delinquency and the suicide rate keep on rising steadily. Man can't do without the irrational. He's not a rational creature finally. He doesn't really want a perfect civilization and a heaven on earth.

She said quietly:

That's because of original sin.

Maybe. But I don't like the Garden of Eden legend either. Man doesn't want to be a sinless Adam in the Garden of Eden. He wants to be a god. Give man another chance, and he'd still eat the apple. He wants to be more than man, and he doesn't give a damn about the misery and filth he has to wallow through. At least it proves he's free. And that's where I made my mistake about Austin. I thought his crimes were a gesture of defiance, like eating the apple. They weren't. He killed for the same reason a dipsomaniac drinks – he couldn't stop.

He stopped talking, feeling curiously exhausted. His tea was still untouched. He leaned forward and handed her the full cup from her side of the table, then stirred his own. It was half cold. He drank it down without lowering the cup. He said:

Do you know why I couldn't help Stein? Because he's really as bad as Austin. Only he doesn't realize it. He wants to see Austin arrested for the good of the organization – for society. But during the war, he probably approved of exterminating the Jews for the good of the organization. He doesn't give a damn about human freedom either.

He was speaking because he could see she felt stunned. It was a way of helping her adjust, like distracting someone's attention from a burn until the pain has gone away. He said:

I've learned a lot from Austin, in a way. I seem to have

536

learned a lot altogether in this past week. For example, that there's no point in running away. There's poor Oliver. I tried to call on him this afternoon, and found he'd left the place – just packed up and gone. That's his way of avoiding things he dislikes.

She seemed to catch at the subject of Glasp as an escape from thinking about Austin.

Oliver? Do you know where he's gone to?

No. He left no address. But I met this girl – Christine – the one who caused all the trouble. She's a sweet little kid – seems rather old for her age though. I've promised to meet her on Saturday.

Meet her?

Yes. I thought I might bring her back to your place for tea? She's obviously pretty upset about Oliver leaving. Anyway, I didn't like to leave her with no kind of contact. I think Oliver's a fool. She's only a child, and he's behaving as if she's an adult who's betrayed him. Typical romantic – he can't be bothered to sort out his emotions. He's like Austin in that respect. Instead of analyzing his feelings, he reacts to them. Only Oliver's reaction is always to hurt himself. Austin's is to hurt other people.

She asked slowly:

Do you really think Austin is . . . insane?

Yes. He's insane.

But would a court of law agree?

I don't know. I doubt it. His insanity's not the recognizable kind.

What do you mean?

It's too much like the insanity of the age. Austin told me this morning that we live in an age of murder. He understands that, all right. Shall I tell you what Austin's like? He's like the rats that die first in a plague. He's been bitten by the virus. He hasn't any resistance. He thinks it's no good resisting. Human freedom's disappearing, and he wants to help it on its way with a little murder. That's why he's insane. Insanity is when you stop resisting. If you put Austin in a mental home, he'd begin to show signs of complete insanity within a few weeks.

Why do you say that?

Because it'd be like taking a drug addict off the stuff. When he feels the strain, he goes out and kills. If you put him where he couldn't kill, he'd snap.

But . . . would he keep on . . . now, I mean?

I think so.

Then . . . I think we'd better do something.

What?

I'll see his parents. You ought to come too. They wouldn't believe it. They've got the money – they could have him put into a private mental home.

He'd have to be certified. And the doctor would have to be told about the . . . the case history. He'd go to prison.

No. They've got friends.

She stared blankly at the fire. She said softly:

My God . . . what a terrible thing to have to face suddenly.

You've managed it.

But . . . I'm not so close to him. And you . . . broke it gently.

Sorme said impatiently:

From the sound of them, they need a good shock.

She shivered:

No one deserves that kind of shock.

I'm afraid it's inevitable now. They might get a worse shock soon . . .

She understood his meaning immediately.

He wouldn't . . . Not now. Surely?

Sorme said, shrugging:

I don't want to alarm you, sweet. But he's quite capable

538

of doing another one tonight out of sheer bravado. It's become a game. That's something I didn't realize when I spoke to him this morning. He can't resist a challenge.

She looked at her watch.

Then we ought to go immediately.

I thought his parents lived somewhere in Shropshire?

His father's in town. I'll phone him now.

Do you really need me with you now?

I . . . perhaps not. But I might want you later. Will you be home?

Yes. I'll wait here. For heaven's sake be careful. Don't do anything that would make us both accessories. If you phone him, don't say anything over the phone.

He helped her on with her coat. The look of bewilderment had gone out of her face; the prospect of immediate action seemed to restore her certainty. She opened her handbag, and put a pound note on the table.

I'll leave you some money. If I phone you, I may want you to take a taxi.

I don't need the money. I've got enough.

Keep it for the moment. I may ring you in about an hour. I shall be at the Albany. If he's not in, I'll wait. Don't bother to come down with me.

She kissed him briefly on the nose, and went out. It was the first time she had offered to kiss him. He stood at the open doorway, listening to her footsteps on the stairs, then the slam of the front door. For some reason, he wanted to be certain he was alone. He poured another cup of tea, and added water to dilute it. In spite of the tiredness, he felt a curious sense of certainty, of order. It was as if he could see inside himself and watch processes that had been invisible before. There was no longer a desire for simplicity; an accumulation of self-knowledge had made it less important.

The phone began to ring downstairs. He hesitated at

the door; when the ringing continued, he went to answer it. There was no point in avoiding Austin now; he felt suspended, waiting for something to happen.

A girl's voice said:

Is Mr Sorme there, please?

Speaking.

Oh, it didn't sound like you! This is Caroline.

He said uneasily: How are you, sweet?

I got your telegram. When did you get in?

About ten minutes ago. Where are you?

At home. What's been happening?

I can't tell you over the phone. I'll tell you when I see you.

When will that be?

He had a sensation like sliding down a slope, unable to arrest the movement. He said cautiously:

When will you be free?

Not tomorrow. I've got a rehearsal. And we may have one on Wednesday. I'm not sure. I'm free Thursday . . .

I'll . . . I'll check in my diary . . .

Thursday's a good day for me. I told mummy I was going to an all-night party, and it's been cancelled. So I needn't go home.

Her voice went on as he stood there, staring at the coin box, using the pretence of looking in a diary as an opportunity to think. Abruptly, he felt irritated with himself. He said:

Yes. Thursday's fine. Will you come over here?

All right, darling. About seven?

Good.

She said suddenly:

I'll ring off. Mummy's at the door.

The line went dead.

In his room, he drank the tea, standing by the mantel-piece. A curious elation stirred in him, an acceptance of complexity. He stared at his face in the mirror, saying aloud:

What do you do now, you stupid old bastard?

He grinned at himself, and twitched his nose like a rabbit.